INFINITE CORNER

LORNA DE SOSA

ISBN: 978-0-578-86665-9

Library of Congress
De Sosa, Lorna, 1913-2009.
Infinite Corner/by Lorna De Sosa; edited by Victor Bonilla-Sosa.
-1st ed.

Published in the United States by Victor Bonilla-Sosa

First Edition

To the memory of my father and mother
and to Kris, Victor, Henry L, Felix, Renee, Salvador
and especially Dwight, whose patience has backed every page of this book
and to that beloved island which adopted me as its own.

CONTENTS

Gargoyle mask from the Camacho mansion

INTRODUCTION

Havana of post-World War II and early 1950s is usually remembered in later anti US accounts as a destination fleshpot and US Mafia gaming playground for American cruise ship and later airline tourists. Similar to Weimar Berlin, 1900 Vienna, Impressionist Paris, and British occupied Hong Kong, these places occupy a mythical status in novels, histories, biographies, and cinema. Focus is often on the Cuban revolution that culminated in 1959 and its immediate precursor of student and middle-class revolt against the dictatorship of former Army Sergeant Fulgencio Batista. Yet, outside of scholarly inquiries, there is a paucity of fictional accounts outside of Cuba that encounter the period addressed in this novel.

My mother, Lorna DeSosa, lived in Cuba from 1940 until 1955 where she occupied a vantage point observing the society and events which presaged things to come. Her marriage to my Cuban born father in Chicago in 1939 after their meeting as freshmen at Tulane University could have taken a radically different alternative had my father not turned down a medical internship in San Francisco and instead chosen to pursue his career in Cuba. There his widowed mother, a native of the Canary Islands had adopted the island as her new "patria chica," or second homeland in the early decades of the twentieth century. It was from my grandmother Julia's accounts of her youth in the Canaries and her family's storied past as innovative farmers (I was told that her father won the Silver Medal at a London exposition from Queen Victoria), relationship to her cousin the writer Ortega y Gasset, and the quaint custom of communicating by whistles that entranced the always creative Lorna to conceive of a novel incorporating these stories and their eventual nexus with Cuba.

The last important colonial possession of a troubled and moribund empire where the "sun never set" (later appropriated to describe the British Empire), the island capital of Havana had for centuries served as the nerve center between the Iberian Peninsula and its vast American holdings. The gold, silver, and precious cargoes of the Manila Galleons and the Veracruz assembled in Havana's well defended deep water harbor from which the convoys sailed for Seville and Cadiz. Strong bonds endured even after the loss of Cuba in the second war of independence from Spain in 1895. Many of the former colonial troops chose to remain and formed new familial bonds with the Cuban population, including Fidel Castro's father, a former Spanish soldier from Spain's Galicia in the underdeveloped northwest. Unique among the former Spanish possessions in the Americas, Cuba remained in many ways close to Spain through immigration, trade, and cultural exchanges. At the time of the 1959 regime change, there were still valid titled nobility at the pinnacles of Cuban society and Galician Francisco Franco maintained Spain's diplomatic relations when most of the Spanish speaking world broke with Castro.

Lorna arrived in Havana in 1940 at a critical moment in the cultural life of the city. Refugees not only from the Spanish Civil War but also from the conflagration in Europe made for a heady injection of fresh ideas and artistic currents grafted onto Cuban life. Musicians like Janos Starker from Hungary, Romanian artist Sandu Darie, and literati like Jose Rubia Barcia from Spain became catalysts for new undertakings. As such, Lorna brought her experience in American theater and radio to great effect and eventually to certain popular acclaim. As she wrote:

"From the moment the SS Florida" docks at the Port of Havana and I descended hearing and seeing the pulse and the colors and the smell of Cuba...it was for me love at first sight. Strangely enough it also seemed to be home for me. Sooner than I expected this feeling led me into a meeting with Rubia Barcia, a brilliant drama professor who had fled from the Spanish Civil War and together, as founders and directors, his project to found a drama academy in Havana became the Academia de Artes Dramaticas. With the enthusiastic collaboration of Cuban intellectuals like Jorge Mañach, Suarez Solis, Luis Amado Blanco and Luis Baralt and artists, like Wilfredo Lam, and Portocarrero, and musicians like Felix Guerrero, the project became a reality."

Rosa Ileana Boudet, writer and journalist, and researcher on Cuban theater in her blog "Lanzar la flecha bien lejos" quotes the late notable Cuban playwright and director Francisco Morín writing in "For the Love of Art" about Lorna describing her as a "gratifying" discovery: "a tall and strong American who spoke a funny Spanish with an accent and who wasted no time in putting us all into action". Pablo Fariñas in the newspaper El Habanero entitled "Un adiós para una querida amiga Cubana" wrote:

"Lorna always valued, until the last days of her life, the characteristics that distinguish Cubans, who in her own words, regarded as brave, bearers of a great sense of humor and joy of living. According to her, she told Fariñas, what she had to achieve in the United States in two weeks of tough rehearsals, Cuban actors could catch up with her in just two hours."

Lorna pioneered new forms of dramatic interpretation unknown at that time in Havana, including Stanislavski's acting method, directing plays from the American, European, and Spanish repertoire seldom seen before. Her weekly drama radio hour included a wildly popular "Dragonwyck," based on the novel of the same name by Anya Seton, and masterpiece productions in the nascent television genre. Her last production was in 1955 of the Italian farse "Filomena Marturano" by Neapolitan author Eduardo De Filippo, later made into the movie adaptation "Marriage Italian Style" directed by Vittorio De Sica with Sophia Loren.

It was in the midst of these undertakings that Lorna came across an abandoned mansion in the Vedado section of Havana next to the Caribbean:

"I was intrigued by a beautiful, old mansion on an obscure point in the Vedado suburb of Havana, which was built very close to the water. I would go there frequently to be by myself and noticed there were several people who evidently occupy the garden grounds there. I wondered about the owners who had abandoned the mansion and how in the world they could have left something so beautiful as this. As I was looking up at one of its towers one afternoon and wondering what kind of story would come to my imagination, one of the wooden gargoyles that seemed an integral part of the wooded tower fell directly at my feet. I picked it up, asked what it was saying to me, and knew I was to write a story about this house and the gargoyle. First I would wish to create people who lived in that garden and why they were there. Who had owned it, left it, and why? What had they been involved in during their lives there? I reflected on the estate's probable historical period. I thought of the "Dance of the Millions" and then perhaps earlier, and I took it from there."

As her last editor Anita Susan Grossman notes in the Editorial Notes to this book, Lorna was foremost a person trained in theater with a critical eye and understanding of character, motivation and the importance of details to convey a sense not only of place but of the characters that inhabit the space. A cardinal rule she observed and taught was the essence of timing in propelling the action. *Infinite Corner* is a time capsule filtered through the imagination of an artist for whom Cuba and its people were always admired and occupied center stage.

Cuba, and especially the capital, Havana, was at the forefront of the currents for social changes brought about by two world wars. At a time when men were traditionally excluded from moral judgment in the male dominated sexual order, in the mid Twentieth Century women already held a special niche in Cuban iconography. Their liberalism, depicted in this novel, were to have far reaching consequences in the as yet unborn Cuba of post-revolutionary 1959. In this sense the struggle of the individual against a structured order bequeathed by Spanish colonialism subverted the accepted norms, opening a new chapter in the island's history.

- Victor Bonilla-Sosa
Vernal Equinox, 2021

1
THE GARDEN PEOPLE

The sun shone brightly on the tin can full of cigarette butts, and its harsh gleam was an alarm clock to Arsenio's trained eyelids. He blinked them slowly, pushed the can out of the sun and looked up at the morning sky. No cloud yet, so he could lie there awhile, watching the little worms and globes that skittered across the pale ceiling. They always floated by in the same direction, and he would follow them with the tail-end of his eyes. Sometimes they would float right through the tree branches like ectoplasmic worms.

He arose, stretching and scratching (and rubbing if there happened to be an ant-line marching over him), ambled slowly over to the broken wall facing the sea, and urinated. He liked to watch the ocean as he did so. The sea's soft familiar voice, its clean breath—carajo! —how much better than coming to life each morning at the side of a woman! Sometimes he would remember his wife, the smell of her all over the place, the sound 'of her quick movements filling the small room where they had lived on the other side of the city in the crowded Old Havana. A woman was much to have all day in your room!

He grinned, showing a few yellow teeth, and thought how fortunate he was now. On the other hand, Chan Li Po, who lived near him under the wild grape tree, wasn't so lucky. Every morning when Arsenio was still snoring, he was up and gone, hurrying to some mysterious transaction in Havana that produced a big can of cooked rice—sometimes with bread, even black beans or fried banana. Once he'd come back with a chunk of pork so big that everyone in the garden had eaten some. Well, that was fine, but it wasn't worth mixing with people early in the morning. People were something that you had to work up to gradually to bear.

Arsenio stretched and looked again. You never knew what kind of ocean you woke up to. Sometimes its foggy covers had already been pulled back by the sun, and then the whole bunch of little waves would rush towards you like children jumping out of bed, with tiny starfish caught in the drifting seaweed. You could see ribbon fish down below, and maybe a small octopus climbing on the rocks.

At times early in the morning or after a soft rain, the mist hung over the shoreline as it curved towards Havana Harbor. Strangely enough, what you could see best from here in the Vedado were the towering Royal Palms. It was as though there had never been anything else here at all—no skyscrapers, no Capitolio, nothing but the great silver palms rising from deep red earth.

But today everything came at you all together and strong! Sharp sunlight cut angles out of the whitewashed buildings and made glaring patches all over town: of the "Nacional" towers; the bronze flanks of Maceo's horse; the gold glistening eagle atop the "Maine"; and the harsh crag of Cabaña Fortress.

Arsenio turned towards the old house, and the shadow of a sea gull moved over the crumbling rock bench that still belonged to the old garden. The breeze was blowing from the north this morning, which always brought hunger, so he walked back to his tin cans and picked out one for mussel-gathering.

First, though, he'd have a smoke. He fingered the pile of butts in the tin can. This was one of the highlights of the day. Butt-collecting, besides being a necessity, had become a hobby. The others who lived in the garden— Chan Li, Marquesa, El Chori—didn't know that he found practically all his smokes right there by the wall or the street that followed the old walls. While they paced the crowded thoroughfares looking for stubs, he stayed here in peace and quiet. Near him servant girls and their men sat on the wall talking and smoking. The girls always left Cuban tobacco, well smoked down, since they didn't have much chance to smoke on their jobs; but their men left cigarettes half smoked, as most of them were a shiftless lot who played around during the working day. They were restless and smoked more from life-hunger than from tobacco-hunger. And that was fine for Arsenio. Good-sized stubs would flip one after the other against the wall, as inadequate as the chatter that flipped through the morning peace, fruitless as the petting of the servant girls that reached no place at all. Well, he grinned, at least he could do something about the cigarettes!

He might have an American brand if he wanted. He would have liked to begin the morning with a taste of the dark-haired woman who drove her own car alone, but she never left cigarette stubs anymore. He missed them. She'd been coming there for years. When he had first noticed her, she was looking out at the ocean, her eyes becoming wings over the sea. Once she'd tried following her eyes, and stepped down from the car. But her high stilted heels didn't let her go very far over the rocks, and back she came, the wings gone from her eyes.

When she returned to her car and was lighting her long cigarette, she saw Arsenio watching her from under a tree a few yards away. He knew that he must frighten plenty of others with the beard, the yellowing of dirt and years upon him, the eyebrows that rambled like sea-moss over his face. The woman glanced over the tin cans, the charcoal and sticks ready for cooking, the newspaper mattress, the dirty rags fluttering happily on the laurel tree. Then her eyes dipped right into his own while she inhaled again. He wondered if she thought he was as lonely as she was. He smiled at the thought, but mistaking his smile, she flung the cigarette through the car window and sped away.

Arsenio had been sorry to have disturbed her. He saved that cigarette with the red mouth on it until it had grown too stale to smoke. He didn't know why he had kept it, except that it was a mouth that needed kissing, and had needed and belonged to him in that moment that she had inhaled—needed his rags, and the tree, and the wings of his ocean.

Shortly after that she stopped coming. He didn't see her for a long time, over a year. Then one day he spied her car. It was parked by the rocks, as near the ocean as she could get. She got out and climbed easily over some boulders, where she stayed a minute or two, breathing in the ocean. Then she walked back towards the vehicle, her face all smiles. When she turned to look at the old house and garden, she saw him, and he felt sure she recognized him. Her eyes seemed to stay with him an extra moment before she returned to the car and drove off.

After that she came by often. It was as though she had to say hello to this place in passing. She was never there long enough to smoke, or to leave a stub, which he greatly regretted.

Other American brands, which cost more than Cuban cigarettes, usually came from couples parked in cars. They spoke in low voices for hours, keeping the driver's mirror in focus always so as not to be surprised from the rear. They kissed with one eye on the mirror and lowered their heads each time someone passed.

Some couples would disappear beyond the rocks, or, uncertain where to love each other, would look with apprehension at the great crumbling house—or what little one could see of it because of its dense vegetation. It was an old gray woman of a house, an emaciated old woman, with crevices running over the face from which the paint had fallen long since. Sightless windows stared defiantly over the sea, empty sockets whose eyes long ago had reflected the splendor of the sunsets. The repulsive old woman yet wore a glory of carved Moorish towers and vines bursting with color. She had fought her destiny with fierce passion. One could tell that from seeing the great wrought-iron gates twisted and deformed, the white curving figures of the fountain, the grotto of the Blessed Virgin, and the cleft marble bench where the moon still stopped to rest.

Nothing was spared but the ocean's voice for her deafness, the sunrise for her blindness. Everything lay broken and maimed: everything, that is, but the delicate Moorish towers and the grey wooden gargoyles—a hundred lewd faces smiling into the sun—guarding against the hurricanes, the tidal waves, cyclones and sun-fire of years: they guarded the last beauty of the ridiculous old woman.

If any lovers seeking their small corner had not already been advised that here were no phantoms, they would know after their first fear. They would know because of the white and rose coralillo that burst radiant from every crevice, and because of the broken marble fountain whose waters sprang joyously from a secret source. It called with a young, clear voice, now buoyant, now plaintive, before returning with a sigh to the sea.

As Arsenio pondered over his early morning smoke, he heard a rustling in the Malanga leaves close by. Marquesa's goat! She had broken from her rope, and, heavy with milk, was wandering about the garden. What luck! If Chan Li could only know what a fool he was, worrying about his rice and beans! If a man had faith, the rocks would give him meat, and the Malanga leaves would grow milk. Miracles were nothing new to Arsenio. Each new sun lit up a few, if anyone had time to see them. This business of hunting miracles by the light of a church candle was like casting a little hooked line in a private pond and turning your back to an ocean. A casting rod of faith, with a new day's sun as bait hooked on the end of it, was the real way to catch miracles.

He burnt his fingers with the last drag and picked up the rope to lead the goat back to Marquesa. That would earn him a nice warm glass of milk. He passed under the arbors that sagged on one leg with their weight of Sun Bells and Piscuala vines and entered the doorless remnants of a kitchen. Marquesa was washing out some towels so frayed that no rubbing could ever restore their whiteness. She smoothed back her black hair that fell over a dress held together by neat patches.

"God guard thee, neighbor," she greeted.

"He has so far," acknowledged Arsenio. The suds hissed as he waited for her to finish the wash. They were no less gray as she hung them on a line above the broken brick stove, but this did not discourage her.

"Sit down, sit down," she indicated, dusting off a wooden crate. "I see that goat has wandered off again. Thank you for returning her to me. If it were some other neighbor now, I might possibly imagine that he'd also untied her rope, so that he could bring her back to me." Her quick eyes smiled at him from under the wrinkled face. He grinned.

They both knew to whom she was referring: Carambita, who occasionally took quarters under the almond tree on the northwest corner of the garden. It was a good morning, so Arsenio did not spit, as he would have done ordinarily, because Carambita was a motherless disgrace, no more than a petty thief who could not understand the common bond between all the inhabitants of the garden.

When suddenly one evening he would appear, moving toward the almond tree, everyone knew that meant hiding everything from cigarette butts to stray pennies—even newspapers if it was a cool night. Carambita would just wink and laugh when Arsenio would try to explain. He couldn't believe that they didn't steal from each other because he was the slave of everything that met his itching eyes. Chan Li's only slavery was rice. And Chori's was missing his kids. Topo made charcoal but wasn't a slave to it. And of course, Marquesa didn't count in that sense because she wasn't right in the head. Who would be, after living alone in an abandoned house for more than twenty years?

"It is a fine cool morning," remarked Marquesa, "Not like when the breeze blows from the southeast. It always seems so restless then. You must excuse me," she said as she went about her cleaning, "but I cannot let Phoebus steal up over a dirty kitchen. To say nothing of the whole house... and what if he should return today!"

"That would be very bad," murmured Arsenio. She was at it again! There were times when, except for her fussing to clean a broken-down house where no one lived but lizards, she seemed as sane as anyone else— which wasn't saying much either. But when she began with those queer foreign names and talking about "Him," then there was nothing to do but humor her. He wouldn't bother to ask who this fellow Phoebus was, or others named Dante and Virgil. They were just sounds that she conjured up for herself, with the screaking boards and the lizards. To be sure, once he did know an uncle who sold lottery tickets whose name was Virgil. But he didn't think it was the same fellow.

"I'll just warm you some milk of the goat which you had the kindness to return, if you will please be seated in the dining-room," she said. To please her, he stepped over the crumbling tiles of the passage-way and entered the dining-room.

At least this room had four walls, and except for the shutterless windows, was quite an elegant thing. He ran his yellow fingers over the mahogany panels that were bumpy with figures from the floor almost up the ceiling. Caramba! What a mess of creatures carved up in that wood: women with something like sheets wrapped around them carrying baskets of fruits on their heads; men with machetes cutting the grass, children dancing about some grapes—for some reason he had to keep running his hand over those creatures, feel them and the smooth wood gliding under. Just like far-off days, when the girls he danced with in the dance halls couldn't understand why he wanted to touch them, and not always kiss them. Maybe women didn't have their hands separate from the rest of them, that wanted to feel things by dipping under. Who could be so foolish as to wonder anything about women, anyway?

He looked up toward the ceiling and suddenly emitted a low whistle. Scratching his tangled head, he looked up again incredulously. Caramba! It was still there. "Marquesa," he shouted, "come here!" She threw down the mop and hurried from the kitchen.

"It's the Company!" she cried. "I saw their car prowling about here yesterday! I knew it! Oh where do you see them?" She poked her head through the open window. Arsenio was too absorbed gazing at the ceiling to notice her alarm.

"What devil of a company," he exclaimed, without altering his gaze. "I'm talking about this 'company,'" indicating the ceiling. Her eyes slowly followed his finger.

"What are you talking about?" she whispered.

"Will you tell me what son-of-a-mare could sit under that woman's naked rump and still want to eat his dinner?" he shouted.

The Marquesa breathed in relief and her shoulders relaxed. She looked at Arsenio gaping at the mural and then burst into laughter. The high notes so shook her thin body that she had to sit on the window ledge for support.

"That is Ceres, Goddess of Fertility of the Fields," she answered. "The artist who painted this interpreted her as sensuous and womanly. Those others are Pomona and—but the milk is boiling over!" and she hurried from the room, her explanation leaving Arsenio entirely unconvinced. She was not right in the head, Marquesa, but then neither was the owner of this house if he didn't mind a thing like that hanging over his plate three times a day!

He noticed that Marquesa's hand was still shaking as she brought him the milk. "What Company was that you were talking of, that frightens you so?" he asked. He wondered if she had noticed those men, after all. He and Chori had invented whatever they could to keep her inside every time men came around drawing lines with sticks all over the place, and looking through some sort of instruments. They'd been doing that for years, off and on, but recently more often.

"It would be a company sent by Leandro's family. Certainly not by him!" she murmured, "Never by Leandro Camacho!" She began to walk about the room, up and down, up and down. "This house is his life, and it belongs to him still. When he left, he did not give it to sell. He meant for them to live here, and to love each other. He went away so that they would remain here. Well, they are gone too. But I'm here. And no one is going to take me from here. Not alive." She leaned against the window and looked out over the garden and the ocean whose voice was part of the silence.

Lost in her thoughts, she continued, "Not as long as I remember the words he spoke. 'If anything should ever happen to me' he said, 'take care of it. You and I built this together, Antonia, and only we two know what we are waiting for. As long as you have faith that it will happen someday, don't ever leave. Guard it for us both.'"

She was still now, and as the morning light carved her profile, Arsenio observed for the first time that she must have been beautiful once.

"So your real name is Antonia, Old One?" he asked.

"I'll show you exactly where we were standing when he said that." Memory had suddenly erased the present from her face, and she was smiling eagerly as she beckoned for him to follow out into the garden, to the long terrace rambling around the other side of the house.

"We had just begun the Cuban Youth Movement, and were celebrating that and the Republic's fifteenth birthday all together. It was the twentieth of May, 1902. A terrible cyclone pulled up the flag-pole long ago, but it was just about here. And over there was the framboyan." She pointed to a huge stump of tree, white with years.

"This was the most magnificent framboyan on the estate," she said proudly. "When it was in bloom, a person could hardly dare look at all its color, all the bright scarlet bursting almost enough to blind one! It's as though the Lord had made a little slip there, forgetting just how much beauty we mortals can endure." She had raised her head as though she were seeing again the scarlet masses all over the house, and she rubbed her scrawny arms in humility before its splendor. All Arsenio could make out was the dead stump on the ground.

He looked up and beheld only the high tower of the house with those crazy wooden faces peering down at him.

"We were standing right here, and we'd looked up, and could see the gargoyles through the branches. Do you see them there? She cocked her head to one side, as though the non-existent tree branches obstructed their visibility. Arsenio gaped to please here, but he didn't know what he was supposed to be looking for.

"No," he shook his head. "I don't see them. They must have flown away."

She smiled. "Gargoyles do not fly, foolish one. Do you not see those faces up there?"

"Oh, I can see those all right!"

"Well, that is what we saw through the branches, and he said 'You, Antonia, and those fellows up there. Wait together.' That was another time, and I really did not know what he meant then, or that he was leaving. But I

7

do understand now..." She smiled.

They both stood in silence, as they gazed at the gray faces grinning at time, faces at once crafty and childlike, wizards whose innocence had not been marred by their knowledge.

"Just look at them," she whispered. "And try to imagine any mortal force subduing them! Not all the cyclones have been able to disturb them; how would anyone else! Any 'Company!' "she laughed suddenly. "I must be a crazy old woman to fear that they could move those up there, or me!" Suddenly she bent and pulled up a small mint plant. Hierba buena. Plant it by your tree. I have plenty of it. Good for the stomach."

Arsenio thanked her. "Getting late" she remarked. "I've almost half the house to clean before lunch time and I must go to the bodega to refill my water pail. It's really very kind of Francisco to let us use his tank, isn't it? God guard you," and she was gone, disappearing just as suddenly as the wondrous framboyan tree that had never been there at all. Arsenio smelled his mint plant and grinned.

"Almost began to believe her there for a while. Gargoyles—" he pronounced at the faces, then slowly made his way back to his tree for a tin can, and from there out to the rocks. He'd better hurry and get his mussels before his neighbor Chori started shouting for him to come and see whatever he'd found in the dump yard.

2
LOURDES AND JORGE

Jorge had finished dressing and had entered the darkened room to find Lourdes still lying there with her arms encircling the pillow. Her face was turned toward the small drawing room whose shuttered calm was flickered into warmth by the altar candle glowing at the foot of the Virgin of the Caridad del Cobre.

He walked to the window and opened the shutter slightly. Like a waiting cat on the sill, a sun-ray leapt over the bed, its perverse claws striping the curve of her body, and absently she reached out in response to it. The sight of her unconsciously caressing her own body gleaming with sun overpowered him. Because the life of her senses was always independent of her conscious intelligence, he could lose himself in these eyes, in the warm mouth under his and the soft yielding of someone who was no longer Lourdes but the incarnation of their own desire, their hunger of creation

He was unable to take his gaze from the light that softly curled and blended with her movements. By the side of the bed where she lay, he bent towards her and slowly raised her to him. He could feel her shoulders tremble at his touch, and when he crossed his hands over her throat, his thumb pressing gently against it, she did not move. His hand moved slowly from her neck and shoulders and rested on her breast, which became hard and small under his motionless hand. Heavily, deliberately, he felt each curve of her body under his darkness, and then slowly he forced her to her knees. The more fury and desire that shook him inwardly, the more it pleased him to exercise restraint. As his dark almond eyes, like those of an impassive stranger, slowly moved over her body, each part of it seemed to assume a separate life of its own. With his two hands he framed her face, memorizing it, as though he would stamp the features on his own.

It was she who first broke the silence with a long sigh. Blindly he sought her mouth again, and his fingers smoothed back strands of hair, damp from perspiration, that had fallen across her cheek. Then he drew away, exclaiming softly, "Don't I ever have enough of you? I have fallen into the hands of one who must surely be a pupil of the witches of Regla."

She laughed, and wished that she might lie there forever, enveloped in his warmth, his hair smelling of the night air heavy with anon-fruit and mango. She would lie staring at the huge factory-renaissance wardrobe, or at the walls with the colored prints of the plump nudes which, having become a part of so many hours of joy, had ceased to be offensive; or watch the tiny white butterflies that trembled like snowflakes past the window; or listen to the soft tinkle of the beaded fringed doorway, beyond which danced the shadows of the darkened little room with the altar light for the Virgin of Cobre.

She could hear his heartbeat mingled with the voices of children and housewives from the small apartments that lined the alley. And somehow, from all these heterogeneous things, there seemed to emerge a harmonious, comprehensive whole. With another sigh she stretched her arms across the bed until her body was taut.

"Qué pasa, mujer?" he asked.

"I am stretching around the entire universe," she whispered. "My fingers reach out and are touching the sea and mountains on the other side of the world. And I am lying in the tall grass under the creaking of the bamboo trees as they rub together, and can hear the conversation of the little lizards and the ants. You have made me part of all this, my darling! Before, when I would pass the Malecón I would watch the people there with such envy— the city fishermen, the mulato lovers, the families devouring hot churros with such relish! All of them whose only diversion and escape from the heat was the Malecón wall. They all belonged to each other and the world because they had nothing else, and I wanted so terribly to belong to them too!" She raised herself slightly, leaning on her elbow, "Have you ever noticed how the fishermen tie empty bottles to their lines?"

"So, they can walk around a little to see how the others are making out," he nodded.

"And they know they've hooked a fish because the bottle jerks and bounces. Well, do you know, dear, that I would stand there and watch them, and every time a bottle rattled on the cement wall, I felt it was myself tugging and calling to them! Because when I tried to mingle with them, there was only silent rejection. I was the dispossessed instead of them! Always flung back into the elegant shadow-box of the world I was born to.

Darling, how cruel the poor are to the rich! They withhold from us even the smallest crust."

He could not answer her about a world unknown to him.

She continued, "But now it's all changed for me! I'm no longer a trespasser, and do you know? I've never been lonely since that day we met and you slammed the door of my car and leaned over, with all the traffic of Calle 23 being held up by us, and said 'I have to take care of you'. Remember, cariño?"

He closed his eyes and lay silent.

"Just loving—without this—" and she pressed her cheek against his arm, "just love—is the best part, isn't it?"

"Yes, my Lourdes, yes," he emphasized slowly as one who reluctantly admits to an undeniable truth. He dragged out the long, weary, hurting "yes," which altered everything; it summoned the almost material presence of tenderness, the cursed gift that turned to significance and beauty and pain everything it touched.

"Don't say it like that," she pleaded.

He pressed his lips to her throat. His words came muffled, "At least I've tried to take care of you. I've always tried." The sadness of his voice told her that reality had taken over. The room was filled with awareness and memories.

"Those were the first words you ever spoke to me," she remembered softly. "I have to take care of you."

"I know," he whispered.

"No one had ever told me that before. No one! It would have been most amusing to others had they heard you—the idea that I needed being taken care of!" Her lips touched his hair and lingered there.

"The others didn't love you." he said. "How could you expect them to know? To me there was nothing strange about saying that. It was so clear, watching you in the Club, surrounded by those dowagers and their complacent men."

"And I scarcely noticed you!"

"How could you? I was trying so hard to be camouflaged amongst the feathered hats, with the Charity Hospital blueprints clutched in my hands. God! How uncomfortable I was. It was the first time I'd ever been to the Yacht Club. I will never understand what made me say yes to that woman—the chairman or whatever she must have been—who called me."

"Josefina Aragon," she prompted.

"You know how I feel about rotogravure philanthropists.

"But you came."

"And you were there!"

"We will someday erect a statue to Josefina Aragon," she announced.

"We will," he nodded gravely, "complete with that hat!"

Suddenly he exclaimed softly "Oh, my Lourdes!" and passed his hand roughly over the back of her head and the long chestnut hair that covered her shoulders. "If you could have seen yourself as clearly as I did that day! That strong face of yours and the simplicity of your every movement. It was like seeing an Etruscan figure in a Louis XIV setting!"

"I have seen Etruscan figures," she observed with mock solemnity. "I am not over-fond of this intended compliment!"

"I've often wondered," she continued, "if you really were so impressed by my 'essential strength' as you call it—"

"And still am."

"Why should you have felt so protective towards me from the first day? I've never quite understood."

"I'll tell you something I'd never mentioned to you before," he said. "I don't know why. Perhaps I've wanted to keep the memory of it just for myself. Do you remember we were all having cocktails? I had been introduced to everyone, which somehow only added to my discomfort, and I managed to sneak out to the terrace and sink from sight into one of those high-backed beach chairs. A few minutes later I heard someone near me and I saw you. You'd wandered away from the others. You stood facing the sea, raising your head as though you were intent upon something, or waiting for a voice to tell you something. I was sorry to be an intruder, eavesdropping on your intimacy. Do you remember at all?"

She shook her head.

"But I couldn't risk moving for fear you would see me. At one moment I would not have been surprised had you walked right into the sea," he smiled and drew her tightly to him. "Then someone from the cocktail party saw you and called your name. You stiffened and closed your eyes as though gaining strength to go back, and suddenly picked up a small shell from the sand. I watched you holding it tightly in your palm as you rejoined them. And from that moment I forgot feeling awkward there and out of place. I didn't know who you were; I only knew that I loved you and that you needed me. If you only knew the schemes, I was inventing to be able to see you again!'

"And I saved you the trouble by offering a lift to anyone going to the Vedado! It's just occurred to me, were you really going to the Vedado?"

"No."

"I should have known" she laughed, "Conniver! And then to say that to me as you left. A perfect stranger! I kept hearing your voice all that night, 'I have to take care of you,' but I don't remember at all about the ocean."

"How would you! You never leave the sea if you can help it! I think you were a little star-fish in some other life. 'La mujer, que tiene su amor en el mar.'"

"Más tiene una estrella en la eternidad."*

12

"Daughter of Chango!"

"Do you know the santeras always tell me that? I'm the daughter of Chango, the sea-god, and of the sea."

"I can believe that."

"Why?"

"Why?" he thought a moment, "Because at times I see something in you—if you ever needed to use it—as austere as the ocean crags. If you were the conqueror of a nation, I think you'd kill off the weak of spirit, and pardon the scoundrels and pirates. Isn't that true?"

"Maybe," she laughed.

"Yet," he added, "at other times you are obedient as the sea which bore their sails gently. You could never be a quiet little pool; you would have to be the ocean, loving one minute, rebelling the next, always carrying sun and earth along with you in the tides. But there would always have to be rocks for you," he cautioned.

"Is that what you are? A rock?" she teased.

"God help me if I were not! Couldn't hold you a day!"

"I believe that's true! Does it bother you?

"I don't know. There are so many other things."

"Oh?" Surprised, she raised herself on her elbow and stared at him. "So there are many things about me that bother you! Why haven't you told me before?"

He pulled her towards him, amused. "I have no need to tell you, little foolish one," he whispered, "because without your ever knowing, I told them."

She knew this was true and lay silent tasting the secret warmth of that knowledge. To feel myself molded gently, silently to his will, she thought, this is the greatest compensation for being a woman. A man can never know this joy. She wished that it were earlier so that she might lie there for hours at his side, trying to make part of herself the scent of his black hair and his browned warm body, even the familiar feel of his muscles she stroked them.

Suddenly, one after the other, like a series of synchronized explosions, the metal doors of the surrounding shops were rolled up, putting official terminus to the siesta hour. Almost simultaneously they could hear the exchange of greetings amongst the proprietors. "Prepared to watch your Almendares Team lose the game tonight?" "Who is saying that?" "My countryman on the right who thinks a 'home-run' is a Jamaican drink!" "Ha! My Havana Team will show you what is a home run!" Their voices were still sleepy from the mid-day rest which had been interrupted by the utterly regretful necessity of bread-winning. Bestirring of housewives and a

---

* The woman who has her love in the sea...also has a star in eternity.

13

mother's ineffectual scolding mingled with the chimes of the neighboring church and a lumbering cargo train.

They both lay there, reluctant to leave, listening in silence to all this that would forever be identified with the deepest hours of joy in their lives.

Jorge rose decisively and, wrapping the sheet around her, knelt to put her shoes on her. "Come on, trigueña," he snapped his fingers and nodded towards her clothes. "If I don't use all my natural cunning against your wiles, we will never get away from here."

Smiling, she started toward the shower, and then remembered. "I can't see you until sometime next week," she reminded him. His hand raised to comb his hair was suddenly stayed.

"Next week!" But his voice was quiet.

"The architects' convention begins tomorrow." Her tone was as expressionless as his. "Being an official hostess means day and night——" She shrugged slowly. It was the only gesture possible before the inevitable.

"Not to see you for even a few minutes, anywhere——don't you think——" he broached hopefully.

She shook her head. "When, dear? There won't be a moment! Besides all the scheduled affairs, there's the sight-seeing for the foreign members; and then the Carnival party has taken a lot of planning. At least that will be the end of it. I think probably by Tuesday it would be all right."

He nodded slowly. "Next week, then."

"Now that you've moved, where can I leave a message?"

"I'm pretty sure I saw a bodega somewhere around there. I'll call to give you the number. In an hour?"

"Yes. But I suppose you don't know yet," she hesitated, glancing around the room. "If only——" she began, but did not allow herself to finish the sentence.

"What were you going to say?" His voice sounded strained and harsh.

"Nothing really, dear."

"If only what?" he insisted.

They stood facing each other in silence. There was pain in her eyes. "Please," she begged, and seeing that he pressed the subject no further, she hurried to the shower.

He lit a cigarette and crossed nervously to the small drawing-room still huddled in candle-light. He knew she had not finished the sentence for fear of his reaction. It was true that this last year he had become exceedingly difficult and over-sensitive. All that Lourdes had meant to say was "If only we were sure that we could return here Tuesday!"—and be spared the scurrying through shadows by being given this illusion of a home. She, who could have anything, dared not hope for this.

He smiled ironically as he looked at the room: the vase of awkward artificial flowers set over a crocheted mat on the center table; the cheap print of the Sacred Heart of Jesus thrust on one wall, and opposite it, staring proudly, the string of faded photographs of the family's heroes in Mambi uniform, fighting in the War of Independence; a small American refrigerator which gleamed in a corner, reflecting the elaborate altar of the Virgin of the Caridad del Cobre, all gilt and embroidery. All tasteless, loving traces of the family who lived here. Yet even this she could not have—nor anything at all, as long as her dogged blind love for him persisted. How could he make her understand that there are lives touched by an evil star that no amount of determination can alter, lives to whom catastrophe gravitates like a loving satellite.

There were moments when her optimism and faith became odious to him. She had been praying before—asking for what? For the plaster figure of a little black Virgin to change the world? To make strong those like himself who were too weak to be unscrupulous? To force the oppressed to relinquish their cherished right to suffer? He loved her more than himself, yet one could more easily wring tears from stones than conformity from him or recognition from the world. Poor Lourdes, who sought special concessions of the divinity with the accustomed optimism of the favored! When would she face the reality which her love refused to look upon?

Suddenly the pretense of this room which was not theirs appalled him. He flung open the shutters, and the crystal blade of the sun shattered everything into fragments of light.

§

After Lourdes had gone, he went as usual to the cafe on the corner to return the key to Oscar. He found him sitting at the table facing the street, as he always did, his sharp blue eyes alert for any trouble. Oscar's face brightened when he spotted his friend.

"Hello, Jorgito! If you have time, how about a rum with me?" There was an almost childish eagerness about Oscar that always touched Jorge. He smiled and shook his head.

"Thanks, Oscar. Next time. I'm late. I'll just have a quick one." He patted Oscar on the shoulder and crossed to the bar. "Pedro Domecq, double," he ordered. Tossing it down, he returned to Oscar.

"Would you know offhand if it's all right for Tuesday?" he asked; but he knew the answer even before Oscar's expression changed.

"Caramba!" Oscar exclaimed, "Usually so far in advance there's no problem. But just this morning one of the regulars, a lieutenant, reserved it for all day Tuesday. Can't make it."

"Monday?"

Jorge shook his head.

"You know, I had a feeling," Oscar grumbled. "Don't like him anyway.

To tell you the truth," he hunched his strong stooped shoulders over the table even more and lowered his voice, "I don't like most of them that come here—like to send them all to the devil! But what's a fellow my age to do, with no children to help me, and a cochino dizziness to keep me from waiting tables or from any other damn land job, and with a sailor's pension that won't feed a termite!"

Jorge could not help smiling at Oscar's face, red as an angry child's. Casting what he thought was a furtive glance at Jorge, Oscar suddenly straightened up and snapped his fingers. "I have an idea! There's a fancy new place I think he'd like. I can reach him and just tell him I made a mistake about the date—"

"Oh, you can't do that!" Jorge protested hastily and added, "It doesn't matter."

"Don't try to fool me, son! I'm just a dumb old sailor, but coño the sea teaches much about men, more than you can imagine." he snorted with pride, "When a man's spent all his life, knowing, just like this," he snapped his fingers, "the difference between blue skies that are fair, and blue skies that are hiding a squall behind them—knowing not just with your eyes, but as though you could smell and touch it, and feel inside of you—when it's so hard for the good Lord or the devil to fool me, just how would a young fellow be able to? Know what I mean?"

Jorge did not answer. No use trying to deceive this man who seemed to sense what it meant to him.

"I'm sure it will be okay. The Teniente will like that place. Just give me a ring in about half-hour to be certain."

For a moment Jorge could only stand there silenced by the unexpected kindness. Then, with a grateful grin that was much more than words for Oscar, Jorge nodded his head, and left...

3
THE BODEGA LA VICTORIA

The heavy noon silence of the streets was just being rippled by early window-shoppers as Jorge drove northwest across the center of Havana. Past Fraternity Park, up Galiano and across winding, bumpy San Lazaro, empty still, except for one wavering street-car; up the hill past the University and across the wide palm-lined avenues of the Vedado which luxuriously stretched and yawned out of its siesta, and down to that indeterminate part of the suburb which curved on the sea.

An occasional goat grazed through empty lots; laundry lines stretched from wrought-iron railings of old mansions, now overcrowded with tenants; and some small new apartments, "estilo moderno," incongruously thrust themselves upon the area.

He thought he remembered noticing the "Bodega La Victoria" somewhere in this section. There it was. Just right: far enough from their new apartment to merit no patronage from his mother or sister, yet near enough for him to receive a message from Lourdes.

There was sure to be a phone. He pulled to the curb, and decided he would wait in the car for a while to give Oscar a little more time. The bodega's lively rhythm splashed out on the hot street. There was always the noise of people buying groceries, dice-players having a drink at the bar, and Francisco, the Spanish proprietor, generally enjoying himself, whether it was talking or singing or attending to customers. The way he shoveled into the shining mounds of garbanzos, rice, black beans, red beans or judias that gleamed from their partitioned glass counter made you think that he liked being a bodeguero.

The morning had been a busy one, and now, as usual right after lunch, two drivers of the corner taxi-stand were playing patas, while waiting to pick up their afternoon "regulars." Why sit around in the taxi, waiting for other calls, when they knew that most Vedado ladies were just dressing now after the siesta and would not be going out until late afternoon? So why not enjoy yourself? Also, Mateo, the neighborhood policeman, would surely be around with a good story to pay for his beer. He never missed.

"La vida es un fandango-o-o," Francisco was singing, as he packed a customer's grocery order.

These new lyrics caused one of the drivers called Pancho to look up from the game and nudge his companion, Isidro. They were familiar with Francisco's habit of improvising songs from old Spanish proverbs.

"Never heard that one before," he called to Francisco.

"—y quien no lo baile es un tonto-o-o," Francisco lustily sang out.

"I like that one," Pancho approved, "'Life is a fandango, and who doesn't dance it is a fool'—sometimes these Spaniards make sense, eh, Isidro?"

"But not often," Isidro laughed.

Undisturbed, Francisco continued his song. An admirably shining pate was more in evidence than the meticulously plastered strands which he thought concealed it, and a flourishing pump-handle moustache sprang from a face which was as rosy as when he had left his native Galicia twenty years before. Havana indolence had neither diminished his earthy vitality nor softened the crisp Spanish accent. His entire person attested to the inviolability of the gallego, son of Northern Spain, land of St. James the Apostle.

"Well, well! Good morning!" he welcomed as Marquesa entered. He treated her with a deference one might have expected for only the best customers. "You must be doing some extra cleaning!" he said, referring to the empty pail she carried.

"Yes indeed, Don Francisco," she answered, "you see, I have a feeling that something is going to happen soon—" her eyes lightened with a lovely secret, "and I must have the house ready for it."

This remark caused Pancho and Isidro to suspend the dice-throwing.

"A feeling what's going to happen?" Isidro asked warily. They all had heard rumors about the house, and if they were true—poor Marquesa!

"Ah-h..." she smiled waggishly.

"I know! You mean 'he's' coming!" Satisfied that she suspected nothing, Isidro reverted to his customary banter with her. But he was not disrespectful. Even though no one knew who she was—except a little crazy—she was a real lady. That was why they all called her "Marquesa."

Francisco took the pail from her and she protested.

"It is my pleasure," he said. "After all, we are both from the Mother-Country, aren't we?" He filled it and would have offered to carry it part of the way, but he knew from long experience that she would refuse. Canary Islanders were as proud and strong as those from his own province of Galicia. "Have a nice day," he said.

"And God guard you too," she answered. The weight of the water pail did not alter the straight tall way she walked as she left the bodega.

"La vida es un fandango," Francisco began to sing again as he returned to his work.

"If your calf is bleating to bring me luck, do not bother," Isidro called as he shook the dice in the leather cubilete. He tossed them out and they rolled over the counter.

"Ha!"

"No runs! No hits! I got four kings!"

"We'll see what we do about that!" Pancho shouted. He scooped up the four dice, and they rattled and shivered through the bodega. He tossed them out.

"Three fairies!" laughed Isidro. "See where they'll get you."

From the radio, the Servando Diaz Trio was playing a guaracha. The maracas and guitar cut the grocery air as clean and precise as the dice. "There's nothing philosophic about Sofia's hips," the trio sang.

Candita's slippers clapped over the floor as she entered. She lived in one of the crowded "solares" nearby. "I've eaten lunch three times today," she announced to anyone in the bodega, "and I'm still wondering what I want for breakfast. I've got tapeworm." She held out a kitchen cup to Francisco to fill with a dime's worth of black beans. "Nothing can ever satisfy me," she complained in a voice like a tired steam-whistle.

"Christ, I wouldn't like to be in your man's shoes" remarked Pancho's cousin Hilario, who had been seated at a table going through Bohemia magazine.

"Does that tapeworm get in on everything?" sniggered Pancho.

"For what you're thinking of, I was the same before I got the tapeworm," Candita retorted. She tugged at the two pigtails that lanced out behind her taut face.

The dice rattled over the counter.

"Try to beat that! Four 'crows' in one!" shouted Pancho. The other scooped up the dice.

"Candita, you read in the paper about the invention of the mechanical heart?" Pancho's cousin, Hilario, called.

"No kidding?"

"So help me."

"That's right," Pancho said. "You'll now be able to walk around with a spare heart in your pocket."

"Americanos make it?"

"Who else?"

"If they can make mechanical hearts, they can make a mechanical anything else," remarked Pancho, "and for Candita's husband, I wasn't thinking about the mechanical heart!"

"Here's your beans." Francisco took her dime. She turned her face towards the players at the counter. "About needing spare parts, Pancho, don't judge everyone from yourself." As her slippers clapped out the door Isidro cawed at Pancho's expense.

The dice were clattering again, with the smell of sawdust and steaming coffee rising towards them.

Jorge entered the bodega and looked around for the public telephone.

"Change for a dime, please," he asked Francisco.

The cash register chimed out, but not as loud as the sound of the dice-cup whacking against the counter, nor as penetrating as the voices of the Trio still singing "There's Not Much Philosophy About Sophia's Hips."

"Buenas," Jorge greeted, "How late are you open every evening?"

Francisco shrugged. "As long as there are customers. And as long as my wife and the neighbors don't complain," he smiled.

"I've just moved near here," Jorge continued, "and I might occasionally need a message left for me when it is urgent. Would it be too much trouble—?"

"Not at all! Be glad to do that for you, señor! And welcome to the neighborhood." Francisco extended his hand to Jorge. "At your service, Francisco Ortiz."

Jorge returned the handshake. "Jorge De Armas. And thank you."

"I'll just lower the radio," Francisco said, at the same time waving toward the telephone.

Jorge dropped a nickel in the slot and dialed. A woman's voice answered.

"Señora de Garcia? Cómo está?" Jorge greeted.

"It is Señor Jorge, isn't it? I always recognize your voice!" she answered. "We are very well, gracias."

"Oscar was expecting my call around now. Is he there?" There was a note of anxiety in his voice.

"No, he just went out a few minutes ago. But he left you a message. 'It is arranged. Everything is fine.'"

"Oh, that's very kind!" Jorge exclaimed.

"Do not worry about it. It was no trouble." Her words visibly reassured him.

"Would four o'clock be all right?" His voice was brighter now.

"Fine. My husband will be there to give you the key as always. How is—" she hesitated, "How are you both?"

20

Jorge smiled. "We are both very well, thank you."

"Bien. Adiós, Señor Jorge."

"Adiós." When he hung up his hand remained on the receiver like a great sigh of relief.

Relaxed now, he looked at his watch then asked Francisco for two more nickels and a Hatuey beer.

Francisco absently gave him the beer, but he forgot the nickels; like the cubilete players he was watching a long, lean Negro stoop over a pile of junk which had fallen into the street from his overturned pushcart. A bedpot, a shapeless mattress, a tin stove without burners, a child's rocker in the shape of a swan, a crocheted yellow bedspread, a toothbrush, and a heap of unrecognizable wearing apparel all rolled out in the street. Quietly, without anger, the Negro was gathering up everything. His woman, a thin mulata with a bright kerchief on her head, was making some kind of joke as she helped him.

"Home sweet home," murmured Pancho, rattling the dice. "That's their entire household in that cart. They're probably going to push that stuff from here across the bay to Regla." The owner of the grocery sucked his toothpick in wonder. It won't be long before old Marquesa and her pals will have to be doing the same thing, he added to himself.

Jorge was watching them too, and he thought, if Lourdes and I had as much of a home as that pushcart! If we could break through as far as Regla! Heavily he slapped down the quarter on the bar then took his bottle of beer to a table. Lourdes was expecting his call in about ten minutes.

On his way to the bodega, Mateo, the neighborhood policeman, stopped to watch the couple, especially the mulata woman who was stooped over. They were too occupied to notice him at first, but as the woman turned slightly, she straightened and stared at him deliberately.

"Don't let me interrupt you," he grinned, without moving. She bristled more from habit than from anger, then walked around the other side of the cart, where the policeman's eyes could not follow her.

"Very funny," she snapped. Her man was too intent to notice. As he followed her, Mateo winked back at Francisco and the players who were watching, and continued, "Planning to move right here on the street?" his eyes fixed steadily on her brown legs.

Before she could reply he picked up the bed-pot lying at his feet and with a sweeping gesture gave it to her. "Allow me, 'Madong,'" he bowed, in his best French manner, and walked toward the appreciative laughter of the bodega.

"A beer, plenty cold," he told Francisco, as he wiped off the sweated blue rim of his hat. "I've had quite a morning of it!" They didn't much believe that he'd had a big morning. When he said that it usually turned out to be nothing at all—making a row about a couple of cars locking bumpers and holding up traffic. Still, they were eager to hear, so he waited until he'd sat at a table, pushed his hat back, tipped his chair and stretched out his legs.

"Well—what happened?" Pancho asked at last.

"Yessiree!" he smacked through the beer foam. "I'm coming from the Crucero de la Playa, and walking down Twelfth Street, I hear a scandal of horns tooting, and a racket enough to be an electoral campaign! Traffic all jammed—you know, there where they're making a new little public square—"

"What, another little square?" exclaimed Pancho. "Now, where is this one being built? In the middle of the car barn?" And the laughter in appreciation of his joke made Pancho scratch his back where it didn't itch.

"Oho!" Francisco's hearty voice interrupted him, "So the citizens of Havana will enjoy another little square!" What a great love for beautifying the city has Pepe, the Minister of Public Works!"

"Why not?" Pancho answered. "Now that his uncle has given him a Ministry, he has to keep things in circulation somehow," he winked. "Else there would be many to complain, eh? A public square is just as good as anything."

"No imagination," observed the other player, sadly.

"Who said no imagination?" retorted Pancho.

"Anybody can build nice central highways and public buildings. But is that imaginative? It is no more than other countries have! But to find such unusual places to make public squares—that is an art!"

"Don't forget also, the streets torn up for repair—"

"And managing to keep them that way—"

"Hooray for Pepe!" cheered the player.

"Hooray for all the Mr. Pepe Plazoletas of the world! If they're smart enough, why not?" echoed Pancho.

"Besides, without them we wouldn't have so many jokes."

Mateo might have enjoyed all this had they let him tell his story first. He hastily picked it up now in the pause. "So, I walk over to see what's the problem. There's only room for one-way traffic on a two-way street, and there's a lady driver in a big parked Chrysler convertible, ready to get out, as calm as you please, with the whole line of cars blowing. On top of that, I see she has no license plates! When I stop her, she says oh, she knows all about that, the car is new and they just haven't given her the plates yet, 'besides' she says, 'you needn't worry about it as I have a Special Driver's License.' She flashes up some painted eyelashes at me and smiles like that was that. Brother, that's where I go blind. When they pull out those Special Licenses! What right has a two-cent-politico to hand out privileges to break the laws? Is this a Republica or what?" His tipped chair righted itself violently as the beer mug hit the table.

22

It was the signal they hopefully awaited. This was the reason, at least the chief reason, for the cubilete playing, the mojito drinking, even going to the bodega at all. And for the daily humoring of Mateo the policeman. The day would be like a beef-steak without garlic if, out of the bodega fertilized with saw-dust and coffee smell and boredom mixed in the joking, there would not spring this flower, this something to shout about, to argue about, and to think about afterwards.

"Is this a Republic or what?" Pancho's cousin, Hilario, repeated, as he sauntered to the bar. "I would say it is an 'Or What.'" His slow, country-cadenced voice issued strangely from the apparition of pink-striped, tight collared shirt, florid purple tie, snug brown suit and highly polished shoes. "But now that I'm used to a country that is an Or What, I have no complaints."

"That's not so!" Francisco clapped down the rag he'd been wiping off the bar with. "Trouble is, you fellows do not appreciate anything. I agree with Mateo about the Special License, but things could be worse. Don't you have free elections in Cuba? Freedom of the press?"

This earned a unanimous snort.

"Compared to what a Spaniard has at home, anything is a republic," Pancho giggled.

"Wait a minute," drawled Hilario, sarcastically, "Maybe Francisco is right now that President Grau has decided he's going to be re-elected. He and the Government are going to make voting nice and easy for us!" He tapped his pocket significantly. "We will have a never-ending term of the 'Administration of Good Friends All,'" he quoted the President's favorite phrase.

"Eddy Chibás won't let him get away with that!" Isidro protested confidently. "Didn't you hear Eddy's Sunday Hour last week? Boy, that was something!"

With an easy gesture Hilario waved the hand with the big ruby on it. "Crazy Eddy and his fairy tales."

"'Crazy Eddy' eh? The only one in this whole rotten country with the guts to stand up for the people and tell them the truth!" Isidro sputtered with sudden passion.

Jorge, seated in the back, had been enjoying the scene. "Keep the faith, Skinny One," he secretly rooted for Isidro. "We will make things different someday." He would be seeing Eddy tomorrow at the meeting and would have to tell him about his "champion" in the bodega. Eddy would love this if he were here now.

"Think all Cubans can be bought like you? Anyone with timbales is gonna fight the bastards that betrayed their own revolution party!"

In answer Hilario, ridiculously pantomiming a boxer, quoted Chibás, "Cubans, take off your coats, loosen your ties, tighten your belts and get in fighting position—" but before he had finished, Isidro sprang at him cursing.

"Muchacho! Muchacho!" Francisco shouted and lunged towards Isidro from behind the counter, managing to hold him by the shirt collar. Mateo the policeman did not stir. Since the grievous interruption of his story, he had seated himself at a table apart, making a great show of indifference, reading Bohemia magazine.

"You're crazy, Hilario," Pancho told his cousin. What the hell you want to ride him like that!"

"He's an idiot taking politics so seriously," Hilario scorned, "and Chibás is another fool. He can't do anything about it. Doesn't he know that? Grau's not going to let go of a good thing when he has it—especially when he plays ball with American investors. Where they are is the winner. Didn't Washington support bastards like Menocal and Machado? They'd never let Chibás be President. He's got too many ideas of his own—like economic independence for one thing. Who can fight the interests of our Yankee brothers? But then, people say the world is progressing. Maybe someday the Americanos will be willing to share Cuba with the Cubans. Who knows?" And he slithered from the bar stool and ambled towards the tobacco counter.

"Nothing bothers that one," Francisco said as the others returned to the bar. In thoughtful silence they sipped their drinks.

"Cynic!" Isidro repeated.

"Aw," Pancho elucidated, hugging his glass. "That's what you don't know. He wasn't always like that. He wanted to be a school teacher once when he lived in the country. I guess he thought he could change things a little, but he found out different. He's happier now."

"Hombre," Francisco reflected after a pause, "there are things in life that will never change. Each place it's something different. Here there will always be liver-trouble, crooks in the Palace, and American businessmen."

"Sure, that's what Hilario says. So he plays it smart now."

"It's not so intelligent to be smart," Francisco shook his head.

"No? What'll you bet my cousin's got a special driver's license too. And plenty of other specials! You gotta be smart! If you don't, someone else will. Like the proverb says: 'Camarón que se duerme, se lo lleva la corriente.'"

"Sí, sí," Francisco assented and grimly slapped down the rag he'd been wiping off the bar with. "'If the shrimp sleeps, the tide will wash him away.' Everyone worrying not to be the sleeping shrimp. That's why the world is what it is today. You must keep awake and steal right and left before the next one does it. Did it never occur to you that the sleeping shrimp at least enjoys his sleep? We all have to drown someday anyway." And he marched over to the pressure-coffee machine, punctuating his wisdom with the hiss of the steam.

24

There was a sudden silence as they remembered Mateo. "Eh, Mateo! finish your story!" But Mateo pretended not to hear as he studied a page of Bohemia. They looked at each other in sheepish amusement as they realized he was hurt. Pancho picked up the cue and walked over to him,

"So, 'General José Martí' Mateo," he winked to the others. "What happened when she said she had a special license?"

"Oh, that," Mateo shrugged in sour indifference, "Nothing happened of interest. I just gave her a ticket."

They were all sorry they had definitely ruined the play-by play account

"So, who was she?"

"The wife of Raul Diego."

"The Senator?"

"Sí."

"Bravo, te felicito," congratulated Isidro. "You're crazy, boy! You dug yourself a grave!" Pancho mourned jubilantly.

"So all right. I buried myself. You can send a wreath." And Mateo walked out, his hurt almost compensated by the admiring glances he felt warming his back.

"Poor Mateo," Francisco clucked. "He should have had the beat near the University. Something is always happening there!"

"Now can you give me change, please?" Jorge, having finished his beer, reminded good-naturedly. He startled the others who had not noticed him seated on the far side of the bodega.

Francisco's hands shot up to his bald head in apology. "Sí, señor! Right away. A little coffee, too? I'm just going to draw it!" He suggested it more from friendliness than from an eye to business. A surge of well-being swept over him. This was what made him happy, the bodega noisy and alive with arguments, cubilete players, and customers coming in and out all morning. He even liked to have people use the telephone. And now there was someone else coming in. This one was an estirado, with his white linen suit, not a wrinkle, and his county club face. But Francisco didn't mind that. He liked all kinds.

"Coffee, please," said the newcomer.

"Just drawing fresh, if you want to wait, señor."

The cubilete players began a new round, and Jorge, seeing it was time, dialed his number. As he waited for Lourdes to answer, he thought, "Thank God it's all right for Oscar's." Today at least, he could spare her the sudden silence that always preceded the question she would try to make sound casual for his sake, as though a game spirit could alter reality or lessen all that the question symbolized.

"Hello, darling," he said as she answered, and his heart was beating as fast as the first time they had ever been together.

The newcomer crossed his long legs indolently and turned away to

25

observe Jorge, whose back was toward him as he talked on the phone at the other end of the bodega. Although the newcomer could not place him, the caller seemed strangely familiar. Slender and of average height, wide-shouldered, sandaled feet crossed, Jorge leaned on one arm that rested high over his head against the wall. There was a tension in the wide back and a flexing of the sun-tanned arm that belied his casual position. The newcomer wondered lazily whether it was politics, money, or a woman that made the fellow so intense. But when Jorge had finished his conversation, he turned suddenly, and his face was illumined with a depth of emotion so unexpected and alien to the man observing him that the latter quickly averted his gaze. It was as though someone had struck him. He felt an absurd resentment toward this fellow who had so brusquely revealed layers of living unknown to him. He could hear him laughing now with the fat Spanish proprietor, and wondered how anyone could carry with a laugh the intense feeling he had just exposed. In spite of himself, the man looked toward Jorge at the cigar counter where he was unwrapping a long cigar, and at that moment Jorge turned towards him and their eyes met. With a vaguely surprised gesture of recognition the man half-waved, but Jorge evidently had not noticed, or, it seemed to the man, had not wished to notice, for he again turned to pay for the cigar and would have left, had Francisco not intercepted.

"Señor! The gentleman at the table was waving at you!"

For a fraction of a second Jorge hesitated, frowning, as though anxious to be off, but now the man had risen, inviting him to his table. Jorge could not now leave without giving offense.

"Mario Guzman, how are you?" he said as he crossed to the table.

Mario, a little confused, shook his hand. He was vexed at the well-meant attention of the proprietor who had forced him into the embarrassing situation of having waved at someone whom he could not place.

"How are you, ah..." he murmured.

"Jorge De Armas," Jorge helped, "Havana Institute, and La Salle School of Vedado."

"Of course!" Mario was relieved, "It's been so many years! I saw you as you were talking on the phone over there."

"Oh?" Jorge said sharply.

"But I couldn't quite remember..."

"Well, that teaches me a lesson. I've been living with the pleasant illusion that I haven't changed at all since high school!" Jorge laughingly thrust the long cigar between his teeth whose whiteness was accentuated by a dark complexion.

Mario smiled. His momentary resentment had been dispelled. One couldn't help warming to this fellow who, as a matter of fact, did have a student-day buoyance about him.

"You really haven't changed," he commented, as he insisted that Jorge sit at his table, "Don't know why I didn't recognize you immediately." Except, he thought, that we had always moved in different circles. He remembered that Jorge had been one of the few boys who was never called for after school. Mario had been impressed, as sitting in the car next to the family chauffeur, he had noticed schoolmates running to catch the bus, even in the near-cyclone weather of October. "And you received a scholarship!" He was glad to have suddenly remembered that, anyway.

Jorge's lips closed over the cigar a moment, but just as quickly his eyes smiled again. "That's right," he exclaimed. A little too gaily, Mario thought, for something that had happened about fifteen years ago.

"And as for you," continued Jorge, "You won last year's regatta from Varadero, studied architectural engineering in the United States, have about a dozen kids, and are Junior Partner of Guzman Realty and Construction, and—" Jorge jokingly scratched his neck, thinking of more facts, but Mario interrupted.

"Un momento!" He exclaimed. "No kids! and how in the devil do you know all this?"

"I was without a car all last year. Had to read the newspaper complete to while away the time in the bus. Even the society page."

"I guess they have to fill up the papers with something," Mario apologized, embarrassed, although Jorge had spoken without malice.

"Here you are, caballeros!" Francisco's round face shone with hearty pride. "If you won't say it's the best coffee in Havana, you won't have to pay me!"

Jorge attentively tasted the dark, shining coffee, the color of his own eyes. "Magnifico," he complimented Francisco.

"Are you still painting, De Armas?" Mario said. "I remember you were the star artist of the class at La Salle."

"Oh, I paint occasionally," Jorge answered, "but it's mostly architecture now."

"Architecture! Funny we haven't run across each other before! Study here?"

"And in Paris," nodded Jorge. "But just a year. Money ran out. Had to come running home to little Cuba the Beautiful for a job. I support my mother and sister. So—adiós, Paris," he added cheerfully. "But we almost did come across each other once. I believe your company was bidding on the Solano Building. I designed it."

"That's right. We almost had the contract for that. Vaya! So you were the architect! Damn good job, chico," he conceded, surprised.

"Gracias," Jorge thanked him, as he shot down the shining black coffee.

"That was quite a problem as I remember," Mario continued. "Required ingenuity."

"Imagination is about the only thing I've plenty of," laughed Jorge.

"Are you with any firm?"

"No. Haven't the money to invest in a partnership, and I don't want to throw in my soul as collateral." Mario knew all right what he meant.

"So, you're an independent?"

"More like a bum," Jorge corrected. The clarity of his eyes and a certain expression they held as he smiled reminded Mario of something he could not define, and it disturbed him not to be able to remember. It was like a face out of the past suddenly confronting one—the face of a stranger, and yet so familiar that one knows intimately the sound of his laughter and the particular way his lips move, even a characteristic gesture as he speaks.

"You manage pretty well for a bum," Mario said lightly to conceal his thoughts. "An important building like the Solano."

Jorge laughed. But he did not add that it was the only one. He didn't mention the dozen of once-beautiful old mansions he had to convert into canned apartments, custom-made distortions. Not to this fellow who wouldn't understand because he had the world in his pocket.

"Sometimes," was all he said. He put a peseta on the table as though to end the conversation.

Mario knew that no question would be asked of himself. The newspapers made impossible all curiosity concerning him and his family. His slender well-groomed hands, smoothing back his hair, also sleeked, in a futile gesture, the pause that suddenly was there. Nothing could be done with this pause. They had said what there was to say from their separate worlds. The point of contact ended there.

"What a noisy place!" he exclaimed, glancing toward the radio which had been turned up to its normal blast as soon as Jorge had left the phone. He rose, holding out his hand to Jorge. "Well, so nice to have seen you, De Armas. Can I give you a lift or—"

"No, gracias. We've just moved near here. And thanks for the café," Mario called back. Jorge nodded through his cigar smoke and they parted.

Jorge went to his car. Here he could at last tear off the mask that so unexpectedly had been forced on him. God damn! He brought his fist down on the steering wheel. Of all the people to run into—and right there, where he had just been on the phone with Lourdes! To turn around a moment later and see her husband waving at him, inviting him to his table! It was obvious that Mario knew nothing, and had not even remembered Jorge's name. But still it was stifling, a situation that demanded this hypocrisy. And to make it worse, Mario was so damn likable, in spite of what he knew about him.

The mid-afternoon traffic was flowing steadily now. There were some specifications he had to pick up and work on that night. He turned towards Havana.

4
GUZMAN & SONS REALTORS AND CONTRACTORS

The afternoon sun shot through the office windows and hurled the large black letters printed on its pane, "Guzman and Sons Realtors and Contractors," upside down over Mario's desk. With a sudden annoyed gesture, he dropped the plans he had been studying and walked over to the window. Every afternoon the same routine! Now because of the heat he would have to open the window and let it all explode from below, all the traffic noises bottled up between the double lines of buildings on the narrow street. A grim perversity prompted him to stand there a moment before drawing the persianas, allowing it all to swarm over him, the cries of the vendors selling fruit, lottery tickets, newspapers; the automobile horns in public warfare at every corner; the monstrous tin buses belching and shouldering through narrow cobbled streets originally intended for the grace of horseman and quitrin. And almost more irritating than the noise was the unawareness of the people who made it and breathed it. Like London fog, noise was a natural element of Havana atmosphere, to be inhaled with singular indifference. Only strangers noticed it. A mute question caused Mario to glance at his brother working undisturbed at the opposite desk. Why me? You know why, he answered himself.

Mario thought back to the first day he had entered a classroom in New England and had stood looking around at it and the professor. For the first time he had been a stranger in the world. No one knew him or his name or even his country. That classroom was a framed space of strange eyes, interesting, whole, dynamic, looking at him with diffident acceptance—planets revolving in an ordered unknown outer space around a dark star. Whether this new star which was himself would become part of the ordered system or be rejected was a matter of complete indifference to them.

He remembered the way he had felt as he stood there. This new anonymity had divested him of all that had never belonged to him, and gave him himself. Those classroom eyes had never seen a Guzman, had never heard of the name of the Cuban empire of city blocks and whole suburbs and highways it controlled. Nor had they seen whole pages of rotogravure dishing up the family with the morning coffee on every late Sunday breakfast table in Cuba and South America: Mama entertaining the Prince of Asturias; Papa playing golf with the Duke of Windsor; his sister devoting herself to the success of the Cancer League Ball; his brother cutting the inaugural ribbons of the new building donated by the Guzman family to the Catholic Charity Hospital; himself, sport-jacketed and casual, attending younger set cocktails; in costume winning the Club Carnival comparsa; attending the Philharmonic; competing in the Varadero regatta; boarding the plane en route to the USA where he was to begin his studies of architectural engineering. On and on, hundreds of Guzman faces since before he was born, being tossed lazily on late Sunday morning beds, fluttering on the country club beaches, covering the sweating heads of sugar-cane cutters, staving off the cold in the guano-thatched huts of the farmers, hastily wrapping newly acquired porcelains of politicians' families in flight.

From the first revolutionaries for independence to the last carnival party, the faces of his family had been part of the Cuban scene. Perhaps during that first struggle for independence in 1868, at the conflagration of Bayamo—that purest expression of Cuban self-abnegation—a paper Guzman face had been twisted into a lighted torch, and quite likely by the very hands of a Guzman patriot. Patriots fighting for something so real, they had followed Céspedes' example without hesitation. With their own hands they had set fire to their palatial mansions and rich fields so that the Spanish tyrant would find but a bleak victory of charred ruins. These men and women of the highest aristocracy had stood there—women so exquisitely dressed, so pampered that the soles of their dainty shoes had never touched the earth, having stepped no further than from marble-tiled patio to carriage, watching the flames consume this flower of culture and refinement comparable to the most lavish salons of Paris, and then they had fled into the wilderness, uncomplaining, fighting side by side with the Negro slaves whom they had just emancipated.

For ten years men, women, children born in the wastelands, and freed slaves fired their own hearts with courage to wrest their land from the Spaniard until with the treacherous Pact of Zanjón the heroic struggle had been truncated. True, it had not been entirely in vain, for their blood had irrigated the land which bore the fruit of independence in the later revolution.

But, what had happened now to Cuba, Mario thought, since the inspiring days of Bayamo and the founding of the Republic? What a desolate void, the dead whiteness on a page of a Cuban schoolboy's history book! With a sudden feeling of revulsion he slammed the window, causing his brother to look up and ask, "What's up, Mario?"

He'd like to know himself, he thought, as he shuffled papers on his desk. What the hell's got into me? Miguel would think I'm crazy if I told I'd been thinking about Bayamo! For some reason he recalled that fellow with the cigar —what was his name? De Armas—that he'd bumped into earlier in the bodega. Evidently that had churned something up in his mind. He should have felt sorry for De Armas—it was apparent that he was having a tough time—but instead it was De Armas who had caused dissatisfaction or restlessness, almost envy in Mario. What a laugh!

"Eh, Mario! What's the idea of closing the window?"

"The damned heat and noise!"

He threw down his papers, and leaving his brother still staring, marched into Guzman Senior's office.

"Papá, viejo, it's too much!"

His father looked up from over the shell-frame glasses surprised at Mario's voice, which, usually calm and easy, had become shrill with irritability.

"Qué pasa, hijo?" he inquired. "What is happening, son?"

"There's no necessity for standing this if we don't have to."

"What? I don't know of anything we have to 'stand.'"

"This noise, Papá! Without an air conditioner we have to keep the windows open."

His father shrugged his shoulders, puzzled. "It doesn't bother me at all."

"That's no answer, viejo, because nothing bothers you!" Mario retorted. "But it does me. I can't concentrate. And since it is certainly not a question of money, I see no reason why I must be subjected to this!"

"It is because you are young, son, that such things can bother you. One day you will become accustomed to concentrating anywhere."

"But why become accustomed to something that can be remedied?"

Guzman Senior smiled as he removed his glasses and wiped them, his small hands moving with deliberate precision. It was a curious smile, Mario thought. The smile and the glass-wiping were pretexts to give himself time to answer such a preposterous question, dropping a hopeless smile into a bottomless well of ignorance. Finally, his father said, "To slowly make every weakness an invulnerable strength," and putting on his glasses, he resumed his work.

Bien! That was that—for today, anyway. Mario knew his father too well to persist. Without another word he turned and re-entered his office. Miguel was terminating an animated telephone conversation which he could plainly hear from the hallway.

"Fine, fine!" he was shouting, "and my congratulations, sir!" He hung up with a triumphant click and swiveled to face his brother. "Mario, the Camacho project has gone through at last!"

Mario stared open-mouthed in his astonishment and momentarily forgot the afternoon's annoyance.

"Who brought about that miracle?"

"Old Salinas! This is quite a feather in our cap, I can tell you!" Miguel's great dark eyes sparkled.

"Wonder how he did it," Mario mused.

"I don't know!" his brother answered impatiently. "All he said was that the Camacho family finally agreed to sign. But who cares about that? The important thing is that the old fox, without knowing it, pushed it through just in time." The cellophane wrapper of his fresh cigarette pack shivered in his fingers.

What zeal! Mario dryly commented to himself. Aloud he said, "Salinas is a wizard. I've heard so many stories about that Camacho family, that I don't know how he was able to—"

"I know all that," Miguel interrupted. "They have never been able to come to an agreement about anything. I've heard they all hate each other. In fact, they've preferred letting the house and estate rot to giving each other any satisfaction in the distribution. But what's that to us now? The point is that..."

"Strange, I was just around that old place this morning. But didn't go there. Just happened to drop in the bodega on the corner for a coffee."

"The point is," his brother repeated with increasing impatience, "Father has been wanting this estate for a long time now, way before he had the inside information on the Public Works Project next to it. And imagine the luck! Old Salinas finally getting the family to sell! Another two weeks, and every real estate company in Cuba would have been offering twenty times what we're paying!"

Miguel was too enthusiastic to remain seated. He had walked to the window overlooking Old Havana rooftops, regarding them with the expression of one who knows that they would also one day belong to the company. Then he returned, half sitting on a corner of his desk, smoking his cigarette with a triumphant flourish. Mario knew that Miguel's satisfaction was not with himself or with the successful transaction, but rather an overflowing of admiration for his father.

He worships Dad, Mario thought. Strange I never thought of it before. "And now that we've made this coup," Miguel continued, "I'm sure Father will want to buy up the small lots bordering it. That bodega you just mentioned, and so on. We'll have to act quickly. Dad doesn't miss much, eh Mario?" At this last he chuckled appreciatively.

But Mario did not respond, had not even heard him.

Miguel turned towards him abruptly with angry eyes. "Oye, Mario! What the devil's the matter with you? You've been strange as hell all afternoon—slamming windows, arguing with Papá, and right now you haven't shown any interest at all! You'd think that—"

"You'd think that I have to account to you for my moods!" Mario took the words from him with mounting antagonism because his brother spoke the truth. "Do you expect everyone to react just as you do? Besides, what is the particular 'kick' to know we've put one over on the public again? That's nothing new for us, is it? What's so wonderful about using stolen information?"

"That's a lie!" Miguel retorted, lowering his voice so that they would not be heard, "That's a lie! No one has stolen anything!"

"No? Then how did Father obtain this information?"

"As if you didn't already know! An intimate friend in the Ministry of Public Works mentioned it to Papá."

"Just happened to mention it, eh? Yes, I know who it is. And just by coincidence, he's a shareholder—a big one—in the Saenz Construction Company."

"Well, if he is, what's that got to do with it anyway?" he bridled.

Mario laughed. "I'll just make a bet with you that the Saenz Construction Company will get the bid."

Miguel's face was flushed with exasperation. "Oh, so you can prophesy whose the low bid will be! What are you, clairvoyant?" he tried to sneer. But it came off badly; his facial muscles were unaccustomed to the exercise of malice.

Mario did not answer.

Miguel continued, "Just because a friend is reciprocating to Papá for a lot of favors, you—"

"Don't pretend to be that much of a fool, Miguel," Mario retorted, "talking about 'friendship' and 'favors.' You mean bribes and 'cuts', don't you? If you have to give double-talk to the world, at least to yourself have the guts to call things by their right names. Or won't Papá-God out there in the other office—let you do that?" He jerked his head in the direction of Guzman Senior's office.

Miguel could only answer with shocked silence. His dark eyes were filled more with hurt than anger, and his long lashes blinked suddenly in one gesture of incomprehension. It was this familiar gesture of his that stopped Mario and suddenly shamed him. He thought, Poor Miguel! He'll never understand anything! It's just as when we were children, when anything more than the accepted appearance of things would confuse him. He believes what he's saying now, and I've deliberately hurt him.

"Miguel, chico," he crossed towards his brother, "I'm sorry. I don't know where the words came from. Certainly, I have never thought of these things before. I don't know why today." He shrugged his shoulders before his inexplicable mood and continued, "Actually what I have mentioned is accepted as ethical business procedure. Why should we be any different?" This last he said in hearty tones of reassurance as he affectionately slapped Miguel on the back.

Miguel smiled and sighed in relief. "That's the way I've always looked at it, Mario. And about now—forget it. I know something's bothering you. Better to take it out on me than a stranger."

"I don't know what it could be, and that's the truth. Funny how a fellow can suddenly behave like this with no reason!" Mario mused.

"Maybe you need a vacation after the Convention's over. You've certainly been working hard for it—."

Mario shook his head, and Miguel continued, "Oh well, somebody just irritated you today then.

"No, I haven't seen anyone outside the office...except," he remembered, "an old schoolmate from the Instituto days."

"Perhaps reminiscing depressed you."

"I'm not that old," Mario laughed."

"I'm sure it's nothing that a good game of golf won't cure, eh?"

Miguel's eager voice caused Mario to exclaim, "What the devil! To be standing here like this just when we've had such good news! Vamos! Let's go and tell Dad!"

They hurried to his office but were disappointed at his lack of reaction to the news. Perhaps he had not heard. "The Camacho deal has gone through, Papá," Miguel repeated, and then with almost childish impatience at not having received the desired response, he insisted, "Did you hear, Papá?"

Suddenly Mario felt that he was observing an interesting phenomenon. Although there was nothing to warrant the impression, he was sure that his father had been caught off-guard. Chin propped in hand, he was sitting motionless when they had entered, obviously in absolute concentration on some matter he had been considering and unaware of their presence. But his eyes were roving in small guarded movements like a camera lens being rotated left and right in search of a proper focus. Finally, he seemed to have found it. He raised his eyes in sudden planned confusion, it seemed to Mario. "Well!" he exclaimed pleasantly, "I didn't realize you were talking to me! What is it, son?" and quietly he folded his small well-kept hands on the desk in complete attention. But Mario knew he had heard.

"The Camacho project, Papa. They've signed," and this time Miguel's face reflected his father's bright smile.

"So! That's very good news! Who did it? Salinas?"

Miguel nodded happily. Guzman Senior removed his glasses and placed them triumphantly on the desk.

"Never thought he'd make it! We old-timers have a way with us," he commented, pleased. "Where is Salinas staying? Tell Gloria to get him on the phone."

"He's leaving for Camagüey, Papa. Can't call him. It's his wife's, Pastora's, Saint's Day."

"Ahhh! We must send her something! Let's see..."

Women probably find him attractive, Mario realized, in a dapper, cool way, with his small hands and feet, his meticulous suits, and a shock of grey hair setting off his complexion. Naturally women wouldn't know that it's more sallow than suntanned because of his liver trouble! But anyway, it looks good.

"Miguel," continued his father, "see that your mother takes care of it. You know this deal has come at just the right moment. Next week the bids will be open and—"

"And fortunately, enough," Miguel cut in, "or maybe because of wishful thinking on my part, Papá, since we certainly didn't expect this, I've already sent the men out there. They've drawn the plots and, oh, by the way! You know where we'd talked about cutting through with an extra block..." On and on it went, their increasing high spirits making them oblivious to Mario's lack of participation.

Mario fascinated, watched the show. His father seemed deliberately to be impersonating himself being pleased, using all his own typical gestures and reactions that one would naturally expect of him. In another moment he's going to smooth his hair and pick up a cigar, Mario thought. He's pretending. But why? When it's something he's been waiting for so long! And as for Miguel, he's an imitation of his father but so much less than the original; not even his childish simplicity can redeem him.

"Do you know," Guzman Senior exclaimed, "this has happened so suddenly, we haven't fixed on an architect!" The mounting office rhythm was momentarily halted.

"Alonso?" Miguel suggested, "He was the one who originally—"

"No, not Alonso. He's too busy as it is with the new Vedado Heights."

"How about Otero?"

"How can you say Otero! This is not for a traditional. It takes someone with real ingenuity, fresh—"

Mario interrupted his father and Miguel. "I know just the one," he heard himself saying unexpectedly, "Jorge De Armas."

"Who? Who's that?"

"A former classmate of mine from La Salle. Very clever. He designed the Solano Building, by the way."

"Oh, he did? Muy bien, muy bien. Style and originality," his father admitted. "Who's he with?"

"No one." Guzman senior raised his eyebrows, but Mario hastened to add, "Oh he's been offered enough partnerships, but he prefers being independent."

"Well, we can interview him anyway. Ask Gloria to get him on the phone for me. But not now," he suddenly added, "In about half hour. First I must finish some other work."

With a pleased smile, his father puffed at his cigar and tapped his slender tanned fingers on the desk. Waiting, Mario thought, waiting for us all to go and leave him alone. Why? What a crazy day!

"Oh, by the way," Guzman remembered, "Saenz Company is going to handle everything for us again, as they did last year on that Varadero job. Our name will be completely disassociated until a convenient time. Don't forget to keep this under your hats. Don't even mention it to your wives! You know how women are," he smiled, "they can't ever keep a secret. Our connection with the project is strictly confidential. You understand, of course," he said in an offhand way.

They understood. As they started to leave, Miguel remained at the door, hesitant.

"What is it, Miguel?" Guzman asked impatiently.

As though reluctantly responding to an imperative voice, Miguel reached a decision. "Dad, I'd like to ask you something."

"Yes?"

Embarrassed that his brother was witness to this moment of doubt, he persevered nevertheless. "Is there anything wrong about Public Works— and Saenz—cooperating with us? Unethical I mean?" The firmness in his voice did not belong to him.

Guzman looked up at him, annoyed as he might have been at the intrusion of an alien speaking a language unknown to him.

"What!" he exclaimed, exasperated.

Miguel interpreted his father's tone as righteous indignation. Reassured, he brightened. "Of course!" he answered himself aloud—quite loud, so that Mario too would hear. "It's only logical that a man as shrewd as you are could be misunderstood!"

Guzman did not know what his son was talking about.

As the brothers walked down the hall, Mario was conscious of an unaccountable elation at the prospect of seeing De Armas again, elation inconsistently tinged with annoyance. At the bodega this morning there had been nothing more to say to each other after the brief conversation over a cup of coffee. Yet ever since, he had been irritable and restless, and had astonished himself by suddenly sponsoring the fellow! Had this happened on a day less uncommon than this one, he might have dismissed it as a generous impulse to help an old classmate. But the special objectivity and heightened perception that seemed to follow him all day permitted no usual deception, even concerning himself. His interest in De Armas had sprung from a source too deep within himself to be severed from his own ego. Well, whatever the motivation, why worry about it? Gracias a Dios, tomorrow would be another day, a nice normal one, he hoped, full of acceptance of the usual comforting deceptions. Today's acute awareness of things-as-they-are was unpleasant. That kind of vision was for revolutionaries and heroes, and he was certainly neither!

5
MAMA

Jorge's second-hand convertible rattled as it labored over the broken-up street of San Lazaro, a condition which obviously had become permanent. No wonder it was a coveted prize to be Minister of Public Works. Who else had this unlimited opportunity to build a private fortune from unfinished highways and unneeded public buildings? He thought: if the conquistadores from the Mother Country had only known how much gold they were forced to leave still lining the Havana streets! They would have envied the spontaneous generation of riches pouring into the private coffers. Like Segismundo in Calderón de la Barca's *Life is a Dream*, they could have exclaimed:

> Válgame el cielo, qué veo
> Válgame el cielo, qué miro!
> Con poco espanto lo miro,
> Con mucha duda lo creo.*

Life must be a dream; else how to explain that despite this age of the clamor for rights, there existed by common consent a fountain of exploitation! He couldn't help remembering the jokes of the bodega, the

---

* May heaven protect me, what I'm seeing
May heaven protect me, what I'm looking at!
With slight terror I see it
With great doubt I believe it

bitter humor of all of them. No wonder there was little racial discrimination here. Cubans, Negroes, Jews all had one thing in common: grim laughter under oppression, and the unsubdued, joyous love of life. Jews and Negroes, the most tragic peoples on the earth, were the greatest comedians. And Cuba, the longest oppressed of all Latin America, its King of Jesters. It was logical because they all knew the gargantuan joke: freedom blared out every morning from golden horns as all bowed to the Northern sun of gold and power. And the yoke of the ploughshares? They might as well have remained swords, for the foreign ploughs were tearing into their native soil, plundering the great forests and the fields to plant oil-wells, mines, and railroads. All the while empty-bellied Cubans shrugged and made jokes as they watched the glittering harvest of their land carried away.

Earlier in the bodega he had wanted brutally to shake them out of their laughter. That excitable, skinny dice-player was right. Enough of cynical joking! It was time to cry out. Eddy Chibás was doing it. He was showing them how.

Jorge finally turned from San Lazaro Street, but was again delayed by the traffic congestion near the Marco building under construction. He had forgotten about it months ago, but now with the morning's despair upon him, his pulse quickened with the old familiar fury. To be born with an instinct greater than that of survival was, he felt, to be unnatural, a monster; one of the sullen ones denied the security and peaceful sleep offered to those who remain within that prodigious framework. His name too, might now have been one of those sweeping across the huge signboard. Oh yes, he had been given the opportunity—that is, with certain conditions. They were not unusual ones. Merely to keep his gaze on the scaffolding, looking neither to right nor left. Easy. And from then on, no more problems. No key to be returned at the corner cafe, no half-formed questions of Lourdes. Simple and logical. Except that nothing in his life had ever spelled those two words. Was this compulsion to look into the abyss below an affront to nature? Was it possible that this was a part of nature's plan? Perfect harmony: the acquiescence of the prey and the sweet sleep of the hunter. Well, bravo for the perpetual motion which kept the world going on its accustomed axis.

As he reached home, before he could use his key, his mother opened the door. No one knew how many hours she spent at the window watching for him. Her large figure filled the doorway, and as she kissed him the familiar odor of old worn silk and talcum clung to her. He made an effort to banter through his annoyance.

"Mamá, when are you going to do me the honor of wearing the housecoat I bought you?"

"We cannot have visitors when we have just moved—Ah, I know! I know!" she anticipated his protest, "'A housecoat is to be worn in the house, just for housecleaning,' you have told me a half dozen times. But, my son, you can't change a leopard's spots. Each time I will answer the same way! It is wicked and wasteful to ruin a new dress for cleaning. It would go against me, and I wouldn't enjoy it at all. How is Manolo?" she changed the subject.

Defeated, he watched her as she took his jacket from him and automatically examined it for loose buttons. Her erect figure had lost the proportions for which she had once prided herself, and the dark abundant hair was greying, but even in this shapeless wilted silk she was still a handsome woman. The cheerfulness with which she sacrificed weighed heavily upon Jorge. If there were but an occasional glimmer of selfish desire in her, or some act motivated solely by caprice, how much it would have lessened the burden! But she had grown to love sacrifice and clung to it as she did to her old dresses.

"What do you mean 'how is Manolo?'" he repeated absently as, after returning her kiss he entered the kitchen directly off the living room. "Yes, Manolo. I thought you were to have lunch with him," she glanced sharply at him as he opened the refrigerator.

"Ah, sí, sí!" he improvised, "I had intended to, but at the last moment I was too busy. I'll see him some other day. I just had a sandwich somewhere."

"A sandwich! Like an American!" she pronounced it with all the contempt tradition held for foreign borrowed innovations. "I could certainly have given you more than a sandwich! And since when do you have to make your own café con leche?" she replied, almost snatching the milk bottle from him. He closed his eyes a moment, looking within himself for patience.

"It's about time I did, mamá," was all he answered. But she merely clicked mockingly at this remark, her good humor restored to be doing something for him again. The enormous energy unspent even after a full morning of vigorous housecleaning was made evident as she noisily moved about. The Frigidaire thundered closed, the milk bottle clanged hazardously on the sink, the coffee-pot rattled sharply to rest on the burner. He walked towards his room, longing to be alone for a short while before he started on the sketches he had promised to work on that evening.

A sputtering sound came from the kitchen. "Ay, your café!" she exclaimed, grateful for the interruption. A moment later she returned to his room, clanging the spoon happily as she stirred the large glass of hot café con leche. She stood there watching him as he began to drink. "Do you know," she suddenly exclaimed, "I almost forgot to tell you that the Baldomero Saenz Construction Company called you!"

Jorge lowered the glass, incredulous. "The Saenz Construction Company?" He knew their buildings, faddish, self-consciously modern.

What could they want with him?

His mother continued: "You know I'm always so efficient about these things! He said that it was urgent too, and ordinarily I would never have overlooked it. Your father, may he rest in peace, used to say that I would have made an excellent business woman if I weren't so attractive!" she laughed at the preposterous idea, and tilted her head as she must have done when he had told her. "Well, it all ended when I lost your dear father. Oh, he wouldn't know me now! Not that I regret it! I'm happy just living for my children, especially—"

Jorge interrupted. "What message did they leave me, mamá?" He tried to sound patient. Faddish or not, it was the possibility of an assignment, if it was not too incompatible.

"Let's see. Please call—'" she tried to remember exactly, "'at your earliest convenience.' You know what must have made me forget? Being disturbed at your having only a sandwich for lunch! I have enough trouble to keep what little flesh you have on you, let alone your eating like a crazy gringo! After all, you're all I have. Oh, there's your sister too, of course— but then, you're my only boy! If anything should happen to you—" She was so engrossed in her words that she did not realize that he was not listening to them, nor seeing the expressive glances which accompanied them.

"Did they mention any name for me to ask for?"

"Oh yes. Baldomero Saenz. Baldomero Saenz! Why, he's very important!" Suddenly she realized the significance of the call. "Hijo mio, wouldn't that be wonderful if there was a big project for you? It's about time! As clever as you are! Why of course, that's what my dream meant! Twice this week I've dreamed of butterflies! You know that always means good luck." She picked up the glass of coffee which he had left almost full and began stirring it for him. "You'll see, Jorgito! Things will begin to happen—You'll see, you'll see," she sang as she stirred. "You were worrying about Berta's tuition and my operation expenses—and here you are! The Lord will provide." Her face was as radiant as a young girl's, and he hated to disillusion her, but she was way ahead of things.

"Viejita, don't jump to conclusions. It might be nothing of interest."

But she wasn't to be discouraged. "You'll see," she sang, "You'll see! Soon we will be able to have an office of your own!" She held the glass towards him. "Now finish this," she clucked.

It   was   good   to   see   mamá   so   happy.

6
CHORI AND CHAN LI

When Arsenio had returned that morning from his mussel gathering, there was his neighbor, Chori, just as he had expected, shouting happy obscenities from the dump yard on the other side of the rocks. He called for Arsenio to come and see all the fine things he had found that morning to use for the house he was making for his children.

"Carajo!" muttered Arsenio, "Don't you see I'm busy?" But just the same he went. Who could resist Chori's enthusiasm? Besides, Chori was from Santiago. Santiagueros would just about die if they didn't have someone to share things with, especially when there was something exciting.

This time Chori was holding up a big sheet of corrugated zinc, acting as though he'd won the big prize of the lottery. "This is just what I needed!" he explained breathlessly. "Something shiny to decorate the roof. So when my little negritos come walkin' up here for the first time, they'll think Santa Barbara sent them a silver cloud to slick up our house! Say, you haven't seen the altar I made for Our Lady of Cobre!"

Arsenio groaned inwardly. "This boy going to have everything so cluttered up with saints a man's not going to be able to talk natural without hiding behind a rock."

"What you think of Cachita helping me finish my house?" Chori spoke softly as he used the nickname of the black Patroness of Cuba. "This piece was all I needed, except for making the doors."

Eight months before in Santiago, Province of Oriente, he had left his wife, first depositing the children with their godfather, and had come to Havana. His wife, who had spent her whole life trying to be white, had neglected the kids and found a white man, a Spaniard, to live with. When Chori discovered this and left, she had seemed glad to get rid of them all. Here at the quiet edge of the sea, he had found just the place he wanted for his children. He had been building the little house ever since.

This perplexed Arsenio. He had long wondered why Chori, having dumped clean all the dirty rubble of his own life and left a job in Santiago, was now working harder than before, sweating and dancing over finding some other fool's trash. Arsenio waved his hand over the shack made of stones, fossils, sea-rock and broken tiles. "Why do you not live as I do?" he asked, "under a fine laurel tree that the good Lord made for me, complete with roof and all."

Chori sniffed at that.

"You laugh. Why, I have not only a roof, but also an apartment. If I want a porch, I go to the sunny side of the tree. My bedroom is on the shady side. It's got a bathroom too," he grinned. "Sí, señor. An apartment all ready-made for me! And I think it is still too much to take care of a laurel tree!"

"That's what's good for you," Chori had responded, "an old goat, happy eatin' tin cans. Got no little kids to take care of, and no woman in Santiago wantin' to bleach out their souls."

"No," Arsenio had admitted, "there you are right."

"Well, I won't stand for no light mulata poisoning my kids against their own blood; and no blacks neither is going to black them up. Just want them to be men. When they been living here where the sun and the cyclones and the ocean teach them who they are, then, if they want, they can take it from there. And that's when I'll go find myself a tree."

Arsenio had to admit it made sense for Chori. "Bien. My belly is singing out more tunes than you ever danced. I'm going to finish my breakfast. I began it with Marquesa. Gave me a glass of milk."

"That goat run away again?" Chori laughed. "Why she always go to you? Why doesn't she ever get lost on my side? A glass of warm milk wouldn't be bad. Well, I guess that goat knows her daddy all right!"

Arsenio snorted a good-natured acknowledgement, but he was thinking of something else. "Marquesa had a name once—Antonia. When she was talking this morning about—" (he couldn't remember "gargoyles") "— about this place and a framboyan tree and the devil only knows what all, her face changed so you could tell she had a name of her own. And didn't sound crazy then. She talked about the 'Company' again."

"Lord!" Chori whispered. "If she'd have seen some of those fellows here yesterday walking all over the garden with those big blue papers, unrolling them, pointing at things—and dammit! —ruining good cigar butts by chewing them to tatters. Marquesa was taking care of Topo's charcoal, and lucky thing there was so much wind fanning up the logs, it kept her busy throwing dirt on them. What in hell they want here?"

He asked that just to help the pretending. Even though it seemed unlikely that anyone would want to buy the property, still, a person never knew, and it was better just not to think or talk about it.

Arsenio wished he had not mentioned it at all. The words they refrained from uttering were like the sudden small flares that darted softly through Topo's charcoal mound. If you did not kill one right off with a bucket of dirt, that whole pile of baking logs would blaze up in no time, and with it would go the days Topo had spent miles away gathering wood, lugging it back in the push-cart; and the loads of dirt he'd dug to cover it; and the days and nights he had tended over it while it baked. All his work would become nothing but a big pile of white ashes.

Words could be like that sometimes. Couldn't Chori or anyone from Santiago understand that? Or any woman? Women could have more things burn down on them just for missing that half-bucket of shut-up! The only woman who knew when to be quiet was Marquesa. And when she did talk, it didn't bother you, any more than the motion of the trees or the waves. A wind would rustle up her thoughts into words, and then let them die off again.

To change the subject Chori said, "Topo's charcoal was setting fast in the middle. Guess he'll be needing us tonight to help stack it."

Arsenio hadn't wanted to talk anymore. "Guess so," he said and shuffled back over the rocks to finish his mussels.

§

Now it was almost day's end, and Chori was still at work making the doors when the sun bobbed ripe on the water. He let his hammer arm drop to his side to stretch his back and look. Wouldn't his kids like this sight! They didn't have any sunsets like this down there, hemmed in by the Sierra Maestra, unless they were lucky enough to get a ride sometimes to Puerto Boniato or Caney.

The sun was heavy and full of juice at the end of the ocean, ready to burst any minute. If Pablito, his littlest negrito, were here, for sure he'd want a pin to bust it open. Anda! There it goes, sure enough! That sun burst wide open and was spilling over the ocean. The scarlet and gold gushed out so strong it even spurted over the clouds a hundred miles high. It stained the whole ocean until you didn't know what was sky and what was water. Even the foam tossed up pink, and the land just the same. All the tin he'd patched into the roof was burning gold, and the whole garden of laurel trees and ceiba and almond were dripping in red gold, too, like those floats that passed by at Carnival time with the colored lights shining over them. Some little children who had been playing and running around the garden looked like darting flames, and their nursemaids' uniforms had turned pink. The nursemaids kept chattering and weren't seeing anything at all.

Caray! He wished there were someone there to shout about it with him. It wasn't fun alone. Marquesa, he knew, was in the tower because she always climbed up there in late afternoons to watch things too. He could see her there now. The old house looked like it was blazing away, and all those crazy wooden faces scary as hell, smiling and staring in the sun-fire. Other evenings, when it was darker, he couldn't always be sure if he was looking at Marquesa or one of the faces.

As he turned, he was glad to see a familiar little figure in the distance, dark against the red sky, hurrying towards the garden. He knew it was Chan Li, because nothing was moving but his tiny feet. Chori remembered then that tomorrow was Chan's big day. He was starting his "business," he had announced excitedly yesterday. "Fellow friend of uncle in market place. I help uncle, uncle help him, he give me peanuts. Two, maybe three times a week peanuts. Sell on Malecón," he explained.

Chori had thought it was a fine idea.

Arsenio had not: "Doesn't your uncle give you rice and fish every day for helping him? 'Business!' Why do you want to complicate your life?"

But it was too much for both of them when they learned that Chan Li wanted to save money, not to get married, as they thought, but to be able to send his ashes back to Canton when he died. This idea had totally disconcerted Arsenio, who just stood with his mouth open; and it had bewildered Chori into wrapping himself around the trunk of a palm tree while asking Chan a hundred incredulous questions. They never did get any answer, as Chan Li merely continued to sit and eat the rice he had brought back. So they had to get over it as best they could.

As Chan now approached, he scooped up a handful of white peanuts from a paper bag to show them. Arsenio had come over to see and said, "You really serious about those ashes?" Finding that Chan had not repented of his folly, he resignedly asked, "What will you carry the peanuts in tomorrow?"

"Must make something."

"Peanut vendor's got to have a big can to carry peanuts and a little can fitted underneath to keep charcoal embers, so peanuts stay hot," Arsenio explained. "Chori, you have any big cans?"

"Francisco from the bodega gave me a big cracker tin to make a burner for my little girl's stove."

Suddenly they heard a metallic clinking under the earth nearby, followed by a great sneeze. Once, twice, three times the sneeze burst from under the ground. "Topo's mighty conversational tonight," joked Chori.

There was no more sun-stain anywhere in the sky, and in the gathering twilight Topo's soot-covered figure was scarcely discernible as he emerged from his subterranean quarters. Only the bright yellow bucket he carried was clearly visible. Topo seemed to find that bucket very special, as he kept it clean and bright, which was more than he did for himself.

"Hooray!" Chori shouted, as Topo approached, "No newspapers to look for tonight! We're going to have a fire!"

Silently, as was his way, Topo extracted from the bucket little mounds of charcoal which was his gift to each of them. "Burned through fine," praised Chori as he examined a cylindrical piece.

Topo doubled the amount for Chan Li. He had not forgotten about tomorrow.

Chan stopped rocking cross-legged over the dried fish he was eating to bob his head, pleased. He could understand well how the sound of words meant nothing to Topo. But later he would thank him by helping with the others to stack the charcoal for cooling.

With ostentatious nonchalance Chori remarked, "Just finished the charcoal on time. For Chan's peanut stove I'm making him tonight." Arsenio tried to keep his yellow tooth from sticking out with pleasure when he heard Chori. "Thought you needed those cans for yourself."

"There'll be more turning up at the bodega," Chori called back as he started whistling over the rocks to his place. He thought, it's getting dark fast now—and quiet. All the rich kids gone home for their supper. Pretty soon that gray Studebaker and the duck-tail Cadillac will be slipping up by the wall facing the ocean for their love-making. Or maybe just to talk.

Going to use both big cracker tins for Chan. Ashes! Crazy little chino! But what does it matter? I do thank you, Cachita, for making us a shack with a shiny roof! Just be sure, please, Lady, that I can send for them soon, my negritos, Chori reminded the Virgin of Cobre.

§

That night there was one more in the group stacking the charcoal to be cooled: Carambita, uninvited. First, he hung around behind the bushes trying to see what was going on in the parked cars along the wall; then he caused a commotion in the garden by trying to steal one of Marquesa's chickens. Arsenio and Chori had caught him, but Marquesa came down the creaking old stairs from the tower, scolding him like an offended school teacher to a child.

The incident had ended by her admonition, "The next time you are intending to steal one of my chickens, advise me beforehand and I will give it to you. In fact, I will cook it for you!" Then carried away by this pleasant idea, she continued, "Enough for all of us—an arroz con pollo, the way we used to make it in the Canary Islands—or, for lack of certain ingredients, more like a paella—if Arsenio could bring some mussels, Chan Li a bit of dried fish from his uncle's—" At this Chori groaned, "Oh Lord, she's going to reward this cretino with a paella every time he comes to steal!"

They had been at work several hours, and the moon was now high enough to shine directly on the tops of the Royal Palms. Marquesa, by the light of a kerosene lamp hung on a stick, was sewing up old burlap sacks into which to pack the dried charcoal. Against the lamplight her strong nose and high forehead formed as impressive a profile as the jagged ocean rocks which surrounded them.

Carambita was still hanging around, not helping at all, just wanting something. They knew that. But they didn't know what until Chori, who had started making the stove for Chan Li, told him that he was going to have the most elegant peanut stove in Havana. He was also going to paint Our Lady of Cobre on it with the paint he was saving for his front door.

That is when they finally learned what Carambita wanted.

He interrupted Chori. "You people all crazy? Finishing your house, making your charcoal, planting garden when you know you're gonna be thrown out in a few days, all of you!"

Arsenio looked up with alarm at Marquesa and Chori. Evidently, they had not heard because of the clinking of the charcoal and the lapping of the waves. "I got some mighty good ideas about what you can do with the eviction money they give you. Oughta be about thirty-five apiece, and there are five of you. That means a hundred seventy-five or more. 'Course I don't have any money, but I got the brains. Wanna hear?"

Arsenio ambled close to him and muttered "What eviction you talking about?"

Carambita admired what he thought was the man's cunning. "Don't want me to know about it, eh? Don't want to let a friend in on anything. I got ideas, I tell you!"

Chori's hammering on the cracker can prevented the others from noticing.

"Answer me, cabrón! What eviction money you talking about?" Arsenio's eyes burned at him through the tangle of beard and hair.

Carambita paused, shifting his gaze in sudden doubt.

"You really don't know?" he squinted. "You're kidding. How'm I gonna know, and not you that lives here?" He was talking loud now, and the others were beginning to listen. "A man didn't talk to you yet about the construction going up here?"

Warmed by their obvious ignorance, he leaped on the pile of charcoal before Arsenio could stop him and shouted gleefully to the others, "For a fact, no one of you knows about the company coming here to knock everything down?"

"Shut your mouth," threatened Arsenio. But it was too late. They had heard. Carambita, perched on the charcoal mound, waited through the sudden silence, enjoying the mighty reaction that his own words had produced. He tingled with the same kind of importance he had felt the time he had been the one to tell some woman that her husband had been shot dead by accident She had looked just the way they the night Manolo Fernandez was murdered.7 did now—like the war pictures he had seen of corpses sitting straight and stiff, their eyes staring sharp at you, their mouths half open as though they were talking, some of them still holding a gun clamped in their fingers.

He noticed Marquesa suddenly gone dead, staring out at nothing, her two arms suspended stiff in the air holding the big needle and burlap sack she'd been sewing. The back of that crazy fool Topo—bent down over the coal, not moving enough to breathe. And the others, the same. Just like he'd put a bullet through each one of them. Of course, he knew it would not last, so his eyes took it all in while it did. Coño! If he could just keep them that way! It was like a game where you could murder for a minute without anyone catching you.

Arsenio began to come to life. He looked at Marquesa out of the corner of his eyes and met the glance of Chori. "What company?" he asked, "coming to knock down—what?"

"Why the whole place! They're a smart outfit! This is a damn good spot to clean up money on apartment buildings. It's sort of by itself but it's not too far from the new buses on Linea Street, and it's about the only corner of the Vedado left. Haven't you even seen how most of the old houses around here have been torn down?" He stared at their silence. "Jesus, where've you all been? They bought the whole big square that the house and garden take up and the whole empty lot on the side. It all belonged to the same family that just sold it. And let me tell you something. You hold out, kicking and fussing, and I'll bet you get thirty-five dollars or more apiece. I heard the man say thirty, but—"

Topo, who had been as silent as the others, abruptly drowned Carambita's words in the clinking coal which he turned over from the yellow bucket.

"Don't be so smart!" Carambita yelled at him, "You're in on this! —this damn charcoal pile of yours, if you don't get it out quick, and that mole hole of a house you made under the ground! Well, come to think of it, they probably wouldn't bother it or you," he sneered. "They just give notice to human beings. The animals get smoked out when the time comes, and that's all there is to it."

Topo did not seem to hear him. He bent vigorously to the work on hand. The others had not yet stirred.

"You don't believe me!" Carambita shouted at their silence. "Well, I'll tell you. I was at that bodega a couple blocks down, watching some fellows playing cubilete, and two others were standing next to me at the bar, talkin' about how they were gonna begin the job on the corner lot. And that it was gonna be plenty work for the bulldozer. I asked one of 'em just to be sure. 'You mean the old house with the tower?' and they said, 'Yeah, that nutty-lookin' old Camacho place.'"

Marquesa suddenly rose, and the burlap sacks and the sewing dropped on the rocks. "It is not true!" she flashed. "In the first place they would not dare, knowing that Leandro will return. And besides, the house is not theirs to dispose of! They—they—" she compressed her despair in her firmly clasped hands and could not go on.

"Eh!" Carambita laughed, "What's biting you!"

Arsenio climbed to the rock where the Marquesa stood, tall and straight, swaying back and forth as though an invisible hurricane were shaking a sturdy tree.

"That motherless cabrón does not know of what he speaks," he muttered close to her. "He has possibly invented this lie for some scheme of his."

"Of course it is a lie!" she continued, swaying as she spoke, "perpetrated not by Carambita, but by the others. It is not true, because they cannot sell what does not belong to them."

"What you think you know about it?" Carambita was becoming irritated.

"Why should I not know about it, foolish one," she cried, "if I am the one to whom it all belongs?"

"Ha ha!" Carambita laughed, not being accustomed to Marquesa's ways.

"When these men come—if indeed they come" she continued, "I will show them my papers I've locked away. They will be forced to leave immediately."

Carambita's loose smile and restless eyes shrank toward the center of his face. "What papers?" he asked softly.

"Never mind. The ones I have kept with my other things in the tower."

"Oh yes," he laughed again, but his eyes turned quietly towards the looming darkness of the tower.

The others, who were accustomed to her, took no notice. Their common fear for her, were this thing true, enveloped them in wordless unity for her protection. They drifted over the rocks, towards the sea, a little apart from her, as she stood lost in herself, swaying and smoothing her hair.

From habit Arsenio stooped and pried a large mussel from one of the rocks.

"Think he lying?" the nervous voice of Chan Li needled through the silence, into the quiet sea. Although they strove to find some doubt, no answer was needed. They all had seen the men coming oftener than ever.

"She will never leave," murmured Arsenio.

At his feet the sea persistently flipped new water into a small hollow, filling it with moonlight. The moon would spill out and then the ocean flip it back in again, like their thoughts, which kept trickling out and returning to the same place.

Finally the metallic grinding of Topo's shovel on the mound where he had not ceased to work broke their musing. They returned to resume their work. They had learned that things like charcoal and a peanut stove would not wait for thoughts.

Marquesa remained seated and almost immobile. After a while Arsenio, who had been glancing at her every now and then, picked up the unfinished burlap sack from the rocks and continued her work for her. At last, El Topo counted the cooling stacks, straightened, and collected the shovels from them. This was his habitual way of telling them that he could finish the rest in the morning by himself.

Carambita's complaining voice now burst from the rock where he had been sitting. They had forgotten he was there. "I believe you idiots are going to sleep without even hearing my ideas for the money. I just been sitting here all along, waiting to hear when one of you would ask me!"

"We askin' you to shut your snout and get outta here fast," Chori threatened. The others began to separate in silence.

Arsenio climbed the jagged rocks where the Marquesa still stood. He tapped her shoulder gently. "Come, Antonia," he said without pausing before pronouncing the name, it came so naturally. "That fellow—" he swallowed hard trying to remember, "Phoebus be coming soon, and find the house dirty if you don't go to sleep." She nodded and permitted herself to be led by him toward the old house.

They stepped over high wild grass whose fuzzy tops filled with moonlight covered the marble benches, the fountain, even the garden statues, in a kind of haze. "It's not true, you know," Marquesa insisted. "Don't allow yourself to believe these lies."

"Of course, of course," Arsenio soothed. He would like to have taken her arm to support her. Once he had had a small boat that he had built himself, and the day it was pierced on the high rocks he had felt as he did now. She was making out to be so strong against the news that Carambita had brought, pretending she didn't believe. He dared not help her, seeing the way her head was raised up under the moonlight, just like the little boat with its broken hull raised bravely over the rocks.

"And if they aren't lies, so much the worse for them. I will have to take action," she murmured. Perhaps she wasn't pretending. That was the fine part of being not good in the head. You could believe whatever you wanted. "God guard thee," she thanked him, as they stepped over the broken tiles of the kitchen patio.

Usually, Arsenio would stop by the arbor to smell the Piscuala blossoms laced with jasmine. Then perhaps he would pick one or two small flowers and continue through the garden, where he would throw back his head and take in the low night sky dense with stars. On occasion it so fascinated him to follow a constellation backwards that he would lose his balance. But tonight, he seemed completely indifferent to the night, shuffling slowly, head down.

"I could light your lantern for you," he offered.

"Oh no, thank you. I have left it upstairs in my room. Since the windows and doors are broken, the moonlight shines through quite enough," she answered.

"Upstairs! Old One, you don't continue to sleep up there!" Long ago he had heard the perilous creaking of the rotting stairs as she had climbed them. But he thought that she had abandoned them by now.

"Of course I sleep in my own room! Where else?"

"Where else!" he cried. "Where you will not discover one night that you and your bed have unwillingly reached the first floor, accompanied by the rest of the house!" Although, he thought to himself, there will not be many more nights perhaps.

She reassured him with a tired smile. "Vaya! That will never happen!"

"But why do you not live downstairs? You have the whole house for yourself. And there is less danger." he insisted.

"I will tell you another time. But now Diana's chase is half over, and there are more important things to do."

Arsenio shuffled, and pulled at his eyebrow. He didn't want her to go in yet. He wanted to tell her something that he himself didn't know what it was. Cofio! What was it?

"God guard thee," she repeated, again waiting for him to answer. But he didn't; he just stood there shuffling. If she were that boat of his, he could have pulled her off the rock out of danger, save what was left of her. But she wasn't a boat and he didn't have any place to take her. Offer her a tree? It was more or less hers anyway.

He couldn't swallow; his mouth was dry. Now he knew what he wanted to say to her, and could not because it was no use.

"And you, too, Old One," he replied gruffly, walking away. For the first time in his life, he wondered if people like Chan Li who got up early in the morning to go to work to be able to bring something back—a can of beans or whatever—might be right.

§

Chori, alone, continued fitting the peanut stove into shape, until it was completed. No one had remarked his unusual silence. No one had remembered his house, completed except for one more door. Or the little niggers who were waiting to live there. Suddenly he sensed movement in his house. He looked up quickly, and alert for Carambita's prowling, hastened toward it. There was someone in his kitchen. He would fix that Carambita! But as he approached, he saw a small flame glowing through the pane-less window of the kitchen, and El Topo bent over the little stove Chori had made for his daughter, fanning the glow. El Topo paid no attention to his entrance but remained there silent, seated on the earthen floor fanning the glowing charcoal embers until Chori finally slept.

Only the small flame spoke for them through the night, as the last car parked by the old wall drifted off, and the moon finally slipped for good from the small puddle in the hollowed rock.

7
JORGE'S INTERVIEW

The Baldomero Saenz Construction Company was clipping along at full speed when Jorge arrived early for his appointment and was ushered into the large reception room.

Every morning the opening of the gleaming aluminum door by Señor Jiminez, the accountant, always the first to arrive, was the salvo saluting the new day. Then stenographers, secretaries, and draftsmen arrived, one by one, to install themselves with an unfurling of blueprints, a brandishing of pencils, and an oiling of typewriters. They had the zest of a ship's crew making last-minute preparations for an expedition whose success was assured. And the large, hearty entrance of Baldomero Saenz, the President, signaled it was time to pull up anchor of this trim vessel.

Success, obvious to a point of embarrassment, would have burst through the seams of his impeccable white linen suit, had it not been carefully tailored with understatement in an attempt to conceal the bulging contours. Upon this man of half-Spanish parentage, modesty sat unfaithfully, serving more to intimate its antithesis; much as the large horn-rimmed glasses he constantly wore suggested more than they concealed.

The large offices and reception room bespoke the same intention. They were furnished with a chic restraint so deliberate as to be almost obtrusive. One could imagine hearing the instructions to the decorator: nothing flashy— plush, but in good taste, toned down.

This morning Saenz was expecting De Armas, the unknown new architect Guzman had sent over for the Camacho project. He was a little puzzled about this until he scanned the briefing sheet of the fellow's record. Bird-seed— except for the Solano Building. Now that really showed flair! Although the style wasn't much in Saenz's line, he could recognize talent. Wonder how he got that break, and no more. Well, Guzman knew what he was doing, he thought.

Some time earlier, over a pleasant lunch at the Carmelo, Miguel Guzman had made detailed arrangements with Saenz, following Guzman Senior's instructions. This was not the first time the two firms had collaborated. Not infrequently Guzman and Sons, like many other reputable old names in the field, had found it useful to accept the services of a man so well disposed as Saenz. Construction is a complicated labyrinth of obstructive regulations, and in certain special situations where misleading attention might be drawn to a respectable company, it was only natural to employ Saenz's facilities to circumvent them. In fact, one might say that the greater portion of Saenz's success was based on his willingness to render service to a friend.

The company offices were housed in a modern building in the smart new business area of the Malecón that faced the bay. Jorge waited in the reception room, wondering why he had been called by this firm. Saenz had been closely linked to the Machado regime and was now part of the clique that monopolized the building industry. Furthermore, the fact that Saenz was responsible for many of the architectural hybrids, so-called "moderns" that were fast perverting Havana topography, made all the more incomprehensible his interest in Jorge, whose work was in an entirely different style. Well, he would see; there was nothing to lose. Besides, he joked at his own expense, probably all Saenz wants from me is to ask for contributions for the Home for Aged Architects.

But the interview turned out to be surprisingly agreeable. From the bridge-deck of his large well-being Saenz was most hearty in expressing his pleasure at this meeting, and his hearty voice extended hospitality to Jorge much as a Captain welcomes the arrival of a new first mate. His six feet two hundred pounds exuded a zesty self-assurance. And he came to the point quite soon. "De Armas, a client of mine, whose name will not be disclosed, has just acquired a large estate on the Punta del Vedado. Quite a beautiful spot, and," he projected his lower lip over his teeth bulldog fashion, "I have an idea it will be quite a busy location. You know how the city is moving out to Vedado now."

Jorge nodded.

"Well, he wants to make a new subdivision out of this. But, mind you, not just an ordinary one. He's keen on creating something that Havana has really never had before—a project primarily directed to the lower middle-class. Small homes, attractive and functional, yet within their means."

He paused a moment as he noticed Jorge's eyes register sudden interest, and then continued, "The other important factor is that, overall, the subdivision must have an organic unity but at the same time avoid the serial number look in the separate units. That's my client's expression, by the way, because frankly," he confided with a many-toothed smile, "I like the neat, purely functional housing. Oh, I don't care about putting names to things—I've been too busy building all these years to have had time to learn them," he shrugged in self-deprecatory fashion, "but I suppose you young people would call me a 'modern purist.' You're familiar with some of my projects, I imagine."

"Oh yes," Jorge mumbled, with an effort to conceal any inflection that might reveal his opinion of them.

"But," Saenz continued, leaning back in his chair with such an explosive gesture that Jorge almost expected to see him on the floor, "my client does not share my opinion—fortunately for you, young man, because that's where you enter the picture. That might partially clarify one of several points for you."

"Naturally I was surprised." Jorge replied. "But this does somewhat explain, sir."

"Ahora, bien." Saenz pursued anew, "A project like this requires an architect who not only has ingenuity, but—" he searched for a tactful phrase, "the time and enthusiasm necessary. Naturally, nothing more logical than to look for these elements in an ambitious young architect. Ingenuity you have demonstrated in the Solano building, and I assume you are ambitious..." he paused.

"Within reason," Jorge smiled. "But I warn you I am not so young as I look. I'm twenty-nine."

"That's very young. But I judge from your answer that you're older than your years as well as your appearance. And that's good. It gives you a realistic approach, which is very important. A fellow who is discriminating and adaptable can go a long way—provided he has talent, of course," Saenz suddenly finished. "That's the story! Are you interested?" He threw both arms down across the desk as though exhausted from enthusiasm, and looked expectantly at Jorge. Or at least Jorge assumed he was looking at him, for the bright light from the window directly reflected on the lens of his glasses, converting them into two glaring discs. It was impossible to know what was behind them.

After a long pause Jorge answered simply, "Yes, sir, I am very much interested. It's a real challenge to the imagination. As a matter of fact, this very idea happens to be a dream of mine!"

He paused again, and Saenz, thinking that he had finished, began to raise himself from the desk with the impetus of hidden springs uncoiling.

But Jorge had not noticed and continued, "To give new horizons to the middle class! Oh, a lot has been done to improve the tenements and housing conditions of the working class. But what about our neglected middle class? The ones who would like to give warmth and interest to their homes and their lives but who find every incentive destroyed because they live in mausoleums dragged over two centuries! It's ironic that just because they have a few extra dollars in their pockets, we justify our indifference. You don't live by bread alone. What aesthetic sense can be developed in people whose slightest spark of imagination is smothered under what's left of a dead era? Damp rooms with walls twenty feet high and more that are constantly humid and peeling because they were never meant for paint! Distribution of space so faulty that even a modicum of personal privacy is denied! The significance goes even further. How can a nation progress spiritually if its people can never know the silence necessary for an inner life?"

He had spoken slowly, with an earnestness that was as disturbing to Saenz as it was foreign. It left him with nothing to say, and besides, it interrupted the sprightly pace of the office and his own inner rhythm. This fellow was certainly overdoing the show, or was greener than he had thought.

"Very interesting," he obliged, dispirited at the prospect of further conversation of this sort. But happily, Jorge surprised him by suddenly concluding. "When are the designs to be submitted, sir?" he asked. Saenz rose briskly and touched off a buzzer. "Our specifications man will give you all the necessary details, and so on," he smiled almost gaily. A moment later a small sprightly man entered the office.

"Señor De Armas, Senor Bustillo," he waved breezily, "Bustillo will be glad to go over the specifications with you—" and Jorge found himself half-waved, half-pushed towards the door. "Good luck to you, De Armas," Saenz concluded with a flourish.

When Jorge reached the street entrance, he stood dazed from all that optimism and attention. Things like this didn't happen to him. Everything had been too simple and easy—maybe there was some mistake. "There you go again!" Lourdes would have said, "Begrudging yourself even a little good fortune!" Perhaps it was true that he was so accustomed to difficulties that he couldn't recognize simple luck. Undoubtedly it existed for others. He wanted to call her to tell her the news. Damn that convention which made it impossible to reach her! Well, at least it would be over Saturday with that carnival party.

A truck pulling up to park splashed mud over his white suit, and he felt better. A touch of reality was what he needed.

If he couldn't reach Lourdes, he could at least have a drink. He went to the nearest cantina and then crossed the wide avenue of the Malecón to sit on the wall and think things out a little.

Jorge felt great confidence. It was a project he had long dreamed of, and now that he had been given the specifications, ideas were already crowding his imagination. He was anxious to go to the Camacho estate to study the location and get the feel of it.

As he stared out at the horizon beyond the little ferries that bounced their way across the bay to Regla and Casa Blanca, he thought, "Hell, this could be the beginning of everything for Lourdes and me." Then he pulled up short. "Wait a minute. Not so fast. Sounds like hope buzzing around! Old Apis mellifera could pack quite a sting." He quickly brushed it off. Not yet. Not yet.

The tide was high, and fishermen dotted the Malecón wall. An old fellow sitting next to Jorge with his legs dangling over the wall was bent over his hook and line, his rheumatic fingers trying unsuccessfully to make a knot.

"Can I do that for you?" Jorge offered. The man handed it to him gratefully. "Any luck?"

The man shook his head. "I've been sitting here since early morning. Haven't even brought in an orange-peel."

"Maybe it's just not your day," Jorge consoled.

"Oh, it will be my day all right!" The fisherman cast his line back into the sea again. "The others are catching, why shouldn't I? No bad luck lasts a hundred years, they say."

As Jorge walked away, somewhere an empty bottle bounced and clanked against the sidewalk, and a fisherman, hearing the signal, hurried back to his line.

"Bravo! I've got one!" he shouted as he tugged.

Jorge remembered what Lourdes had told him about hearing the fishermen's bottles rattling on the cement wall of the Malecón, and smiled.

8
DON CIPRIANO GOES TO HAVANA

Don Cipriano Salinas was certainly not in a mood for a carnival party, but out of consideration to so many old friends and clients, he had accepted the invitation to attend the closing affair of the Pan American Architects' Convention.

Although it was evening, he drew out his linen handkerchief, lifted the crisp, straw jipi and wiped his forehead. Perhaps it was his state of mind, for even the breeze flowing through the taxi windows did not seem to help. And far less, the staccato voice of the Negro driver, who was more voluble than eloquent. But then, "voluble" was hardly the word—hysterical. Havana always seemed hysterical to Salinas, reluctantly persuaded by his clients to abandon the cool dignity of his patio in Camagüey for the capital three hundred and fifty miles away. Try as they might, neither he nor his wife, Pastora, ever succeeded in preparing his nervous system for the shock that was Havana. Pastora always reminded him before he left, "Now please remember to take care of yourself and try not to notice the people and the noises—Ay! And the gua-guas! Be careful, dear Cipriano. Those Havana bus drivers are all assassins."

He had sighed and looked longingly at the tranquil patio which he already missed. The cockatoos swinging softly in their cages, shaded by the large banana and malanga leaves, the great earthen tinajón whose stolid roundness had stood firmly for a hundred years catching the rain which dripped from the gently sloping roof. All converged and sat firmly in this patio like the very tradition and order which was its center. And Pastora, still fresh-eyed and fair, handing him his walking stick, his portfolio, and his jipi as she had done almost every day of the thirty-five years of their marriage.

"To think," he had protested suddenly, "that I have vowed time and again that I would not take another case in Havana. I have assumed I am retired, and have a right to——"

"——to serve the grandson of a friend you loved," she had finished softly, concentrating on the linen handkerchief she was folding in his breast-pocket, so that he would not notice her interruption, but think that he had spoken the words himself. Ah, those endearing transparent tricks of hers! Of course, she never succeeded in taking him in, but it was her attempt to do so which he loved! That was something women of this generation no longer understood. That all the knowledge and independence of their new world was only a liability if acquired at the price of their mysteries. From those monstrous handbags of theirs they zipped out their desires and opinions in the same impersonal manner with which they extracted their former boudoir secrets.

"Yes, yes, that's right," he had agreed, a little ashamed of himself. "This time it is different. The boy's letter has quite touched me, and I am going to use all my wits as a lawyer to help him. So, I go to Havana. But, my dear, I promise to return home as soon as the sale of the Camacho estate is completed—that is, if I can succeed in effecting any transaction at all!" he added, as he kissed her good-bye.

"When you have made up your mind about something, you generally succeed," she said with admiration.

He had not been quite so confident as his wife. For years now Guzman Construction had been offering a fair price for the estate, and Leandro Camacho's heirs had maintained their degrading feud amongst themselves, preferring to let it lie fallow (the house had already gone to pieces) rather than yield to each other in equitable solution. It was ironic that the house which Leandro Camacho had so loved and through which he had hoped to keep his family united had served only to estrange them more and to emphasize their egotism! Poor Leandro!

But now that Salinas had accomplished his mission, the memory of Leandro was not so sad. It was gratifying to know that his efforts had put Leandro's extraordinary grandson on his way. Salinas had heard of MIT, and if the boy's family had not been so indifferent to its prestige, as well as to the boy's talent, Salinas' task would have been much easier. Their excuse for having squandered the cash Leandro had left them was preposterous: "They had lived abroad most of their lives." As though an enterprising spirit is dependent on geography!

But thank heavens it was done, and although one never knew what that sly fox of a Guzman was up to, pursuing the property so many years,

Salinas hoped he had obtained the best possible price for it. Certainly not for the family's sake, but for the boy. Remarkable, the resemblance to his grandfather—Leandro's same irregular features, powerful physique and magnetism. Yet there was a serenity which Leandro had never possessed; instead of his grandfather's vigorous, ample gestures, this boy, who wanted to be a scientist, moved with quiet resolution. But the mark of greatness was there. Who knows what he would accomplish?

Well, it seemed everybody was happy now. And so would he be if he could just go home soon. There were only the formalities of the negotiation to settle, and he had assured Pastora that he would be home on time to celebrate her birthday with her. Meanwhile here he was, still in Havana and on his way to a party!

It did seem cooler as they drove down Fifth Avenue, through Miramar and the country club section. He could remember when this constituted a "trip to the country." But now it would not be long before the ocean itself would be invisible, with so many homes built on the coast.

The jabbing voice of the driver was causing him actual physical pain.

"So you've just come from Camagüey, doc," the voice shrilled. "Then you've certainly heard the news about the first prize of the lottery!"

"I don't believe I have," Salinas murmured without interest.

"What!" He thrust his gleaming black head toward the back seat. "Didn't you know that Camagüey drew the 'gordo'? Ha, ha, ha! A really fat prize! Get it?" And he flung his right arm over the back, the better to see Salinas.

Evidently the fellow was going to drive indefinitely with his eyes fixed toward the rear, awaiting a reply.

"Quite amusing," Salinas speedily agreed. It was one of those political jokes the masses enjoyed. He knew, of course, to whom "the gordo" referred.

"I thought you'd get it, doc!"

With relief, Salinas noted that the driver again faced front, but neither the heavy Saturday traffic nor Salinas' marked inattention served to diminish the flow of conversation. The animated hands had practically abandoned the wheel to gesture with every word. Thank heaven Pastora could not see this! The red fringed balls lining the interior of the car bounced forward, and suspended from a red satin ribbon, a medal of St. Lazarus, complete with crutches, clanged against the windshield.11 He could not pay the fare fast enough when they reached their destination.

The taxi rolled up to the drive, and as the butler opened the door for him, he could hear music coming from the rear grounds of the house. He was led to the portico where he lingered to observe the lively scene.

Good-naturedly relinquishing any hope of finding the host, he walked toward some friends who had recognized him and were waving enthusiastically. He reminded himself that he must try to observe those little details of a party that ladies seemed to relish so much, so that he could recount it all to dear Pastora.

9
VIVA CUBA LIBRE!

The music from the orchestra crept up the softly illuminated palm trees. From the tables dotted over the lawn, the laughter, the click of glasses and snap of ladies' fans, the tilt of a head or the quickly concealed provocation of a glance, formed, with the dancers and the music, a component part of a vast orchestration. The gourd hissed, the trumpet cried incitingly, the senserro and marracas spilled over the lawn and twirled the dancers into renewed heights. Intricate, incisive and male, the heels of the men as they spun and darted in and out were a counterpoint to the easy voluptuous cadence of their partners.

But with the heightened impulse of the music, these entities of flesh and blood that ordinarily awakened to desire at the slightest contact had been transported. Touch no longer mattered; partners had become one, like metals fused by the white heat of that which all had in common—the joy of life.

Born of the sun, children of the sun, they did not worship but became a living part of their god. Other peoples might try desperately to imitate, only in sad travesty, that which could never be acquired. And if the sun corrupts and destroys even as it impregnates, no matter. They had retained that inestimable gift of joy which had been conferred upon them.

A burst of laughter from one of the tables caused Lourdes and her partner, Rafi, turn towards them. "You can be sure that's Juanito still recounting the Countess Santa Marina's latest adventure!" he smiled. "I was there a few minutes ago when he was just beginning. Have you heard that she's getting a divorce again?"

Lourdes did not immediately answer, as a blade of sound from the trumpet separated her from her partner. Her eyes were shining and her face was flushed as her steps led her to him again a few bars later. "No, I haven't heard," she resumed, "but what an impression of us the foreign members must have from Juanito's stories. What's this one about la Santa Marina? I didn't know. Has she already divorced the poet?"

"Oh, you're way behind! That was last year. She divorced him and married a sculptor. But that's over now, too! she says that—oh, I could never tell it as Juanito does! I won't spoil it for you. Let's go over and listen when this number is finished."

Another shout of laughter from the same table completed a coda for the orchestra. Lourdes and her partner hurried over.

"Lourdes, it's a wonderful party, but—this terrible man!" someone pleaded, "I haven't been able to finish one drink!"

"That's exactly why I've come," Lourdes laughed, "to salvage the last poor shreds of our honor in the eyes of the foreign architects! Fortunately for me, a hostess' sacred right of sanctuary protects me from Juanito's tongue! In fact, I am probably the sole possessor of an intact reputation!"

The laughter increased.

"Ay, poor Lourdes!" gasped one of the party. "Did you really think that would deter him? Juanito has already finished with you!"

Lourdes laughed and shook her head in mock wonder. "Satan could not have found a more perfect decoy. Just look at him." And indeed, as Juanito sat there graceful and relaxed, his boyish smile and disarming blue eyes made it inconceivable to associate him with the cynical quicksilver of his amusing gossip.

"Are any of these fantastic stories of his true?" protested the wife of Quintana, a member from Venezuela.

But Juanito answered for himself. "Anatole France once said, 'To know is nothing. To imagine is everything!'" he smiled.

"What an inglorious retreat! Lourdes has frightened you!" someone exclaimed.

"Oh, I feel safer when she intimidates me," laughed Juan. "It's when she pretends not to be angry with me that there's any danger."

Well then, finish your story about the wedding. You were saying that the Countess Santa Marina was converted—"

"Oh, yes, she was converted to the simple wholesome life of her sculptor, who detested money. It was the only thing that stood in their way—her money. Of course, he didn't make a cent himself because he not only hated money but he abhorred people even more. So naturally he refused to sell any of his work— that is, supposing anyone could be found who wanted it. He worked mostly with black lava stone. He said that all life was but a writhing agony, and that is just what all his figures looked like—except to him they were sweet. He maintained that we were incapable of seeing beyond their appearance into their reality, which was in a sublime state of transition, a rebirth into death, or some such thing. Called them 'children of my cold loins of the tomb.'" Juanito contorted his features into fierceness, at the same time lisping ridiculously as he imitated the man.

"Ay, qué loco!" Lourdes protested laughingly. "I certainly know of no such creature in Havana!"

"But this is the one I was telling you about," Rafi affirmed, "the one she's just divorced. I've met him and he speaks exactly like that, lisp and all. She likes it. Says that it is the one imperfection that proves he's human." This was met with another outburst. Juanito resumed, "She was so in love that she decided to relinquish all the comforts of her past life, marry him and live in his bohio. To celebrate this decision, she gave a farewell-to-the-world party and spent seven thousand dollars on the orchid decorations alone. You were there, Rafi," he nodded. "I was with her a few days ago. She called me to console her. She was nostalgic now that it was all over, and—"

The orchestra had begun again, and at another table a group of men waiting for their wives to rejoin them had been discussing President Grau's intended reelection campaign. The theme had naturally drifted to the communist-controlled labor groups flourishing under his administration.

"Communism in Cuba?" protested a jovial architect from the United States delegation. "I hardly think that would be an issue!"

"It's not inconceivable," demurred a Venezuelan. "Now that the last war has made the world so much smaller, our people can compare their standards of living with those of other countries, and believe me, what they've discovered has been a great shock for many of them. Then too, with the war effort, they've seen how industry needs them. Oh, they're awakening very fast to their rights. Medieval resignation doesn't belong in this atomic age."

"Caramba!" grumbled a corpulent, usually genial, Cuban, "What more rights do they want? They are certainly getting them with Grau. Caramba!" he exclaimed, but his tone of voice was far more trenchant than this mild word which the occasion demanded. "Higher minimum wages, holidays with pay and per diems: A man can't fire his own employee anymore!" He puffed out his jowls and looked toward the others for confirmation.

"That's the other extreme," answered the Venezuelan, "and specious. Just the administration's vote-getting. Besides, it doesn't affect the lower classes or the farmers or even the middle class, who can't ever better themselves because of other very real factors. From the long elliptic of his face his sharp black eyes looked unequivocally toward the American. "All this is used for communist propaganda."

"Oh, I know President Grau has not been as forceful with them as he should," Mr. Langdon, the American, interrupted. "But then, gentlemen, I have visited Cuba often enough to know that it could never take Communism seriously." He waved his highball glass confidently. "Why, this is a Catholic country and a liberty-loving one—"

Several of the men nodded agreement.

"That's just what the Russians are relying on!" pursued the Venezuelan, "your over-confidence. If you will forgive me, Mr. Langdon, besides the— ah— more chronic causes, you also obligingly furnish them with such choice morsels for propaganda as the way Negroes are treated in the United States, destruction of surplus crops while half the world is starving..."

"Also, they ask, 'What is the United States doing about Somoza in Nicaragua?'" Mario suddenly added.

"Anything can be misjudged if the factors causing it are overlooked," Langdon said curtly.

"Well, sir, you can be sure the Russians are not bothering to explain your reasons," the Venezuelan laughed.

"True, true," agreed Mr. Langdon.

The brief discussion seemed to have concluded. Mr. Langdon, as though to reassure his table companions of Yankee good-sportsmanship under fire, declared admiringly, "Well, now, I don't think any people who know how to enjoy life as you Cubans do—and that includes the poor—could ever fall for Commie propaganda. We Americans envy you. Dammit! We take everything so seriously. Without realizing it, we are always conscious of our 'moral heritage' and our mission in the world. Sort of weighs on us. Have to drink to let our hair down. You fellows here don't need drink for that!"

The others laughed with him at his frankness. But Mario suddenly asked, "What exactly do you mean by this 'mission' of the United States?"

The American looked astonished at the question.

"Why, championing freedom, of course, and the underdog who fights for it! Certainly, Cuba is a proof of that!" With fraternal warmth he turned to Mario for corroboration. But Mario was silent. Fortunately, the American's burst of comradeship was undampened.

"What I mean is—we won Cuba from the Spaniards—could have taken her as a colony—but instead we cleaned her mess, got her settled, and gave her complete independence. Never took a thing for ourselves—which was only right," he conceded breezily. "And since then we have brought in millions of dollars to build up her industry, given people work, have always paid a higher price for her sugar—and the only thing we want in return is app—" He was going to say "appreciation" but corrected, "—is friendship..." with his voice trailing off. Had the orchestra not been playing, the eloquent silence at the table would have been more marked. "Hell, I'm sorry, gentlemen, if I sounded patronizing," he shook the ice in his empty glass. "Didn't mean to go into all that; merely brought it up to clarify my statement to our friend here."

Miguel added quickly, "Of course, we know that Franklin Roosevelt has helped us a great deal with advantageous trade agreements and so on, and that Truman is advocating—"

"A mere drop in the bucket," Mario interrupted. "More realistic help is needed than a handful of dollars that usually never get past our big brass! We need agricultural equipment, machinery, technicians—"

To Miguel's great relief, Dr. Matas, a pompous member of the Ministry of Education, interrupted. Miguel was becoming troubled at his brother's growing indiscretion. Not only was Mario offending the American, but also the others, good friends, who were themselves identified with the "big brass." Dr. Matas' verbosity could always be counted on to take the edge off anything.

He was expounding, "Ignorance, exactly! It is the core of all our troubles! If we were to investigate, we would discover that even the labor problem we were discussing before is in the final analysis a responsibility of the Ministry of Education. Distorted perspective, lack of understanding of—"

"Precisely," echoed an eager assistant in Dr. Matas' department. "If Dr. Mata's School Bill were passed, it would inculcate a true concept of democracy in the future labor problems. Don't you think so, Mario?"

Mario's habitual smile was tinged with gravity, "Do you really want to know?" he paused.

"Of course!"

"I don't think anyone believes a word he is saying. We just like to hear ourselves talk. We are all deliberately avoiding the real issues." The finality of his gesture as he finished his drink made them wonder whether the accustomed humorous turn of such a remark would be forthcoming. It was not.

"It's a national sport," he continued, "to toss around words that have high-flown ideas glued to them like feathers to a badminton shuttlecock. Whether it's a bus driver eating in a fonda china or one of us, it's all the same game. Nothing's going to change. We Latins can be heroic at Bayamo or a Guayaquil, but in everyday life?" he shrugged his shoulders with good-natured contempt. "As the old saying goes, we can die for our principles, but as in our case, it's not dramatic enough for us to live by them."

An architect from Argentina protested, "Why 'we Latins?' I don't think we have a priority on hypocrisy! Certainly, we have only to look at the policy of—"

But with a winning smile, Mario extricated himself and turned the conversation, "Of course, of course!" he conciliated, "what I meant was that we Latins, strange as it might seem to others, have a greater sense of reality. There is only one life, and the goodness of life. As our friend, Mr. Langdon says, 'We leave depressing abstractions to be carried out by others!' Caball-eros!" he toasted, languidly holding out his refilled glass, "I drink to our priority in happiness!"

"And to our Cuban hosts!" someone responded.

The older men present were not offended. Mario was, after all, a Guzman, and one of them. And the visiting architects did not know him well enough to detect a certain note in his voice which belied his flippancy.

"And to our hosts of this evening. It's a wonderful party, Mario!"

"Where are our wives? This music is too good to waste!"

"Well, I'm glad to hear you say that!" Elena Montero, on her way to her own table, twined caressing arms around Mario's neck as she leaned back of his chair. "You were all so serious a moment ago, I thought it was no wonder your women had abandoned you! I certainly would have," she teased. The diamond earrings hanging from the small pierced ears sparkled in contrast against her long blond hair and bare tanned shoulders and breast. The fragrance of her hovered as part of the warm carnival night of which the men themselves were a part.

"How wrong you are!" Mario defended, "It is only our faithfulness that keeps us here waiting for them! And since this might be the last dance with the orchestra, we've hired a comparsa from the Carnival in town to continue out here after they've finished." He rose and led her to join the dancers.

Only the lawyer Salinas and the American remained. The latter had lost his jovial air, and puffing at a cigar, from time to time sent up a smoke screen of aggressive bewilderment. His large, loose frame, clear brown eyes, strong jaw and rather bulbous nose briskly set on a ruddy face somehow reminded Salinas of North American states unfamiliar to him—Texas or Montana or Wyoming. He wondered what chain of events had led this man here to an environment so obviously alien to his nature. And to this particular table which had given him such an awkward moment.

Salinas remarked, "Difficult to understand. More difficult to believe."

Mr. Langdon raised his head, surprised to discover that he was not alone at the table. At the sight of the elder man's kindly face, he realized the remark was in answer to his own thoughts. He suspended the cigar hopefully and looked slightly relieved. "You felt this way too, sir?"

"Not quite," Salinas smiled, "I am speaking for the many Americans I have had the pleasure to know. I may not always have agreed with them, but usually was able to understand them."

"Well," the American impatiently slapped his hand on his knee, "I wish I could say the same about your countrymen. If we were not at a party— our host seems to have forgotten that for a while—I certainly would have answered some of those not too subtle inferences. Actually, I was ready to blow my top! Would have lost my temper, that is," he explained a little apologetically.

"Oh, I am familiar with the expression," Salinas assured him. "I am also familiar with your reaction. Believe me, you are not the first of your compatriots to be perplexed at this..." He waved his hand toward the table.

"Then I trust I am not offending you, sir," Mr. Langdon said, somewhat mollified at the other man's obvious sympathy.

"Not at all! You see, although I have not succeeded in my effort to retire from law practice, I have at least attained one enviable attribute of old age, objectivity."

"I appreciate your invitation to speak frankly," Landon replied. "I'd like to think that I'm objective too, but it seems my compatriots and I have been harboring some pretty one-sided illusions about the cordiality that exists between Cubans and Americans."

"I wouldn't call it 'illusion.' It is not an entirely unfounded feeling. The Cubans admire American enterprise, although they do not wish it for themselves," he smiled, "and they instinctively like the American spirit—the friendliness, sense of humor, and—"

"Oh, that," Langdon exclaimed. "The good-natured, gawky, blundering Yankee!"

"No, no," Salinas objected.

"Then why that resentment at the table? My own grandfather fought in the battle of San Juan, and since childhood I have been raised to be proud of this friendship between the two countries. I don't want to sound boastful, but I've always thought we have a right to be proud of it." He paused, suddenly defiant, waiting for Salinas to deny this.

But Salinas nodded. "You have every right to be proud of the majority of Americans who wanted and truly believed that the faith would be kept. You are yourself an example of the people's sincerity."

The compliment exasperated Mr. Langdon. He wished the nice old duffer would come to the point. But he supposed that was impossible. Latins were never capable of just plain talk. They had to use that damn irritating language of implications and subtleties.

He made an attempt to talk this same language. "You imply, of course, that it is naïve to think that altruism motivated the Americans."

"Much more than that. And I'm not implying; I'm stating."

The American laughed in spite of himself. Salinas had beaten him at his own game. "Oh, I know we didn't get into the Spanish-American war just for love of Cuban liberty the way we learned it at school," he replied.

The dancing in the garden had become increasingly animated and the two men decided to escape to a more secluded area at the side of the house. They walked slowly along the garden path and Langdon continued. "Oh, yes! I know about the Maine incident being something of a manufactured Pearl Harbor. It stirred up the American public and made it easy for McKinley and Hearst to ignore poor old Spain's humiliating overtures. I know too that when Cuba asked us to help only with money and arms the United States took over the whole war instead."

Salinas expressed surprise at Langdon's familiarity with these facts.

"Well," the American explained, "most of this I learned from my grandfather. I'll never forget the stories he told me about the way the Cuban soldiers were so glad to see their Yankee brothers disembark at Daiquiri that they waded into the water and carried them to shore on their shoulders. But not the Cuban generals. They wanted to win their own war. And there are other stories, too, how—I forget the name of the general down there in Oriente—"

"General Garcia."

"How he was so offended at the cool invitation of the Americans that he didn't attend the signing of the peace in his own Province. My grandfather said he'd never forget the faces of the Cubans when the American flag was flown over Santiago, and their own general wasn't included in the new government. As you might have gathered, my grandfather loved Cuba and remained there afterwards to work in the reconstruction. One time when he was telling me about that period, he described what some American businessmen had done to the hardwood forests and farming lands, pulling them all up to make quick money planting sugar cane—well, he became so incensed and his face got so red you would have thought it had just happened."

The American stopped walking and faced Dr. Salinas. "At any rate, you see I know some facts that are not very pretty. But my grandfather felt, and so do I, that no great things can be accomplished by a nation without having certain amount of scoundrel hangers-on. But the main thing—and that's what he was proud of—is that we did keep our promise. We did get out. And certainly, in spite of all the advantages gained for the United States, there was a hell of a lot of good done for Cuba. And there still is!" He swayed back and forth on his heels and relit his cigar. Evidently, he felt better for having unburdened himself.

"I must say your grandfather was a man of rare exception," Salinas remarked. "I also fought in Cuba's war of Independence, the 'Spanish-American War,' as you call it, and I know that most of the Americans who came ignored. all this. Perhaps in their excitement of the adventure and glory they lost sight of the real issues. Just as your grandfather recounted the story of Daiquiri, so too the Cuban people figuratively had borne on their shoulders what they thought to be their big brother, emancipator, friend and mentor. Now they are hurt, resentful, betrayed."

"But you yourself admit we've done a great deal for Cuba, Langdon exclaimed in exasperation. "Then why do you say that? And what interests me even more," his tone was raised excitedly, "is why those men at the table react as they do. After all, you were talking about past history. I want to know about now."

Salinas placed a quieting hand on Langdon's arm. "I wish we had time now to explore this thoroughly. Your concern deserves our attention. But I'm afraid we're not behaving very well as party guests, are we? So I must content myself with hoping that if you ever come to Camagüey we may resume this conversation." He paused and sketched his cane on the gravel path as he meditated. Then he continued, "You helped us win our freedom and then took it back with the Platt Amendment. You gave us employment, but your billion- and-a-half dollar monopolies of almost everything—public utilities, railroads, banks—has taken away the possibility of ownership for us. You talk to us about democracy and finance our dictator.

"Certainly, one can't deny that we had great friends too, like Brooks and Welles and Franklin Roosevelt, but alas, they do not balance the scale! Indeed, the American people are our friends, but how can the Cuban understand this? He knows only what he sees. Well, forgive me." He waved his cane apologetically. "You wanted to know. In view of all this, can we be so sure that one day the Communists will not find willing ears? I pray it will not be so. There is still time to change things, but it's running out." He smiled, but a note of sadness tinged his warning which trailed into the pause.

The American with arms folded had been listening attentively. Occasionally he puffed at his cigar. Several times he had made a slight gesture of surprise or protest, but as the commentary progressed, he became more and more intent, almost withdrawn. And when Salinas had finished, Mr. Landon was motionless, remote, as though searching within himself. The cigar between his fingers had gone out. Finally he looked up at the older man and smiled somberly as he extended his hand. "Thank you, sir," he said. His voice was vaguely troubled.

Salinas noted that as the American slowly walked away, he did not return to the party, but continued to the front of the house, where he signaled for his chauffeur.

The pungent odors of paella and suckling pig crackling with golden chicharrón rose from the long buffet and wafted over all the traditional dishes.

Old Pancha presided. In deference to the foreign members of the convention, she had been persuaded just this once to relinquish her shapeless old skirt and beige cotton stockings for a uniform. But as she took respite a moment to look out over the garden and observe with pride that the party was "going fine," her old myopic eyes squinted as she perceived something in the distance. She forgot the dignity of her uniform as she waved a potholder to attract her mistress' attention across the lawn.

"Señora Lourdes!" she shouted, "They're coming!"

From beyond the hills there was a glimmering of lights, green, red, and gold. Lourdes had seen, and signaled the orchestra to stop playing. Against the gaunt outline of the royal palms the moon revealed the swaying figures of the comparsa, undulating slowly, rhythmically, all one body, like the curving sinuous ceiba trees whose roots their bare feet touched as they passed. Their minor chant grew more discernible... "Ae-e-e, Ea-a-a." It might have been the voice of the night itself which a hundred years ago had curtained the slaves' laments. "La conga va rolla —" the conga will run over you. Stepping high and proud, their backs curved from the weight, the men who bore the long faroles spun and twirled them until the sky became a vortex of flame and color. As they approached it was evident that there was no formal organization in this haphazard mingling of all shapes and heights. These were no performers. Their dark faces were rapt; they were unconscious of all else. As the comparsa reached the garden, the leader stopped, and the group fell into silence. No one moved. The guests too were caught in the moment's tension. Only the leaves rustled, waiting, as though straining at the same call, and the austere palm seemed to have become articulate in the nervous dry cry of a peacock. A bongo hollowed a warning, and suddenly, as though it had burst from the red earth, a trumpet broke into the shrill call of a conga.

"Anyone who wants to, join in!" Mario invited, taking the arm of Elena Montero.

Soon the house-guests followed, gathering behind the comparsa. Sharp, high-heeled shoes caught into the grass and were flung—satin, brocade, jewel-studded—into the hedge. Their feet, black and white, beat with the pulse of the earth.

§

The Pan American Architects' Convention had come to a close with this party. A crest of voices, perfume, and glances careless at this late hour broke over the terrace and into the living room. Lourdes stood in the entrance hall saying goodnight to the departing guests. Don Alberto Velasco, taking advantage of finding her alone a moment, pressed her hand. "It was a wonderful party," he whispered, "but then, wherever you are is wonderful. I only wish it would not always have to be with so many others—." He waited and she felt one of his fingers move across her palm.

"I'm so glad you enjoyed it," she smiled as though she did not understand, and as she withdrew her hand, she found a small scrap of folded paper.

"Do you have my wrap, Alberto?" his wife interrupted. "Call me," he whispered as he left.

Lourdes could not repress a glint of amusement as she observed him placing the stole about his wife's shoulders as though wrapping in old newspaper a distasteful bundle to be quickly disposed of.

"This has been an unforgettable evening," Señora Quintana's small fingers patted Lourdes' arm impulsively.

"Not only this evening, but the entire convention!" her husband added.

"It's true! You cannot imagine how we appreciate everything you have done for us. Why, in just these few days all of us have felt that we are not strangers here at all!"

"I only hope that when the convention is held in Venezuela, we will be able—" her husband began, but someone interrupted. "Oh, will it be Venezuela next year?"

"It hasn't been decided yet, but if it is, we will have to look sharp, you may be sure, to give you as interesting a program as we have had in Cuba!"

"I might safely add," Don Carlos Mendia said, joining the group, "that Havana has been made doubly delightful for you because of our hostess!" He raised Lourdes' hand to his lips, and she smiled fondly at him. No social function was complete without the warming sight of his small perfectly groomed figure, the regal head prematurely silvered, the mellow voice and winning smile. His very presence evoked with nostalgia the fading era of Cuban society which had been untouched by the outside world, where the cultivation of friendship had been a career in itself, more esteemed than material success; and where conversation was a flowering of the spirit.

"But what about our host?" someone protested, loud enough for Mario, who was approaching them, to hear.

"Oh, anyone knows that the host is the least of it," Mario laughed, putting his arm around Lourdes.

Lourdes smiled and held the pose.

Elena Montero's voice interrupted. "Mario, dear, please help me find my shoes, or I can't go home! I threw them in the hedge and I've looked and looked..."

§

Lourdes was relieved to see the departing cars flowing down the long driveway. She had exchanged a last few words with her sister-in-law who was waiting in the car for Miguel, and as she entered the house several stragglers of the reception committee, tired and content, were commenting on the success of the convention as they prepared to leave.

Pancha entered, happy once again in the beige cotton stockings that were always half falling under the long shapeless skirt.

"Perdone, señora. Juan wants to know if he should take the tables from the garden now."

"No, Pancha, he can clean up in the morning."

"'The morning!'—today, you mean, Señora Lourdes! It's five o'clock. What a party!" She looked at the others with satisfaction and folded her hands over the long denim apron, her only concession to a uniform, but resembling more an alchemist's smock of multicolored stains from mysterious ingredients known only to her. There was nothing Pancha loved so much as a party, and although as cook she should have had only a remote kitchen view of it, her many years with the family since Lourdes' childhood gave her the right to wander in and out at will.

"You're right, Pancha, it certainly was a fiesta," one of the men remarked, "and as usual the grand climax was your paella. Was that one of your chickens I recognized in it?"

"Ay, Señor Ramon!" she threw up her plump hands in horror, although she knew he was teasing. "You know those chickens are part of the family!"

"Are you raising chickens now, Mario?"

"No," Mario laughed, "Pancha does. When we built this house there was no way of separating her from those hens!" Lourdes' father has a finca, and as far as Pancha is concerned, there is no difference between the Biltmore residential section and the countryside." Pancha stood there nodding emphatically.

"With so much land here, señor..." she protested.

"Oh, she refused to come with us otherwise! So here we are with a functional, ultra-modern home, and a built-in poultry yard! And with her self-appointed title of graduate architect. You can just imagine when we built the house—." Smiling, with a downward tilt of the head, he smoothed the side of his hair and raised his eyebrows in measured exclamation. He did not know that the restrained gesture was typical of his father.

"Señor Miguel," Pancha appealed to Mario's brother, "did you ever eat a filete that was cooked in one of those—" her upper lip, wrinkled from the loss of teeth, curled with scorn, "electric stoves? Can you imagine my paella tonight if I cooked it on that!"

"There you have it!" Mario appealed, "and Lourdes just as bad, encouraging her!" His fond, teasing expression as he looked at Lourdes made palpable to the others their companionship and the little jokes they shared together. But it was really all a sham, she thought, a public deception which she could no longer abide.

As they laughed, Mario, whose arm hung over the side of the sofa where he was comfortably relaxed, lightly patted her thigh. It was not a vulgar gesture. He would be incapable of that. On the contrary, it was the feigning of tender possession which was intolerable. With the pretext of seeing to the tables she rose and escaped to the garden.

The carnival illumination had been turned off, and all was hushed and drawn into itself. Only a few crickets speckled the silence, the twittering of the tomeguín family that nested in the almond tree, and the trickling of the rock-garden pool. The tops of the royal palms like giant spiders sprang at the pre-dawn sky, and a heavy dew was settling on the grass and on the tables that now looked so out of place. Their center decorations and cloths drooped with dampness, limp white shrouds of the ephemeral gaiety that had hovered over them an hour ago. She had enjoyed the party because the secret by which she lived gave meaning to every detail of her life. But what if there were for her, as for many others here tonight, nothing more than this? — the desolate reality for all the heroic little attempts to clutch at life or to conceal its blight. She could feel the pointed edge of the carefully folded note pressing against her bosom where she had been obliged hastily to conceal it. She drew it out now, and without looking at it crumpled it into a tiny ball and threw it in the pond. No need to read it. She knew its message only too well.

She turned and drank in the deep seclusion of the garden, but the sound of Mario's voice soon penetrated her thoughts. The guests had gone. He walked jauntily down the path towards her. "Well, look who's here!" he said expansively, "I thought you'd gone up." He stopped a moment to survey the scene. Undoubtedly, he had made quite a success in handling the convention, and the moon was shining down on his success, his house, his garden, his wife. As he inhaled his cigarette, she felt that he contemplated the very moon with proprietary pride.

"A shame Dad's liver attack prevented him from being here. He would have been very pleased. Many of them had had no idea of the progress our National Association has made. And then, of course, their naming me as one of the editors of the international magazine..." he put his arm around her carelessly. "Aren't you proud of yourself?" he asked, suddenly looking at her. "You had quite a hand in this, milady. I congratulate you and thank you. We make quite a couple, don't we?" He had drunk a great deal, as they all had, but she felt that the intimacy of his tone was not due to that. Without looking at him she knew that at this moment he was bathed in self-satisfaction and contentment. This was the first time in two weeks that she had so much as seen Mario for more than ten minutes, and that was not unusual. But the truth did not matter to him at all. Only the picture they made of a happy young couple surrounded by admiring friends; or was it tomorrow's social column shining in his eyes? "The last evening of the Pan American Architects' Convention was celebrated for foreign delegates in the home of Mr. and Mrs. Mario Guzman, junior partner of the well-known firm Guzman and Sons, and chairman of the Havana Reception Committee for the Convention—"

If he would just save the false picture for the public! At least it would be a nice honest hypocrisy! But what disgusted her most was the cynicism when they were alone, the ease of self-deception, the enjoyment of these empty scenes.

"I'm glad you're so pleased," she managed to say.

There was a pause, and then he leaned quite close to her and added "and you're very attractive tonight, Señora Guzman. That gown, by the way is a Bernabeu, isn't it?"

She nodded. How well she knew the way his eyelashes instinctively lowered, and the almost imperceptible dilating of his nostrils. How often she had seen it used! They both stood there silent, as though before a grave for which one could feel only faint regret for something that was irrevocably lost. But it quickly passed. He suddenly withdrew his arm and exclaimed, "I forgot that Juan is waiting for the car keys!" and hurried toward the house.

Did he really imagine, she wondered, that she could go on for the rest of life like this, content with the appearance of a life? The thought had occurred to her that perhaps he imagined that she had a lover, and that he thought it was all right as long as no one, including himself, knew. As long as the picture was unmarred.

One of Pancha's roosters had begun to crow. She slipped up to their rooms. He was still below. Before she undressed, she hurried to turn down the cover of his bed. It was of white linen, from her trousseau, with the beautifully embroidered initials. She turned it back slowly.

10
LOURDES AND MARIO

Lourdes, half awake, stretched out a languid arm which just reached the cream brocade drapes of the French door. She pinched back a corner of it to make a hazy guess at the time. It must be after noon, as the young bamboos were already spindling shadows across the lily pond. The knowledge that the outside world was at this moment involved in its endless machinations heightened the luxury of this quiet, zealously guarded by the household. Even Pancha's ebullience was contained until the sound of Lourdes' stirring would release the charivari of kitchen activity. The green silk under drapes swayed sleepily, the unwound clock muted time, and in a low bowl a small wood-carved fawn posed serenely within a miniature woodland of fern and moss. It was an island of silence protected from the moving sea of sunlight and outer life.

She could indulge for a while in the drowsy luxury of being. If her hand happened to touch any part of herself, she loved it, because she belonged to him, and loved everything that was his. She had never thought much of herself before, considering her physical being too unclassical: long legs, full thighs, slender neck, plump shoulders. Once she had complained that she was neither sport model nor classical, neither sensual nor chaste. To this Jorge had responded, "Exactly. You are all of them." He had scolded, "From the beginning of creation you are the only you. But until you learn to love yourself a little you will only be half you." Well, if he had succeeded in teaching her, it was not by his words. She had learned to cherish all things that an unloved woman finds absurd. Her toes; the back of her knees; the belly roundness; the silky mound; the pleasant consciousness of her full mouth curving as she spoke; and the baptismal sweat of two bodies in union. All had taken on beauty because of a love that rose beyond carnal gratification.

Her room, too, was beautiful because it was the room of a woman loved. The very world was a corporeal part of themselves. Because she was his, she loved all the lovers in dark corners, the men who looked at her, the women whom his eyes admired.

Across the room the mirror reflected a faint reproach from the Christ who hung above her bed. Did He not love all that was truth, and scorn the letter of the law when it killed the spirit? Surely the sinners and publicans would not have listened to Him had He not known how to understand the turmoil of the human heart. And had she not remained faithful to Him in all the years of her disillusionment and loneliness with Mario, until an affliction of body and spirit had sucked her into a phantasmagoric world close to death?

But when neither faith nor life-force had seemed adequate, Jorge had come, direct instrument of her salvation, to pull her from the vortex of annihilation. Ironically it had been Jorge, himself ill-favored of life, who had retaught her of its goodness and of her own useful place in it. She had never abandoned God although she had felt abandoned by Him. Now, by giving her the gift of this love, was it not His way of repaying her faithfulness?

The priest, with an understanding smile had called it rationalizing. Well, perhaps it was. Who could distinguish between theological nicety and one's personal, honest communication with God? How could the same instrument be at once salvation and damnation? For all her respect, she could not understand; and if the flower possibly bore a parasite somewhere in its foliage, nonetheless it flourished, and she was able to forget that uncertain blight.

Suddenly, an amen to her thoughts, from the upper sun room her beloved canary Trigo's song, spilling over the window ledge, flowed into her room. From his little cage came the wisdom of God's world, love bursting from the separate cages in which we live, fusing into everything that surrounds us, just as his song, even now, was dissolving into the tinkle and whisper of the caña brava leaves outside the window. Luminous her room, herself, the world!

Why had Mario never made her feel this way? Ridiculous thought! Mario had always been too busy being in love with himself—although no one else remotely suspected this. People assumed that the man they knew was relaxed, affable, attentive, unpretentious, and with a subdued taste in clothes. In fact, his male attractiveness was enhanced not only by his innate aristocratic bearing but by his apparent indifference to the impression he made. Delicious joke! If they could only guess the time that was consumed in the creation of this effortlessly well-dressed image!

His tailor, a Spaniard who enjoyed the patronage of Madrid society, was delighted with the discovery of Señor Mario, who did not bend with every new breeze of fashion but whose natural elegance could afford to shun caprice. He reveled in the challenge of imported fabrics which Señor Mario brought him from Spain, France, and sometimes Italy. He could mold to this client's handsome figure a suit that could be a work of art in its sobriety and unobtrusive perfection. He highly approved of Mario's subdued ties and the unembellished hand-sewn shoes. Even the guayabera, which respected no man after an hour's wear, behaved differently with Mario. That male coquetry of hand-stitched pleats and diminutive mother-of-pearl buttons somehow miraculously retained its linen freshness for him.

Once Lourdes in a burst of optimism returned from a shopping excursion at El Encanto with some printed beach shirts for him. They were smart prints, not too dashing, that had just made their appearance from the United States. Mario, amused, had tried them on to please her. They both faced the mirror to contemplate the results, which proved to be inexplicably droll. Lourdes had to agree with Mario's comment that he could wear them with success at the carnival. No doubt about it—Mario's unobtrusiveness could not be tampered with.

He abhorred rings for men, and wore only a watch. He considered professionally manicured nails effeminate, but daily she had observed him fastidiously care for them himself. And the pressing demands of neither heaven nor earth could accelerate the ritual of his daily toilette. At the expense of the waiting Lourdes, family, or friends, or business appointments, his calm absorption would remain unaltered until the last defiant strand of hair, the last natural wave, surrendered to the desired picture of manly simplicity.

He and Lourdes shared several jokes concerning his acknowledged narcissism. "I will be faithful to you, Cynara in my fashion," he often enjoyed quoting, his heavy eyebrows arched half-jesting, half cynically, and his high forehead wrinkled enigmatically. It was not only a playful hint of infidelity, but an admission that his infidelity to her was with himself. He was his own first true love.

Even in bed, there was the joke of his narcissism. He would stretch out his naked body, with the long, well-proportioned limbs, small waist, wide shoulders, and strong neck, and with a secretive smile faintly suggesting the mysteries and joys of self-love, would beckon her to approach him. It was not a command, but rather an overt act of generosity that would share the privilege of his beauty with her.

"You could never deny that you are of pure Spanish descent!" she had once exclaimed. "The Super-race! Conquistador! No Creole blood in you! I can see a Castilian in all his arrogance and pride lying as you are now, and saying to his doña, "Look at this splendor, you fortunate woman; I give you permission to enjoy it!" They had both laughed. He recognized the fault but did not swerve in his steadfast devotion to himself.

It had been different before they were married. Friends from childhood, they had suddenly awakened to each other in adolescence, and from then on they had been official novios. They had been inseparable except during the convulsive period of the Revolution which ended the Machado dictatorship, and the savage reprisals which followed. Mario and Lourdes, secure in their teenage world, had been blissfully unaware of almost everything. Newspaper stories of violence and horror were concealed from her as inappropriate for a young girl's eyes. Then schools had closed, visits and outings were curtailed, and Mario, accompanied by his mother and brother, had suddenly been whisked off to the United States.

Although she missed him terribly, the flight had lent Mario a new glamour which almost compensated for his absence. It mattered little that no patriotic act of Mario had motivated the flight. He was in danger, and that was thrilling! It was much later both he and Lourdes learned that it was his father's identification, astutely concealed, with the overthrown regime that had caused their exile. And after the orgy of avenging passion had spent itself and Mario could safely return, life resumed its customary enchantments—even more than usual, since school had not yet reopened.

There was the summer season in Varadero of sailing, swimming, riding; and the winter of parties in private homes, country fincas, and clubs. The two were inseparable but never alone, at least officially. Even for the movies, there was the inevitable chaperone. But that doughty symbol of propriety was well-trained. Chaperones remembered the days of their youth, and by unwritten protocol, a book, or a bit of needlework suddenly became the object of such absorption that the good lady would seem bereft of all sense of her surroundings! With a smile, Lourdes recalled the innocence of their delighted wonder when, one evening that Mario was visiting, her sister, who had taken their mother's place since her death years before, should have required so much time in the kitchen to prepare chocolate and churros.

With reckless courage they experienced the tremendous enchantment of their first kiss, and it never occurred to them that her sister need not have left the room at all, as she could have summoned Pancha, whose quarters were adjacent to the kitchen!

But most unforgettable was the farewell party at the Club honoring Mario his last night before leaving Cuba for college in the United States. It was May 29, 1934. Many of his companions also were preparing to resume abroad their long-interrupted studies, as the University was still rife with political unrest. But more importantly, this night everything was forgotten, differences and woes both public and private, in the unbounded rejoicing over that event for which generations of Cubans had yearned, the abrogation of the Platt Amendment! At long last Cuba was to be the master of its own destiny! For good or for ill, it would be their own success, or their own disaster. Henceforth no nation would have the right to intervene!

Even the youth, ignorant of the transcendence of the occasion, could not help being caught in the feverish mood of the three-day celebration.

Lourdes remembered that after dinner, all the guests, in a procession of cars, had attempted to drive into the city, as they had been invited to attend the reception in the Palace. But the overflowing of the deliriously happy populace had made it inaccessible. Nevertheless, they were able to behold the Capitol blazing lights, the dancing in the streets, the wild cheering to the banners which flaunted "Viva Cuba Libre," Viva Mendieta," "Viva Roosevelt." The street-singing, the shots fired into the air, the whistling of boats in the harbor all seemed to be swept to a frenzied climax by the port sirens.

As the revelry of the masses increased, the party had returned to the club. They were all in high spirits, for the excitement of the town was infectious. Certainly, Lourdes and Mario, already stirred by their imminent separation, were affected. They had observed the customary methods of others to evade the chaperones, and this night they dared avail themselves of them. Separately disappearing from the dance, they had met at the dock near the boat house. There, on the softly swaying pier, protected from the May moon by the anchored yachts, she had known that first desperate embarrassment, that first frightening wild joy, as he kissed her breast; and his hand, with more experience than she could have suspected, slipped under her dress.

Now surely, having shared the shame and wonder of this new intimacy, she belonged to him forever! The shock of discovering that she could feel repugnance and desire at the same time—and that the person whom she had known all her life was really a stranger in a warm-breathing world of his own mysteries, bewildered her. Her emotions, the swaying pier, the plopping of the boats made her faint. She opened her eyes, and suddenly the night sky held, not stars, but galaxies of saints who were witnessing this wonderful and terrible scene. With a sharp, low cry which startled Mario, she pulled herself away from him. "Go back to the dance...please...please," she whispered, trembling. Mario, relishing the new role of indulgent man of the world, consoled her. But she could only answer, "Go away...please go away."

"All right, but do you love me?" he asked. Saints or no saints, she threw her arms around him, and more horrified than ever by this added gesture of consent, she ran from him, endeavoring to compose herself sufficiently to re-enter the ballroom. She managed to slip unobserved into the women's lounge, where she smoothed her dress a dozen times and looked at herself anxiously in the mirror.

To her slight relief, she could detect no visible change, but she was not convinced. By some diabolical mark, her transgression surely would be apparent to all! With a shudder, she returned to the dance. It was worse than she had thought, for it seemed to her that the large pavilion was filled with the saints: Saint Joseph (the chaste—how awful!), La Caridad Del Cobre, Our Lady of Lourdes, Saint Teresa, Our Lady of the Immaculate Conception, but above all, Saint Anne, the little grandmother of the Child Jesus! For a grandmother to have seen what happened on the pier! For some reason, Saint Anne was a greater reproach than Christ. Wanting very much to die, at that moment she saw Mario, who to her amazement was completely at ease, gaily dancing among the saints! His poise should have been reassuring to her, but somehow it was not. She had not then understood why she would have preferred seeing him less composed.

But the next day he had left, and, after an interval incredibly brief for such unparalleled love and woe, a new world had begun for her.

Lourdes had heard about Eddy Chibás. In Cuba, who had not? Almost daily the newspapers carried stories of his quixotic exploits and blistering polemics waged against public figures. He had rejected the affluent society into which he had been born by claiming his sole brotherhood with all the Cuban people. The sound of his name had become as much a part of Cuban life as baseball and the black market.

Eddy the "loco," the "Revolutionary," the "quijote," the "psychopath" Eddy had brazenly and publicly defied Machado during the dictator's most violent period of terrorism; had literally armed himself with a horsewhip, and like a myopic, bifocaled Galahad, had avenged the honor of Cuban womanhood by pursuing its defamer, a prominent publisher, across the noonday Havana streets; had fought duels at the drop of a hat; had delivered shrill tirades against the economic monopolies of the United States in Cuba, but written in burning defense of the American people and their way of life.

Corrupt government officials called him a compulsive troublemaker; capitalists called him communist; the communists called him millionaire bourgeois; the middle class chuckled at his mad illusions; the resigned masses, fluctuating between incredulous amusement and sudden hope, were increasingly devoted to him. No one, neither government, nor gangster, nor foreign power dared silence him, "madman" or not.

For Lourdes, the half-heard references to his escapades were as unattended as any other dull topic of the adult world—until the day that she met him by chance in an art store. She had stopped in, accompanied by a friend on the way home from an afternoon movie. As they were introduced, his shrill voice and manner of peering at them through heavy bifocals caused them to suppress a giggle. They chatted a few minutes about mutual friends; then suddenly he looked quite gravely at Lourdes and asked, "What are you doing?"

"Just coming from the movie."

"No," he smiled, "I mean what are you doing with your time, your days?"

Lourdes had never thought about that. She shrugged, a little puzzled. "I suppose silly things that all girls do."

"I noticed you were examining some of those figurines on the shelf. Are you interested in sculpture?"

"Oh, yes, but just for a hobby. I take wood carving classes at the Lyceum."

"I see, I see."

She could almost watch him thinking through those magnifying windows of his eyes. There were worlds within them. She forgot that he had seemed comical.

"What are you thinking about?" she asked, suddenly self-conscious.

"I am thinking that it is exactly you we need."

"Who is 'we'"?

"Cuba."

She laughed uncertainly. "No, no. I'm serious."

"Está tomando el pelo," she chided.

"No, I am not pulling your leg. I'm dead earnest. Let's put it this way: we need you to help us carve our history."

He was not at all surprised at the hilarity which his statement provoked. Amused at his own expense, he suggested impulsively, "Let's have something at the café next door and I'll explain."

As they sipped their refrescos he continued, "Every country, as well as every human being, reaches one critical moment of existence when a particular attitude or action determines the entire future. We Cubans have reached that moment now. It is what we will do with it that counts." He hunched toward them over the table, and his index finger poked the cloth vehemently as though to pinion that transcendent moment. "The Revolution now has rid us of dictatorship, but that is just the beginning. We must learn that a democracy must be governed by its constitution, not by the strength of its army. You know from your studies that this is what Martí wanted above all. When that little boat, which was ultimately to carry him to his death, secretly bore him towards Dos Rios, he was reminding us that even in the thick of the battle we were fighting for our right to live by our constitution. But no matter how idealistic our leaders, nothing can be accomplished without the cooperation of the masses.

"Look at him out there!" He had turned so suddenly that he startled the girls. Bewildered, they gazed at the crowded thoroughfare. "The man in the street! That is where the truth lies, with all of them! If the people out there are good, it is worth giving your life for them. And all the more if they are not, so that they can be helped to understand what goodness is!" He had become exhilarated as he spoke, and his face glowed excitedly as he watched the crowd. They are like wine to him, Lourdes thought.

"And now, my encantadora señorita," he smiled at Lourdes, "that is where the wood carving comes in. You know what it is to pick up a piece of rough wood and feel its hidden potential beauty, don't you?" His gaze sharply confronted her. She nodded. "And then what do you do? Draw a design on it, select your sharpest knife and cut into it?"

"Why, no!" Lourdes protested. "The most important thing is first to look at the markings and the grain of the wood so that you can bring them out. Your knife has to move along with it." As though she had just realized it, she exclaimed, "That's the part I enjoy the most!"

"And that's why we want you." he retorted.

"Eddy, there you go again!" She called him by his first name because everyone did.

"That's right!" he shouted. "Because without knowing it, you understand. Don't you see, señorita, that the people's potential beauty has been locked in ignorance and abuse? They have been forced to live with mediocrity and egotism. If we would help them bring out what they feel is the best in themselves, we must give them dignity, teach them to think in a new way.

"But we can't force this, no matter how good the intention. We can only care and work patiently so that a new Cuba will be carved—but by no other hands than our own; especially by the strong clean hands of our youth. Oh, it will be a long, long struggle unless you young people care!"

As they parted, he mentioned directly to Lourdes, "We are having an interesting meeting tomorrow at the University. You just might like to attend."

And she did attend, compelled by some force in this strange man who was at one moment attractive, direct, dynamic and the next, serious, shrill, and eccentric.

Lourdes was transported. Life held so much more than she had ever dreamed of! The clash of minds in combat was stirring, but even more was the discovery of something she wanted to help make right. How much less exciting now seemed the beat of the dance bands, although she loved that too! And more vivid than the characters of any movie were those of history, good or evil, as they began to come alive on the screen of her awareness: Maceo, Céspedes, Bolívar, San Martín, Washington, Weyler the-Butcher, Machado.

She was struck with remorse as she realized that she, Mario, and their friends had been frivolously dancing through such violent pages of their history. Why, it was something special to be a Cuban, to belong to this tiny island which over and over had risked everything for freedom! Somehow, listening to Eddy, the word freedom began to have meaning, still faintly, but excitingly. For how could she have known the meaning of freedom, she puzzled, if she had never been deprived of it? It was necessary to make an effort of extreme concentration to imagine herself someone else, a person who was not free. She was learning that not all Cubans were really free. And when she was able to accomplish this, she found such a state unbearable, and shared Eddy's anger and his desire to do something about it with the "Auténtico" Party. She was eager to join the Youth Movement he had formed. But her family was dismayed and forbade her participation. They found it completely improper for a young woman to interest herself in such things. "Why," protested Ana, her sister, "even Father remains at the cattle ranch in Camagüey to avoid the degrading political atmosphere of the Capitol!"

Lourdes realized that as part of a Cuban family even she was not as free as she thought. She would have to wait until she was older and could be more independent. Her only support and companion in ausencia of new horizons, was, happily, Mario. His letters were full of excitement. He was finding it a great challenge to be at a large foreign university, eagerly applying himself to his studies, absorbing attitudes, and admiring the enterprise and self-reliance of the American people, which was even more pronounced in those years of the Depression.

"What an adventure," he exclaimed in one of his many letters to her, "that together we have awakened to the world. If at times I write you about all that I am learning with an excessive zeal that is almost passion, please blame it on my youth of which you are a part. Your adoring 'Mayito.'"

To this Lourdes had answered, delighted, "Don't apologize for our impassioned tone. And rather than attribute it to our youth, I would like to think of what Eddy has said: "The 'apasionado' are the first-born of the world. Viva la pasion!'"

When he returned to Cuba for the Christmas holidays, she glowed with pride as she listened to Mario's effusive accounts. His family too enjoyed the harmless ardor of their son as he spoke of new ideas in architecture, building techniques, and the American way of life; but when he denounced Franco, or spoke of the New Deal and labor's right to organize, it was another matter. Señora Guzman would raise her eyebrows and look at her husband. She did not expect him to voice an opinion now. He never did among the family. But there was no doubt of his reaction.

Friends of the parents dismissed their worries. Didn't all the students attending American schools return with crack-brained enthusiasms about one thing or another? "No se agiten, don't get excited," they consoled. "All that wears off as soon as they come back to stay."

There were, however, a few who engaged in heated discussions with Mario. Lourdes found it difficult to remain properly inarticulate. Once, during a pleasant holiday dinner, someone asked her what she thought of all this. "What Mario thinks, I think," she said demurely. The guests approvingly interpreted her answer as the expected womanly deference to her fiancé's opinion. But Mario, who had not missed the sparkle in her eyes, enjoyed the secret joke. They both knew that she had meant it.

These little subterfuges would not be necessary if she were in the United States, Mario told her, where a woman has the same right to express an opinion as a man does. Before he could finish the sentence, they looked at each other, both struck by the same idea.

Shortly after, to the credit of Mario's persuasiveness and the fact that Havana schools had not yet reopened, Lourdes was permitted to attend Sacred Heart in New York.

Now, in retrospect, that period which followed seemed to Lourdes like an amnesic, whirling prism that flung drops of fantasy and reality across her memory. Only the iridescent impressions remained—new ideas, places, hopes, names, enthusiasms—all chromatic globes. For her marriage to Mario soon after his graduation terminated this halcyon life within a life. They acceded to their families' insistence on an elaborate wedding, but society was perplexed and amused at the remainder of their plans.

Over the dinner tables:

"Dear did you hear about Lourdes and Mario Guzman? They're not going anywhere for a honeymoon—just a week at Varadero beach—that's all."

"Not very exciting. They could take a trip around the world if they wanted."

"But they don't want to. Mario is too eager to open his new architect's office."

"New office? Isn't he going in with his father?"

"Not he! He's found a little place of his own and is absolutely thrilled. Wants to make his own way, Lourdes tells me."

Amused chuckles.

"That's a new one! What will these youngsters think of next? Arturo must be furious."

"That's not all. They've rented a little apartment."

"It can't be true. I know Arturo and Maria are planning to build a wing on the estate for them."

"Not any more. They will accept no financial aid. They refuse to have servants and they're making most of their furniture themselves."

Explosive laughter.

"That isn't all. In their spare time, they're both working in the Auténtico Party."

"With that crazy Chibás? I don't believe it!"

"This comes of sending kids to the U.S. If I were Arturo, I would put my foot down."

"He won't have to. They are accustomed to every luxury. How long do you think their crazy caprice will last?"

Amused clucking, head-shaking, raised eyebrows as the brandy is poured.

Lourdes and Mario were themselves amused by the general reaction. They thought that Cuban society, for all its continental sophistication, drowsed in Colonial lethargy. It needed to be ruffled into progressive thinking. And if their own lives could serve to ruffle it a little, well, so much the better!

Oh, they were so sure that it was not a "caprice." The adventure of those brief months of independence could never be forgotten. The freedom to choose new friends who shared their attitude, if not their background, had opened new vistas of life's promise.

Trigo's singing, like an uncanny accompaniment to those memories, had been flooding the room. But now its joyousness became an irony. How sad to relive the past while knowing its future. It reminded her of the times Christ must have foreseen its ruins as He beheld the fair hills of Jerusalem; or the moment a bomber pilot simultaneously contemplated beneath him the living heart of a city and its destruction.

She rose, vexed that her lovely awakening had led her into the past. But the mood was broken now. She slipped on a negligee and wondered what time it was. When Mario had moved to the other room, he had taken his clock, and she had never replaced it.

She could hear no sound in his room. Evidently, he was still asleep. She carefully opened his adjoining door to see the time. It was after one, but no matter. They had made no engagement until late afternoon, when, as usual, they were expected at his mother's—hardly a thought to draw her from her lethargy. After the busy week and last night's party, she felt a disinclination for anything. And she hated Sundays.

She looked at his darkened room. Not a cuff button out of place. She could not help thinking how different it had been in the old days, when they slept together. It did not look like this. Their clothes, so cared for before the party, would now be in happy, revealing heaps all over the room, and they would be sleeping in each other's arms. Well, undoubtedly, he was much more satisfied this way, with his sterile room. She wondered whether his mistress or mistresses were bored with this over-fastidiousness. But then she thought wryly, it might assume only secondary importance for him in that other environment.

As she looked at him asleep, she resisted that insidious pull which she frequently experienced. Only when he slept did Mario resemble the man she had loved. His complexion seemed fairer, and his exasperatingly groomed hair—always perfect at the sacrifice of others' time—fell in carefree waves and invited rumpling and laughter. But there was a different expression now in the way his arms stretched out in a sort of helplessness and the long fingers curled like a child's. Something about him seemed defenseless against himself. Contrary to all logic, she felt a compulsion to strengthen his weakness, to comfort the perpetual loneliness of the Mario that was; to fill at least partially his desperately concealed need. That former daily Calvary of memories stirred within her.

As though aware of her presence, he opened his eyes. She stood there waiting and marveling at the mystery of herself as a woman, born with the need to give. They looked at each other. He seemed disconcerted. Then to her relief, he smiled at her blankly as he went back to sleep.

This staring at the illusion of his true self in repose reminded her of people who deliberately return to a once significant place, knowing that its emptiness will pain. The neurotic surrendering of oneself to the luxury of sorrow was a self-indulgence which she loathed. She returned to her room revolted by her moment of sentimentality. How absurd to have imagined that Mario could ever feel the need for anyone but himself! "What a fool I am," she muttered. "Probably a manifestation of frustrated maternity. This burst of generous compassion might have been excusable if I didn't know him so well."

At least there was one consolation: hopelessness rewards with peace.

Well, bien. A cold shower would wash off this banality. Today was not for the drowsy embrace of steam bath and perfumed oils. Sunday was the day of neutrality, the day to be the sexless, charming wife and daughter-in-law. Amusing that her mother-in-law thought that she was the cold type, easily satisfied, like the Americanas with whom she had lived for three years, who had sold their fulfillment for the right to labor in competition with their men; who traded love's ecstasy and mystery for the quick orgasm (if that) and had undeceived their men of the illusions of love even as tomorrow's children will never know of the moon's mystery. Uninspired, the men drifted into the quick, the casual, at most the unleashed passion— and proud of that. Under the smart clothes and trimmed-off, measurement-obsessed flesh, the glamour careers, the efficiency, the barbecues, the interior decorations, the tailored pajamas and the easy-to-launder underclothes—was the hunger of something lost. To have buried your joy under this efficient nothingness! She admired American women in many ways and considered it a pity that in trying so hard to obtain happiness they dissipated their great potential for it. She had been content to return to her own country, although that, too, was an extreme. But she preferred it. At least here in Cuba woman had not lost her identity. A true woman is deliciously conscious of being a woman twenty-four hours a day, no matter what her work or interests.

She slipped off her gown and sat lazily on the chaise to feel the breeze fluttering through the French window. She looked at herself in the mirror. If you saw me now, would you still think the same, Doña Maria Guzman? Carnivorous Doña Maria and Don Arturo, have you seen him asleep, your son, looking like a child—a shining beetle caught in a web? Oh, I remember your thin spinning fingers that were too much for me, weaving the threads that would invisibly entangle him. And when the day finally comes when he discovers his prison, it will be too late. But that day has not yet come, and probably never will!

Would it have happened without you, Doña Maria and Don Arturo Guzman, this tragedy of waste? Who knows? He drifted into the old ways so easily. It must have been fertile ground. But still, would it have happened? I can see you sitting there, on the furniture he had built and of which he was so proud, sitting stiffly on the edge of the chair as though it would contaminate you. Your furious eyes belied the benevolent smile. But he was so busy being happy he did not notice that you curtailed the visit in an aura of maternal sweetness. But I did notice. And how long after that was it that I found an unwanted cook in my house, generously pre-paid and delivered by you? And Don Arturo, you were as transparent as the Baccarat champagne glass which you raised. A toast to Mario on his birthday! Junior partner of Guzman Construction and Realty (Guzman and Son it would be now). The first modest office bursting with all the new ideas to be executed was abandoned. And shortly after, the little apartment too. It was logical, of course.

"They're right, Lourdes," Mario had commented, as they moved into the beautiful home which he could now afford. "Now that I'm a junior partner of the Company, we'll have to live normal lives. All that nonsense about making your own way is fine for the Americans. But let's face it, we're Cuban. Besides, this is a practical world. The way we were living would now be an unthinkable affectation."

"Nonsense" was a stab in the heart. But he was right when he called it affectation. For there was little left of those first dreams.

Soon everything changed. Mario thought his father was right, after all, concerning the Auténtico party. Eddy Chibás' reforms were good for "crack- brained bohemians," like those new friends they'd been seeing. He wished Lourdes would understand why he didn't want her to continue with them. Business activities drew him into their former social circle. More and more frequent were the messages "Señor Mario will not be home for lunch" and "Will not be home for dinner." There were business trips to the interior of the island or to the United States ("Better for you not to go, Lourdes. It's just boring business meetings and so on.")

Upon his return he would take her suddenly and savagely. This was a new Mario whom she could have understood had there been any sustained intimacy in their relations. But their life together was devoid of any such allusions. She would have responded to a suggestive glance from Mario in some unexpected prosaic moment of daily life, or an inflection of voice that told her she belonged to him. There was never any such message from him. Thus the suddenness of his violent sexual expressions seemed a violation. She wondered if this might be his desperate effort to save their marriage, but, after the first heartbreaks of rumors-turned-facts, a protective cynicism suggested to her that perhaps his behavior was a reflection of his relationship elsewhere.

From one of these moments without tenderness a child was conceived. Surely now everything would be different. Mario's delight and pride were apparent, and he was quite solicitous of Lourdes. Feeling wise in her new estate, she thought, "If I had only realized that a young husband's philandering is a strange male phenomenon which cannot prevail against love and parenthood. What hold on him now can a mistress have, or frivolous companions!" She recalled Benavente's play Roses of Autumn and agreed with the playwright. If young wives had patience and feminine tact they could spare themselves much needless suffering, for a man always returned to a good wife.

But as the months passed, she was forced to acknowledge that it was not Mario and she who were drawn closer by this new bond, but Mario and his mother. She would observe them together discussing the child's name, how it would be raised, what it would be like. Occasionally she expressed her own ideas. She did not want the child to be pampered. He must be taught self-reliance. With an overtone of something more than jest they laughingly called her "Americanized" and "cold-hearted."

One day, unable to contain herself, she suddenly cried out, "If my baby is not going to be mine at all, but your mother's I would rather it wouldn't be born!" She herself was shocked at the words and immediately apologized to Doña Maria, saying she had not meant it at all. She could not tell them that it was but the twisting of hurt and despair. If Mario had only understood, had taken her in his arms and reassured her. But from the appalled silence of his stare, nothing was ever right again. He was courteous, solicitous; nothing more. With increasing intensity, she loved the child she was carrying. Oh, it would be hers, all right! This love was the only thing that gave meaning to her life. And when it was born, fatherhood would endow Mario with understanding. She could not help breathing optimism in a world that was so young.

She was in her eighth month. They had been invited to an intimate dinner at a friend's. Because of the inclement October weather, they had brought their raincoats. As they were having cocktails, the butler approached Lourdes and gave her a folded letter with no envelope. "I was putting away the wraps, and I think this fell out of your coat pocket, Señora Lourdes," he said.

Absent-mindedly she unfolded it. "Irresistible Mario," it began. The impassioned, intimate tone of the brief letter left no room for doubt. Struggling to conceal her distress, she walked quietly from the room and replaced the note into Mario's raincoat. She felt suffocated and faint. She must have air. And she must be alone! Unobserved, she slipped from the house through the French doors of the library. She would go to the sunken garden where no one could hear the sobs she could not control! As she stumbled over the lawn in the descending, twilight she thought brokenly, "Oh, Mario, Mario, how could you have done this! Could you have cared so little with our first baby stirring within me?"

She had reached the marble stairs leading to the garden, and as she took the first step, dizziness enveloped her. She swayed, her arms flung out seeking support, and the last thing she could remember as she fell headlong was the wild effort to protect her child.

Days...weeks...footsteps...comforting voices...Doña Maria pinning a rosary on her pillow...Mario's white linen suit and his large slender hand holding hers...perfume and tinkling charm-bracelets as friends quietly leaned over to kiss her cheek...Pancha, thinking no one sees her pin a black azabache charm next to the rosary (dear Pancha's gleaming dark face always there) ... Don Arturo's gentle voice and small feet as he sits concerned and embarrassed to be in the intimacy of a sick-room. She lies quietly but, like her, the bamboo and palms bend, sway, grieve under the fierce October rains. November brings sunshine, but November Second is All Souls' Day. Her baby would have been coming soon into the light; but not now, not now. Today it is included in the prayer for the departed. The Monsignor has come to visit her. "Does it not comfort you to know that the soul of your child will enjoy a natural happiness for eternity?" he asks.

"But I want him here with me here. To have seen his face just once..."

November sun is heedless of grief. Lourdes can sit up now, even walk about the room. Health is returning. Mario's hand grips hers so tightly when with her first real smile she exclaims softly, "He is right. No need to dwell on sorrow. There will be other babies. We will make up for this little one." After a few days at home she feels strong enough to go to the nursery, and for those first minutes she would like to be there alone. Pancha and Lourdes' sister Ana have heard her too late. Lourdes has already opened the nursery door.

"Niña Lourdes! It is too soon for you to be walking around."

"Who has moved the nursery!" she gasps, as her eyes wander over the improvised sitting room. Ana and Pancha helplessly look at each other.

"Pancha, answer me! Who has done this!"

"Ay, dios mio, mi niña, mi niña," Pancha is chanting, her eyes tear-filled. "It doesn't matter who, Niña Lourdes...and you were not supposed to know so soon..." Lourdes, white and trembling, is leaning against the wall. "I will not able to have a child again, will I, Pancha?"

Ana's visit was abruptly shortened by their father's illness. "But you won't be lonely," Ana comforted before she left for Camagüey. "Mario is devoted. And of course, you have so many friends..." This was true at the time, but Mario's affection, which had been the chief source of her progress, seemed to wane with her partial recovery. Friends, relieved that her life was no longer in jeopardy, assumed that there was no further cause for concern. Lourdes learned a strange lesson. The concrete, the tangible—physical illness, financial distress, bereavement—were the world's common denominators. But illness of the spirit, the soul's bereavement, the daily bankruptcy of purpose, were considered hypothetical ills, which were indeed a luxury when one has wealth and a handsome husband who is attentive in public.

Gradually those public functions became the only occasions where she and Mario were together. She had thought that the gnawing void of frustrated motherhood would be compensated in great part by a happy marriage, but in this her hopes proved chimerical. Again, the irresistible force of habit possessed Mario. When she tried to talk seriously about it with him, he was patient and perplexed. True, they had just suffered a tragedy which they would never be able to forget, he said. But now that Lourdes was out of danger they ought to pick up "their old life." What life? she wanted to ask him, as he was saying that "it was a very pleasant one. Why clutter it with imponderables?"

She had never spoken to him about the note she had read, thinking that it belonged to the past. Now that she knew she had been mistaken, what use to speak of it? To combat a growing restlessness, she tried to resume her former activities. But this attempt was self-defeating. The more she simulated an outward affinity with the real world, the less real did she become. It was a camouflage that only heightened the deception. She felt separated from the living.

She began to have a recurrent nightmare, always the same. In it she was lying on a cold tile floor, and ants were marching across her towards a thousand glass doors, behind which streamed blazing lights, beckoning hands, and disembodied voices calling many names. She would try to flee from the ants but bongos thundered, waves of darkness covered her, and the swamp began to suck her into its slimy black belly. A hand reached out to pull her from the black mouth, but although she touched it, she could not be saved. She would awaken terror-stricken, muffling a scream into her pillow.

It was at this time that she had met Jorge, whose name she had heard in connection with the reform movement. Gently, almost imperceptibly, he had entered her life, and she had understood then why Christ's miracle of Cana had been the first. Joy and love were the greatest gifts of life, the miracle that could change water into wine and from an empty heart draw abundance. Now it seemed to her that all the past desolation had served only to enrich the soil for the dormant seed.

Pancha, carrying a tray, entered the room without knocking. "Señora Lourdes, por dios! You haven't finished dressing. You know you mustn't be late for your mother-in-law. For once it is Señor Mario who must wait for you!" she joked. "He's downstairs. Take your jugo before you go. She held out a large glass of orange juice, which Lourdes drank hastily as Pancha zipped up her dress.

Lourdes whispered, "Getting into my costume for the Comedy of the Week."

"Niña!" Pancha chided—unconvincingly, for her mouth puckered a restrained smile.

11
SUNDAYS

Sunday at the Guzmans' was a languorously balanced mobile suspended from a comfortable sky. At times a sudden gust of animated conversation or trivial disagreement might stir it into movement, but never precariously. The nice placement of its components always ensured safe return to the center. As far back as anyone could remember, excepting such occasions as illness, golf tournaments, special social events or travel, Miguel and Mario and their wives had spent Sunday with their parents.

It was a day lazily interspersed with a usual trickle of the same friends dropping in: Mario's meandering gossip, Miguel's earnestness, the fluttering gold charm bracelets, voices and fans of his wife, Luisa, and her friends; cigar smoke veiling the even, measured voice and gestures of Don Arturo Guzman in conversation; the softness and graciousness of Doña Maria Guzman (easy, because it flowed from entrenched security); Lourdes' uncommitted charm, which could have been eliminated without altering the flavor, joking, card-shuffling; the sudden shrill interruptions of Miguel's small children and their equally shrill tata. But the motif running throughout was the intimate relationship between Doña Maria and her two sons. Somewhere during the course of their private language of jokes, references, and facial expressions, they unconsciously became two happy, preposterously large children at her knee.

But today there was an imbalance. Mario's reflection of general well-being, which had become a necessary Sunday element, was missing. Everyone noticed that he was restive, monosyllabic, and so bad at bridge that Luisa, his sister-in-law, was delighted when he good-naturedly offered his place to a friend. Nor was he interested in the late afternoon merienda. He had a few drinks instead.

"Lourdes, whatever is the matter with Mario?" his mother asked in a low voice.

"Nothing that I know of," Lourdes replied.

"Well, I know there is something. A mother senses more about these things. Of course you wouldn't understand that." There was no guile in Señora Guzman's tone, merely an insensibility to anyone but her sons.

"I'm sure," Lourdes answered indifferently. There was no rhythm at all to the evening. Only Guzman senior, talking earnestly to a friend, did not seem to notice.

The day had been peppered with comments of the brilliant party of the preceding night, and Luisa remarked that the Mayor and his wife had left quite early, before the comparsa.

"I can tell you why," Miguel remarked. "And it's no wonder they left, since the Mayor is getting so touchy. I saw what happened. Reinaldo Vasquez had been drinking too much. He offered him a highball and said, 'Have another, Mayor, it's easier to get in this town than water, these days, right?' He didn't at all realize what he was saying. He winked, and laughed as he walked away."

"Certainly, very poor taste." Doña Maria's fan clicked disapproval.

"It was brutal!" Lourdes couldn't refrain from exclaiming. "If people only knew what those supposedly humorous remarks are doing to him!"

"Well—" the fan hovered mid-air, reluctant to accuse, "It is really terrible. Thank heavens we have our own private tanks. But to think that in the very capital one must measure the water for his garden!"13

"We have a regular schedule on our street," added Luisa, "and have you seen the people waiting in line for hours to fill their buckets at the street hydrants? I think it is shocking! Supervielle certainly hasn't kept his promise!"

"But how can he, Luisa, if he is trapped on all sides!" Lourdes protested.

"Lourdes, my dear, why such sympathy?" Guzman senior turned to her pleasantly. "He could easily spring the trap if he wanted. Havana would have water if he were not so stubborn. We have tried, or that is, I have friends in the Cabinet who have tried to help him. But the man is unreasonable."

"With all due respect to your friends, father, perhaps he doesn't approve of their kind of help," Lourdes replied.

"Their method in no way differs from that of all politicians," Guzman shrugged.

"Maybe that is just what he doesn't like," Lourdes looked up blandly enough, but she was trying to control herself. She had been at the Mayor's home often, and knew well enough what those methods were: help us to keep our thriving black market, share the pork barrel with us, and you will have your water.

"If that is so, he is a fool for entering politics at all," Arturo Guzman leaned towards her and continued. "A man has no right to venture into an area for which he is not suited, especially when he knows that his temperament and personal convictions disqualify him. A man can't fight against himself. He is an intruder, a meddler, and in a way just as unethical as the system which he deplores."

"Oh, let's not go on with politics," Luisa exclaimed, "Mayito, do you think you'll be able to play any better?" she laughed, and began to shuffle the cards.

Mario raised his eyebrows with a hopeless expression and made himself another drink.

"I think he must be tired. He has well earned a rest," his mother said proudly, and as an afterthought, "and Lourdes too. I think that instead of having any more of those highballs—and on an empty stomach—they ought to go home."

Lourdes brightened at the suggestion, but Mario walked to her, and with a display of fondness, put his arm around her as he said, "Dear, you don't mind if Miguel and Luisa take you home later? Mother's right. It must be a reaction to all these weeks of work for the convention. I'm going to take a long walk, or perhaps just wander a bit. Don't wait for me."

The inevitable joke came. "Allá! I wonder where he is going!" Someone waved a waggish finger, and they all laughed.

It never failed to intrigue Lourdes that people could pretend to joke about such a matter that they knew to be true. It was not from malice; rather, they were so accustomed to the game of lies that they had no remaining delicacy or awareness. She smiled at her joke within a joke, for she was laughing at it all. She would live through the bridge game. She could do anything with Jorge's invisible presence enfolding her.

Mario was glad to stand alone on the gravel driveway and breathe in the night air for a moment. In the distance on Fifth Avenue, which fringed the Biltmore residential section, he could see the steady procession of cars and buses returning from their Sunday. He wondered if there was anyone seated in one of them, unfulfilled and restless, pressing his nose against the window-pane, staring enviously through the darkness at Mario, and muttering to himself, "One of the lucky bastards who lives in these expensive Biltmore houses." Mario smiled at himself and the unknown unfulfilled one. They were both envious of each other, or so they thought. What they were doing was to use envy as a hopeful crutch, pretending that if they could be this one or that, the gnawing would cease. But it was only a postponement, not a solution. The envious flattened noses actually didn't know what they wanted.

He would go to Silvia's. Now there was a person who envied no one. She was probably expecting him to drop in, as he usually managed to do after what she called another "Fandango of the High Life."

It amused her to hear Mario's descriptions, anecdotes, gossip. Reclining on the sofa and faintly smiling, she would listen quietly, her handsome brown legs crossed, only her manicured toes occasionally wriggling her enjoyment. Her heavy black lashes partially concealed an enigmatic gleam, half amusement, half satisfaction in the knowledge that she was involved in this complex human comedy about which she enjoyed hearing. Her own life was simple and clear.

But today when Mario arrived, he found that even in her salutary, voluptuous, real presence he could not throw off his mood. It was at once apparent to her that he had been drinking. No, he did not want food, he did not want coffee but he would like a drink. But when she gave it to him he still stared off into space, and in his hand, untouched, was the highball. He did not seem aware that he held it or that she was there at all.

"Mayito," she drawled, "there's something you haven't noticed."

In response he inclined his head slightly without looking at her, as though reluctant to abandon his own thoughts.

"My Jacques Fath suit." (She pronounced it Yok Fas.) As she stood there in the fashionably tailored wool crêpe which she had insisted he buy her—for a joke, as she put it—he found it difficult to conceal any expression of his that might reveal how ludicrous it was that this glowing common Creole figure should try to disguise itself in the severe lines of the suit. The full throat and luminously copper shoulders were made to be seen above the low-cut embroidered blouses she usually wore, and her high rounded hips were not intended for the restraint of a girdle, which in her case only disfigured.

"Well...?" she was laughing at herself as she waited.

"You are beautiful," he said. He had spoken with sincerity. Something in her attitude made it true. Despite her almost maternal acceptance of realities, despite her free, casual way she stood there now with a wistfulness behind the self-mockery, a shy hesitance of the wide mouth that dared not break into a full smile until certain that he found her pleasing. "Ready for the Champs- Élysées," he said.

She laughed uproariously at the joke. He smiled, but he was thinking, strange how some women were born with all the primitive womanly instincts, while others have a beauty and charm...yet...

The arm which he had half extended to her dropped indifferently, and his eyes returned to their distant thoughts.

"Mayito, qué pasa?" She turned his face towards hers and looked squarely into his eyes. "The devil with the suit and girdle—I thought it would be a little variety, but you're not in the mood. I was going to wear it to celebrate tonight with Dulce and Carlos."

"Celebrate what?"

"Why, your triunfo, mi prieto. I've been waiting for you to say something about it. Saw it in the paper. The Diario has a whole page of pictures of the party and an article about your being appointed Editor of the International Magazine. There's a picture of you dancing the comparsa that's terrific, and another where you look very serious and important!" She picked up the page which she had clipped from the Sunday paper. "And by the way, doesn't Lourdes ever say anything about your being so much with Elena Montero? In all the photographs you are together.

"Are we? I hadn't noticed. I see what you mean," he said, scanning the page, "but it's just a coincidence. Well, not precisely a coincidence, I suppose. She has always been restless and unsettled, and she drinks too much. We have known each other since we were children, and she has an idea that she loves

me merely because I'm the only man she's known so long! People seem to drift in and out of her life, and suppose I represent some sort of stability to her. You see, this is what keeps most all of us in bondage. But you wouldn't understand that."

"No, I suppose I wouldn't," she answered.

"That's interesting!" he exclaimed suddenly, and looked at her searchingly. "Why don't you understand?"

She returned his gaze, submitting herself to his scrutiny. It was gratifying that he would find something new about her to intrigue him.

"Why don't you need what so many others find necessary?" he persisted.

"Like Elena Montero, you mean?"

"Yes."

She flung her head back against the sofa-arm in one of her unpredictable seizures of laughter. "Forgive me, dear Mayo!" she exclaimed, "but it's very funny—that one should think of holding on to people—of all things, people—to find stability! Why, you might just as well say that you are going to give a gun to an assassin so that he protects you! One's life is stable enough, but it's the human beings entering it who cause the confusion! Like swimmers at a beach—a wave throws them together, they talk, maybe kiss, and then the next wave separates them! And that's how it goes! Can you hold on to a wave?" She leaned forward, her hands resting on her thighs with a compact positive gesture. "'Stability'? I am my only 'stability!' she said softly now. "Me! That's all!"

She stretched back in the sofa again, and they sat in silence, regarding each other, smiling, and unable to penetrate those two disparate worlds. She would like to help him. So many problems that didn't sound like problems at all prevented their enjoyment of life. But she had had very rich friends before, poor things, and this was nothing new to her.

He was sitting at the end of the sofa, contemplating her words, looking for meaning in them, and listlessly resigned to his failure to capture it. He was searching for something, but he would not find it here. Suddenly he discovered the drink in his hand, and with a resolute gesture, as though determined that this would solve his problem, he finished it. Quietly, almost sadly, he stroked her leg, that beautiful extension of her womanliness and strength, and with a tired smile, rose abruptly.

"I'll call you," he said, and left.

He began to walk aimlessly through the narrow streets of old Havana. Its Sunday afternoon quiet was changing pace now. People were coming home from the long day at the beaches, the dancing and picnic grounds of the Tropical, or the ferry rides across the bay to Regla, Guanabacoa, and Casa Blanca. Families descended from the buses and streetcars in straggling streams. Husbands in wilted guayaberas which curled and wrinkled over the hips dragged their feet as they carried children too tired to walk. Women, high breasted, full hipped, balanced precariously on spiked heels and longed to free their flesh from the girdles that have bound them since the morning Mass. Those who had remained at home leaned over the flowering wrought-iron balconies, fanning and chatting as they watched the scene below. Small children, naked except for their sleeveless undershirts, crawled on the floors and poked plump feet through the railing. And from every kitchen a sofrito of garlic, onion, green pepper and olive oil released an invisible cloud which merged over the street with the strains from the radios of the ubiquitous bolero and guaracha. In spite of their activity, to Mario they seemed as aimless as he, on a treadmill, marking time for nothing.

As he continued down the street, the music became less apparent. Slowly, simultaneously, the balconies emptied, and from almost every open door and window a man's shrill voice prevailed.

Good Lord, Mario muttered, No me faltaba más! That's the last straw! He realized now that people had taken places around their radios, for the "Sunday Hour" of Eduardo Chibás had begun. The voice gradually took possession of the street.

Mario quickly turned the corner. He could think of nothing less welcome at this moment than Eddy's strident exhortations and diatribes, and he looked for a neighborhood bar. Perhaps another scotch was just what he needed. He sat at the empty bar and had just begun his drink, when a group of men noisily entered, swarmed next to him and one of them called to the bartender, "Eh, Chico! Tune in on Eddy, will you? We're late." Mario was intently staring into his glass, as if nothingness was a thing you could see through the clear amber. At first, he was not aware of the voice from the radio, but gradually the words seeped in.

"One who has been your most devoted follower for twenty years, Mr. President, now asks twenty minutes of your attention, one minute for each of the years dedicated to defend the great principle which since 1927 you yourself have inculcated in the youth of Cuba...The corrupt politics which we have so combated has now infected all the ministries of the government. It is true that your first compromise with reality seemed insignificant, merely the means to attain an ideal upon which your vision was still fixed. But, sadly enough, with time you had become so familiarized with the malodor of the corrupt methods which once offended you that you no longer notice them. In fact, they now seem to you an agreeable perfume. One day your advisors employed bribery as a means to attain the public good, and when you discovered how well this method worked, you began to use it for less elevated purposes. The people chose you to represent an administrative morality, regulation of public works, and an end to wasteful spending; housing for workers; agrarian reform; and struggle for economic independence. You corresponded to the stature of the leader. But now you are betraying the illusions of the many Cubans who had placed their patriotic hopes in you."

This was not the harangue Mario had expected. With restraint and simplicity Eddy was giving expression to disenchantment. Mario was impressed by the men's faces as they listened. They utterly identified with Chibás and with each other. The physical process of having their drinks, occasionally moving about, or exchanging comments seemed automatic; they were committed only to that voice which was speaking for them, and nothing else mattered.

Only at high moments of a world series or a regatta had Mario seen men so freed, projected on something outside themselves. And even then it had been a purchased, vicarious freedom. But for these men at the bar, obvious followers of Chibás, the moment was sustained, an integral part of their life.

With new curiosity he began to listen.

"Why, Mr. President, have you opened your arms to the old politics, and turned your back on those who had been at your side in the hour of sacrifice? Why have you submitted little by little to the improvised friends who have finally convinced you that you could not remain in power without compromising our revolutionary ideals?"

As Chibás continued, the heads at the bar bobbed vehement approval. Each felt that he personally was before the microphone. When the speech was over, they enthusiastically compared it to the memorable letter of 1915 written by Maso to President Menocal. Then too, an intrepid patriot was giving voice to the people's disillusionment.

Now they were finishing up their drinks, going somewhere. Going somewhere very much alive. Mario smiled at himself. He was certainly flattening his nose against a window pane right now as he watched them! He had another scotch, and as he left the bar he almost bumped into a hurrying passerby.

"Well," he exclaimed, "Jorge De Armas! This time I remembered your name. Glad to see you."

"Hello there, Guzman," Jorge stopped, disconcerted and surprised at the hearty greeting.

"I guess you wonder what I'm doing around here in this part of town, eh? And on a Sunday, too," Mario continued with unexplained intimacy. "Well, I'm here because, uh—" his arms waved vaguely since he himself did not know the reason. "How about having a drink with me?" he concluded illogically.

"Thanks, but I'm late for a meeting."

"Oh? Well, if you're already late, one drink won't matter, will it?" He smiled and placed a hand on Jorge's shoulder.

The eagerness manifest in the gesture was puzzling.

"Sorry, but I'm afraid it would matter," Jorge answered.

"Aha! Meeting of the Auténticos, eh? Group of your compañeros there in the bar listening to Chibás. You know," he said suddenly, "I think I'll come too!"

"Fine, fine. I might see you there then," Jorge disengaged himself.

"How about a drink after the meeting?"

"Fine," Jorge answered equivocally, certain that Mario would not be there at all. "Hasta luego," he waved, and was off hurrying down the street.

Mario continued after him slowly. It was not difficult to know where the meeting was being held, as there were others coming from various directions. Each face had that same look of definite motivation.

An acquaintance of Mario's was among the latecomers standing in the doorway. "Caramba! Who would ever think of finding you here, Guzman!" he whispered. "Glad to see you."

"Well, don't ever say there is nothing new under the sun," Mario smiled, "although I must confess it's just curiosity that brought me."

"I warn you that's the first step," his friend joked. Then turning to his companion, a tall, quiet young man with dark moody eyes, he said, "I'd like you to meet an enthusiastic University student, Fidel Castro, Mario Guzman."

They turned to listen to the meeting which was in progress. Mario was aware that his unaccustomed drinking was making it difficult to concentrate on the discussion. His thoughts were drawn to the people there whose vitality was contagious. He could feel his own blood circulating. They evidently

knew what they believed in, an important element that he lacked.

He firmly hoped that De Armas would get the commission for the

Camacho project, as then they would undoubtedly see each other more often. The fellow was a shot in the arm. However, he cautioned himself, he must make no mention to De Armas that he was in any way connected with the project. That was taboo. What was that father of his up to again?

When the meeting was over, Jorge was disturbed to discover Mario waiting for him. It was evident that he had been drinking and his insistence made Jorge apprehensive. Certainly an interest in Chibás could not have motivated his coming! Had Lourdes made a slip somewhere? Or had he himself been careless about anything? He thought back quickly, wondering if Mario could possibly suspect his relationship with Lourdes. On the other hand, what a relief it would be if Mario did know. Jorge half-wanted to tell him the truth then and there, but that would be at Lourdes' expense! Above all else, she must be protected until he could provide for her.

Mario refused to be put off. "All right, Guzman, but just one. Then I must leave." Jorge's determined expression was lost on Mario as he proceeded to give his impressions of the meeting and to express his admiration for Jorge, who was "really accomplishing something."

Although Jorge was on his guard, Mario's genuinely nostalgic tone prompted Jorge to remind him, "But it seems more in order for me to be congratulating you, Guzman! I read in the paper this morning about your election and the success of your convention. It's a personal one for you."

To his surprise, Mario shook his head and replied with a melancholy smile, "There's nothing very thrilling about a success that is not really mine. It is made in advance, because I am a Guzman, and because everything I do is so easily accomplished. Sometimes, De Armas, think how exciting it must be to achieve something difficult on your own." As he hunched over the table, Mario's tall figure, always poised and prepossessing, loomed as a heavy presence of insecurity. His sincere melancholy was baffling.

"You don't know how much I envied Monche Marquez last night," he remarked.

"The band leader from Pogolotti? I wasn't aware of your secret ambition to play in charanguitas at the Playa," Jorge joked.

But Mario ignored the pleasantry, and continued quite somberly, "That is just what I mean. Despite the necessity of playing for those 'charanguitas' and grinding musical backgrounds for high-class orgies, he has made enough money to study music, have his own band, and play in the Philharmonic Orchestra besides. He knew how to rise above all that. All on his own! Do you know what a sense of achievement he must have?"

Jorge could only suspect Mario of pulling his leg, but he answered, "Just by coincidence, I ran into him last week. We know each other from the old days, when we were kids. He was always a happy-go-lucky fellow. But now I hardly recognized him! I told him so. He said it didn't surprise him. He wished that he had never heard good music that had 'set him off' like that.

Before he was content to play poker a couple of nights a week, have some beers and conversations at the cafe. But now he reads books about atonality, sweats at concerts at the Lyceum, spends his afternoons at orchestra rehearsals, and is always wanting to do better. He ended by saying, 'I don't belong with my friends at Pogolotti anymore, and I don't belong to the elite. No roots.' It was touching. Certainly he is not happy."

"Oh, but I'm not talking about happiness. Who is happy?" Mario's strained eyes looked disarmingly at Jorge. "No," he continued, "I am referring to people who—" he searched for an explanation, "who can walk the face of the earth carrying their homes and their world with them, like turtles, wherever they go. They are not bound to their own inadequacy. Oh, and there are others besides Monche..." You, for example, Mario was thinking, with that good-looking strong face that hasn't aged at all, and those wrinkles at the corner of your eyes. Are they from many griefs? Or from laughing at yourself and the world? With all your talent, you haven't had a chance, and yet there is an air of freedom about you—dammit—as though you had figured it out so that something makes sense to you.

Jorge listened with mounting disbelief and resentment. Guzman envious of him! It was a farce. If Guzman knew something about him and his wife and thought Jorge would submit to a cat and mouse game, he was mistaken. And the technique he had employed to lead up to it was repugnant— whimpering poetically about inadequacy. Jorge had had enough. "1 don't know what the point of all this is, Guzman, but if you have something to say to me—"

"To 'say' to you—" Mario repeated, perplexed. "Not 'say' exactly, De Armas, but just to talk. You know, this is a rare event, a phenomenon. A person can really talk to you. Do you think I could do this with other people I know? I'm supposed to be the happiest man in town. Why, my wife and I symbolized hymeneal bliss—" he pronounced the words with a grim smile—"but the truth is, nothing exists between us. You won't believe it, but if she knew that I had a mistress, she would not be at all disturbed. Perhaps some men would call this enviable."

Jorge rose brusquely. "Guzman, you've had too many drinks."

"No, no, De Armas—" With an unsteady hand, Mario detained him. "It is not 'in vino veritas,' but we could call it 'in miseria veritas' or 'in friendship' or 'in an understanding face.' Christ, but you have an understanding face! I'm going to tell you something," he said thickly as his insistent arm drew Jorge back to the chair. "That day we met in the bodega remember? Before we had recognized each other, I was watching you. You were talking on the telephone. You should have seen your face! I was so envious I hated you. What the hell woman have you found who makes you feel like that?" He did not see Jorge pale with rage, for suddenly he closed his eyes, turned from the table and kept shaking his head, as though such an experience surpassed understanding. "How is it possible?" he mumbled incredulously. Then he opened his eyes and said, "No offence meant, chico. I envy you, that's all. You own yourself, and you know how to give yourself. I don't know how to do that. I suppose if a man has no identity, he has nothing to give." The sound of his voice was thin and dry back in his throat, and there was no doubting his sincerity.

Jorge's apprehension faded, but he sat in pained silence. How had this fellow rejected Lourdes when he needed her so much! It was difficult to imagine this was the man who had so neglected her, been so indifferent to her despair, to her very life. Oh, weakness could be as dynamic and destructive as evil!

"...and you know what love is. More power to you," Mario continued, still moving his head from side to side in wonder. To say something, Jorge answered, "Certainly you have known it too!"

"Love?" Mario repeated the word as one who discovers a strange piece of furniture in his own house. "The love that I mean, I have never known. I might have, but perhaps that also came too easily. Why have I never experienced anything intensely?" The smoke from his cigarette rose wearily, following the unknown answer.

Damn it, Jorge cursed. He liked Mario. And his own responsiveness was loathsome to him. Always feeling sorry for people! How many times had he vowed to tighten up! Would he never be quit of it, this malady which softened the brain, this soggy, fatuous inclination to pity? Who was he to think of weakness in others? Pity is a termite, he thought, destroying from within, an obscenity posing for compassion. If I am truly compassionate, I will not gratify my own instinct to indulge him. I will let him fight it out alone—or let him croak. It's the only way a man can ever know if he has it in himself or not.

"Guzman, I think you had better go home," he said.

Suddenly Mario felt extremely tired. "You're right. Appreciate your company. And your patience. 'Night." He rose from his chair and walked out slowly but quite erect. He would show people that at least he was man enough to know how to hold his drinks.

12
JORGE AND THE MARQUESA

Arsenio had been thinking and he hadn't noticed the quiet rain until a tomeguín, taking things for granted, alighted on his knee and shook itself out. Arsenio had been sitting there for so long with his knees drawn up, leaning against the good part of the wall, that the bird must have thought he was part of the heavy old vine. Well, maybe he was! It went roaming in and out of the curling grilled gates, around the crumbling rocks of the wall and over the broken columns.

Amused, he had watched women or children who sometimes came running over, seeing the big red blossoms bursting, and thinking they'd just take some along home. First, they'd discover they couldn't take the flowers without stems, and there weren't any stems, or any ending to them. Root and stem were all one. So then they'd settle on pulling up a root too and plant it in their patio. It would pull up out of the light top soil easy enough, but for such a thin thing it was tough as the devil, and it wouldn't break off no matter how they pulled and yanked, and it wouldn't end, unless, he grinned, they'd take the trouble to follow it in and out, up and down, till they cleaned up the whole damn estate! They'd finally give up and walk away, mad at the vine.

He remained motionless until the bird had had enough of him and then he stretched out his arms to the rain. He loved the feel of this quiet misty drizzle that brought the breath of the earth, and that was as soft as the spray that would drift up on his face from the sea foam. He tasted it on his lips out of habit. Something was missing. He liked the salty water better. Still, this was good too, and the way it ticked hollow on the big malanga leaves helped him to go on with his thinking.

But a woman's voice coming from somewhere, and not belonging to the rain, spoilt it. It was a fat colored nurse scolding two small children and spoiling it for them, too.

"Mira que lo van a coger y bien! And just wait till I tell your mother you won't come out of the rain!"

"It isn't raining!" protested one of them.

"It's just wet air, that's all," her brother said.

"Desobedientes!" she fussed. Then she noticed the garden ahead and giving them a little jab in the back she exclaimed, "Hurry up! Run over there and stand under that big tree by the wall!" But they just continued walking slowly, and looked sideways at each other, disgusted.

"Anda!" They could feel the familiar point of her fingernail this time, and, deciding to make a game out of what was a lost battle, they raced each other down the block to the wall. When they scrambled over the corner of it, they suddenly discovered Arsenio and came to a quick stop. He made out he didn't see them, and just sat still so that he wouldn't frighten them.

"Look at him!" the little girl whispered in awe. Arsenio almost didn't breathe. The two children stood transfixed, their mouths open in wonder. Finally, admiration exceeding caution, the little girl began to smile and, pointing a finger toward Arsenio, exclaimed "You're dirty!"

"Yeah!" added her brother with marked envy.

Arsenio tried just the smallest twinkle of a smile in his eyes, and they both smiled rapturously back at him,

"Don't you ever take a bath?"

Arsenio risked answering, "Sometimes, in a sea-shells." Their burst of laughter tinkling in the garden sounded beautiful to him.

"Who are you talking to?" the nurse puffed, catching up. Then she saw him.

"My God, what's that?" she stared and clutched their resisting arms to pull them away.

"He only takes baths in sea-shells!"

"You crazy talking to him? Come along now!"

"I don't want to go!"

"His beard's all different colors!"

"Don't you know the coco when you see him?"

"El coco!" Their reluctance changed to panic, and in horror they broke from her grasp and fled from the garden. As he regarded their retreating figures followed by the triumphant nurse, Arsenio thought how nice it would be to have Chori's kids there. No one would trick them into being afraid of him. But when the devil would that be now?

He never saw Chori any more, ever since the night that motherless-son-of-a-Carambita came where they were stacking charcoal and told them that story about the sale of the place. The morning after, the Marquesa acted like she didn't remember a thing, but worked away so hard polishing and sweeping that the little green lizards, scared to death, darted out from corners.

But the rest of them had stayed quiet by themselves, not knowing what to say—even that talkative Chori, quiet for once in his life—until Chan Li started getting nervous and asking them all what they thought was happening, so Chori went out to the street to find out.

They'd hung around, acting busy while they waited and hearing the Old One in the house singing a Canary Island song. As most of the walls were down, it was like giving one of those blasted free open-air concerts that he used to sneak away from, where women perched on the stage and squawked away. God a'mighty! Marquesa didn't sound like that. Maybe she sang good, something between a Galician bagpipe and a church bell after it had shaken itself out awhile.

And then finally Chori returned. He found them all standing around the warm deserted street, pretending not to be there and looking like a pack of fools. Even Marquesa managed to be sweeping nearby. Chori began to say something. When he saw her, he started coughing. It could have been the dust she blew up, sweeping. Anyway, he finished coughing and smiled big and showed her two large cans of water he had brought from the bodega so she wouldn't have to bother today getting it for herself. And there—oh, as far as that talk about the construction company, nobody out there had heard a thing. Carambita must have just made it up to feel important. Marquesa stopped her sweeping long enough to stand straight as her broom and say that naturally there hadn't been any truth to it. She was the only one who could give consent legally, and of course she never would.

Chori answered, "Of course, of course," and with bright big eyes began to whistle and take off the red checked shirt he had put on for the street, and said he was going over to his shack to measure for the door.

The others went back to work too. That's when Arsenio followed Chori up to his place to see if he was really going' to work. He didn't like several things, especially Chori's bringing Marquesa water today so that she wouldn't go to Bodega La Victoria. They all knew she enjoyed getting it herself so that she could chat with Francisco. Arsenio lay down on what was going to be the little garden and just watched Chori. With a long string he was measuring the space where the door had to go, and having a hard time trying to write it down on a piece of paper. But every now and then Arsenio could feel those shining white eyeballs shooting over a backwards glance towards him and then the whistling would come louder than ever. Oh, Chori was mighty busy whistling and looking out of the corner of his eyes and making a big sound of working but he was not working. Arsenio thought maybe by the sound of his voice he would know what was up.

"You've got wood for that door?"

"Yeah."

"Without holes in it or nothing?"

"Yeah."

There was something wrong all right when the Santiaguero just said "Yeah."

Topo, who had finished tying up the rest of the charcoal sacks, came over to them. They weren't used to seeing him much in the bright morning light, as he was always gone off early. In the places where the soot wasn't, you could see his skin as white as an eggshell, and come to think of it, there wasn't anything about Topo that was like a mole except his name and the place he lived. He walked over quiet and serious, but his eyes were smiling like he wanted to say something but was too shy. They both watched Chori fighting with that pencil. He kept licking it like the answer would come out of the point. Nobody said anything, but finally Topo walked over to Chori and held out a pretty little box under his nose. Chori was surprised at first but then he got the idea and opened it. The first thing he found was a card with words on it. Chori spelled it out: "For Chori's daughter Cachita—while—-she—waits—every week—I will carve you a new little figure to put on your bracelet."

Then Chori slowly unwrapped the bracelet and looked at it. Arsenio thought that black Santiaguero was surely going to cry; he kept shaking his bent down head from side to side and holding tight to the little box. But when he looked up, Topo had gone. Arsenio too pulled himself up and was walking away, going off to the ocean that was slapping and banging around and didn't bother about anybody. There he felt strong, but when he was with people that had so many feelings caught in nets like crabs—!

Before he got very far Chori called, "See you later, Arsenio." He was putting on his checked shirt again.

Arsenio stopped as he hurried towards him. "You're not finishing that door?"

"Oh sure, sure," Chori said. He said it so hard Arsenio knew it was a lie. "But I'm going to find some work."

"Thought you already had wood for that door. What do you need money for?"

"Oh sure, but—uh—." He was looking around for an excuse. "Need it to finish up. And Public Work's looking for so many streets to tear up and put together, I might as well get in on it."

"You're sure you didn't hear anything about—"

Chori kicked at nothing a second and couldn't look at Arsenio. "See you later, old goat."

And none of them had hardly seen him since then, gone digging ditches, and he never went near that little shack, all finished except for the door and garden.

Suddenly the light drizzle changed to a downpour. The newspapers Arsenio was going to sleep on were getting all wet, and he ought to put them under the tree, out of the rain, but he remained seated against the old wall because he liked the feel of the wet, red earth splashing up on his legs and the rain washing it off again. If that noisy Chori were here, he'd say, "Hurray! Old goat getting one more bath in twenty years!" Maybe if the rain kept up, they'd have to stop working on the street, and he'd come back early.

Arsenio noticed that an old red convertible car had parked by the garden ever since it had started to rain. From under his shaggy brows his glance darted suspiciously to the driver. Lately, instead of taking the cigarette butts that they threw, he'd been looking hard at the drivers, wondering if they'd be getting out with those long rolls of blue paper under their arms or those three-legged things they'd been looking through a while back when he had to keep the Marquesa from seeing them.

"Vaya una cosa!" He suddenly thought, "Marquesa and the others busy working and not bothering at all, and it's turning out that I'm the one beginning to worry about things. A fine way to change now!" Just the same, he looked hard at the fellow in the car. The man didn't notice Arsenio, though. (No one ever did; he looked so much like the rest of the place.) From what Arsenio could see of him through the hard rain, he didn't think he'd have to worry about this one. Gentle looking, like the Topo, but more fighter in him. But not the kind that wanted to knock the house down. Besides, he'd moved over to the other seat just to be able to enjoy the rain, like Arsenio. He was smiling at it, sort of washing his mind in it, and a shame that the rain would mess up the cigarette butt he threw out. Arsenio would have liked to have this one's cigarette.

"Anda!" Rain was coming down now so hard that the zinc roof of Chori's shack sounded like a steam engine. Maybe it was pouring in that little old place. Better go see, the way that crazy nigger wasn't paying any attention to it these days.

As he splashed through the wet bushes toward the shack, he thought, "Chivado de verdad!" He's really screwed! Here I am worrying about things again. What's the matter with me!

§

When the rain stopped, Jorge got out of the car. He had been eager to see this land which he felt was going to mean so much to him. The project was his chance, the one he had waited for so long. If all went well, others would follow and he could then support Lourdes. She could get her divorce. Since the accidental meeting with Mario the night before, continued deception seemed unbearable to him.

He had sped through the heavy Vedado traffic to the Camacho estate. It lay on a coastal strip which was to have been an extension of the Malecón Drive. But the road had never been completed, and the area had been relatively neglected in recent times. Many of the old mansions built during the sugar-boom of 1918 had been boarded up or had degenerated into crowded tenements, as investors were more interested in the commerce near the main thoroughfares across the city and in the outlying suburbs.

By the address he knew that the Camacho property was somewhat removed from the rest of the area, jutting out into the sea. As he parked the car the light rain which had begun to fall turned into a downpour. He would have to wait, but no matter. He loved the rain and, like the fisherman's bottle singing on the Malecón wall, he felt that it was a good omen. He moved to the other side where, through the streaming window, he could see a haze of tall pine and ceiba trees extending to a small rocky area that turned softly to the sea beyond.

What a perfect spot to fulfill this dream of his. He could envisage the little houses with their horizontal sweep, their patios and their cheerful interiors catching the right kind of light as well as providing cool escape from the blazing afternoon sun. They would erase from memory the old vault-like renovations and the so-called "modern" gingerbread boxes. A detailed concept of the project in its entirety appeared before him almost of its own accord.

Those of limited means know all too well exactly what they want. He could hear again his mother's disappointed voice and his sister's and his own as, worried, they trudged with her through the long years of moving from one inadequate dwelling place to the other. "Nothing at all on the esquina de fraile, the Friar's Corner Street? These rooms will be so hot," or "Nothing with a little more light?" or "Mamá, nothing where I could have a room of my own sometimes where people don't have to walk through it to the bathroom?" "Nothing that has walls that the paint will stay on?" "Nothing that has windows you can put curtains on?" Nothing...nothing...Small wonder that the stunted instinct for beauty flowered in such distortion that the Frigidaire is given place of honor in the stiff Renaissance dining room. Well he knew!

He made some mental note of what he wanted. The certain angle of exposure, distribution, and architectural line would take up more than the normal frontal space granted small homes, but he would plot the streets in such a way that it would be possible without land-waste. Above all, there would be decorative simplicity, so that the money could go into the quality of materials used.

The rain had stopped now, and as he walked toward the high iron picket fence surrounding the estate, which he calculated instinctively approximated two large city blocks, he started to look for an entrance but found it unnecessary. A few yards from his parked car, a high arched wrought-iron gate hung open, twisted and broken on its great rusty hinges. Stepping over the low crumbling wall which it enclosed, he entered what once must have been a garden but which was now so densely overrun with wild shrubs and trees that no semblance of any order could be determined. He paused a moment to breathe in the heavy fragrance of jasmine, piscuala, and prickly guanábana. As he gazed at the maze of colors so clear and pure after the heavy rain, it seemed that a joyous hand, taking advantage of man's absence, had wantonly festooned all with the brightest vines and creepers in Cuba.

Slowly, as his eyes searched for traces of the original plan, he distinguished through the foliage a double row of Doric column with a very simple architrave, now covered by vines forming a long arbor. At the end of it, almost hidden, was a niche in the wall, and as he parted the thickets that had undoubtedly saved it from cyclone and vandalism, he discovered a marble figure intact. It was of a young Grecian woman of radiant expression and with a certain lithe forward inclination of the body that conveyed an impression of movement, as though she were just about to approach someone or something. Arm half bent, she held in her hand a budding twig which she might have just plucked or might be relinquishing—one could not say which. At her feet lay an open pomegranate. The figure was beautifully executed in strong archaic style, and Jorge had no recollection of ever having seen it before either in reproduction or print. It was not, of course, ancient, probably made within the last fifty years, and carried no name. He surmised that it represented Proserpina because of the popular pomegranate symbol. It might have been casually acquired; or perhaps it had been commissioned of the sculptor, since the colonnade seemed to have been designed to give it prominence. He guessed it might have held some significance for the owner. With a protective impulse he bent to push the concealing vines back in place, and as he did so, he was surprised to discover at the base a small glass containing what seemed to be the remains of a votive candle. Although it might have been there years, protected by the niche and shrub, neither cobwebs nor foliage grew over it. Someone knew of Proserpina's hiding place. Who would be lighting candles to it, the goddess of Spring, and Queen of the Underworld'? He suddenly replaced it, feeling ridiculous at his fanciful flight. Religious figures exercised an irresistible attraction on the people, amounting almost to fetish, and certainly someone stumbling across it had mistaken it for the Blessed Virgin. And as for the statue, classical motives had been a popular feature of all the great mansions built in the era of the fabulous sugar-profits during the First World War. They had called it, appropriately enough, the "Dance of the Millions." One could still see them in what had been the exclusive residential sections of that period—the Víbora, El Cerro, and of course, the Vedado. And too, his work had frequently introduced him to another ghost of the period: bare foundations, or half-built palaces, suddenly interrupted as though the lava of some economic Vesuvius had ruthlessly stopped the hands of the builders. These remains were imperishable witnesses to that terrible catastrophe, the crash of 1919. So, there was really nothing unusual about this! Perhaps the unexpectedness of the encounter had lent it enchantment.

He turned back to inspect the rest of the estate. Because of all the high bamboo and massive ceiba trees, it was difficult to know exactly where the house was. He suddenly came upon it, an imposing grey phenomenon in spite of its state of decay. Whatever it had been, it was not neoclassic, as he had half expected, but what—? he asked himself, smiling at his own bewilderment. The frames of its high paneless windows and rotting doors suggested the Moorish arch, but as his eyes travelled upwards past three stories, he beheld a lofty gothic tower studded by large grey faces or a kind of stylized gargoyles which dominated the entire structure. Indeed, their expression, even from that height, was so compelling that he could not refrain from staring at them, fascinated. Wisdom, mirth, and something timeless and indestructible looked out upon the world from those wooden faces that were almost alive. What a contrast to the atmosphere of that simple Doric garden!

He followed a rotting wooden verandah, the vestiges of whose intricate arabesque pattern still boasted an airy grace. It led around to the other side of the house, which appeared much less abandoned. Broken Moorish tiles, unexpectedly bright and clean-swept, directed his steps to an open court enclosed by a low wall that had been lavishly encrusted with hand-painted tiles rich and subtle in design. Most of them had been stolen, but enough remained to convey the original impression, at once sensuous and delicate. In the center a goat grazed at the ruins of a fountain, now overrun with vines.

He stood there perplexed. What manner of person had he been, the owner of this house, to have defied all the laws of architectural aesthetics with this unheard-of combination of styles? Certainly no architect would have gone along with this. And because of the loving care evident in each detail, it was obvious he must have built much of it himself. Jorge was eager to examine the interior of the house. Undoubtedly it would reveal still more of the man. He retraced his steps toward the back of the house, where rotting boards had fallen away, half exposing a large kitchen. He was about to enter when he heard a movement on the narrow staircase from within.

"Is that you, Arsenio?" a rather high, very clear voice called. Jorge did not have time to answer, for the next moment a tall, very thin, large-boned woman entered the room. She was past middle age, but her erect carriage and clear green eyes were a striking contrast to her nondescript dress worn and washed past all suggestion of original shape or color. When she saw him she stopped abruptly, obviously alarmed.

"Excuse me if I frightened you," he apologized quickly, and noticing an old kettle steaming on the charcoal stove, added, "I didn't know that anyone lived here."

"Have you come on any particular—business?" Her thin fingers nervously closed an imaginary collar.

"No, no. I'm just looking around. The house is so unusual—I hope you don't mind."

She seemed extremely relieved, and her attitude immediately altered. "Oh, that is quite all right! We occasionally have visitors who enjoy browsing around. It is beautiful, isn't it?" She smiled proudly. He wondered who the "we" were to whom she referred, but something about her discouraged personal questions.

"Do come in. You are welcome." Her gracious manner seemed to take no cognizance of the crumbled wall that made an invitation to enter superfluous.

"Thank you." He stepped over the broken tiles and hesitated, indicating the kettle. "Perhaps I'm interrupting?"

"Oh, no!" she smiled. "I wouldn't think of eating until I've finished up. It is quite a large house, as you can see, although I've shut off some of the rooms until he returns. Now if you will excuse me—" and she disappeared up the stairs.

From their perilously deteriorated condition, he wondered how she dared use them. He could already hear her on the creaking floor above, which meant that she must be familiar with every broken board, to be able to pick her way about with such agility!

As he crossed the kitchen to explore the interior of the house, he wondered what new style he would find. Surely nothing would surprise him now! But he was mistaken. In general, the intricate Moorish mood was continued. Spacious arched doorways, ample windows with delicate arabesque grilles, and traces of lavish marquetry and tile incrustation must have lent to the rooms an aspect of lightness and fantasy. The dining room, however, was paneled in a richly carved mahogany depicting mythological scenes. And strangest of all was the graceful stairway he found in a small room, probably a sitting room, which led to nothing but a short passage with a dead-end. There was no doorway, nor aperture of any kind. But in the wall was an empty niche. What had been there? Obviously, the stairway had been devised for no other purpose. An incredible house, a nightmare for an architect! And yet there was something so personal about it, so much loving attention given to each detail, that it was difficult to understand its present abandoned condition. Undoubtedly he would be able to find out more about it in Saenz's office. Perhaps too, the original plans were still in existence. He would like very much to see them.

He did not try to inspect the upper floors, which he would like to-have done, for fear of alarming the woman again, but as he left the house, he noticed a small group of people in conversation at the far side of the Moorish patio, and recognized her tall figure among them. He would have waved goodbye to her, but none of them had seen him.

As he reached the garden on the way to his car, he stopped impulsively and turned to look back. The effect should have been monstrous, this conglomeration of gothic, classical, and Moorish, yet it was not. On the contrary, as he looked around again, the beauty of it seemed to grow into a harmonious completion, and he experienced a peculiar kinship with whoever had created it.

Of course it could have been the ceaseless waves of time and the elements beating down its contours that had lent it an appearance of unity. But it was not that. Every line seemed to lead logically into the next, just as the random musing of a fertile mind will flow into an organized thought. Here he could feel a presence, an abundant and rebellious spirit that had been faithful to its own concept of beauty, and indifferent to the world's sanction.

Now more than ever Jorge burned with desire to see his project realized. He felt that the vital spirit so palpable here would not be resentful. On the contrary, it would understand that instead of crumbling ruins there would be a place for people who could for the first time live with beauty too! Above all, he would plan each step with the same love that had created this, and although others would submit designs, he knew his would be accepted.

Suddenly he experienced the same desperate impatience to get to his drawing board as he always did to meet Lourdes. It was the same! It did not matter now that Lourdes was busy with the convention and that he could not see her. At moments like this when he was in his true world, her physical presence was not important. She was here with him now, closer to him than she could ever be with her body.

He made note of a few measurements before he turned to go. He would like to preserve some of these old trees. He would also call Saenz's office on his way to' work to find out if they knew anything about the original plans. They would not of course, have any bearing on his designs, but if they were in existence, surely the owner himself would have made them. To see them would be like a conversation with him—or a handshake.

As he began to walk towards his car, a short fat fellow in shirtsleeves had left the group talking on the other side of the house and came hurrying across. the garden towards his car parked behind Jorge's. As he caught up with Jorge, he seemed eager to talk to him, or to anyone. Sighing to attract attention, he pulled out a handkerchief and wiped his face. Jorge opened the door, but the man could not resist conversation. "Compadre!" he exclaimed with over-familiarity, as if they knew each other. "You know I always wanted to be a public accountant, but my old man didn't have enough money, and I never finished school. Had to get out and work. And wotta job I found!" He waved. some sweated papers in his hand. "If I had any more like these people today—" nodding in the direction of the house, "especially her—"

"You mean the tall lady?"

"Lady!" he tapped his head significantly. "All of 'em!" Then leaning against the car, he took out a cheap cigar. He was enjoying himself thoroughly. "It's all gonna be torn down. I came to serve them notice of eviction. They're squatters and every blasted one of them crazy!" With broken tobacco-stained teeth he zestfully spat out the tip of his cigar and looked toward the garden. "Christ! You'd have to have all your screws missing to sleep in a place like this! Ghosts and them wooden faces—Hey, I wonder what goes on there at night! All those nuts together! How do you think those screwballs do it? Must be something to watch!" With his head thrown back and shoulders jerking up and down, a spasmodic sound, evidently laughter, came from his vocal cords. Jorge, who experienced an absurd impulse to destroy this revolting face before him, made a move to get into the car, but the man put a familiar hand on his shoulder. "Know what they did when I told 'em? Nothin'. I've handed plenty of these eviction papers, and the people usually cry, or get sore and fight, or try to get real crafty and wangle out more money. But these locos say they won't get out and won't take any money. Say that the place belongs to the old witch! Ha, Ha!"

Jorge managed to free himself and get into the car. The man shut the door for him, laughing and sweating. "Well, it's their funeral, eh?"

Driving into the busy thoroughfare, Jorge almost wished he hadn't seen the old woman, whose eyes reflected a lucidity that he had seldom encountered. What would become of her in this outside world? No doubt she was unbalanced—look at her choice of domicile! —yet she made sense, even as the house did. Still, she would be much better off elsewhere. They would probably send her to Calixto Garcia Hospital, where she would be taken care of. Besides, there were so many others who would benefit, he hoped, by living there. They were waiting, even now, without knowing it.

13
SEE YOU IN CAMAGUEY

Jorge seated at a table, recognized Don Cipriano as soon as he entered. He was unmistakable from the spats on his shoes to the cane and white hat and, above all, to the inherent dignity that this was Don Cipriano Salinas. The Carmelo itself was a tradition, and several of the old waiters who must have served him here years ago came to greet him. Jorge waited until the old gentleman was comfortably settled at a table and then approached him.

"Dr. Salinas, sir?"

"You must be the young man of the telephone conversation. Sit down," he invited, cordially shaking hands with Jorge.

"Jorge de Armas. Thanks, sir. There was so much outside noise when I called you at your hotel, I doubt whether you were able to understand exactly who I was or my reason for wanting to meet you."

"I did succeed in making out something about Saenz's office. And you are quite right about the noise," he chuckled. "I never expect it to be otherwise in Havana."

"When Saenz's office suggested I might call you I had no idea you were leaving early tomorrow morning. It's quite a trip to Camagüey. I hope I'm not imposing?"

"Not at all. The business matter that brought me here is finished, and I'm merely waiting for some old friends with whom I'm having dinner. I'm delighted to have this opportunity of talking to a young man of modern Havana. Everything has changed so—even this." He smiled and unfolded his thin hands to indicate the shining glass wall of the remodeled Carmelo.

"Just between us, something of a slight betrayal—" he joked. As Jorge observed him against the glittering modernity, it seemed to him that the anachronism was not Salinas but the Carmelo. He was impressive enough to make a century seem out of place. "Therefore, I have the pleasure of knowing a modern young man in a modern Carmelo. Do you care for a glass of manzanilla?"

"Thanks. But I'm afraid you'll be disappointed. I'm not quite a perfect sample of a modern young man."

"Indeed! How so?"

Jorge looked into his eyes that were so young, and smiled. He felt a great rapport with this man, but words did not come, especially when the subject was himself. "Oh, for several reasons," he shrugged. "Not necessarily flattering, in comparison—"

"Come now! You don't look like a befogged champion of tradition."

"Hardly!" Jorge laughed. "But I don't reject it, either. After all, what is tradition but a kind of springboard into the future, a bridge. Why shouldn't one use it?"

"Well, there are many people today who want to find their own way."

"Certainly. But they don't have to discard their heritage, which is the thing that distinguishes them from everyone else, do they? Look what's happening to Havana! Pretty soon it will look like Miami or Los Angeles or Caracas or even Milano." He laughed and vehemently rubbed his head at the preposterous idea that had some truth in it. "This is happening all over the world."

"Certainly you would not have us ignore all the great technical improvements?"

'Of course not. But they have to be adapted to our own expression. They're only the instruments to help us transpose the Cuban tradition into modern idiom. The Seagram building or the Lever building may be masterpieces in New York because they're a true expression of its spirit and its needs. But transplant them even on smaller scales (as they are doing) to another country, and all you have is a meaningless imitation. So many people want to merge with an anonymous present! Wouldn't it be more interesting if they emphasized their national experience?"

Salinas' hands waving silent mirth interrupted him. His eyes twinkled. "This is most refreshing and, I must admit, rejuvenating," he exclaimed, "to find myself, whose future is past, if you will forgive the preciousness, defending it against a young man whose life is only of the future." Jorge laughed good- naturedly and would have protested, but the elder man continued: "Most people think the achievements of the past should be duly admired as such and lie sweetly buried. But you imply that we should carry its bones around with us."

Jorge knew he was joking and was also touched by his obvious delight at this reversal of position. "We'll leave the bones undisturbed," he smiled, "but the achievements live in us today. Isn't the real meaning of tradition a transmitting? A sending forth? That's why it is always new. An uninterrupted leading towards the future. Values never change. We just translate them into our own terms." He paused a moment and leaned across the table, his dark eyes sparkling with intensity. "I don't think the free expression of any great Master ever suffered because of his adherence to that continuity. The strength of what he has to say will always make it new. When the Renaissance Italians, for example, picked up the inheritance of their past, they didn't wear it like a seedy old coat one finds in a trunk. Their tradition was the kiss that awoke the enchanted princess. With it they found new life. Their artistic restlessness found its modern individual expression.

Don Cipriano, happily aware that the friends with whom he was to have dinner were late, poured Jorge another glass of manzanilla, and with much inner amusement observed that, unconscious of everything around him, without a thank-you, Jorge had downed the small glass of wine as though it were a shot of rum.

"Oh, there are sensationalists, too," Jorge continued, "who really haven't anything to say, so they plunge off the bridge just to create a splash! If they—" but a waiter interrupted him.

"Don Cipriano, excuse me, but will you be having dinner?"

"Not yet, José. But perhaps Señor Armas—"

Jorge shook his head with a blank smile, and as the waiter left, he straightened in his chair and looked around him, confused. His hand shot to his forehead in embarrassment. "So terribly sorry. I didn't realize—"

Salinas looked at him questioning.

"You were kind enough to see me your last day in Havana and here I've"—he made a hopeless gesture—"been making speeches! I'm sorry. Why, usually I find it difficult to express myself, let alone—"

Salinas interrupted. Slowly, but with a precise movement that marked sincerity, he folded his hands on the table and leaned towards Jorge. "Please," he remonstrated. "All the more reason for me to feel flattered. I am enjoying this immensely."

"Why, I haven't as yet explained the purpose of my call! And your dinner engagement..."

"They are late." Salinas nodded. "It is very comforting," he joked. "At least there are some customs in Havana which have not changed! And as to the purpose of your calling me, we'll get to that in due time. Let's finish our conversation." As Jorge hesitated, he exclaimed, "Ah, but I am the thoughtless one, detaining you from something far more interesting than an antiquated—" he paused to stress waggishly, "—revolutionary."

Their eyes met in an embrace of friendship and they both burst into hearty laughter. "Of course you would not approve," Salinas teased. Jorge smiled. "That you're a revolutionary? Perfectly compatible," he replied.

"How so?" Salinas prodded him with a pretended surprise. "Isn't this a plunging off the bridge too?"

"Not really! The kind of revolution I'm talking about is the culmination of the progressive thoughts, needs, and actions of generations. The classical examples of the French and Russian Revolutions were ripened by years-of preparation. And our own—yes! —by Lopez, Céspedes, Aguilera, before it reached Martí in art—the revolt of a Beethoven, Debussy, a Schoenberg, a Picasso evolved from their knowledge of all that preceded them. Naturally, I don't include the opportunists, fanatics, and demagogues who make the blind angry gestures without offering a real solution, whether in art or in politics.

"Ah, my friend," Salinas interposed. "Do not underestimate the fruitful effect of an angry gesture, even blind, when made at the proper moment. Narciso López, for example. He was thwarted but he served a—"

"Served a purpose when and only when—" Jorge vehemently shook his finger at Salinas to stress his point, "the slow process of development produced a mature generation."

How delicious! Don Cipriano thought. He has snatched words from my mouth, he is shaking his finger at me, he has completely forgotten my seniority; in fact, he has made me a thirty-year-old companion.

"Cuba has reached that point of maturation now. Try to stunt it and there will be violence." Jorge spoke the words slowly and looked significantly at Salinas. "The 'angry gestures' have been made—and the protests, if only there are ears in the United States to hear them—"

"Not only in the North—Cuban ears also," Salinas countered.

"Yes, of course!" Jorge affirmed. "Otherwise what recourse is there but violence? It's necessarily the fruit of our own self-interest. A cancer is allowed to spread," he shrugged. "A knife must be used—unless we begin improving the world by changing ourselves first. The choice lies within us." Jorge leaned back in his chair with eyes lowered and arms folded, still absorbed in his thoughts. He did not seem aware of Salinas' presence. His youthful buoyancy had vanished. In its place was a dark brooding.

"You are quite right, my friend," Salinas nodded, touched by his earnestness. There was a heavy pause which was incongruent amidst the frivolous chatter of the Carmelo diners. Aware of this, Salinas changed the subject. "But tell me, in view of all this, how is it that you are connected with Saenz? I believe I understood you to say that on the phone."

"Oh no!" laughed Jorge, "I'm free-lance. Saenz just asked me to submit designs for a project of his which, as a matter of fact, is to be built on the newly purchased Camacho estate."

Salinas raised his head in surprise. "A project of Saenz?"

118

"More or less. Actually, an unnamed client of his."

"I see, I see." He suspended the glass of manzanilla he was about to drink and considered this information with a puzzled expression.

"I went to look it over, get the feel of it," Jorge pursued, "and I must confess that what I found, the remains of the building and the gardens, and above all, the personality of the man who created it (who must have been extraordinary) so impressed me that I was curious to see the original plans, if they still exist. The office didn't have them, but they suggested I contact you.

At last we arrive at the purpose of my call!" Jorge smiled, a little embarrassed.

"For which call I am most indebted," remarked Salinas, graciously, "although I'm sorry to say must disappoint you. The plans are not among the papers turned over to me." He leaned back, quietly folding his hands, and only the slight tapping together of his thumbs suggested a more personal reaction than mere reminiscence. "Yes, yes," he nodded, "I haven't been to the house for many years—God knows what is left of it— but I can understand how you would be drawn to it, now that I know you.

"I was there the day that it was opened," Salinas continued, "the housewarming—unforgettable day! That house meant so much to Leandro Camacho. It was, in a way, the symbol of everything he had fought for." Jorge longed to be able to see in his eyes the images that memory was projecting. "Except for one person who understood (and goodness knows what has become of her!) people called it a madness——as they always will when a man has the courage to create his own world."

"You knew him well?"

"Yes. Quite well. We were comrades in arms during the last years of the Independence, and our friendship lasted until he—disappeared. 'Peace you will never have,' Christ once enjoined. What an astounding remark to make to one's disciples! And how well Leandro Camacho knew that truth, although he was not a religious man in the conventional sense—nothing about him could be conventional."

"Did you say 'disappear,' sir?" Jorge could not refrain from interrupting.

"When he felt that he was an obstacle to his own dream—but it's an involved story. Perhaps some other time—"

The belated arrival of his dinner companion put an end to the conversation.

"Cipri! Here you are!" Jorge was amused to hear him called by his nickname. He rose as he watched the two old friends throw their arms around each other in a hearty embrace. The waiters and other diners could not refrain from stretching around to share in this happy reunion. Their delight was contagious, and smiles spread from one table to another. The impersonal, antiseptic elegance of the redecorated Carmelo and its well-dressed clientele was suddenly converted to its former family warmth.

"Qué tal, Carlito!"

"Estás muy bien, Cipri! y Pastora, cómo está? Tan dulce cómo siempre?"

"Qué placer!"

They made a wonderful contrast: Don Cipriano, whose dignified sobriety could carry his extreme height, and Don Carlos, compact and silver haired, whose tiny hands and feet and slight stature only enhanced his jaunty elegance. His voice was suave and melodious as a courtier's. Together they were the essence of Cuba, combining the dignity of the Spaniard and the charm of the Creole.

"Terribly sorry I'm late!" he said gaily.

In answer, Salinas chuckled. "I would have been disappointed if you had reformed. And especially today! Thanks to you, I've had a delightful conversation with an exceptional young man. He turned towards Jorge. "Señor De Armas, Don Carlos Mendia."

"Excuse me, caballeros," a waiter interrupted, "the mayor just phoned and asked me to give you the message that it is impossible to keep his engagement with you. He regrets this very much, wishes you a good trip, Don Cipriano, and asks to be remembered to Doña Pastora."

"Thank you, Pedro," Dr. Salinas said. His smile faded and he and Don Carlos exchanged a troubled glance.

"Do you know, when I saw him the other night at the party, I found him quite changed. You remember how his eyes always twinkled with wit? It's gone now." He shook his head sadly.

"I don't like what they're doing to him, Cipri, I don't like it!" Don Carlos echoed.

When Jorge took his leave of the two men shortly afterwards, Salinas accompanied him to the door.

"I wish you luck on the project. If Leandro Camacho were alive, he too would wish it so. But also—" he looked concerned, as though there were something he wanted to communicate to Jorge, "it would be well not entirely to forget what our Lord once said, 'The children of this earth are wiser than the children of light.'" He shook his hand firmly. "My wife and I would be happy to see you in Camagüey. Adios."

Coming from Salinas, the words puzzled Jorge. They would have puzzled him anyway, he smiled. He was scarcely an avid Bible reader. Meanwhile his contact with this exceptional man exhilarated him. And too, he was amused, because Don Carlos had invited him to lunch the following week. It was the first time he had been recognized socially.

14
SOME VERY STIMULATING PEOPLE

Jorge knew it must be close to six a.m. He could hear the soft hollow sound of charcoal which the cook next door was gathering from the patio bin for the day's cooking. Soon the comfortable smell of alcohol and wisping smoke would float up to him as she fanned it into flame.

In spite of having walked about Havana for—he did not know how long— possibly hours, after the party had ended, he was not yet tired. He closed the door very softly so as not to awaken his mother and sister, but the motive was not purely unselfish. His design for the project had been accepted and he wanted this moment undisturbed. As he leaned against the closed door, he could feel his heart beating rapidly, and his entire being was transported in a feeling of oneness within himself. There was no sound now anywhere, and through the window, in that hour before the dawn, even time had become nothing but a ghostly outline, like the insubstantial traces of the roof-tops and grilled balconies, all transparent shadows of unreality. But here in this room was the world. He could almost feel the live tree within that wooden door and his drawing board. Except for him and those two pieces of wood, nothing existed.

He walked towards the drawing board and turned on the small light over it. He knew now that every line he made there was a living thing. It would exist in the rain and the sun; it would be a cosmic part of the hands that accidentally touched it, the thoughts that it would shelter, and the lives it would directly influence.

Even before they had called him today to tell him his design had been accepted; he had felt sure of it. Ever since he had gone to the Camacho estate—in fact, from the first time Saenz had told him of the project—he had known. This, amazing enough, for one who had become accustomed to expect nothing good of life! Was the law of averages finally catching up with him? He grinned at this new-found optimism. He was anxious to begin working. There were some slight changes he wanted to make, but as he picked up his pencil he heard with regret, the slapping of his mother's old bedroom slippers on the tiled hallway and her muffled knock on the door.

"Se puede?" she asked, in a whisper so vehemently intended to be secretive that it hissed down the hall. He had called her that evening to tell her the news, and her excitement was plainly visible as he opened the door. She stood there in an old bathrobe, the silver-streaked hair as yet uncombed reaching below her hips, and for once she was rendered silent by emotion. The wordless joy and pride with which she regarded him emphasized her strong features and reminded him of a Roman matron. Suddenly unable to contain herself any longer, she threw her arms about him in a fierce embrace.

"Hijo, hijo!" was all she could say. "My son!"

He felt ashamed at his desire to be alone. At last poor mamá, to whom he had been able to give so little—. He kissed her on the forehead, and noticed tears in the corner of her eyes.

She rubbed them away roughly with the palm of her hand as she

exulted. "Didn't I tell you, when I dreamed of butterflies!" she said triumphantly, as if the butterflies had been responsible for the whole thing.

"You certainly did, mamá."

"It never fails. Two months before the death of your father, may his soul rest in peace, I dreamed that..." A distant cockcrow caused her to glance through the window. Horrified, she realized the time. But the occasion was too happy a one for scolding. She put her hands on her hips, and tapped her foot playfully. "It is after six!"

"That's right," he teased. "Isn't that your usual hour? I thought I'd follow your example."

"Ha! My example is to get up at six, not to go to bed then! Don't think that because you won that 'contest' that you are to start carrying on!" He had never been able to dissuade her from associating him with children's activities. She somehow visualized all architectural projects as school contests, with a prize for the best student.

"You probably waited up half the night for me."

Closing the shutters, she pointed to his pajamas, always folded on the bed which she turned down for him every evening.

"I'm not going to bed now mamá! I was just going to make a few corrections—." He looked longingly at the drawing board.

"Don't be silly," was all she said. "It's nervous excitement. While you're undressing, I'll make you a tilo to calm you." Before he could protest, she was gone.

"Tilo!" he smiled to himself. Much good chamomile tea could do when there were still nine hours to endure before he would be meeting Lourdes. The thought of her joy, and of what this meant for them, was almost unbearable. It was strange, in a way, to realize that she did not know. She had been with him every moment.

As he hung his jacket over a chair and absently brushed off the smudge of cigar ashes from his lapel, he remembered the big fellow at the dinner he had just attended who had slapped him on the back so heartily that Jorge's cigar-ashes had fallen all over his suit and into his drink. The man had winked and remarked, "Nothing like a talented head with feet of clay!" And then there was Hernandez, the specifications man at the dinner, who had looked astonished upon learning that Jorge had been accepted and had remarked, "Pretty nice to have a godfather," which had amused Jorge very much, and he was going to tell him so, but someone from the office changed the subject. Now as he buttoned his pajamas he frowned, momentarily puzzled by these remarks, but the mood was quickly dissipated under the score of hazy yet exhilarating impressions that tumbled by.

"Mamá, I was with some very stimulating people tonight," he commented as his mother sat on the side of his bed with the steaming tilo.

"Now tell me all about it, while you sip this."

"Well, I was called to Saenz's office late this afternoon, and when I arrived, he immediately saw me and told me the news! It's a big project; I still can't believe it. Everyone in the office was congratulating me. Some friends of Saenz's happened to be there, and also several of the biggest contractors in the country. It was around closing time, and they suddenly decided to go to the Yacht Club for dinner, which turned out to be in my honor, more or less."

"Vaya!" she exclaimed as she hung up his jacket.

"Most of them are far different from what I expected."

"This suit needs dry-cleaning."

"Are you listening, vieja?"

"Sí-í-í?" she said.

"It was a revelation to me. They're not what I thought at all," he mused as he sipped the tilo. "One of them gives three nights a week to the San Lorenzo Charity Hospital—not his money alone, but his time! He actually works there. Another is a music fanatic. I think he's more interested in his chamber music rehearsals than in his concrete. He invited me for dinner next week. You know, a friend of mine"—he almost said "Lourdes"—"once said that the poor don't give the rich a chance. Can you understand that? Mamá, I don't think you've heard a word I've been saying. This is no time to be cleaning out my closet!"

123

"What?" she called from the depths of it.

15
PARKED ON REINA

It was early when Jorge arrived at the cafe where Oscar was waiting to give him the key, and he was glad there was time to please the old fellow by having a drink with him.

"This time I invite you!" he exclaimed gaily. "I've just had some great news, Oscar, and I came early hoping that you would be able to celebrate with me! The best part of a happy moment is to share it with a good friend, right?"

Oscar's round, shining face blushed with pleasure. "That's right, that's right," he beamed, as in his enthusiasm he squatted rather than sat on the chair. "I'm mighty glad to hear something good has happened for you. You know—" there was something unusually eager today in his childlike expression, "—my wife Rosa and were talking about you both—high-class. No! Don't laugh! I mean really high-class. In here," tapping his heart. "Not in money—oh! we've had plenty of those, too— 'gente fina'—so-called high-class.

Oh, not too bad," his voice lowered to the intimacy of this pride which touched him. "You know yourself I won't have anything to do with anyone who I didn't know, was, well, respectable, you understand. But you—you're a real gentleman."

Jorge laughed again.

"No, no. Don't joke, I'm serious!" His index finger chased the ice around the inside of his glass of rum and lime indignantly. "Listen to me, Jorgito! No one in the world can get to know more about people than us that's in this business. We've had plenty of high-up government people, society—" he shook his head and gulped down his drink, "not like you! Why, you'd never even know anybody'd been down there after you leave! But Caridad del Cobre! If you'd see the way the others leave the place sometimes! No more, though," he announced and then had suddenly shut up, and stared into his half empty glass. Jorge, amused, had waited for him to go on. But he noticed that the old fellow was stopped by something. "Compadre, what's the matter?" He leaned over the table to see what was going on in that downturned face.

Finally, the face squared up at him. "All right, Jorgito, I'll tell you something." Whatever it was, it was costing him a lot of effort to get out. He looked away, paused, and began to pull at his ear-lobe. Finally he said, "In my business, I shouldn't talk about what I'm going to talk about now. Especially to you! You know we're supposed to be struck deaf, dumb and blind. It's got to be that way. But we don't miss anything—not even our own selves. Oh, maybe I never would've got round to it—to thinking—if it hadn't been for my wife. She used to get pretty upset, being religious the way she is. You've seen all her stuff in there," he nodded towards the door down the street.

Jorge thought, "All her stuff in there," and suddenly in spite of everything, he found himself thinking with tenderness of that crudely painted statue of the Caridad del Cobre and the way Lourdes, lying in bed, looked at it as she prayed.

"Quite an altar!" he said aloud.

"Yes! Oh, she takes a great pride in it! Why she worked for several years steady on that lace thing the Virgin's standing on! And no cyclone or Machado police ever kept her from daily Mass. Does a lot of charity work and never meddled in anyone's business in her life. So, you can see this business might've bothered her some time at first. She'd say to me every now and again, 'Oscar, I just don't think it's right. We can't go on doing this.' I'd remind her, 'What does that priest keep telling you every time you confess? Have you forgotten, woman, that he's told you a hundred times that he knows and the Lord knows, from all the bother you give them, that you don't want to do it? That it's your motherless husband's fault? That you've tried to make me find something else and I can't find it? And that I'm the one to blame and will have to take the rap for you in hell?' That would usually quiet her, because you see, Jorgito, I've got Plenary Indulgence that was blessed personally by the Pope. Old ship-mate of mine got it especially for me when he was in Italy. So she knows I'm safe! Or when that doesn't work, I tell her that if we did quit, all the others all over town would go right ahead just the same, and at least our place is clean and decent. Well, so anyway, she goes on sometimes worrying, sometimes not.

"But mostly the worrying. Until—" There he ran into a wall again, pulling at his ear-lobe.

"Until...?" Jorge asked.

"Until you came here, boy."

It surprised Jorge.

"You both come here for a different reason than the others. Time after time with the same mate—yes, son, you can see it's your real mate, not just a woman to spend a time with. Why, my wife shows me how you keep fixing up the place, like it was a home of your own that you could never have. None of my business, of course. Anyway, my wife's changed. A few days ago, she said to me, 'Oscar, may the Lord forgive me, but I don't rightly see how I'm going to confess being sorry for having them here! I feel more like it's a Christian act, getting to think they're children of ours we are giving a home to in a queer world where they can't have any home together. When I know they're coming, I always clean up the house double clean and light a candle to the Blessed Virgin for them. They bring flowers to her often, have you noticed? I feel like helping them, makes up for all the others. Except I wish there wouldn't be any others,' and then she said that if there are any things you'd like to leave so that you would feel more at home, she'll put them away locked up. But, Jorgito, I was thinking of something else," he hesitated painfully and then went on. "I feel she's right. And I was thinking, well, fact is, you coming so steady gives us enough. We don't need to have anyone else come. Fact is, I'd be mighty glad to turn away the others."

He stopped, waiting for Jorge's reaction. Oscar's face was shy, as a child's offering a gift. Jorge could only nod his thanks in answer. There was a tight knot in his throat. These simple people who knew and understood!

"And then my wife said," Oscar continued, "'I just don't seem to be troubled in my conscience any more about what we're doing. It may be a sin, and I'll confess it, but I don't think it offends the Lord.' You just consider it your own home," and he lowered his head again, fumbling around with the lemon in his glass to conceal his embarrassment.

"Your own home!" In the pause that followed, Jorge was grateful that Oscar did not notice his own emotion. So short a time ago that he had scorned Lourdes' faith. And here it was! Someone more civilized would call the sudden changes of fortune "coincidence." But he had enough blood of Andalusia and Cuba to know it was not coincidence. He knew it! "Gracias," he thanked silently. Aloud he managed to say, "I am very grateful to you and the Señora Rosa. You do not know how much." Suddenly Oscar, over his down bent glance, sensed Jorge's emotion. He jerked himself to his feet and held out his plump hand to Jorge.

"Well, I've been talking too much and it's about time for you to go. You know I'm expecting someone this evening," he explained, "but since we both agreed, it will be to tell him that it is the last time, whoever he is! You don't know how glad l am," and he clapped Jorge's back softly, "that after today my place won't be choked up with perfume anymore! Caray! l never was seasick in my life, but sometimes this..." and he waved away the imaginary evil, "I know nothing of what is fine taste or bad, but whether it's the perfume of elegant ladies coming here or the smell I remember at the port-cafes, it's all the same to me! l only know I was mighty relieved to pull out of those ports and get back to where I could breathe again! Madre de Dios! Love is as good and clean as the sea—if it's love! What do they have to go hiding it with that perfume-stink for? Unless maybe with them it's not much love. Well—" His clear blue eyes met Jorge's and they both stood looking at each other and smiling, saying more than all words ever could.

Jorge said goodbye, paid for the drinks, and left the cafe. He didn't have much money in his pocket, but he was going to buy flowers, wine, and candles to celebrate with Lourdes as he surprised her with the news. Today he could buy the world for a few pennies.

Like a gay shawl, the smell of garlic spread out warm and reassuring over the narrow street, and as he passed the small shops his heart filled with an almost giddy neighborliness. Unaccustomed as he was, this dram of good fortune had gone to his head! He made his purchases and then arranged them on the table of the little drawing-room. Then he lowered the shutters and leaving the door ajar very slightly for Lourdes, he sat waiting for her, visualizing her entrance, her surprise, her eyes as he told her about the project, Oscar's offer, and that at last everything had begun! He almost prayed that she would not be late, for such joy of expectancy could not long be endured.

§

It was too much! This was the last time! She had sworn it so often before and always forgot afterwards, but this time, this time! She was fed up with lying to the maid, lying to her friends, lying to Panchita (who certainly suspected something), lying to Mario (even though he didn't care), squeezing her brain dry for just one more lie, always in a hurry, never able to make the hour she and Jorge had agreed upon.

She always parked the car on Reina, whose strident heavy traffic served somewhat as a camouflage against any chance familiar eyes. She hastily locked the door and was about to look for a taxi when a voice called, "Lourdes!" Of course, it had to happen sometime! But today, when everything was so unbearable, and it was already so late...

"Hello, Amelia!" she waved. Hello, relentless Amelia; inexorable world.

"Whatever are you doing in this neighborhood, Lourdes?"

"I come here often. Working with Father Bonifacio on the Comité Auxiliar." She nodded towards Reina Church in the middle of the block.

128

Bravo! She could finally use that one! It had been prepared and waiting for a long time.

"Oh, then you're not going to the Gomez-Molas' Carnival party at Varadero?"

"No, I've promised to spend the afternoon working here. Besides, Mario couldn't make it." Mario. Who is 'Mario'? A shadow on another planet; two hands in space towards which her hands had stretched and never touched.

"What a shame! You remember what a wonderful time we had there last year? Which reminds me, I hear the party you gave for the Convention was stupendous! And we read that Mario's been named director of the Revista, and I don't know how many other things. You must be very proud of him. But, after all, you've had a hand in it, too."

Yes, Amelia, yes! Not only I but his father, cupping power in his palm and his name gently, oh so gently, possessively, knowingly, stroking his forehead, luring him to the comforting paralysis of the delightful, easy world as it was, as it is and ever shall be, world without end, amen.

".-but of course you and Mario are so close." The beautiful mascaraed eyelashes of beautiful, chic Amelia fluttered their hypocrisy at her, fluttered the sad lie, the secret blood-pact of the world.

"Oh, I've had nothing to do with it, really. But thank you, we are proud of him." Prick your vein, smear your blood with hers, complete the pact.

"Never mind being so modest!"

Damn, she couldn't be rude, and it was so late. If she were not so tense, she would have been amused wondering if at this very moment Amelia were not also on her way to a secret meeting with someone. But no, she was chattering on unmindful of the traffic noise and the scorching sun, and with no hint of an approaching coda in her voice.

Fortunately, the church bells rescued Lourdes.

"Oh, I'm keeping Father Bonifacio waiting! Amelia dear, you must forgive me," and so forth and so forth!

She dared not take a taxi although her friend was already walking in the opposite direction. Amelias have eyes in their backs. Now she would have to enter the church, at least for a few minutes.

As she genuflected in the rear of the darkened, silent church, the conflict of all beings seemed condensed into one moment. "God, I love You. Forgive my earthly loneliness."

Out into the street again. See if you have change for the taxi fare, so that you are not delayed before curious eyes. She fished in big purse. Not enough small change. That meant lengthening the agony, pushing through the hot, thronging, gasoline-filled street to find a shop and make an unnecessary purchase. What if she bumped into Mario now! Quick, another invention to explain why she was walking in that direction. Damn!

The purchase made, she now stood on the street corner looking for a taxi. Five minutes, ten minutes, there were scores of them going by, but on the other side of the street. She must stay on this side, where she could be lost in the line of people waiting for buses, for what pretext could she have for taking a taxi instead of using her own car? A hand-pushed frita-wagon stopped directly at her side, a strategic spot to sell hamburgers and croquettes to the impatient bus-waiters. The smell of onions and cheap meat frying in rancid lard nauseated her. A thousand buses vomited black fumes into her face. The horns, the people, the sun of midday flamed in her throat, soaking her face with sweat, staining her dress, wilting her hair, which only a half hour ago had been arranged just as Jorge loved to see it.

Never again! Never again! She had absolutely no desire to see him now. She would like to phone him and say that she was not coming, but looking for a phone would only prolong the torture of dirt and noise and heat. The quickest thing would be to wait for a taxi. At last she saw one approaching on her side. She shouted, but her voice was drowned in the shrieking brakes of a bus. She was already three-quarters of an hour late, and they had so little time together. But when she arrived, she wouldn't care now, anyway! Was she mad, going through this absurd, cheap tragedy of a thousand pulp stories? Had she lost all sense of dignity and perspective?

Finally a taxi! Do not yet remove your sun-glasses. Hold a handkerchief before your face. You might be recognized. The taxi stops at the address. As you walk to the door, look indifferent and unhurried before the eyes of the housewives leaning over their balconies, and the idle curious of the corner cafe.

A dios gracias! The door is slightly ajar. A place to hide! A place to remove the sun-glasses that make two rings of perspiration on her face, and a place to curse aloud! She pushed open the door of the little sitting room. The lowered shutters blessed it with a welcomed, almost complete darkness. She knew that he was standing in the shadow by the door, but deliberately she turned away from it, and without a greeting strode to the dining-room, tearing off her sunglasses and dropping her purse on the table. She did not notice that the centerpiece of clumsy artificial flowers had been replaced by a delicately arranged bouquet and that there were two festive lighted candles on either side of it, whose dripping mound of wax marked Jorge's patient waiting.

Two dimes were still clutched in her wet perspiring palm. Half sobbing, she threw them across the floor. "Never again! Never again! If you knew the ludicrous hell I've gone through! That horrible woman, the lies, the noise, the smell of those fritas! It just isn't worth it!" Her gaze fell on a book and she hurled it in the corner.

Jorge had remained motionless, watching her in silence. Now he walked towards her. His voice, emerging from the cool shadows, was soft and deep and tranquil. "Hello, my darling." He did not touch her. His voice impelled her to face him. She turned slowly, involuntarily. In the penumbra she could discern only the whiteness of his smile, the gentle hands, and the pinpoint of light in his eyes, so bright to be in this darkness! As she turned, he laughed softly, "I've had the electric fan fixed for you, and there's a good breeze from the persianas, too."

She looked sarcastically towards the thin trickle of air stringing through the shutters.

"Well, maybe it is not exactly a 'breeze,' but it's air!" he added with indulgent amusement. Offering her a chair upon which she sat resentfully, he adjusted the fan, so that it would not blow on her too directly, and wiped her face with a handkerchief he had dipped in cold water. "Poor little one," he smiled soothingly, "my kitten that thinks itself a raging lion!"

Her agitation subsided with the stroking of his voice and the cool refuge of the shadows. But her decision was unaltered. She would have a drink with him and then tell him.

"Are you more comfortable now?" he asked after a while. "Yes," she acknowledged grudgingly.

"That's good. Now I want you to go over and pick up that book you threw." His words elicited a provoked smile.

"Do as I say, Lourdes."

The voice gentle; here was no need for assertion that betrayed insecurity; she belonged to him, in a belonging of which the body, the flesh, was but a poor inadequate instrument. All that she had suffered that day, the anger and the indignities became, as always, insignificant. How little a price to pay for that which had been given her! What is it to be a woman? That the alchemy of one voice alone can dissolve the brittle rage into life-fluid!

She rose and recovered the book from the floor. "I'm sorry," she whispered, and with her back to him walked slowly to the shuttered window. Her skin glowed dimly under the black chiffon dress. She could feel her body trembling. Each second seemed an hour. Suddenly, for he had come so silently, she felt his lips on her neck. His dark head as he bent slightly over her was the only reality in life. She could scarcely stand for the faintness drifting through the black ocean, praying he would not face her, for to look into his eyes would be dread and ecstasy unbearable. With calm fingers he unbuttoned her blouse. His mouth slowly fluttered over her shoulders and her back...in her ears...she felt his firm hands on her cool quivering waist as he turned her to him, and put his mouth to hers...warm wine mingling with the roots of the earth... descent, descent, all her being pinioned to the heart of the earth...

§

The little candles sputtered on the table before they extinguished. Lourdes, whose head had been resting on Jorge's chest, raised herself slightly.

"What's that?"

"Candles. And flowers, red ones. And a bottle of wine, that is now warm."

She sat up mystified and looked towards the drawing room. "Who put them there?"

"I."

"No bodega rum today?

"No," he teased

"This is April; it has no particular date for us," she protested. "Have 1 forgotten something?"

"No, but it's a celebration," he smiled. "Quite a celebration."

"Stop teasing! Tell me why!"

He merely looked at her in response. They both laughed. Then taking her hands in his, a deep joy filled his eyes." My darling, my darling! I can't keep it from you any longer! If you only knew how 1 had been waiting, bursting to tell you, two wonderful things to tell you..."

16
CARAMBITA

Carambita's eyes were two shining beetles moving on his face. He had led the junk man directly to a clump of bushes which he parted, revealing a bronze sundial with a marble base and an adjacent marble bench.

"Didn't I tell you!" he whispered excitedly, and kicked the bench to prove how solid it was.

The junk dealer nodded. "What else?"

"There are about four more of these benches. Then there's a fancy bird-bath over here." In his eagerness, Carambita took a quick backward step, forgetting the bushes and fell into them headlong.

"Ha ha!" the other man laughed, giving him a hand.

"Shhh!" Carambita warned as he scrambled up and looked around them cautiously.

"Thought you said none of 'em was around!"

"That's right. But you never know when one of 'em's gonna crawl out from the bark of a tree!"

"Ha ha!" laughed the junk man again loudly.

"Shhh!" pleaded Carambita. "Wanna see the others?"

"What else is there besides the wrought iron and this heavy garden stuff?"

"There's plenty."

"Want to see what's in the house." He made a step towards it, but Carambita pulled him back.

"Wait a minute, viejo," he whined, "'lemme see if it's OK."

"We've got to hurry up," the man whispered impatiently. "That article in the newspaper says the company's going to begin work right away. They always have their own dealers. But if I can go right away and make a deal with them for the little stuff, it's okay. Otherwise I haven't got a chance."

"And me, too—" Carambita reminded him. "Don't forget my part."

"No, I won't forget your part. If I ever saw a bastard that looked like he'd never do a favor without getting something for it, you're it," he commented.

Carambita grinned as though proud of this truth.

"Well let's go!" resumed the junk man, but Carambita plucked at his sleeve.

"Wait just a minute!"

Hiding back of an almond tree, he squinted over the sea rocks and made sure Arsenio was still out there picking mussels. He knew the others were never around at this hour, and he'd seen the Marquesa up in that looney tower of hers. She didn't much matter, and anyway they could always hear her in time if she came down.

"Vamos!" he waved.

"Christ! I think you're scared stiff of them," the junk man remarked, amused, as they walked cautiously to the house.

"Me scared of them? They ought to be scrapped with the rest of the junk! Naw, I just don't want them to see us and waste our time. Here, just step over this, and we'll go look at those painted tiles and things in the hall."

They had not been there more than a few minutes when the sound of a policeman's club thumping on something quite near them caused Carambita to grow pale. That all too hollow sound! His unusually long dirty fingernails—no doubt convenient instruments for his particular profession—unfortunately had succeeded in prying loose several painted tiles from a center panel. He nervously attempted replacing them.

"How did the police know l was here!" he panted.

"But you aren't doing anything!" protested the junk dealer, surprised at his terror.

"There are a few other things." Carambita started towards the paneless window of the dining room, but he saw Arsenio approaching in that direction. Thump, thump, sounded the club, and before Carambita could dispose of himself or the tiles, Mateo the policeman entered, followed by a corpulent perspiring man.

"Well, why didn't you answer?" asked Mateo, not unfriendly.

Carambita was quick to perceive that. "I was just making a visit," he tried to smile jauntily, "me and my friend here, to see the Old One. Was just tryin' to put these things back for her when I heard you. They must've dropped out." Since Mateo hadn't come for him, he could have left on

134

some pretext before the others saw him, but he remained out of curiosity. For once the law was a friend! Nothing much that black devil or the old cabron could do to him with the policeman here.

"Hola! Hola! Anyone here?" shouted Mateo up the stairs. They heard the Marquesa descending from the tower. He inspected a few of the steps and returned to them, shaking his head in wonder. "Beats me how she hasn't fallen all the way through. I wouldn't set foot on one of them."

"Now would you please go out there and pull in the rest of 'em?" asked the fat man. "I'd go, but like I said, they won't pay any attention to me."

"Here comes one now."

"I know, but get the others. One's got the shack out there near the rocks, and the Chinaman—"

"—and the mole livin' underground." There was more eagerness than cooperation in Carambita's voice.

"You're kiddin'! Underground?"

"That's what I said. I've been in it. Christ, you oughta see it! Got three rooms down there, all wall plastered. Old pictures hangin' up on the walls, and flowers, and stuff he carves, a whole wall full of it."

Mateo went out to round them up.

"Any good?" asked the junk-dealer.

"He's got a crucifix there," Carambita's eyes looked meaningfully at his temporary associate. "Could get plenty for it."

"Yes?"

"Yeah, but he wouldn't sell. Gives it all away, the bastard." He was remembering a long time ago that Topo had caught him selling one of those carvings he'd given him. He never let him in that mole hole of his again.

When Chori came straggling in after Mateo, he stopped suddenly upon seeing Carambita. The muscle of his arm instinctively flexed. "What you doing here!" he menaced. Carambita stepped back as if to run, and then remembered Mateo's presence, "Just came to pay you a visit."

"Bring a present to the Old One, eh?" Arsenio looked calmly at the tiles in Carambita's hand.

"Why, you!" Chori took a step towards him, policeman or not. With guilt plainly visible on Carambita's face, Mateo became interested. "I found them on the floor. Was just putting them back," Carambita whined.

The Marquesa intervened. "Of course, of course," she said comfortingly as though speaking to a child, and took the tiles from him. She turned to Mateo. "He's not bad really, you know. He's just never been able to find himself, officer."

"Thank God for that!" mumbled Chori. Arsenio, arms folded, leaned against the wall, his yellowed eyeballs looking up from under the shaggy eyebrows. He had the patient half-smile of one who knows that this is not the moment. But it would come later.

"This is getting me nowhere, and I'm way behind. Been held up by those damn Holy Thursday crowds," the fat man protested.

With a sudden stiffening they turned towards him. They had not noticed him until then.

"OK, OK, take it easy," Mateo the policeman said.

He tipped back his officer's hat, not to look too serious, and coughed before he began to speak. This wasn't the kind of audience he liked. In the bodega it was different. Fellows drinking beer, arguing, playing cubilete, bragging about their conquests with women (mostly invented), listening to their own voices talking politics, with them it felt real good to walk in with boots, revolver, and club easy-like and feel their admiring glances as he had a beer and invented things too. But with these people here, it just wasn't fun to be important. Wouldn't matter to them.

"Now, this is not police business," he began. "I'm here just to try to help all concerned. Mr. Díaz, who's trying to do his job, says that you won't pay attention to him."

"Forgive me, officer, but we have already discussed this with him. I think there is nothing else to say, isn't that so?" Marquesa turned graciously to her companions. They looked at each other, and in the silence, Topo nodded his head in answer.

"Me cago!" Díaz cursed. "Here we go again!"

"Calma," Mateo admonished. He didn't like this sweating pig too much. "Now listen. This man works for a company. I know it's tough on you people, but in a few days they're going to come. Big machines." with sweeping gestures he drew one in the air for them. "Know what bulldozers are? Ever see a war movie with tanks—fffffssssdh!" he pantomimed a tank in action.

"Chori work consluction," Chan Li's little voice was indignant. "We all know bulldoze "

"Ok, chino. You work in Public Works?" he addressed Chori.

"Yessir. "

"Then what the hell! Oh sorry, ma'am, why don't you tell your pals that a couple of bulldozers are going to knock this place to hell before they could even pick up their belongings! Trees, house, everything! This is their last chance to get the money. How much is. it?"

"$150 apiece," Díaz said.

Mateo whistled, and a vein stood out like a cord on Carambita's forehead.

"That's a real decent company, hear that, you people? Lots of outfits just throw you bird-seed. They're giving you $150 bucks!"

"You don't understand. That would be very nice of them if the property were theirs. But it isn't. And we are not leaving. It belongs to me." The old woman spoke calmly, and with such conviction that Mateo could almost believe her.

"See what I mean!" Díaz, exasperated, rolled the soiled handkerchief which he always had in his hand. "First time I came here she told me all that rigamarole and I've come two times since then and they just don't bother. Think she's the only one batty? Just listen to the others. Go on!"

Mateo turned to the others. "You don't believe what she's saying, do you?"

No one spoke. He felt himself surrounded by the silence of those eyes that looked through him. Carambita might have joined Díaz's sudden derogatory snicker except that he couldn't really enjoy all this because the thought of all the money they were going to lose gave him a belly-ache. If that money went back to the company, it wouldn't give him, Carambita, even a chance to get near it!

"Do you?" Mateo repeated, incredulous. They remained silent. Turning his back to the Marquesa, he beckoned Arsenio, Topo, Chan Li, and Chori to one side, "Listen," he said in a low voice, "it can't be like that fellow says, that you're all touched in the head as the old lady! You know the poor old thing is imagining that story of hers. You're all going to find yourselves without a place to lie down in a few days. But if you have that money, you can get along. Bet none of you ever saw more than ten pesos at one time in your life, eh?" No one answered, but he saw Chori swallow hard. "This is no joke. Today's your last chance. And if you're a friend of hers, you ought to make her understand too instead of going along with her screwy talk. Or she'll be out in the street.

Well...?" he waited.

Silence. Then Chan Li said, "She leave here, she die."

"She don't have to leave here. She's got papers to prove it," Arsenio added.

Mateo raised his hands in a hopeless gesture and was ready to quit. But he tried once more. "If that was true, don't you think it's funny no one ever saw them? If she had any kind of document, which is impossible, of course, where would a pobre loca like her get any documents! But just supposing she did, don't you think she would have shown them to—"

Chori interrupted. "Three times that fat tub came, she asked him to get a lawyer. He just laughed."

Mateo groaned and turned to the old woman, "Where are those papers you're talking about?"

"They're right here, up in the tower, where I keep all my personal things."

Arsenio did not miss Carambita's glance that roved toward the stairs.

"Suffering Christ! Is this catching?" gasped Díaz. "I asked you to help me and instead you're startin' to talk about those darned papers too! I've had enough! And with this holiday, I'm way behind! People with nothin' to do but fill the buses goin' from one church to the other," he grumbled. "I'm goin'. You gonna take the money and carry that trash outta here or not?"

"You watch your tongue," the Marquesa spoke sharply as she drew herself straighter than ever. "We are not leaving. And I demand that your company read these documents."

"All right," he smiled to call her bluff, "just go up and get them. I'll wait."

"Certainly not. You have no authority. You communicate to the company that someone authorized come, and I'll give them to him immediately."

"Mal rayo!" he cursed as he stamped with Mateo "Didn't I tell you?" "You'll have to tell your boss."

"Damn right I'm goin' to tell him! Crazy bastards! Anyway, that settles that. This is the last time I come out here. Where's a phone around here?"

At the bodega. After you call, I'll invite you to a beer."

Mateo didn't like the fat pig, but he couldn't help feeling sorry for him, so worked up and sweating.

§

"Can't he give you the message? I'm busy now," Baldomero Saenz smiled blatantly at Guzman Senior and Mario as he spoke through the intercom to his secretary. "All right, all right, put him on." He shrugged in good-natured boredom. "One of the office boys, Díaz, she says, is all worked up. Something about trouble with squatters. Excuse me," he commented to them as he picked up the phone. "What's the matter, Díaz? Sí...aha...aha..." As he listened, he took off the lid of the humidor and offered Mario and his father a cigar. He looked amused, "Calm down, man, you're talking so loud I can't make out what you're saying."

They could hear the man's voice from where they sat. It sounded like an excited mouse in the desk drawer. "They won't! Well, if they're such fools, that's their look-out! Nothing we can do about it." Mario lit his cigar for him. "Documents! That's a good one!" The row of huge teeth drew a smile across his face, which suddenly changed to an impatient scowl. "Ridiculous! Tell them they'd better take the money while they can and get their belongings out. We have no time to waste on a couple of muertos de hambre! As it is, you're late. Jimenez wants all those back catalogues and samples to be filed. What? All right, all right, don't waste any more time now!" he ordered, and turned in disgust to Guzman Senior. "Sorry to keep you waiting. Half-wit old squatters giving him trouble. They claim they have documents proving the place belongs to them; that's a new angle! And they

138

want someone 'authorized,' nothing less, to go there and read them!" He spoke into the phone again angrily, "You tell them they'd better—"

"Baldomero!" Guzman gestured to him, "It's always preferable to avoid unpleasant incidents, especially now. Evidently, they're mental cases. Don't you think it would be better to humor them and—"

"All right," Saenz nodded to Guzman, adding. "But I wonder that they're allowed to roam around loose, eh?" Then he instructed curtly into the receiver, "Listen, Díaz, tell them someone will go by there and read their documents. The demolition crew can start afterwards, provided all is in order." He hung up but continued the conversation, addressing it to Mario and his father. "Within a week there won't be a stone left standing of that old eyesore! Well!" His chair swirled the great smile towards the Guzmans, completely dedicated to them. "Where were we? Ah, yes!" He sprang from his chair. "If you both would like to step into the other room where I've set up the work schedules. Shall we?"

He opened the door for them. Mario rose but his father remained seated.

"Coming Papá?"

His father did not answer but seemed struck by some thought that had just occurred to him.

"Arturo?" Saenz called.

Realizing the two men were staring at him, he said suddenly, "Baldomero, you and Mario can go over the preliminaries without me. I hadn't realized the time, and there are some urgent matters at my office. Since we're meeting tomorrow—"

"Fine. Let's see...I'll be going to church with the family at noon, how about my house at five?"

"Muy bien," Guzman answered absently.

"Five o'clock all right with you, Mario?"

"Yes, I'll be free then. Lourdes takes the day rather seriously. She always goes to the procession." Perplexed, he was still observing his father.

"So much the better," laughed Saenz. "Oh, with all due respect to our ladies, of course! But we can work much better uninterrupted. My family will be at the Club at that hour." As they began to walk out, he smiled brightly and clapped a large hand on Mario's back. But something about his father's behavior prompted Mario to ask before he left, "Is there anything the matter, Papá?" Perhaps it was the new olive brown suit that made his father look so pale.

"Eh?" he murmured absently to Mario's question, "Why no, not at all." Not a stone left standing.

Arturo Guzman had never believed it would really happen.

17
LEANDRO CAMACHO

When he was sure Mario and Saenz were in the other office, Guzman quickly left. He wanted to be undisturbed. His chauffeur was waiting, and they drove down the Malecón towards his office in the old section.

For years he had taken this same route without being aware of it, but his present thoughts caused him to note that they were passing the very spot where his father had taken him, a boy of ten, to witness the lowering of the American flag of the Intervention. He had seen the American occupational forces set sail, and the Solitary Star of Cuba—flown, solitary at last—over the Republic which had waited three years since its birth to be invested with the rightful dignity of autonomy. It was only natural that his generation, growing under the sun of those first stirring years of hope, inspired by the still fresh accounts of heroism, would retain its illusions unmarred by the reality of humiliating disasters that had already led to a second United States intervention lasting for two years.

Guided by the noble teachings of the great educator, Enrique José Varona, Arturo had plunged into youth activities with all the blind ardor of inexperience. His father, struggling to remake the fortune which had been sacrificed to the Independence, had audaciously risked their only remaining funds to invest in the land boom following the stabilization of the Cuban Republic. Descendant of a highborn Spanish family, Arturo's father had inherited his former estate and was untutored in business. But armed with Asturian shrewdness, he had learned as quickly as the foreign private investors who were invading the country in steadily increasing numbers, casting covetous eyes on the vision of sugar plantations rising from charred, uncultivated lands. The land boom was temporarily checked by the Second Intervention of 1905, but resumed three years later with the re-stabilization of the Cuban government. At this time, having made a considerable profit, Arturo's father decided to limit his interests to the development of the residential sections on the outskirts of the old Havana which was expanding rapidly. His affairs prospered.

Although eager for his son to join him, he did not press him. He regarded Arturo's patriotic activities with compassionate indulgence. Only too soon would reality undeceive him! Moreover, youth's exaggerated idealism was a wholesome manner of sowing wild oats. He waited.

By the time Arturo was nineteen, his father had subtly guided him into the business without placing too much limitation on his other interests. And, strangely enough, it was a business negotiation which occasioned an interview with one of Arturo's childhood heroes of the Revolution.

His father had said with an unaccountable twinkle his eyes, "There's a man who has returned to Cuba to liquidate a number of investments he has held during the years he has spent abroad. One of them—some land of considerable size—was practically worthless until recently. But the fellow has had a lucky break. Now that everyone is leaving the Cerro and Vibora for the Vedado, his land is worth a small fortune. I thought you just might be interested in dealing with him yourself."

Young Arturo wondered why.

His father cleared his throat and slyly added, "His name is Leandro Camacho."

In spite of his nineteen worldly-wise years, Arturo gulped. He could not believe it! He had never identified Camacho with the practical world. In fact, it was a shock to realize that he existed at all except in the legends of his revolutionary exploits. If he was a man of flesh and blood, where had he been all these years? With nervousness combined with a fear of disillusionment he hurried to their luncheon appointment at the Hotel Inglaterra, but he need not have worried. The man was captivating.

When he rose to greet Arturo, people in the lobby instinctively turned to watch this figure of towering proportions and ample gesture, rugged features, and leonine head. Arturo half expected that at any moment he would burst from the subdued tones and conservative dress into the irrepressible giant of defiance and energy which had marked the legends concerning him. But as they continued talking, and Arturo had recovered sufficiently to observe his companion, he realized that the inner spark which he had expected to emanate from the grey eyes was missing. On the contrary, there was an indefinable quality of meditation which had led to weariness. When Arturo, no longer able to contain the impulse, impetuously confessed his admiration of Camacho, the man had not seemed pleased, but frowned and remarked, "Such idealization can only belong to those who were cut down in their greatest moment of truth. Martí, Maceo, only they remain pure for eternity. Somewhat like Keats', 'All, happy, happy, boughs! that cannot shed our leaves, nor ever bid the spring adieu!' Do you know this poem?"

"No, I don't. But although if I did know it, I'm sure I would still protest at your excessive modesty."

Camacho's frown deepened, and Arturo hastened to a more impersonal terrain. "Surely you will agree that there is one hero very much alive and who is going to accomplish wonderful things for Cuba." His enthusiasm caused him suddenly to break out of his formal manner to exclaim boyishly, "Wasn't it great that Menocal was elected?"

"We will see..." Camacho answered blandly.

"Why, I would think you would be more overjoyed than any of us! You knew him personally. Fought under him at his great Victory of Las Tunas. And since that time his record of honesty and patriotism has been spotless. Certainly he is recognized not only by all of us Cubans but by the United States as well as our natural leader!"

"I don't deny any of this," Camacho assented, unmoved. "But all men change. One can only hope that he may prove to be the exception. For your sake," he added, with a trace of compassion, "for you, who can still believe."

Camacho's remoteness disarmed him. He had hurried to the meeting as one who hastens to renew an old friendship only to discover that it was a delusion. The man did not know him at all! Like the reader of a biography, he had foolishly assumed that his feeling of possessive familiarity with the subject was reciprocated.

He had wanted to blurt out, "Don't you know that we are old friends? What has happened to you? Where have you departed from yourself?" Embarrassed, he trespassed no further, but guided the conversation to superficialities, and the business matters which had brought them together. Camacho intended remaining in Cuba only as long as his affairs necessitated. He had not "returned" at all, as Arturo had imagined. In fact, a casual tourist could not have been less concerned over national affairs. They parted with the understanding that Arturo would contact him if there were any developments regarding the sale of his property.

Left alone, Arturo felt foolish, indignant, and betrayed, not by Camacho, but by the world. What had they done to this man? Why had he so changed?

After gathering whatever information he could, he soon began partially to understand. In every controversial issue during the early years of the Republic, he had been active and had given evidence of a man who refused to temporize, who had fought first with ardor, then determination, and

142

finally with a stubborn tenacity that eventually alienated the very men who fundamentally agreed with him. There was a revealing little announcement in the newspapers, the last one mentioning his name: "Carmen Aguirre, wife of Leandro Camacho, accompanied by their children, was moving permanently to Manzanillo, Oriente Province." He had lost his family as well!

The issues involved gave Arturo Guzman much to ponder. Certainly Camacho had not always been right. His stand at times seemed impractical, straining often towards the unattainable. Wasn't it sometimes wiser to temporize and be prudent for the sake of the ultimate goal? Martí himself had never striven for the impossible. But then, much that Martí achieved had seemed impossible to others! Perhaps it had been the same with Camacho. This was something young Guzman would have to think about, but later. What interested him at the moment was that he considered himself a match for Camacho in one sense: obstinacy. His faith in him had not been touched, and he was almost obsessed with the desire to revive the lost hope of this man!

Using business matters as a pretext, he managed to see Camacho several times, and was rewarded by discovering a mutual interest in theater. Nothing could have been more propitious. Havana, prospering under Menocal, had become a glamorous host to world-renowned theatrical companies, ballet, zarzuela, and opera. Nightly audiences packed the theaters which were focal points of a dazzling society. Arturo Guzman and Leandro Camacho became part of it. Responsive to the environment and his young companion's enthusiasm, Camacho was expansive. His store of tales gathered from his wanderings in Europe and the Orient was endless, and his observations delightful.

However, any attempt Arturo made to interest Leandro in national issues met with failure. At most he would listen, indulgent but silent. And when the corruption of Menocal's administration could no longer be concealed, Leandro's eyes seemed to say, "Do you see, now?" More than bitterness, they reflected sorrow for his young friend's disenchantment. But Arturo, far from despairing, Arturo, like his contemporaries, thought only with impatience of combating the evil.

It was then that Leandro had received the delayed letter from the Canary Islands, advising him of the arrival of his recently orphaned cousin, Antonia Monte de Oca. He was her only surviving relative, the letter informed him, and it had been her father's last wish that she seek Leandro's help to begin a new life in Cuba. Arturo never forgot the day Antonia arrived at the Havana docks. The vision of that young woman in the outmoded clothes of the Canary Islands touched him as she marched down the plank, erect and with definite intrepid step, straight into a new world with the matter-of-factness of a teacher entering a new classroom. Her uninhibited gestures and natural bloom contrasted curiously with the olive-skinned, assiduously groomed and perfumed Cuban women. It was not long before he discovered how deceptive was that amusing air of sobriety, for in the weeks that followed as, two cicerones, he and Leandro, showed her Havana, she revealed a gay imaginative flair that was captivating.

And then a memorable day arrived which had a lasting effect on their lives. The three had made plans to drive to the countryside which Antonia had not yet seen. At the last moment Arturo was unable to accompany them, but had agreed to meet them later. He never learned what had happened, but a startling change in Leandro had been affected. He had decided not to sell his property in the Vedado, and he was going to build a house the likes of which had never been seen in Havana. For its style would be subject neither to prudence nor to fashion, but to the dictates of a free spirit.

As Arturo stared openmouthed, observing the longed-for change in his friend, Leandro impetuously embraced him and exclaimed, "Yes, I know what you are thinking. I look the way you have wanted me to ever since we met, because I feel that way! Mi querido Arturo, do you see how all your patience has not been in vain? Another would have given me up long ago! But not you, and now the disagreeable old man has rejuvenated. You are right, of course. We must all work for the redemption of Cuba." He laughed at Arturo, who looked confounded but hopeful. "Yes, I've come back to work with you; and with this Antonia, this Canary Islander who looks so demure and has such a terrible temper, and the will of a mountain-goat! She is going to work with us, too. And I'm going to Oriente to see my wife and ask her to return with my sons. It is time I made up to them for the lost years! Oh, I yearn for my own sons to be a part of the movement. Well," he continued, "I am going to begin on the plans of the house at once."

Unable to digest all this so quickly, Arturo could only ask, "What architect are you going to have?"

"Architect? Why, no one. Myself."

"Leandro! You're not an architect."

"I am now!" Arturo had shaken his head, delighted and still overwhelmed by it all.

§

But many years had passed since anything had succeeded in overwhelming Arturo Guzman. Until today.

The car reached the Guzman Building, and as his chauffeur opened the door for him, he hoped his unsteadiness would not be noticed. He felt almost desperate to be alone. Fortunately, today being Holy Thursday, no-one would be working.

In closing his office door, he was shocked to observe that his hand, usually nerveless, trembled as it rested on the doorknob. With what effort he had concealed his confusion when first his sons had marched in with the announcement "The Camacho deal has gone through!" If they had known what their words had affected! And now, today, Baldomero talking about the demolition crew leaving "not a stone." Guzman had simply not expected it to happen, not after all these years of waiting. It was his now, the house that had been Leandro's and, in a way, Antonia's. He closed his eyes for a moment, and thought of nothing at all, a spectator impassively observing the reactions of another person. Emotion—this feverish, involuntary response of cells, glands, bloodstream—was indeed a stranger to him, and he did not know how to cope with it. For the first time in many years, he was not master of himself. Leaning against the door, his nostrils pinched as he breathed with difficulty, he could only stand bewildered and helpless as this thing took possession of him.

Finally, he managed to cross to his desk, and the usually agile figure dropped heavily now into the chair. His glance absently focused on the familiar letter-opener which he used daily. It had never occurred to him to remember where it had come from, for it was like so many objects that from long use lose their identity. But now, with amazement, he slowly picked it up. Of course! Antonia had given him this. But when? He had disposed of everything pertaining to her, but had probably withheld this for which he had a particular liking until with time he had forgotten. It was difficult to try to remember. Memory's function had become atrophied from long, deliberate disuse. As he stared at the old object suddenly new, it came back to him because of the griffin head on the handle. And then he did not want to remember, for a world which he had successfully buried became alive; and most unpleasant of all, the layer of being which was himself had been brutally uncovered. He struggled to close it over again, and it exasperated him that the instrument of his will which he had perfected through the years would not now obey him.

That griffin head....

§

It was the occasion of Leandro's birthday. The three of them had been seated on the cement bags which were being used for the construction, just begun, of Leandro's house. His enthusiasm had been such that they had been unable to take Leandro from it long enough for a birthday celebration. So they had brought the celebration to him. They were decorating an improvised picnic table of wood planks set on a tree stump when a huge wave, crashing against the nearby shore, interrupted them. As they paused to admire its explosion high in the air, Antonia suddenly ran to snatch some packages from the spray which the wind flung towards them.

"Why, I'd almost forgotten!" she exclaimed breathlessly as she returned to them. "Here's a present for you, and one for you, too!" She laughingly faced Arturo as she waved the two small boxes.

"But why for me?" he exclaimed.

"When I was looking for something for Leandro, I came across this. It reminded me so much of you. You will see."

"If it's like him, I'm afraid to look at it!" Leandro joked in pretended horror.

"But why don't you save it for my birthday?" Guzman protested.

"Vaya! Listen to the dreamer becoming practical! Wanting reasons!" Leandro scoffed.

"Look who is talking about dreamers!" Antonia shook her dark head in mock gravity. "Really, between the two of you!" They smiled. "And you want a reason? Muy bien." She stood stiffly at attention, cleared her throat and formally pronounced, "Señor Guzman, I present you with this gift because true friendship is the greatest gift of all, and should be remembered on a friend's birthday." She relaxed her pose, and her clear green eyes looked fondly at them both, the towering, rugged-featured Leandro, whose face was marked and strengthened with lines of suffering, and the yet unlined face of the young Arturo, who adored him.

The broken rays of the sun held the three friends in a net of warm silence. "You have worked together so intensely for something you have believed in," she added softly.

"And you too, Antonia," Guzman reminded her. "You know, it is difficult for me to remember that you are not Cuban. If it were not for those odd expressions you use sometimes of the 'Guanches'" he teased, "and that little song in your speech."

"I know. I cannot imagine that I arrived such a short time ago. But I am Cuban now. This is my land."

"No Cuban woman has worked more for our country in so short a time," Leandro said.

"Being around you, what else could one do?" she retorted. "Do you know, I was only a little girl when I heard about my great patriot cousin who was fighting like a tiger!" She sat down as she spoke and demurely smoothed her skirt, but her eyes were shone brilliantly. That was the fascinating thing about Antonia. She was all warmth and life, yet her gestures were moderate and smooth, as though no passing outer element could interrupt her fluid serenity. She had startled them both today by appearing in the typical costume of the Canaries, with her eight skirts and white linen cap that sat so adorably on her black hair. She was always unpredictable in that sober little way of hers.

Now she was primly smoothing her skirt as her voice and eyes continued animatedly. "I have two memories of childhood about the Cuban war with us. You know that although my father was Spanish, he was in sympathy with the Cuban struggle for freedom. I don't know how he managed to receive Cuban newspapers there in the Canary Islands. Probably through one of the ship captains he knew so well. I remember I was trying to milk a goat on the mountain, when Papá came hurrying excitedly to me with a newspaper. He motioned to me to hide behind the rocks, and with such pride read me one of the great battles and showed me the name of my cousin Leandro, one of the youngest and bravest of all! It said that his daring was becoming legendary.

Then Papá put his finger to his lips and whispered, "Don't tell anyone about this, not even your mother. You know how they all feel about it." I was so proud! And of course I loved my secret with Papá."

Arturo exclaimed, "Why, that's also one of my first childhood memories! Leandro Camacho was one of my greatest heroes! And he still is," he added in a low voice so that Leandro would not hear.

Leandro, with mock indignation, thumped down the Spanish sidra he had begun to unwrap. "I must say, this is a fine way to celebrate my birthday, recounting your babyhood memories of me."

"Of course you're an old man, didn't you know? Thirty-five years today!" Antonia teased.

"Well, never mind telling your other story, because I'm going to feel too feeble to work anymore."

"Listen to him!". She pressed her lips together so severely that one would think she was in earnest. "He thinks all our stories are about him! I said about Cuba, not about you!"

"Well, all right then proceed," he said, and picked up the champagne bottle again.

"I can remember so clearly," she continued. "I was about seven. Mother was angry because I had not worn my dress of eight petticoats, like this one, for the visitors. She complained, 'What curse has the Blessed Virgin not protected me from! To have the only daughter in all the five islands of the Canaries who is not proud and happy for an excuse to wear her feast-day dress.' And she called my mountain clothes savagery. My father covertly approved of me by the twinkling of his eyes as he filled his pipe, and his expression, which was quite serious, always accentuated those fluttering lashes of his at such conspiratorial moments.

"Then the Spanish captain had arrived, and after him the English colonist bringing the news of the transfer of power in Cuba from Spain to the United States. Everything became so silent that I could hear my donkey, Rosario's, little bells tinkling from the tamarind tree where she was tied, and the crinkling of the papers as they were passed around the table. That was the first time I had ever seen a man cry. I was so impressed as I watched those tears rolling without shame down the captain's cheeks. Through the dimmed eyes he kept staring at one newspaper photograph in particular. It was the procession of men passing through the gate of the Plaza de Armas in Havana, before the Governor-General's Palace. He looked up, suddenly meeting my childish, awe-stricken stare. I think no one's eyes can absorb another's pain as a child's can. He felt that, and beckoned me to him. 'Look well, little one,' he. said with a choking voice. 'Do you see this Palace?'

"I nodded, too awed to dare speak.

"'For four hundred years this has been the home of our country's rulers in Cuba. For as many years we have discovered new lands, conquered, ruled, created civilizations from jungle, made known to all men the wisdom and culture of East and West, and carried at least the seeds of Christ's love to unknowing hearts.1f we erred many times, the good we accomplished should not be forgotten. And now...this is the end...'

It was very sad, and I was about to cry, but the captain blew his large nose just then, such a glorious, foggy blow that it reminded me of the mighty conch-horns of King Neptune." She interrupted her story to add, "My father had made me one. I'll show it to you sometime. I brought it with me."

"So that is where you get your love of mythology!" Arturo interrupted.

"Oh yes. You know, Leandro, Arturo always teases me about that. But you see, my father was an avid student of mythology, and as he grew older, I think he lived more in that ancient world than in this one. And he raised me too in that world. Oh, how I loved those early days spent high up in the mountains with him, as he would tell me about our own Canary Islands which the Greeks called 'the Blessed Isles.'

"Anyway," she continued, "the captain's nose-blowing was so startling that I forgot to cry. And with everyone but me so sad that no one seemed to breathe, suddenly, with a small voice, my father whispered in my ear, 'Viva Cuba!' Oh, how difficult it was to keep from laughing! I had to swallow very hard."

The little story had been amusing but impressive. Antonia rose to help Arturo empty the baskets of food and wine they had brought. Then Leandro broke the silence. They did not know whether his voice, resonant with mixed feelings, was sarcastic or not.

"Very touching," he said, "The death knell of the Spanish empire. I was there that day, in official capacity," he smiled drily. "The transfer of power was at noon. The American forces slowly began to occupy the city from Colón to the Alameda de Paula. The people cheered General Lee's division as they took their places from San Lazaro all the way to the Punta. I was part of the Cuban commission which accompanied Commanding General

Brooke and the other generals. A little before twelve we entered the Throne Room of the Governor General's palace. I remember the pallor of the Spanish General as he and his staff prepared the last details. And as the bells began to toll twelve o'clock, the Spanish forces marched to the dock, where the ships were waiting to return them to Spain. They moved as swiftly as possible, so as not to prolong the unendurable scene. All the populace, of course, was aware of the terrible solemnity of the moment. In the Throne Room, General Castellanos faced General Brooke and officially relinquished the sovereignty of Spain. And after a farewell message from Brooke, the Spanish officers and all the remaining forces boarded ship. The last Spanish station before leaving fired a twenty-one-gun salute, and as the last shot was fired, the Spanish flag dropped as though it had been hit. And the Spanish Armada was lost on the horizon."

Antonia and Arturo had stood spellbound listening to his description, but they were surprised to notice the sudden bitterness in his voice as he continued. "And then, reality. Oh, there was great rejoicing! But your weeping captain did not know what else was taking place in the hearts of a people who had fought for fifty years, who were looking at their devastated lands, where not one crop, nor one stalk of sugar cane, nor one head of cattle broke the desolate monotony of ruins. Where starving ragged specters wandered over the countryside looking for roots and grain to devour raw. Where the very birds perished of hunger. Those people not only had to celebrate their victory by flying another foreign flag, but, worse still, our psychological victory had been taken from us! Do you know, Antonia, that Cuba was not represented at the Peace Treaty in Paris? It was made between. the United States and Spain. Not one of our statesman or generals was invited. The Americans had helped us give the death blow to what we had almost achieved alone, and then excluded us from the treaty of our own armistice! And after all those tense years of sacrifice, we did not have the release of even the most childish but understandable satisfaction of knowing that there were headlines throughout the world reading "Cuban Victory," or "Spirit of Martí Victorious!" Nor even of seeing one Cuban general photographed, seated in an elegant chair in Paris at the Treaty. The pent-up emotions of a people and their dignity need these compensations. We were forgotten in our own country. Our army was disbanded to give way to the Americans until, frustrated and confused, we were finally permitted to have our own Constitution, but only if we would accept the Platt Amendment. We were victors without victory, begging. What alternative had we?"

"But Leandro!" Arturo protested, shocked. "Surely you don't deny what the Americans did for us!"

"No, no; no-one can deny that," Leandro laughed harshly. "They give, but isn't it strange that they always manage to get even more?"

Antonia and Arturo were alarmed at the mood which seized him. "I thought you were not going to live in the past!" Antonia reminded him.

"Is the present any different? What has changed in the thirteen years since our independence? Is graft less? Elections more honest? Has the United States' tutelage taught us democracy, or rather the special vices which can flourish as weeds in democratic soil?"

"Well," Antonia's voice was sharply matter of fact, but it carried a strident quality which betrayed pain. "Evidently it is all quite hopeless, and frankly I see no reason for us or anyone else to continue struggling for what can only end in frustration. Don't you agree, Arturo?" She walked stiffly toward her place at the table and picked up the champagne bottle, ready to uncork, as she said, "And now, shall we get on with our 'celebration'?"

"Don't!" Leandro exclaimed angrily and he turned and strode toward the large rocks on the shore.

Arturo had been appalled at Antonia's attitude. When he would have spoken, she shook her head to silence him. They waited. After a short time, they saw Leandro return.

Even from a distance the sight of the swift agile figure climbing over the rocks told them that it was all right.

"Forgive me." He took Antonia's hand in his and raised it to his lips. "Of course she is right," he said to Arturo. "She knows that 1 would not be building this house if she had not helped me to understand..."

Arturo was puzzled at this reference, but he exclaimed proudly, "And she must not minimize what she has accomplished. It has been much!"

"Enough to inspire hundreds of young people," Leandro acknowledged.

"What a pity, though, that they can't yet put into practice what they are learning."

"Why not, Arturo? Why not?" Leandro impatiently interrupted, "The future is made now. Isn't that what we've just agreed? As the sapling grows, so grows the tree. Isn't that why Antonia is teaching her classes the power of strength and freedom that is in their hands? Isn't that why we're fighting to break Menocal's dictatorship?"

"But Leandro," Arturo demurred, "this is the first time Cuba is prospering. You must remember that human nature needs time."

"Who is prospering?" Leandro retorted, "Certainly not the people! And it is the weakness of human nature that needs time, you mean! Why 'time'? We are always pampering that weakness, looking for excuses, feeding it, waiting, compromising, and nothing happens! But now things will be different.

"Even the American people will be made to realize the kind of dictator their State Department has been supporting. I tell you, we are going to gain a dignity we never had before. We are fighting for it," Leandro turned toward the naked construction of his house and added intensely, "This too will be a stronghold for so many things. Our own work, Antonia's classes, the youth movement."

"To which your own sons will belong!" Antonia reminded softly.

The thought almost took his breath away. He paused, and then asked almost wistfully, "Do you really think so?"

"I know they will. Haven't they written you so? And your wife too? You will see." She looked directly at him, trying to imbue him with her own confidence.

Leandro smiled, and then, with a dramatic gesture, swept back the straight brown hair which had fallen across his forehead, and exclaimed impulsively, "Do you know! The house will be completed in time to have the opening for the 20th of May celebration! And your saint's day is the following month, isn't it, Arturo? You'll have the next party in our new house!" He looked like a happy tanned giant, standing astride the mound of gravel.

Arturo certainly had not agreed with Leandro's reasoning, but no matter. It was wonderful to see him like this. Tempestuous, vital, determined.

"Let's drink to that!" Antonia poured the sidra champagne, and as she filled the glasses, the bubbles rose like their own spirits ascending again to life. Then they opened the gifts. Arturo's was this letter-opener of delicately carved deep brown tortoise-shell inlaid with mother of pearl and silver. When held to the light, a glowing amber, almost scarlet, burst through the deep clouds like a burning autumn sunset. The handle was a carved griffin head whose open mouth was just ready to seize a globe, inlaid with pearl and silver, revolving on a silver axis.

"Beautiful!" he had exclaimed, "But do I remind you of a dragon?"

"Silly, that's a griffin."

"The symbolism is perfect," Leandro admired, "Toni, Toni," he said with delight. She and Leandro looked at each other, that smiling secret look of things shared. Guzman felt out of it,

"Well, what is it?" he felt himself say irritably. "Not everyone loves mythology as you two do."

"A griffin is half lion and half eagle, and he has a special instinct for finding hidden gold with which he lines his nest."

Guzman frowned, a little puzzled.

"Naturally," Leandro amended, "the allusion in your case, is to gold of the spirit!"

"And that's you, devouring the world!" Antonia teased in a whisper, close to Guzman. "But be careful, it might be indigestible!"

And while Leandro was occupied opening his own gift, Guzman had suddenly drawn her towards him and kissed her. It was then he had realized that his love for Antonia was the only thing in the world that mattered. The

151

dreams, the continued struggle for the cause, had only been fired by this love.

But she had been wrong, he smiled dryly, as he contemplated the letter-opener lying on his desk. He had known how to devour his world without suffering undue consequence. True, it was not the same world to which she had referred that day—and thank God for that! —or he might now have been one of those loathsome failures, a hybrid, wandering between the worlds of non-conformity and necessity. A race of fools like Leandro who thought they could forge a republic shining and pure without counting on the human condition, stubbornly wasting their lives; and Antonia, whatever had become of her, fool enough to follow him! God only knew.

No one observing Arturo Guzman at this moment could have suspected what contempt filled this quiet silver-headed figure as with measured movement he seated himself at his desk.

Well, in spite of everything, he was indebted to them, who, all unknowingly, had changed the course of his life. Thanks to that day of the housewarming! As Leandro had promised, it had been completed for Independence Day, the 20th of May. Guzman, who had worked enthusiastically the preceding days helping his friend with last-minute details, had gratefully found a lonely bench back of the trellised arbor where he could rest a few moments.

The orchestra had exchanged the traditional danzon for the new American two-step, and the guests were thronging the grounds, admiring, stupefied, or scandalized by the strange house Leandro had built.

Two women seated themselves on the other side of the hedge, unaware of his presence. He ignored their identity but he had never forgotten their voices and the strident clicking of their fans.

"Oh, 1 was so embarrassed!" one of them was saying in a low voice, "which one is his wife, then?"

"The one with the flowered chiffon."

"Oh, very chic. But I congratulated someone else. She was very quiet until she began explaining all about the house, and naturally I thought she was the wife! You know, the girl with the high forehead and green eyes."

"Of course. That's just his cousin from the Canary Islands, an orphan, who came here about a year ago. She planned most of this preposterous house with him, and is going to live with them now that his wife is back."

"Is back?"

Out of delicacy, Guzman had found himself an unwilling eavesdropper. He could not have risen without their seeing him.

"She's been with her mother in Santiago for almost two years. Took the children with her. 1 hear that is one of the reasons he built all this. To bring them back."

"Nena, how could she leave him? If I had a husband that attractive...

Oh, but I suppose that was the trouble," she insinuated,

"Heavens, no! He's very serious. Besides, since when does a woman leave her husband because he's unfaithful? She would have understood that!"

"Well, I certainly wouldn't understand it!"

"Just wait until you're married," her friend laughed. "Oh dear! I forgot you're active in all that—what do you call it—woman suffrage! But then I'm surprised you don't know about him. He's the one who's been organizing against President Menocal, and insisting the American people should be told that their government is protecting a near-dictator, all that sort of thing."

Her companion's fan clicked to a sudden halt. Proud of his friend, Guzman heard awe in her exclamation. "'Camacho—Nena, is he Leandro Camacho? How thrilling! Carlota brought me here for fun, and I just hadn't associated the name. Why, he's one of our real heroes of the Independence! And he's still devoting all his time to—"

"Exactly!" the other interrupted. "That is why his wife left, and I don't blame her! She just wants a normal comfortable life. He should have married someone who—"

"—who could share his dedication. Like me!" whispered the girl, "or like his cousin!"

"What!"

With difficulty, Guzman had refrained from committing the social transgression of openly protesting, but as they continued, loyal indignation gradually ebbed, and a sudden fear took its place.

"No wonder that I confused them: they might not know it, but they are in love. Didn't you hear him speak of the work they are doing together, the new Youth Movement, and the way, she looked at him as he spoke, as though he were a saint."

"Ridiculous. She's a quiet nice girl, and I'm sure she has very strict morals, raised on a plantation in Tenerife. You know how the isleños are!"

"Anyone could be inspired by a man like that! Morality has nothing to do with it."

"Cuidadito," teased her friend, "speak for yourself!" There was a pause during which their rustling fans voiced their thoughts. Guzman feared they would hear the very thumping of his heart.

"Besides," the one called Nena concluded, "I hear that she and Arturo Guzman are practically engaged, and he is also in that crazy Youth Movement. So, you see!" but her voice held less conviction than before.

He had not heard the rest of the conversation although, almost suffocating, he was compelled to remain there until the women had left.

He was ashamed of his disloyal suspicion, yet his heart pounded with increased violence. He rose, furious at his own weakness. He would look for Antonia. He knew that the moment he saw her, everything would be all right.

And it had been! he thought with gratitude, as he leaned back in his desk chair, it had been, thanks to that one last moment of his immaturity, when, not having found them among the guests in the garden, he had looked up towards the house, and there, in the tower high above, was Leandro, and he had seen Antonia's white lace shawl fluttering in the wind; shortly after, when they both had returned to mingle with the guests, it was enough to see the expression of their faces.

Without a word to them, he had literally crept from the party. Outraged and stricken by what he was sure was their duplicity, he groaned, remembering the way they had used him, patriotism, and, yes, even Leandro's family as a front for their loathsome affair! In the days that followed when, bewildered by his behavior and then alarmed, they attempted to see him, he had blindly refused. The skin of adolescent illusion had been torn from him and he swore that he would never be so humiliated again, nor would love ever possess him, nor any causes. Causes? Then only "cause" was one's own!

He began to give all his energy to support Menocal, who, no matter by what means, was bringing prosperity to Cuba, and to himself. Arturo also experienced satisfaction in combating measures championed by the political "idealists" (ghastly hypocrisy!) represented by Leandro. And he was highly amused to hear that Leandro's family, instead of being "taken in" by him, had entered the dizzying dance of the millions, spending his money as greedily as they could.

He avoided all mention of Antonia. "If thy right eye offend thee, pluck it out." It was as though he had never known her.

§

The unexpected ringing of the telephone startled him. Automatically he answered. It was Baldomero Saenz.

"Arturo," he blared, "I've just finished going over the stuff with Mario, and I was thinking how about stirring up a game this evening after you've finished whatever the hell you're doing in your office—"

"No, no, can't make it," Guzman answered.

"Too bad!" Saenz shouted. "Well, maybe we can fit it in tomorrow after the meeting. Be sure and come before the Good Friday procession starts; otherwise they won't let you cross Calzada." He hung up.

In the silence of his office, the ticking of his old clock was a voice that shared an intimate secret with him. He turned towards it, his heavy, high-slanting eyebrows raised in the suggestion of a smile that is exchanged between accomplices. Why did so many people fear that sound? Do everything possible to avoid the awareness of it, discreetly ignore its existence, camouflage it? Time had been his only trusted friend. It was not without profit that he had studied and beguiled it, and sleeked it into domesticity. It had been working for him, and had arranged that the bulldozers' work would be finished only a few weeks before May 20th, the day of Cuban independence and the decades-long anniversary of his own private revolution.

With a shock, he realized that he had spent his entire life vindicating himself to a man who had been dead for years.

18
THE BOX IS NOT THERE

After Mario had gone over the work schedules with Saenz, he was about to leave the building when he saw a familiar figure approaching. "Hola, De Armas!" he called out, surprised at the heartiness in his own usually lethargic voice. He also found himself grinning, which was not habitual.

Evidently De Arms had not heard him, for he would have continued past, but Mario clapped him on the shoulder. "Jorge De Armas," he repeated, "You are really absorbed in thought!"

"Oh hello, Guzman."

Mario did not mind the half-hearted greeting. One shouldn't take offense at the reactions of artists, and no doubt about it, judging from his designs for the project, this boy was a real artist! He felt proud of the fact that he, Mario, had had the perception to recognize an unappreciated talent, and had been able to give him a boost.

"Well," continued Mario, jovially, "one doesn't have to ask you why you are here! I read it in the papers. Congratulations, chico!" and he shook his hand, almost proudly. A warm pleasure was spreading over him as though he were being congratulated himself. It made him feel good.

"Thanks, Mario."

"Your designs must have been damn good to have won over some of our top architects." Mario wished the Guzman Company connection didn't still require secrecy so that he could tell Jorge that they were really working on it together. "How about having lunch together at the Club? I certainly owe it to you after boring you stiff the way I did that night after the meeting. My rush of confidences must have swept you off your feet," he joked apologetically.

"Forget it," Jorge smiled. "And about lunch, thanks, but I have to go over a few things with Saenz."

"And after?"

Jorge shook his head. "Sorry. Thanks just the same. I usually don't have lunch. And when I do, it's generally an ajiaco at a fonda china," he winked. "My stomach is not conditioned to country club food!" He was glad his mother could not hear him!

Mario laughed. "Never mind, De Armas! Now that you've really begun, there's no knowing where it will take you. I think you'll have to recondition your stomach! And I sincerely hope so," he said earnestly. Jorge did not answer. Mario wondered what he was thinking of, with the distant look in his eyes and the muscles of his jaw contracting. "Well, some other time, eh? I guess I'm detaining you. Oh, by the way, you can find Saenz down there in the drafting room."

But when Jorge entered, Saenz was not very happy to see him.

He had been watching the already festive spirit apparent in the lines below waiting for the little ferries to take them across the bay. Many employees had been given the afternoon off, since it was Holy Thursday. It was a beautiful day and Saenz was thinking what a shame it was that he couldn't get up a game with Arturo. Too bad that Arturo had been too busy to spend the weekend at their beach home in Varadero. The family had certainly grumbled, and he couldn't blame them.

And listen to this idiota, De Armas, stressing specifications! Going on with his blasted intensity!

"...want no danger of the wood being undersized, two by twelve for the joist and roof-rafters...."

"...aha, that's right ...yes, indeed..." Saenz interjected from time to time to humor him. Damn fool, did he think they'd never built a house before!

"...and then, of course, such things as large enough panel boxes, and the wiring. These are details, but very important ones, after all."

"Of course! Naturally..." Saenz mumbled as he thought, "as soon as I get rid of him, I'll call Arturo. Maybe at least we can have a quiet game in the patio.

§

"Now listen folks, she's taking a long time up there getting those papers. I've got to get on my way," Gomez the Saenz employee complained impatiently. They did not answer. He wished they would say something. All of them just standing there silent, helpless looking, waiting for the crazy old woman to bring down documents that didn't exist. Not knowing what to

157

do in the pause, he offered them cigarettes. They silently shook their heads in refusal. "Gracias," the big Negro murmured courteously for them.

Gomez cleared his throat for want of anything else to do, and looked at his watch. Then they heard her feeling her way down those rotted stairs. He hoped they wouldn't cave in on her while he was there! In silence, all their glances were riveted on those stairs, their faces of powerless, mute loyalty.

And then she appeared. White faced, her nostrils pinched as though it were difficult for her to breathe, she struggled hard to maintain that straight-backed look that he had noticed when she had invited him in. Her empty hands trembled.

"The papers are not there," she whispered. "The box is not there. Yesterday evening I had it all in order."

"I'll look again." Chori made a move towards the stairs, but she raised her hand slightly, "No, It is not there."

"Don't go up there, man. Would never hold your weight," Gomez cautioned.

But it was the finality in Marquesa's voice that detained Chori. It caused him and Arsenio to exchange glances. It was only a slow half-look they dared because of the pain.

Gomez cleared his throat again. Then with an effort to cheer things up, he said "Well, ma'am, after you get over the shock, you'll see it's all for the best. Why, you will be much better off in... uh..." he was going to say "Mazorra," Havana's psychiatric hospital, but caught himself, "in some charity institute! They're real nice." He stopped, suddenly feeling foolish. The brightness of his voice was like a paper hat at a dull party. And she was not hearing him at all. He addressed the others in a more sober tone.

"Here's the address where you fellows can go to collect your money. I've got to be on my way." He held out the card to El Topo, who stood nearest him. Topo shook his head.

Gomez looked at the others, and in consternation realized that their reaction would be the same.

"Díaz told me about you people. But you don't seem to realize. This is your last chance! You're going to be out in the street, and you will need this!" He might have been talking to himself, and he was fed up with the whole thing.

"All right! I'm going. But one of you ought to tell her the truth. There never was any paper. You can't all be crazy!" And then he left.

"Maybe box down here," Chan Li's words fell into the silence.

"That's right," Chori exclaimed. "Maybe you brought it down here, and just don't remember."

"No, Chori, it was safer not to. I purposely did not bring it downstairs; my goat might find it, or some stranger out of curiosity."

Arsenio and Chori reacted at the same time, "Carambita!" Of course!

How had they not noticed? He had been hanging around for days, smelling money and grief in the wind, and this morning he had disappeared. Like a panther, the Negro sprang over the crumbled wall.

"I know where he hangs out! That cabrón, when I get hold of him..." but Arsenio lunged after him.

"Come back, Chori. I'm going."

Chori paused just long enough to shout, "No, no! I'm quicker than you!" and would have continued, but Arsenio's roar stopped him,

"Chori, come back. I said I am going." No one had ever heard his voice like that before, a command powerful and angry. "You stay here with them, I'll find him, and I'll bring back that box. I will not return until I do. Do you hear me, Antonia?"

She lifted her head, and her clear green eyes looked straight into his. "I know you will," she answered.

No one dared speak as they watched his great shaggy figure push through the underbrush. He moved slowly and heavily, like something that only God could stop.

At last he could do something for the Marquesa.

19
RENDEZVOUS

All of them remained with her, waiting for Arsenio to come back. They were relieved to see that most of the time she forgot why they were there.1 She made café con leche for them, and even some little merenguitos as though it were a party. Occasionally something would break through and Marquesa — or "Antonia" as they had been calling her lately, now that they knew it was her name — would suddenly look perplexed, then almost agitated, and they held their breath, hoping she wouldn't remember. But she would sigh and the half-thought would slip away again. Finally, when the moon was climbing, they decided to leave. They tried to conceal their oppression, but it hovered over them as, reluctantly, they said goodnight.

Marquesa sensed their mood and it reminded her that she too was burdened by some thought; or was it something that happened? She could not quite remember. Like the wake of an unidentified vessel which has disappeared, emotion would remain with her although its cause had already slipped from her mind. Continuity always was difficult to sustain. She realized that her mind skipped back and forth indiscriminately through time and events, and she had acquired the habit when perplexed of smoothing back her hair, as though the soothing rhythm might coax back lucidity--or lightly brush away the shadows.

Now she wondered what was troubling her. She picked her way over creaking boards of the corridor to the tower stairway which led from the study. An impulse guided her to the tower, but she hesitated. The moon had shifted, thrusting the stairs into blackness, and shooting ruby through the remaining fragments of the stained-glass window of the study.

She sat on the bay window, startling a small sleeping lizard that scurried over the empty bookshelves and fled through the window casement into the garden. From here she often enjoyed watching the sea and, far off, the Old Port of Havana where so long ago she had arrived in Cuba from the Canary Islands.

Waiting on the pier were cousin Leandro--a handsome, tired, bitter man he had seemed when she first met him--and his friend, Arturo Guzman. Dear Arturo! What terrible thing was it that later was to have robbed him of his youth so suddenly and turned him against both them and the Movement? Well, she could not have married him anyway, because Leandro was alone except for her. If only his wife and children had cared about what he was trying to do! She had done her best to keep them all together. Or if he had expected just a little less of himself and of them! She understood him because he was so like her father, who had died on the snowy peak of the Teide Mountain. Except, of course, Leandro would come back some day.

Now she remembered what was troubling her! Some curious tale about a "Company" wanting her to leave the house! Leave indeed! What were they thinking of? Why, she had helped Leandro build it! And that little statue of Proserpina at the bottom of the grove, hidden now under all the wild bushes, was the very first thing he had asked the Italian sculptor to make. "It is for you," he had said, "because you have brought Spring to my world again." Then he had looked troubled a moment. "Be careful, Antonia--don't let me carry you into the darkness," he had said quite gravely.

"Even so," she had answered undismayed, "we know that Proserpina always returns, don't we?"

That was before the house had been built. And it was here in this room that she had hidden, the unforgettable day of the house-warming, to escape the party awhile, to be alone with her happiness. Oh, there had been so much hope! She had been watching the guests clustered in bright groups over the garden. Some were being served buffet at the merendero, others were dancing on the terrace. There were two orchestras, one playing the danzón with violin, flute, guayo, horn and clarinet; and the other had brought the daring new "fox trot" or "two-step" where the couples danced close, to the strange jazz sounds of trombone, saxophone, banjo, and piano.

As her eyes had roved searchingly over the crowd, she realized that she was not looking for Arturo but for Leandro. And when she did not see him there was a sudden desolation, an emptiness that terrified her. With a pounding heart, she had fled to the tower. And a moment later she heard his step on the stairs, light and youthful as it had never been before.

"Antonia!" he almost laughed in his joy of finding her.

"When I didn't see you with the others, knew I would find you here having a rendezvous with these fellows." He laughingly clasped one of the wooden gargoyles. "I'm going to be jealous of them one day!" But suddenly the laugh caught in his throat as he said, "This is all your work, Antonia. Without you——" and she was in his arms, enveloped in his strength. She felt his mouth against hers, trembling in restraint.

"Antonia..." The torment with which he pronounced her name fell strangely on this joy. "This once only you will hear me say the words, and never again," he whispered. "I love you, Antonia. I didn't know until now! I didn't know!" The pressure of his hands stressing the words was pain that surged from his fingers through her whole being. "Forgive me! It won't happen again, but, thank God, it can't be taken from us--the one moment we will have in all our lives!"

Suddenly they were aware of the high sweet sibilance of the flute and the clarinet and the women's laughter in the garden below. They were the sounds of reality that separated them.

"Nothing has to be changed. We'll go on as before, the work we began can never be destroyed," he continued, "and through others it will be completed. I promise you that. No matter how long it takes."

All that could never be said filled that moment of silence as they stood looking at each other. And then she had fled from the tower.

But she could not escape the party. She was obliged to be there amongst the white linen coats, bonnets, saxophones and the two-step, the speech-making of Resurgence of Cuban ideals. And she had to be looking at Leandro, knowing that never again could they share the same closeness. Although they would be living and working under the roof, this one moment in the tower had been the last. And it must be forgotten.

How many years ago had that been? What did "year" mean? The thousands of days and nights that had slipped rhythmically over that day, over the word "year"? Did it mean the cyclones, the blistering sun that bleached all color and reality from the world? The revolutions, the changes, the trees that had grown with her? Only the vaguest attempt to think of what "year" meant caused her to smooth her hair in confusion, but that day of the tower and those two words, "I promise," and the silence afterwards were as living now as then. And although other things she had learned to forget, this she had locked in the heart of the sea. It was the song guarded under the house.

She rose from the bay window of the study where she had been seated and found it suddenly strange to see the empty bookcases and the peeling walls, which the moon illuminated. But outside in the garden was the little statue of Proserpina. No one else knew it was there, under the wild bushes, in the darkness. "Only I knew its secret," she smiled as she slowly went to bed.

20
GOOD FRIDAY

For several hours, crowds had been lining the Paseo and adjacent streets of the Vedado suburb waiting for the Good Friday procession to begin. All know it is a solemn occasion but are grateful they can count on the old people to wear the outer solemnity. As for the young women, all their lace mantillas and rosaries cannot contain their festive spirit; and how can the men be grave, surrounded by this spectacle of feminine beauty? It cannot be otherwise on this bright Havana afternoon, where the leaves of the Royal Palm are glistening banners waving against a brilliant blue and white sky, and the candy man's high twirling poles spiked with sweet piruli explode their crystal rainbows.

"Papi, when is the procession starting? Papi, look! I want a piruli! A green one! No, not a green one, a red one! Call him, papi-i-i!"

The little girl's father is too busy joking with a friend to pay her any attention. It infuriates her to behold their great open mouths with cigarettes happily dangling at the corner since her own joy is yet unfulfilled. "Pa-a-pi! I want a piruli!"

He looks down. "What do you want, child?"

A little finger points, the reflections of many more desires yet unknown burning in her eyes.

"Oh, all right. I'll get you one. Eh, pirulero!" he calls after the candy man.

A little boy watches them enviously.

"Mamá, that little girl over there is getting a piruli! Why can't I have

163

one?"

"I told you before. This is Good Friday."

"Well?"

"Didn't I just explain to you at church? Today Christ died on the Cross for us. We have to sacrifice a little something, too. How are we going to eat lollipops and ice-cream? This isn't a party!"

"Well, it looks like one, and everybody else is buying things!"

"Well, they shouldn't."

"Will they all go to Hell?"

"Of course not! Most of them haven't been taught to realize what they are doing. So they don't know they are doing wrong."

"Then, if you hadn't taught me, I could...have a...lollipop...now..."

"That's right."

The boy's voice trails off, and with it his thoughts, and the whole world, down a misty long road, where some people are happy because they don't know anything. And others...it is all mixed up, so he begins to pick his nose.

Lourdes and Jorge, who had been part of the crowd lining the Paseo, crossed the wide intersection where traffic had been blocked, and joined others in animated picnic fashion over the grass of the center promenade.

They had openly walked across the street together. It might have been premature, but they were too happy to be prudent. The beginning of success was making their waiting bearable. They enjoyed this little recklessness today because they could almost afford it.

As they settled on the grass, Jorge squeezed Lourdes' arm, already warm with sun. A faint breeze helped him breathe her in, delicious as the sparkling churros and hot peanuts that were sending forth their exciting smells. The ice cream man's bell tinkled. Jorge looked at Lourdes and at the people of Havana whom he loved; they were so noisily, unashamedly alive.

Neither he nor Lourdes spoke. Words would have been redundant.

A Negro family had just approached and were gaily looking for places. The eldest, husky, bald, and toothless, with good-natured indignation waved away the offered help, as with a show of agility he seated himself on the grass next to Lourdes. But his grunt at the effort did not escape his family.

"Just look at your grandfather! Thinks he's still fifteen!" laughed his son, spreading a handkerchief on the ground for his wife to sit on. The two little girls giggled delightedly. Their white organdy dresses, embroidered by hand, spotless and starched, the luxurious taffeta ribbons caught into shimmering bows that crowned the carefully combed little heads, and the great wondering eyes shining and black as the jet azabache charm around their necks recalled to Lourdes, watching them, the wistful words of the popular song:

Artist, whose brush paints heaven,

164

Why do you always forget
That there are little black angels too?

The little girls ceased their giggling to look up in awe as a lottery vendor intoned grandiloquently, "Here comes the Procession! Ye-e-s! It's on the way! If you buy number nine, your luck will be coming too!" He pointed dramatically to the large red number nine placard fastened to his straw hat. "Nine stands for death. Just the thing for Good Friday! Ni-i-i-ne!"

Before they could see the procession, the solemn measure of the funeral march was audible. As it drew nearer and nearer, the muffled monotone of the drums became unnatural and eerie. A drum arouses and incites. But today it was muted as though there were something wrong.

The sandaled Carmelite priests appeared in their long brown robes chanting the rosary. Behind them, looming over the throng, the holy figures advanced slowly, and at times a little unsteadily, on the velvet draped catafalques, for they were borne on the shoulders of the faithful who had marched a long way under the hot sun from the Carmelo Church. The Nazarene, in robe of purple velvet and crown of thorns; the Dolorosa, Mother of Sorrows, weeping diamond tears; Mary Magdalene; but no Holy Sacrament in the procession today. It had been guarded in the Church, concealed from all eyes, for today the Christ was not on earth. Of all the days in the year, this was the most sorrowful. This was the reason for the muffled drums and the piercing cry of the horns. The same lament was even now being played from Seville to Barcelona on the ancient streets of Spain whence it had derived. The eyes regarding the moment with reverence were the eyes of the New World, but this was the legacy from the Mother Country.

There were other eyes paying homage, but with a different ethnic memory. Sometimes many of them still confused these symbolic figures with their own lost gods from the bitter heart of Africa. Ochun! Chango! Yemaya!

The procession solemnly turned on the wide Paseo while the Army, Navy, and Police bands intoned the funeral dirge.

All have been stirred by the transcendence of this moment, but here with the rich red earth, the burst of flowering bushes, the radiant sky, how could one think long of the Cross or the smaller, more real agonies of one's own hunger or insecurity or disillusionment? It was enough to be alive and intact, to be there on this beautiful day with bodies to move, dance, and gesticulate, voices to laugh, eyes to see a pretty girl, hands to feel the warm clasp of a child's small fingers perspiring with wonder.

A musician looks up from his sepulchral drum as he winks to a girl and pays a different kind of homage. "I too would give my life for a beauty like you," he murmurs as he passes.

And another one, who plays for tourists every night at the Rhumba Palace, had done as much penance as he can. He leans towards his companion as they march and murmurs, "Couldn't we sneak a little mambo into this without anyone noticing?"

"Try your lucky number! Nine! Dead Man!" exhorts the lottery vendor.

"Well, triqueña, I must leave you to join the High Life," Jorge grinned.

Lourdes looked at him and wished this moment would never end. He was so happy, sitting cross-legged in the grass with a clean new cigar clamped playfully, exaggeratedly, between his white teeth, and merriment lightening the color of his normally thoughtful dark eyes.

"When you look like that," she said, laughing, "especially with the ends of your eyebrows raised in that lewd point, you remind me of a Buddha."

He scowled at his flat stomach. "No Buddha yet," he corrected proudly." Almita, my little soul, how I hate to leave you! All day I'll be hearing that voice of your yours. Sometimes people think I am absent-minded when they speak to me. It's just that I'm hearing you!" Then he suddenly jumped up and, pulling her with him, said, "I've got to push on and meet my buddies!" They laughed at his reference to the affluent group of contractors meeting at Saenz's country home.

"Hasta mañana!" she waved.

§

As the chauffeured limousine sped over the country road, Don Emilio, close friend of Saenz, and Morales, the lumber contractor, were delighted with the refreshing wit of their young companion. Jorge's high spirits, combined with his amusement at finding himself mingling socially with these hacendados, had prevailed, and the spontaneity of his humor mottled the routine comfort of these men much as the bright sunlight flickered and danced through the car over the arbored highway.

"You're quite a story teller, De Armas!" chuckled one of the men, his belly shaking under the white guayabera.

"The credit goes to my grandfather, who was a Curro."

"Andaluz. That explains it!"

"Most colorful rogues in the world come from Andalusia," Jorge admitted.

They were about to cross the main square of a small village, when a rural policeman suddenly stopped them. He gestured towards the church.

"Procession," he explained.

The chauffeur turned off the ignition and they waited good-naturedly. The villagers bordering the shabby plaza suspended their talk, for the procession had already descended the steps of the old church and was approaching. Here no ice-cream bells, no souvenirs, no laughter of festive

166

indifference. Each face reflected the sobriety of the funeral dirge. It was out of tune, but no matter. Their eyes were fixed on the scene of the crucifixion and the Dolorosa, Mother of Sorrows. Jorge's light-heartedness faded, as he caught a glimpse of their "Dolorosa." Her once resplendent robe, vestige of a long dead prosperity, had been mended and re-mended, and a cheap netting resembling cheesecloth had been carefully draped over it in a futile effort to conceal the splitting velvet and near-tattering brocade. With what devotion they followed her, their Lady in rags, and the crude wooden crucifix! He suddenly wondered what he was doing in this car, where he did not belong.

"Hombre! Is this what we were stopped for?" exclaimed Don Emilio, amused. The resonance of his comfortable world carried through the open windows of the car, and several of the villagers hearing him looked with new eyes at their shabby procession.

"Their Dolorosa could stand a good bowl of soup," joked another. "She' s ready to fall apart!"

"Poor things! I'd like to send some money to their church so they can have a decent procession next year."

"Excellent idea. Why don't we make it our business to take care of that sometime soon? It's pitiful."

"Agreed."

Jorge had remained silent. An unreasonable fury mounted within him. He knew that a Cuban could not refrain from making a joke about anything at all whenever there was an opportunity. And to be sure, there was no serious mockery in their words. On the contrary, the Cuban sense of life's absurdities made them more apt to joke when most deeply touched. But today it was different, perhaps because he felt more accustomed to being among those ridiculed. It was all very well to change the wooden cross for a handsome one, and clothe the ragged Lady in splendor. Such measures were the prerogatives of the rich, who chose to cleanse themselves of poverty's contagion. But it never occurred to them to wave their antiseptic wand to eliminate the roots of the disease by providing schools, employment, and honest government.

Even now, as they neared Saenz villa, the men were enthusiastically formulating their generous plan. The fumes of self-righteousness clung to their clothes and filled the car. How was it possible that only a few moments ago he had been comfortably joking, feeling at one with them? Oh, the unbridgeable abyss between the rich and the poor!

Somehow, he was almost prepared for what occurred shortly after their arrival. Out of deference to Lourdes' constant plea ("Darling, don't waste yourself on the little things that can't be helped!"), he concealed as best he could his change of mood as they arrived at the finca and were greeted by the others who were already there. And during the pleasant repast (light, in

167

observance of Good Friday) served them on the wide veranda shaded by a flowering framboyan, he even tried to dismiss this mood as neurotic, conditioned by his past. That was something else Lourdes often stressed; she would observe impatiently, "I can understand how your past has made you hypersensitive to some things. But really, there are times when it seems indulgence, too! For a person as strong as you, relishing a bitter cud seems shockingly near self-pity."

For her sake now he tried, until Jimenez, from the office, arrived with the modified plans. Over the past few days Saenz had demanded an increasing number of changes, the majority of which Jorge had reluctantly conceded after spirited defense. He felt that it was prudent to yield on the minor issues as long as the fundamental concept remained intact. But now, as they bent over the working plans Jimenez had brought, the afternoon's foreshadowing had only partially prepared him.

"Jimenez," he had interposed at first glance, half smiling, "you've brought out the wrong plans."

"Hardly," Jimenez laughed. "I drew them myself. Pretty easy for some people to make all these modifications at the last moment." he remarked waggishly to Jorge, "as long as it's just the draughtsman got to copy them again; I stayed up all night finishing these last ones. Really sick of looking at the damn things!"

"Jimenez," Jorge corrected," I drew the last modifications myself." He gave another cursory glance at the plans and dismissed them. "This could never be mine," he smiled.

"Well, hell, they're somebody's," Jimenez replied.

The engineer and several of the contractors peered at them. "It's the project alright, De Armas."

"Oh, it's the Camacho project, but I think it must be one of the early trial-and-error plans made by Saenz when he was working out possible changes. Sort of throwing them all in at once. There's just some mistake."

Jimenez' voice became a little shrill, as he insisted, now nervous, "I told you Saenz gave me this list of modifications just the other day. You can see it yourself attached there underneath. In fact, I remember now, he mentioned that if I had any questions, I shouldn't bother you about it, but refer to him—"

"The other day," the sudden dryness of Jorge's throat made it difficult for him to swallow. "I know nothing of the other day." Desperately trying to steady his hand, he picked up the list. The other men exchanged glances. "For example," he pursued, "I see here: the frontage is decreased to less than its minimum. And here's a fine one! Studs in walls spaced at thirty-two inches on center. Specifications, of a necessity, call for sixteen."

"That's right," the engineer broke in, I went over this myself with Saenz."

"That is not right!" Jorge retorted, "You know perfectly well it isn't spaced at the given load! Why, the upper floor could collapse! And look at this! Undersized! Ceiling plaster would crack, the paint would fall off."

"I think you're exaggerating, De Armas. And as far as the cracking, well, in twenty years, maybe."

"When it wouldn't matter to us, eh? Damn it! The people who buy these houses are not going to be sold short! And what's this about the wood that hasn't been—"

"Don't get so excited, De Armas!" the lumber contractor tried to reassure him. "You're very new at this. It's true the wood isn't kiln dried, but there's something new that is much less costly. It's called—"

Jorge was not listening. He had let the plans drop, and swung around regarding them one by one. His voice was scarcely audible as he asked, "Is it possible, that knowing the facts, you are defending—"

The face of the lumber contractor darkened as he reminded curtly, "You are forgetting yourself. Our companies were established before you were born. Our only responsibility as reliable firms is to see that the quality of materials complies with the contract." Realizing Jorge's youth and his agitation, he added more gently, "We are not the builders or the engineers, son; and besides, you are exaggerating."

"Exaggerating!" Jorge wheeled on him. "Perhaps you have been too accustomed to collecting from the government on public works to be capable of shock anymore!"

White-faced, Morales took a step towards him, but Don Emilio intercepted. His back towards Jorge, he made a conciliatory gesture to the others.

"Young man, we will not take offense at your words. We realize that this is your baptism of fire, so to speak, and that you are too inexperienced to be immune to the first shock of certain realities that are actually quite normal."

Incredulous, Jorge regarded them in silence. There was almost friendly compassion written on their faces.

"I'm going to see Saenz." He rose from the table.

"Hombre, calma! We were all young once, too!"

Jorge refrained from brusquely shaking off the well-intentioned hand on his arm.

"That's right!, you must sleep over a thing like this," Don Emilio added.

"A thing like this is precisely what I don't sleep over."

"Besides, this is Good Friday. He's probably at Veradero," one of them observed.

"I know he is at home." Without taking leave of anyone, he strode towards the door.

"How will you go? You don't have your car with you."

Listen to them! he thought. They're like a ward of the incurably diseased, sympathetic and attentive to a newly stricken arrival. And beneath the solicitude, see how they gloat as they recognize the first symptoms. How well they remember those first pains, the neophyte horror as the first pus begins to ooze. Dogs licking each other's sores!

"We'll be leaving soon and can drop you right there if you really intend." But Jorge had already left.

He hurried over the narrow, cobbled streets of the miserable little town to the nearest bus stop. It was almost more repugnant to him than the place he had just left. Which was worse, the latter, or those shivering wretches of the village, happy for the scraps of consolation thrown in their empty plates? Christ, if you ever existed, the resignation you meant was not this rotting acquiescence but resignation to accept the fight! With fingernails, to dig out—each one of us—the little corner of our infinity!

He thought of all the sweet countryside of Cuba, "fairest land that mortal eyes have ever gazed upon," Columbus had exclaimed. The dust of its fallen Martí flowering in vain as long as this apathy to corruption endured.

When would they realize that if only they believed in themselves they could change all this?

He caught the first bus going to Havana.

21
SOCIAL VISIT

The butler asked him to wait in the drawing room, and a moment later, with a breeze-stirring entrance, Saenz came to greet him.

"Well, well, well! This is a surprise."

Without returning the smile, Jorge said, "I've come to see you about something urgent."

But Saenz did not hear him, so taken was he with himself, with the hand-shaking and back-clapping. Talking all the while, he propelled Jorge across the sumptuously carpeted room, past the wide marble stairway, to the entrance of the living-room furnished in Renaissance splendor with heavily carved bargueños, tapestries, and paintings. His arm still around Jorge's shoulder, the irresistible mass arrested long enough to wave, "Not modern, you see! My wife is the boss at home!" and then turned back to the stairs, "This way to my study!"

Jorge had to come to a dead stop to make the man listen to him.

"Saenz, I said I've come here to talk about something urgent."

"Fine, fine, come along." He was already half-way up, giving Jorge no alternative but to follow him. As they entered the study, a pleasantly surprised voice said, "Well, hello there, De Armas!" It was Mario, comfortably seated at a work table across from a dapper grey-haired man. Mario rose amiably, but Jorge, barely acknowledging him with an unsmiling nod, turned to Saenz.

"I haven't come here on a social visit."

"Muy bien, De Armas. Sit down." Jorge's somber attitude had suddenly registered on Saenz. Unpleasant prospect. Caramba! He'd had quite enough of this fellow's earnestness, and he hoped to God that Guzman would now take over. As he introduced Guzman Senior and Jorge, he remarked significantly, "Architect for the Camacho project..." It was up to Guzman to make his relationship known, but Guzman said nothing.

"These are old friends of mine, De Armas. We can talk freely."

"All right, Saenz. All I want are the facts."

The three men were alert at this behavior.

He had not accepted the chair offered him, but stood there doggedly. "I just left the meeting at your finca, where Jimenez brought plans that could no longer be recognized as mine. They all seemed surprised that I was ignorant of what they called 'alterations.' I told them there was some mistake," his eyes leveled at Saenz, "and I've come directly to you."

At the mention of Jimenez's name, Saenz reacted. "He mustn't have received my message," he muttered with annoyance. "He wasn't to have gone out there today."

"Oh, I see. Because I decided to go?"

"Not in the way you mean." A smile quickly covered Saenz's momentary confusion. "You see, ah, because of the holidays and all, I hadn't had the opportunity of consulting you about some last-minute changes that were found necessary. Naturally, I didn't want Jimenez to take them out before I had discussed them with you myself." He waved off this very logical statement by picking up a crystal decanter of brandy from the table. "As a matter of fact, I'm very glad you've come! Sit down and we'll discuss it over a brandy. Mario? Arturo?" He looked significantly at both as he poured them a drink.

"You will remember," Jorge pursued, ignoring the invitation, "that only yesterday I was in your office, and again stressed clearly the principal specifications, to which you agreed. Am I to understand that these 'changes' were made subsequently? Between yesterday afternoon and today, precisely when one is working?"

Saenz made a last effort to control himself.

"My dear young man, I do not keep a time schedule of every conversation I have. Besides, the religious holidays have interrupted things, and—"

"Señor Saenz," Jorge's sarcastic smile accompanied a gesture towards the empty highball glasses, "I hardly think that your religious devotion could have erased the memory of yesterday's conversation!"

Saenz rose violently from the chair and faced Jorge.

"De Armas!" Mario exclaimed, rising also.

"This is not your affair, Guzman!" Jorge cautioned.

"But that's just it! It is my affair!"

Jorge looked at him uncomprehendingly.

The cool voice of Guzman Senior intervened. "Caballeros! Please! This young man's agitation is understandable, Baldomero, but I'm sure I can straighten things out. You see, De Armas—"

"Sir, this is a matter strictly between Saenz and myself. Although you are a friend of this house, I see no—"

"That is exactly what I wish to clarify," the elder man cut him short. "I am not speaking as a friend, but as Saenz's client. You see, I am the one responsible for the Camacho project."

Jorge's head jerked towards him. "You?"

Guzman Senior smiled and nodded.

"I wanted very much to tell you when we met yesterday at the office," Mario added, evidently relieved, "but it was not my place."

They all looked as though they expected him to be pleased. "I don't understand. A 'client' of Saenz? How is that possible if you yourselves are contractors, and construction—" he did not finish. He was beginning to sense a dark nebula of reasons, but that would come later. Now it was enough to know that Mario... "In other words, you are the ones behind this. Saenz is the front for you."

"I wouldn't put it like that, De Armas."

"In other words," he persisted, "it was you, and not Saenz at all, who accepted my designs."

"That is correct." Correct! Somewhere inside he had to have known all along that it had been a fantasy, this hope, this optimism that he must have worn so ludicrously, like a top-hat on a clerk!

He continued dogging them and himself.

"Why me? Why did you take my ideas? What was the real reason?"

"What's the matter with you, De Armas? This is inconceivable, something that doesn't concern you at all!" Red-faced from imposed restraint, Saenz turned to the others. "I told you he was impossible!" He had removed his heavy

rimmed glasses, and waving them in a gesture of exasperation, he strode towards the window overlooking the garden, leaving Guzman and Son to cope with him. "This is the kind of bore I've had to deal with right along!"

He was glad to be able to wash his hands of it.

Guzman placed his detached smile as he did everything, with the powerful precision of a chess-player. "Frankly, De Armas, your reaction is uncalled for. The information we have given you is about internal business arrangements which do not concern the architect at all. Naturally, your enthusiasm and youthful impatience—"

"De Armas, whether it's with Saenz or with Guzman, it really doesn't make any difference, does it?" Mario put in.

Jorge did not answer. The irony of the situation made speech impossible. His and Lourdes' future life together in the balance...it would be unthinkable to work with Mario, but then, there would be no occasion for that to happen. His dealings were exclusively with Saenz. And old Guzman controlled him. If Guzman would guarantee that no significant modification would be made, and none at all without his, Jorge's, consent...why, then, let them go on stealing from each other as long as it hurt no one else, play their intra-mural sports. He turned to Guzman Senior.

"As you said, internal business arrangements do not concern the architect. My sole concern is the design and safety of the building. If you will absolutely guarantee—"

Mario's eagerness did not permit him to finish.

"But of course, De Armas! That is our concern just as well!" He looked at his father for corroboration. "It's a beautiful project," he continued, "and I really thought it would be a pleasant surprise after all these years." His smile wavered under Jorge's unresponsiveness.

Oh, no! Jorge thought. What was done was done, but not that, too! That voice of Mario's like a child's fingers fondly stroking a cat, stretching out in timid friendliness. Jorge ignored Mario's remarks and addressed his father.

"And now, concerning the purpose of my coming here this evening, I assume I can deal directly with you."

Guzman waved him toward a seat which he accepted. "Quite so," Guzman replied.

Mario, who had noted with some relief that Saenz had left the room, chose to remain standing in the background where the two men could not notice the concern he felt. He knew there had been some minor alterations, but certainly nothing as serious as the ones to which Jorge had alluded. Had Saenz dared to take this upon himself, or had his father consented...but it was unthinkable!

"I will begin by answering your last question, De Armas. Why did we happen to call you, and why accept your design over the others?"

Mario turned towards the table, alarmed. But no need. His father was saying, "I will answer you frankly and briefly. I am no fool. I recognize unusual talent when I see it. And when it is comparatively unknown?" He gracefully waved a jaundiced hand. "Let us not mince words. We all know that capacity and ambition go hand in hand. You impressed Saenz at your first interview as someone with a realistic attitude. He has evidently changed his mind since then," he parenthesized, smiling, "but I'm sure that could be only a problem of personalities. The fact is, our company has an important place for a talented man who knows how to adjust himself."

"Adjust? To what? What are you trying to say, Guzman?" Jorge's impassive face had completely disregarded the praise. Arms folded, shoulders and dark head thrust slightly forward, listening, he waited.

Guzman was beginning to feel that Saenz's annoyance was not wholly

174

unjustified. "That the unusual facets of the project are certainly worthy of carrying out in the future, when we will have had more time to study their practicability. But I am sure you will understand my regret when a few days ago we discovered that certain of the ideal specifications were completely inadvisable. The cost of—"

"So you did make those changes!" Jorge violently pushed his chair from the table at the same time that Mario exclaimed sharply, "Papá! I can't believe this!"

Guzman chose to ignore his son. "De Armas, from the architectural point of view very little has been affected. You probably have not quite understood."

"I'm sure I understand." Jorge leaned forward again, his eyes penetrating Guzman's, emotion resonant under his incisive speech. "I understand only too well. The outward appearance has been untouched—oh, perhaps with the exception here and there of such an 'insignificant' detail as proportion or distribution—but what undiscerning eyes of a ninety-dollar-a-week family would notice that you have changed only the invisible! What does it matter that the people who live in those homes find themselves without water during a dry season, or that they are once again disillusioned with cracking ceilings, peeling paint, walls torn up because of inadequate wiring or even fire hazards? If the appearance is attractive, what does it matter that the guts will be rotting? Have I understood correctly, Guzman?"

The older man stared back at him with cold detachment. "You disappoint me," he said. "These remarks of yours, which are intended to be extremely offensive, indicate that my judgment of people, which rarely errs, has done so now. But then, it could be the impetuosity of the artist in you. I hope so; because, I repeat, I think your ideas for the people are excellent, and you would have a great many more opportunities with us of carrying them out."

Jorge's fist struck the table, as he rose furiously. "'The people!' 'Opportunities!' The words sound filthy in your mouth. Bribing me to become a procurer for you! If you try to go through with this, Guzman, I'll fight it!"

Guzman smiled. "You wouldn't get very far. And of course, you will have finished your career. At least, in Cuba."

"That won't stop me."

"And I'm going with him, Papá."

Jorge wheeled furiously on Mario. "I told you before, keep out of this."

"You!" Guzman, full of contempt, looked at his son. "Your life has been so easy that it amuses you to play at heroics! Now I understand why you insisted on my calling De Armas for the project. Your hero. He reminds me of one I knew once..." His measured voice faded into a pause, and his gaze seemed to be focusing on some distant but clearly defined past. But as though it were distasteful to him, he quickly dismissed the vision and continued with a grim smile, "...and dozens of others with the same face. Oh, useful enough in war because they are in their element fighting. But what happens to them when they have to face life's complexities? Instead of meeting it half-way, they are so absorbed in their incantations to love and honor that the damn fools commit the greatest dishonor of all: they wantonly throw away their usefulness. The world is full of these puling failures."

Jorge started towards the door.

"Listen to me, De Armas!" Guzman called imperatively. Seeing that Jorge had stopped, he rose, walked over to him, and said in a more modified tone, "I have been patient with you because of your talent, inexperience, and because I too was once an idealist. Until a shock opened my eyes." He put an unsteady hand on Jorge's shoulder. "Listen to me, young man," he repeated. "The world is not absolutely black and white. It is better to accomplish less than the ideal than to achieve nothing at all. You are young. You have a whole life to open doors if you will face this reality. Don't shut yourself out!" His urgent tone that was almost a plea stayed Jorge. There was unsuspected emotion in this calculating man, almost as though he were seeking vindication within himself for his way of life. Then, assuming his habitual remote manner, he sharply withdrew his hand from Jorge's shoulder, and walking back to the table said, "Since we will never see eye to eye on this project, I am going to release you from it. I will pay you for the plans but will not use them now. I will withhold them to use unaltered," he stressed the word, "on some other occasion. There will be many such opportunities, De Armas." He paused. There yet no reaction from Jorge, whose face was somber with restrained anger. He apparently remained only in deference to Guzman's age. Guzman continued, "Unless the damnable nuisance of the CTC labor syndicate row and the strikes force us to postpone everything, work will proceed on schedule. Whatever your decision, telephone me without fail."

Jorge heard him through, and his own hand trembled as he picked up his briefcase, threw a curt good-night, and hurried from the room.

To Mario, who was following Jorge, Guzman said, "If you leave now, don't ever come back to me." Mario, ignoring the threat, continued after Jorge.

It was not until Jorge had reached his car and suddenly felt a hand on his shoulder, that he realized Mario had followed him.

"I'm going with you." he said. Jorge angrily shook him off and would have opened the car door, but Mario stared at him in astonishment and repeated, "But I'm with you, De Armas."

"'With' me!" The bitterness in his voice was like a blow.

"You don't seem to understand. I've left my father for good. I believe in you. Together we can fight this."

Mario's words seemed further to enrage him. "Who asked you to believe in me? I don't want you! Go back where you belong."

"You don't know me at all, De Armas. I've been wanting this my whole life."

"Don't be a fool. You rich make me sick 'playing at heroics,' as your father said." He spoke in such a tone that Mario did not know if he was mocking or not, but Mario retorted indignantly, "Do you think you're a privileged class? Perhaps you do not know that there is another kind of poverty that has nothing to do with money or success!"

Jorge's laughter was startling. "Oh, I know! The poor of spirit! Who can ease their suffering by yachting at the French Riviera, or sponsoring charity balls, or drowning themselves in art collecting!" He opened the door of his second-hand car and slapped the top of it fondly. "Have you ever driven a tin-can like this? That is what you would have to do if you left your father. He'd see that you didn't have a cent! I assure you this would not give you the same satisfying outlet for your present mood as your Continental will. Your father knows you better than you think."

Mario hung on. "My mind is made up."

Jorge, entering the car, paused and turned to look at Mario, whose hands were clenched, and whose eyes shone with determination. They regarded each other a moment, and then with a smile more of weary compassion than mockery, Jorge said softly, "No, little soldier, go home." He slammed the door and was gone.

Mario, left suddenly alone, absently looked up at the soft night, where a thin moon floated over the sleeping hills. Strange setting for the bitterness he had just seen in De Armas. What things he must have suffered in his life to lash out like this!

For the first time in years, he really hoped Lourdes would be home. It was crazy but he was remembering the day he had returned home to Cuba from college for Christmas vacation. Family and friends were waiting at the pier to welcome him. He had almost bounded down the gangplank, suddenly realizing that it was Lourdes alone he was hurrying to! She was the only one who would want all the ideas and enthusiasm he had brought from that other world. How hard it had been to make sure that he embraced his mother, father, and Miguel before running to her! And as soon as he had looked into her eyes, he had known how much she cared.

Now even as then he sped over the road from Barandilla, he pushed down the accelerator-as far as he dared. The few cognacs he'd had could not be responsible for the power and exhilaration he felt. It was a special kind of levitation, an abandon that reminded him of the people in Chagall's paintings who floated through doors and windows in a euphoria which emancipated them from natural laws. He discovered that his former contempt of artists' sudden moods as "cheap exhibitionism" had been nothing but a personal resentment born of envy. With great satisfaction he noted that he too was capable of experiencing these transports! He actually felt that he could reach Lourdes more quickly if he were to park the car and run to her—or float to her—all the way! Lourdes! Those first years together had been wonderful! He was not driving through space but through time, going back to where he had stopped living.

At last he was turning up the drive. He was home! There was a light in her sitting-room. Pancha stared open-mouthed at his retreating figure as he hurried up the stairs. He had not given her time to open the door but had used his key.

"Lourdes?" he called, not waiting to reach her room. She was on the chaise-lounge reading, and looked up in alarm at the urgency of his voice. Very seldom did he have the inclination to come to her room at this hour, and much less the eager impatience to call her from the stairs.

"Mario, what's happened?"

He stopped abruptly in the doorway. He opened his mouth to speak and could not. The shock of reality had rendered him inarticulate. For this woman in the green satin negligee, seated across the room, self-sufficient, collected, was completely unaware of all that had just happened to him. She was ten years away from Lourdes of the pier. What had she been living these ten empty years? It was unutterably sad to think that she had not shared in their encounter with the living past. He longed to rush to her, toss the suspended book from her hands, hold her to him as he had never embraced anything in his life. But she would think he had gone mad.

"Mario," are you ill?"

His heart was bursting to cry out, "Lourdes! Years ago I returned to Cuba like a home-coming traveler laden with gifts, and I gave them all to you, but I went away. Now I want to share them with you, Lourdes. Meet that day with me again. Please!"

He wanted to say this but he could not. Aloud he could only answer, "No, I'm all right." He sauntered in, trying to cover the hopeless silence with a smile he knew must have seemed idiotic.

"Did you have a nice time?" she asked, although she did not have any idea where he had gone, and was indifferently wondering what he had been up to now with this strange behavior.

Her room seemed different tonight, although he could tell at a glance that nothing had been altered. The combination of period, functional, and unclassifiable had always disturbed Mario. Then there was the same confusion of books (some opened), record albums, curios collected from travels, and, above all, that jungle of flowering vines entering crazily through the opened door of her terrace and through the windows. There must have been a dozen varieties. But as he looked at it all now, he thought it rather amusing. In fact for some incomprehensible reason, he found her room tonight delightful, crazy, happy, amusingly full of many interests! So this was her private world! And he was an outsider filled with yearning to share this with her. If he didn't make an attempt, just one attempt, he might never have the opportunity again.

His glance fell on a stack of architectural magazines. He picked up one and walked toward her. "I didn't know you were so interested in architecture."

"Very much," she smiled, but she was observing him warily as one does the sleight of hand of a magician, tolerantly amused and expectant. It was enough to silence him, this expression of hers. But he couldn't afford to be silent, not now. "Then if you're interested in architecture," he repeated stupidly, "you might be interested in the project that we are going to...that is, that I am going to..." he faltered.

Lourdes closed her book. "Mario, I have never seen you so confused before. There is something the matter. Please tell me."

If unable to reveal his new emotions toward her, he rejoiced that at least he had been given this opening to tell her about everything else. With a rush of words he began, from the chance meeting with a former classmate of his, an architect, to this evening's decisive break with his father and all that he represented.

As she listened, Lourdes' curiosity gradually changed to astonishment. The diffident agreeable voice, the characteristic easy gestures were no more. He was emphatic and glowing. She had not seen him like this since the first year of their marriage! Like a series of time-exposures, a metamorphosis seemed to take place before her very eyes.

"Then he shook me off pretty violently," he was saying, referring to the architect, "but I understand. He will see that I'm not 'playing at heroics'! Playing!" he laughed vehemently. "If he only knew how he has stirred up everything in me that I thought was dead, and has helped me find myself again!"

He had been walking back and forth, then seated himself on the edge of a white leather pouf, vigorously clasping and unclasping his hands, as though his newfound energy could not be contained. Now, as he abruptly raised his head and looked at Lourdes, her perplexed expression checked him. "Well?" his smile was almost of embarrassment.

It was now Lourdes who found words difficult. Finally, she shook her head in wonder, "I could never have imagined. Why, I thought life for you was—"

"No, Lourdes. It wasn't," He anticipated. "It was pointless. Everything was made for me. God, a man needs to feel that he can do something on his own! Yes, even I," he smiled at her. "How many times have I been shocked at—let's call it 'company policy'—but when I tried to do something about it, I was called naïve, disloyal."

"As your family will call you now," she admonished.

"As everyone I know. That's why I was glad you were home." He hesitated, for he scarcely dared more. "I had the feeling that you would understand, Lourdes."

"I do." She rose and walked towards the terrace door, deeply touched.

He wanted to go to her but he was still too uncertain of her reaction. How easy it had been all these years to put his arms around her, when it had meant nothing! But now, to span the few steps which separated them, that gulf between the need to communicate and the action itself seemed the most challenging obstacle he had ever confronted. His heart pounded, his hands were damp with perspiration and he felt an agonizing hollowness in his stomach. So this is what it felt like! And what he had seen in De Armas' eyes during that telephone conversation with whoever it was in the bodega that first time they had come across each other. Oh, being alive was not easy! Yet he

was going to lose Lourdes because the moment was passing, and he could

do nothing about it, only stand there paralyzed, with his heart thumping until it burst; or excuse himself, casually say good night, and leave without her ever knowing how he felt about her!

Just then Lourdes dropped the book which she had absently brought to the terrace. Mario quickly recovered it glancing at the title as he gave it to her. "Poetry for a lady who inspires it," he bantered with mock gallantry and then quite unexpectedly quoted, "I have been faithful to you, Cynara, in my fashion."

Lourdes could not believe what she heard. This joke belonged to the old days. She looked at him bewildered.

"It's true, you know," he continued, "I think I have been more faithful to you than to myself."

"Oh?" she remarked easily. But his deliberate lightness made her uncomfortable.

"Well, that is a euphemism," he laughed. "To be quite honest, I should have said, "I have been as faithless to myself as to you.""

Lourdes, shocked at his unwonted honesty, took the book from him and would have turned, but he held her hand.

"Lourdes, I know I've startled you enough for one evening with my outburst, but there's more," his smile was self-mocking.

"As I was on my way home after the argument tonight, I began thinking about you and me, how it had been at the beginning, you remember?"

The smile became wistful. "Remember that little two-by-four office of mine, and how important I felt?"

Yes, Lourdes remembered silently. And the framed engravings I never had a chance to give him. The ones I had collected secretly all during college years to hang in that first office as a surprise.

"And remember our first apartment," Mario was saying, "where I made sofas out of crates? It was a pretty good job! So deceptive that I'll wager more than one guest's sacroiliac remembers! And the first breakfast you made. Eggs in an uncured iron skillet! You asked me if I was all right because I   looked green. I felt green!"

With increased misgiving Lourdes had withdrawn her hand from his, and now suddenly in spite of himself Mario's protective merriment was gone and he said quite seriously, "What happened to us, Lourdes that everything changed so? What happened? Oh, don't try to answer," he hurried. "It doesn't matter anymore! What is important is that we are still young enough to correct our mistakes. We can start all over, the right way!"

Lourdes was distraught and at the same time embarrassed for his sake, for this typical overconfidence. She was seized with a terrible desire to shout, "'Start all over!' But I have! Long ago, when you left me to die of waiting and someone else restored me to life!"

But as he stood there, she felt again that compassion, almost tenderness, for this man. She remembered how much she had loved him. How long she had waited for him! A haunting line from the poet Emilio Ballagas almost burst from her: "What if you come too late,/ And find only the frozen ashes of waiting?"

No, she could not tell him. She turned from him and leaned over the balcony. Her visible emotion, misinterpreted, encouraged Mario, and he continued more impulsively, "After what happened at Saenz's tonight, I know that we can do whatever we really want to do! The fellow I was telling you about taught me that! Oh, if you could have seen him! Imagine, Lourdes, after discovering that he had been completely deceived, that his plans had been distorted, and that he was being used; and after my father tried to tempt and threaten him, he had the courage to walk out, knowing that this meant ruin for him in Cuba! All my useless life, without realizing it, I needed to know a person like this! If I had only met De Armas long ago, our whole life might have been different!

A lightening pain pierced through Lourdes's body. "'De Armas?'" she repeated, thinking she had not heard.

"Yes, Jorge De Armas," he answered.

"Is he the one you have been talking about?" she managed to ask. It was still not believable.

"Why, yes! You will understand what I mean when you meet him."

The metal pattern of the railing cut into her palms as she clung to it to control the trembling and to keep from falling. Somewhere under the shock her mind was trying to make her comprehend the words that were only sounds: "completely deceived... using him...ruin..." That means Jorge, he's talking about Jorge, she kept saying to herself, his work...our life...

"Even worse," Mario was saying, "was the sort of brutal way he discovered that I had sponsored him, as though his design was not accepted on its own merit. He didn't give me a chance to explain that they never would have been interested in him if he hadn't shown great talent. They intended giving him plenty of opportunity in the future as long as he proved himself 'adaptable' on this particular project. You should have seen his face when Papá used that word!" Mario glowed with admiration. "You never heard anyone talk to the old man as he did. I'm eager for you to meet him, Lourdes. You will, of course, as we'll be working together."

"You what...?" Inconceivable that a part of her brain was functioning, interpreting the sound-symbols!

"Oh, naturally it will take a while for him to recover from this blow. Right now, I suppose he hates everything, and especially me," he admitted regretfully. "He thinks that it was only from a favor from me that he was given this work. It's amazing that a man as gentle as he really is can be capable of such raging pride!"

"Oh stop!" Lourdes cried harshly. Mario looked at her astonished. She had brusquely turned from the balcony and was pressing her fingers against her temples.

"I'm sorry," Mario faltered, "boring you with so much talk about someone you don't even know! But you will. Once he gets over this shock and I can convince him that I'm on his side, he'll be coming here often."

Lourdes' unexpected laugh alarmed him. It sounded a bit hysterical. He crossed to her swiftly and would have put his arm around her but she cried, "Don't!" and jerked herself from him almost savagely. For a moment he was stunned. But then he smiled, suddenly reassured. He followed her and exclaimed delightedly, "You do still care, don't you? You would not have reacted so strongly if you were indifferent!" This time he embraced her with more confidence.

"No, Mario, no!" she whispered, but her protest now incited him.

"Do you see what I mean?" he whispered excitedly. "You want me, Lourdes, don't you! God, now I realize that just a short time ago you came to my room, remember? That day after our Carnival party. You came to me, and I was so damned blind!" he held her more tightly and continued, "but it will be different this time. I promise you now that we've found each other again!" He no longer knew what he was saying. He forcibly turned her face to him, and she felt his large hands moving over her body, the moist familiar mouth covering hers. "This is someone else, not I, not I," she clung to the thought as though it were a talisman to preserve her sanity.

A knocking at the door was accompanied by Pancha's apologetic and sleepy voice. "Excuse me, Señor Mario, your mother and brother are here. Must be something important for Doña Maria to come here this time of night."

The knocking had aroused Lourdes from her trance-like state of shock, and she saw Mario carefully combing his hair before the mirror. He said, "Well, we know what this is! Mother must have found out about what happened tonight." Just before he went downstairs, he turned to Lourdes. "You come

too!" he said impulsively.

For years he had not asked Lourdes to participate in any personal discussion with his mother. This invitation was a sign of rebellion against his former life and a kind of pride in his newfound "friend," Lourdes.

She could not refuse. "I'll be down shortly," she nodded. In sudden playfulness Mario winked at her as he shut the door.

Limp with relief she remained with closed eyes, unutterably grateful for the moment of solitude. If she could only have a few moments to herself.

The rise and fall of voices from the library below swelled on little waves growing ever higher. Even now Mario was calling her impatiently. She descended, not caring how she looked. Her mother-in-law never saw her anyway; she would notice nothing now. As Lourdes entered the library, the wave of conversation fell and they all looked up. Miguel and his wife were there too. Doña Maria's voice greeted her.

"Good evening, my dear Lourdes. It was really inconsiderate of Mayito to disturb you. There wasn't any need." She offered her cheek for the meaningless ritual of Lourdes' kiss. "I wanted her here, Mamá," Mario protested, "and there is a need." He took Lourdes' hand gratefully, and his face was flushed and agitated. "Dear," he explained "Papá has had a severe liver attack because of our argument, I'm afraid. Naturally, Mother is upset too. She came here as she did not want him to overhear our conversation on the phone. But I can't make her understand my position. Perhaps you can-"

Doña Maria interrupted. Her voice and eyes were glacial. "I am sure that if there is any explanation, it can be made by you, Mario. There is no need to involve a third party."

"Lourdes is not a third party, Mother!" Mario retorted. "It concerns her life as well as mine!"

"As well as all of us," his mother corrected softly.

Mario ignored the inference. "We have plans," he continued. "Lourdes feels about this as I do. She always has, as a matter of fact!" he added recklessly. "She has been very patient. There were so many things we wanted to do. But we never did." Warmed by his convert zeal, he expanded. "How could we have? Everything was made for us, ambitions invented for us. Papá has always overwhelmed me, wanting me to become another imitation of himself," he looked fleetingly at Miguel, "suffocating me with his own plans instead of leaving me to follow my own!"

To Doña Maria's credit she limited herself to a reproach. "But why have you never told me this before? Or is it, perhaps, that I too have 'suffocated' you?" Her tone was gentle, casual, with no trace of resentment or sarcasm.

"But, Mamá!" both Miguel and Mario protested in unison. Mario hurriedly crossed over to her and took her hand. "Don't ever say that again! I'm sure you were joking." He kissed her on the forehead. "Of course I would have told you but I didn't realize it myself. Although I think Lourdes has, for a long time now..." He looked at Lourdes questioningly.

"Oh?" his mother observed softly.

"But I didn't know until tonight. When I saw a man who has nothing but his talent and his honesty stand up to my father, lose everything he could have had, and walk away owning the world, I was looking at the man I should have been! The Guzmans have been like this in other generations. They skipped over my father. But why can't we pick it up again?" He was facing Miguel now, and it suddenly sickened him to see his brother's and sister-in-law's obtuse detachment. They were looking at him as though he were some rare specimen in an aquarium, puzzled, slightly troubled but with no suspicion of its relevance to themselves. He turned from them. "At least I will try," he muttered.

"But not at the sacrifice of your father's life, Mario!"

"Let's not be dramatic, Mother. I'm sorry about Papá, and I'm afraid it couldn't be helped. He's outraged because he's been defied for the first time, and by his own son, who finally has the impudence to think for himself! Oh, no conflict of principles is troubling him, don't worry! He is indifferent to the moral implications involved in this entire affair—defrauding the public, deceiving the architect, making accomplices of his sons. Let's be honest. Nothing can really touch him, not inside. We all know that!"

"No, that's not true. He was not always that way," his mother said after a silence. "You're not fair to him. He too had 'things he wanted to do.'"

"Papá?" Mario exclaimed scornfully.

"Have you ever bothered to find out? To ask him about his youth?"

Doña Maria sat very still but her hands trembled as they folded and unfolded a small lace handkerchief in her lap. Then she looked directly at Mario, and her face was quite pale as she spoke. "I will answer you honestly, Mario. Do you think you and your architect friend are the only ones to be deceived and disillusioned? Did you think so? But when your father confronted his crisis, as you evidently have tonight, circumstances and his own nature demanded a different solution. For him, the only way to survive was to be practical, to focus on one's capacity to accomplish. And he has accomplished much! I have loved your father all these years, and you, my two sons, who have been my only true life."

She struggled to maintain her composure, but her voice quavered, and as Miguel and Mario started towards her, she began to sob. Mario would have put his arms around her, but she shook her head, and with a forgiving pat on his shoulder, she left the room. Miguel's wife hurried after her. As they waited in the uncomfortable stillness, Miguel and Mario began wandering through the entrance hall and the library. Lourdes saw their eyes meet and Mario accept his brother's wordless reproach. The bond that held them was stronger than any disagreement, and there was a fleeting smile of reconciliation as they turned toward their mother's approaching footsteps with an expression of concern and reverence.

When the time came to leave, Doña Maria turned and placed her hand on Mario's shoulder. She had nervously dabbed her face with powder, but the uneven patches only emphasized the eyelashes still wet. "My darling son, if you want to be so stubborn, you will kill your father. Don't underestimate his love for you. He has denied himself its joys, but it exists in him nevertheless. He has only desired to make you invulnerable against life's deception. This is his way of loving. We are all too overwrought to discuss anything now. But if you will only give it thought, you will find a way to compromise with him. Otherwise, not even his love will make him retract."

"Of that I am sure," Mario answered drily. "Poor Mamá," he murmured as he watched the departing car, "What at a wonderful person she is! But don't worry, my dearest," he took Lourdes' arm as they re-entered the house. "This discussion has only clarified the issue for me and reaffirmed my resolve. Oh, I know they are all going to use every means to persuade me! But they will fail, for I've found myself, thanks to De Armas. Perhaps what I thought was a useless life was a seed lying dormant, waiting for this moment. Who knows? It may be my destiny to perpetuate the Guzman tradition that was sidetracked with my father. Lourdes," he stopped short and faced her momentously. "I think my star is ascending."

This was a new note! Lourdes listened to this unprecedented flight of rhetoric with fascination. He continued, "I will not disappoint you this time! We're going to recapture everything we almost lost. But now we have the advantage of being a little older, having a better sense of values. Besides our own happiness, there are so many things, social and political issues, to fight for right here in Cuba! Oh, I don't want to bore you now. I know you don't know about these things, living as you do in your own world of—" he paused, caught short. "Well," he smiled lamely, "I really don't know what your world is, do I? But I can find out." He squeezed her arm. "We're going to grow together. I tell you what I'm going to do; I'm going to say good-night to you now and pack my bag. I'm going to leave in the morning for Santa Clara. There are two fellows there, brothers. One of them is the best estimator Dad ever had. But they both left. I know why now. They were too honest to play along. If they would come in with us, they, De Armas, and I will really make a team! I'm also going to look for a small office to rent when I return." Resolve animated every gesture and inflection. He was glowing. He held both her hands in his and said regretfully, "I won't see you in the morning, as I don't want to disturb you. I'm leaving very early. I wish I didn't have to. There is so much for us to talk about."

All night he had been experiencing this exciting sensation of really seeing Lourdes as a woman: the slender neck which gave her an air of natural aloofness, the abundant dark hair that he would like to loosen at this very moment and see it cascade over the cool green satin negligee which, despite her regal bearing, suggested voluptuous form underneath; the graceful assurance of her movements. She was a provocative combination of strength and femininity. What a fool he had been! Silvia couldn't compare with her. He did not think that Lourdes was the sensual type, although she certainly looked it. But perhaps with a little guidance...Undoubtedly, he had not bothered to teach her much, he reproached himself.

The expression of his eyes did not escape Lourdes, and she was infinitely relieved when he shook his head quickly in dismissal and kissed her on the forehead. "We will have a lifetime ahead of us," he promised softly and went to his room.

22
SUCCESS

After a sleepless night for Lourdes came the waiting. Waiting for Jorge to call. Hearing the collage of normal morning sounds, indiscriminate fragments assembled in the frame of habit as though nothing had changed.

At last his voice. Yet not his voice at all. Apathetic. Toneless.

And when they met that same morning at Oscar's apartment— "their" apartment—his eyes had seemed burnt out. Nevertheless, with the strength his presence always gave her, she had heard herself even now speaking with optimism about "together working things out."

Her optimism astounded Jorge. "Work what out? That my career in Cuba is ended? That I have a mother and sister who are forced to depend on me? That any hope I ever had of attaining a position worthy of you is gone, and as for supporting you..." The very thought was preposterous.

Why must his career be ended? she had vehemently demanded. Mario's father was not the only builder in Cuba!

"When he is an enemy, he might just as well be the only one."

"Surely you and Mario must have misunderstood!" she had insisted. "I know my father-in-law has never been very ethical. But to be this unscrupulous? He has no need! Why would he do such a thing?"

She remembered how Jorge had raised his arms slightly in a gesture of bewilderment. "Who can answer that?" he mused. "I doubt whether he himself could. Maybe strong men like Guzman act without knowing why anymore. They follow one objective—success or whatever—until it ends by hypnotizing them. I don't know," he said with weary impatience. "I'm the last one to have the answers. If I did, we wouldn't be in this situation now!"

Lourdes remembered feeling lost and betrayed, she did not know by what. Did he really mean this? Were all the plans suddenly shattered like something struck by those freak summer lightnings of the tropics? Was it to be the same all over again, before she had met him?

After a while Jorge continued, "I was beginning to think I was an architect. I couldn't know that my designs were accepted because I was your husband's protégé! Amusing, isn't it?"

It was painful to hear this unwonted sarcasm. "That's not true!" she hastened to explain. "Mario feared you would think that! He said his father was very impressed by your work. Mario merely suggested your name. You did the rest." Lourdes thought she saw a faint look of relief on his face as he considered this.

But then he said tensely, "Yes! They gave me the job. They thought an unknown architect with ambitions was their man." Suddenly he flared, "I wish I could be, Lourdes! I swear to God wish I could! Then I would have known how to make my way!" He seemed to be twisting desperately inside himself. "Every man who has accomplished anything has had to close his eyes one time in his life! But I can't! I'm too weak. I can't learn to stop caring!" He emphasized each of the last words slowly with a self-mocking smile. He could not be freed of himself.

"Of course you can't," Lourdes had responded. "It's exactly that quality that makes you you. What else do you think it was that so inspired Mario?"

She wished she had not said that, seeing the tormented look on his face. Since entering the apartment, she had forgotten about Mario. Now, with sickening clarity, she remembered. She had no choice but to tell Jorge of Mario's new attitude towards her and his life. "But it won't last!" she hastened to add as she saw the effect her words had produced. "All this is only a new hobby for him!"

Jorge turned from her, shaken. "You can't be sure of that, Lourdes."

"I tell you I know Mario!" she protested nervously. "Oh, at first he'll be caught up in thoughts of what he calls his 'ascending star.' The challenge will be an exciting game. But when he discovers that he's not—what is his other expression? —oh yes! that he's not a 'man of destiny.' Or when his mother tempts him with some small compromise, he'll return! You will see!"

Jorge shook his head. "Everything you say may be true, but we don't know if it is. This may be a real turning point in his life."

"What if it is!" Lourdes retorted. "I don't believe that's true, but what if it is? I ceased to exist for Mario long ago. After all these years, am I expected to give up my own life—our lives—because he just might need me now? He has no right!"

"It's not that, Lourdes," he said harshly. "It's that I'm not strong enough to live with that doubt. Every day of our life together I would be thinking, "Maybe Mario's life paid for this.""

"And what of all the other lives that have been the price of Mario's games? He's had all the chances since he was born. He could have done anything he wanted. Inside himself, too, he had everything it took, but he chose not to use it. And every time he tires of those games, he throws lives away too, of the people who believed in them, including himself, and me, and..." She was thinking of her baby.

"I know, I know," Jorge said softly. "Maybe it's because there were always too many chances, they cancelled each other out. Maybe it's as bad as not having any, unless you're very strong. Maybe it's worse, because then you can blame only yourself."

The long silence that filled the room seemed already to separate them a little. "And now something has made him believe again, and it does not seem a game at all," Jorge finally added.

"You," she whispered.

Jorge closed his eyes, almost as if in prayer.

She had not wanted to say it, but she owed him that truth. And she knew that after that, there could be nothing more.

For his sake she would not cry out.

Suddenly, fiercely, he drew her to him.

When she could speak, she said quietly, "Give me time to understand and to get used to the idea." She faltered, then continued with an effort, "Maybe something still could happen."

There was grief in his eyes to see her still cling to a hope.

23
EASTER SUNDAY

"But Señora Lourdes! You don't look like Easter Sunday," Pancha protested unhappily. "Why, what will the sombrero say when he hears that you haven't worn the new hat that he made you especially for today! And you can be sure he'll hear about it!" She wagged an admonishing finger. "He delivered it himself last week, and if you had seen how contento and proud of it he was! He had to take it out of the box to show me when he explained how every detail of it was designed to go with your new suit!" Pancha held up the hat, and her dark knobby fingers fluttered, poked, and pointed out its virtues. Seeing that this had no effect on Lourdes, who, pale and listless, was buttoning a simple black crêpe she had chosen to wear, Pancha raised her voice as though its very loudness might evoke some interest. "This beautiful new suit! You would look like a queen!" She dangled it on its hanger before Lourdes, who merely looked without seeing it and then quickly returned it to the closet. Pancha took great pride in considering herself above superstition, but that unworn suit suddenly looked headless and legless and not quite Christian, as anything did that was not used for what it was intended.

She changed her tactics, grumbling, so that the upstairs girl could not eavesdrop. "And not going to church with the family! Even if Señor Mario isn't here, the rest of them will be very offended..." her voice quavered off in futility.

"If they call," Lourdes answered, "ask them to excuse me, that I had to go early to a christening at Reina."

"Bueno, bueno, Señora." Pancha did not believe this, but at least it was an adequate excuse for the family.

Lourdes folded the black lace mantilla into her purse and turned to leave, but she saw Pancha's troubled face and came back to kiss her on the cheek. "Don't worry, Panchita," she whispered.

She had chosen a Low Mass at Reina Church in order to avoid seeing anyone she knew. Strange request this day of Resurrection, Saint Paul's words, "Purge out the old leaven," asking her to relinquish all that meant earthly life to her! Was she to pretend that she was not of the earth? She could not.

When it was over, she stood on the side of the wide entrance steps leading to the street as the parishioners flowed past her in a gaudy stream. Those to whom the day meant more than a festive occasion were walking into a new whole life. The world had just begun for them. Others, unconscious of its deeper meaning, nevertheless carried it within them. They were born to it as they were born to the good smell of garlic, to sun, to laughter. They did not stop to thank God for garlic! Yet they could scarcely live without it.

On this block she had parked so many times to meet Jorge, had cursed her fear, the subterfuges, and the noisy, sweating streets. How could she have thought it sordid, this road that led to life!

She hurried to the car, and, as always when she needed to find strength, drove to the ocean to the abandoned Vedado Point, where the waves plunged and where the wild growing garden gave another kind of strength in anonymity, a kind of nameless belonging.

She had been dismayed when she had first learned from Jorge that this was the site of the Camacho project, and the coincidence had seemed extraordinary. Jorge had spoken to her of the significance of the project and his hopes that, if this were to prove successful—and he was confident it would—a new way of life would be opened to the lower middle class, a new attitude towards living whose example might spread throughout the island.

Now she did not want to think of what would be there in its place! And today the coincidence did not seem coincidence at all.

She parked near a corner of the garden and took a long walk on the beach. When she returned, a woman was sweeping the garden path. Lourdes had noticed her at a distance on previous visits, and thought she might be the one of whom Jorge had spoken.

As Lourdes approached the car, the woman straightened, and her eyes met Lourdes'. Although they had never spoken, never seen each other except from a distance, a look of recognition passed between them. More than recognition, it was as if each was looking at her own mirrored reflection. They stood looking, saying nothing, and were aware of the startling experience. Suddenly they smiled, and then the woman turned and continued her sweeping.

Ever after, for Lourdes, the remembrance of the woman's eyes and the breath of the sea were one.

24
MATEO! COME QUICK!

Francisco the Spaniard was glad it was Monday. He had kept the bar closed since Holy Thursday except to serve café. But that wasn't very lively. Besides, he liked to work. So it was good now to see one of his favorite customers coming: Señor Jorge.

"Buenos Dias!" Francisco's hearty greeting bounced unheard off the counter he was polishing.

Jorge had driven aimlessly around town, finding no place to be alone that did not hold the expression of Lourdes' face at their last meeting. Pain, bewilderment, and still that speck of preposterous, unrelenting hope shone in her eyes.

What if she were right that somehow they could work things out and be together, no matter what? But then, she had not yet realized that they would become two different people. And eventually if they lost themselves in the metamorphosis...well, by then it would make no difference.

This thought pursued him as he drifted on a wave of habit which had brought him to the bodega.

"Eh, Don Jorge!" The respectful title which Francisco conferred upon Jorge failed to evoke the usual cheery grin. Francisco appreciated that "Don." Jorge was a quiet man and educado, yet Jorge never let that get in the way. And then, what a gift from God he had for telling jokes. Or just inventing them. They had become the main source of Francisco's own repertory, which was a very important thing for a bodeguero to have, especially at the bar, when the political discussions or baseball arguments got too hot! One of those remembered jokes had saved more than one head from being cracked, not to mention damage to the bar!

But today there would surely be no joke. "Don Jorge" had seated himself in the farthest, darkest corner of the bodega.

With what he thought to be tactful naturalness, Francisco walked towards him and boomed in a round Galician voice, "Well, well! What would you like today?" Jorge looked up at him absently and shook his head; then, because he must order something, asked for cognac.

"If you have no desire for it, there is no necessity. Here you are a friend." Francisco was grieved to see him in this state. "I tell you what. I have some fine albariño wine from Galicia that I save for myself. For sorrow, it is also a good friend. You will be my guest."

From far away, Jorge shook his head.

Francisco busily began to wipe off the table near Jorge, trying to think of some way to cheer him up. Then he remembered what had happened that morning. It was enough to make anyone laugh. "Don Jorge," he said brightly, "you know who came here this morning? A tonto, por dios, what a young fool! He was connected with a construction company. Wanted me to sell this bodega to him!"

Jorge looked up, appreciating Francisco's efforts.

"I told him, sell it? What would I do if I sold it? It was my father's and now it's mine. He told me I wouldn't have to do anything, that I'd make a big profit on the sale and I'd have more money than I needed. Now what would I do with more money than need?" He waved the polishing cloth in exasperation. "When I asked him, he had to stop and think a moment about that. 'You could travel.' I told him that Galicia has changed since I left, and everyone is dead. Then he said I could travel somewhere else, to Rome or China! Now can you imagine that, Don Jorge? He knows I don't know anyone there. What would a man be going so far for just to see strangers?"

Jorge could not help but smile.

At another table Pancho, Isidro, and Mateo the policeman in their late morning dice-game were just warming up to the usual polemics when they were interrupted.

Suddenly, as though bursting from under the sidewalk, the wave of excited voices surged over the street. Their bobbing heads and gesticulating arms looked like darting sea-creatures under the whitewashed sun. The wave swelled nearer, and a small Negro boy was spawned from it. He sprinted breathlessly toward the policeman.

"Mateo!" he shouted, "Come quick! They lookin' for you! Here he is!" He waved to the others. "Someone killed at the abandoned house, Mateo! Squashed like a cockroach!"

There was no pity in his child's voice, nor in the faces of the others as they approached, sharpened with excitement that warmed the thin blood of their unfulfillment. Violence had broken them free. Only later, when they picked up their lives and remember themselves, pity perhaps would come. Pity for themselves in the form of one who had been squashed like a cockroach, the one that might someday be themselves.

"At the construction?"

"Sí, sí!"

Mateo tossed on the policeman's hat with the blue sweat rim on it. The hat was also very important now and much envied, especially since the accident was no political street shooting and presented no danger.

"Who was it?" Pancho asked the boy.

"Don't know."

As the policeman hurried towards the crowd, Pancho called out to Francisco, "I'll be back," and followed Mateo. The other players joined him; and Jorge followed them absentmindedly, as one who can go nowhere follows shells on a beach leading nowhere.

The sharp cry of a woman standing near him cleaved him from his thoughts. "I can't look!" she gasped, and turned away, her trembling hands covering her eyes. It was then that he became aware that he formed part of a fast-augmenting crowd standing before the house that had just been torn down. The hard midday sun touched up the disintegrating cloud of cement dust that still hung over the shattered mass.

Raw cement dust ate the eyes and the delicate tissues of the nostrils, creeping down the throat and clinging there.

Two-hundred-year-old laurel and ceiba trees lay torn from the ground, their powerful arms contorted against death, their roots still alive with the fresh earth trembling in clots on them, writhing under the nakedness that was their dying.

And giant pine trees torn from life so suddenly that they had not had time to taste death. They lay sweet and green, believing that their branches would forever be the harps upon which the sea sang.

Fresh red soil spurted over fragments of marble and plaster and painted tiles; the gray bones of old shutters and doors and arbors, flung over the ruins; in the center a great yellow bulldozer; and under the broken columns which it had just felled was the one all had come to see, the one who had shaken out this moment for them; the one who looked no different from the uprooted ceibas and the red earth and the broken marble.

People began to cough and choke from the dust. "Doesn't anyone know who it was?" inquired a bystander. "Sure," another answered. "The old lady who lived here. Sort of crazy."

"Oh yeah!" exclaimed the bystander. "The one they called Marquesa. How did it happen?"

"Workers weren't looking, she climbed up into the tower again, she just wouldn't leave!"

Jorge was stunned. It was the unforgettable woman with whom he'd talked only a few days earlier.

"Vámonos de aqui!" someone cried. "Let's get out of here!"

"Qué horrible!"

"Qué cabrona muerte!" "What a hell of a way to die!"

Jorge stood motionless, involuntarily identifying with the scene, as one pursuing his work unconsciously pauses listening to the chords of familiar music. The cement dust piercing his lungs was nothing new. That was the only certainty with which he lived: that sooner or later, a bulldozer always crept by to destroy anything he had. He should have expected it. But whatever else he accepted in his life, he was not going to let Lourdes be destroyed with him, like this one under the columns.

For a horrible moment he had thought that it was Lourdes.

The crowd was growing fast. Its rhythm became insistent, as though deliberately choreographed. One dancer would jostle his way out and three jostle their way in. One out, wiping the sweat from his forehead as one wipes his mouth after a satisfying banquet; three in, hunger filling their eyes. One and three, one and two, one and one, all feasting their unfulfillment on the one lying there.

Jorge turned to leave when a shrill staccato sound which had persisted somewhere adjacent to the columns took on speech.

"It cannot be, cannot be, cannot be," it said. "She is our friend. Police no take her away. We bury her."

The voice came from a small Oriental who was attempting to communicate with Mateo, who stood near—but not too near—the remains of the woman. For all his revolver and hat, he was not much of a realist, Mateo the policeman.

He and the interrupted construction workers, while awaiting the arrival of the judge, had succeeded in holding off the crowd, with the exception of the Oriental and two others, evidently his companions. The policeman looked down on the Chinese and in helplessness scratched his head.

"I repeat, Chan Li, that no one is permitted to touch her until the arrival of the judge. Then she will be taken to the morgue, and there, if you so desire, you will be—" but he suddenly interrupted himself. "But why do we waste words? I doubt there is anything sufficient left to take anywhere at all!"

"Cannot be, cannot be," Chan Li answered. Mateo shrugged his shoulders with good-natured impatience. "Can't one of you quiet him?" he asked the two companions, one a Negro, the other white, although the charcoal soot covering him made his features indiscernible. They did not answer him or seem to hear him.

"Suéltame ya, chinito! Let me go!" He wiped his forehead and turned to one of the workers. "Jesus! This fellow's got a death hold on me! Can't any of you talk Chinese? How long are we going to have to wait here for the judge? What sun!"

A cry we all carry with us on this island, cursed Jorge. What sun, what sun! We eat it, our bellies swell up on it cheap with bitter jokes, and then it eats us. Sucks up our blood and the marrow of our spirit.

"You said it! Surely is hot!" the construction worker answered Mateo. "You feel it worse when you're not working under it."

But the arrival of the judge and the doctor interrupted them,

After the legal proceedings had been completed, Chan Li, who had hovered nervously at a distance, shadowed by the silent charcoal maker El Topo and the Negro Chori, poked at Mateo's uniform.

"Now? Now?" he asked. The judge was hurrying to his car.

"For the love of God, the chino again!" groaned Mateo. But Chan Li had not waited for an answer. He was scurrying towards the judge.

"Juez! Juez!" he intercepted. "Must talk to you. Now accept. Now yes. $150 I, $150 he (indicating his companions), $150 Topo, $150 Chori. Bury her, the Marquesa."

His Honor had not understood. "What does he want?" he asked Mateo, who had hurried to detain the little man. Mateo's handkerchief waved a wilted exclamation. "Your Honor, these people have made a nuisance! These are two of the squatters we told you about. They're all sort of crazy. They're friends of the old lady who was killed. They've been pestering me here not to take her remains to the Fosa. They want—"

"Fosa no!" Chan Li poked again. "With money we bury her. Maybe forty I, forty he, forty."

"Ah, now I get it! He—"

"—forty Arsenio—"

"Hold it, will you, chino! Judge, it's the eviction money from the company. None of these wanted it because they refused to vacate. But now I guess they're willing to take the money to be able to give their pal a funeral. That it, chino?"

"So," Chan Li nodded.

"Refused the money for themselves, and now are putting up a fight for it to bury their friend," the judge observed. Yes, officer, naturally these people would be called mad. How many are they?"

"There are five living on the estate grounds, Your Honor. They refused to move and refused to appear at the court summons."

"And their possessions?"

"Duly disposed of, sir."

"Tell them they are legally entitled to the money. Take care of it for me. I'm in a hurry. Going to see Almendares beat Havana," he winked and was gone.

197

Chan Li's eyes had not left theirs during the conversation. He stepped forward nervously as the judge left.

"Never mind, chino," Mateo said. "You can accompany me to the Mortuorio. There you can find an undertaker. You will be given the money to bury her." Chan Li's expression did not alter, but he looked at his silent companions and nodded.

Mateo turned to the crowd. "Go on home! Let's clear this up!" Mateo and the other policeman had had enough.

"Ice cream!" the familiar bells tinkled through the dispersing crowd.

Then Jorge and some of the stragglers heard the voice.

It came from the rocks that sloped from the ocean. Had the day been less calm, it could have been the shout of an old wave caught in the hollowed rocks. But the sea was immobile. The voice rumbled above the various small noises of the waning crowd. Then Jorge heard it plainly.

"Es-a-a!" it called, "Marque-esa-a! Es-a-a!"

He saw the ragged old fellow climbing up the rocks against the horizon, an imposing figure despite the dirt and the beard so unkempt he was tempted to doubt its authenticity. The man seemed to be in an exalted state which made him oblivious to the scene into which he had broken. Held firmly under his arm was a medium-sized lidless crate of the usual grocery variety. The tall Negro saw him and, running towards him, shouted. "Arsenio!"

"Where's Marquesa, Chori? Hurry up and tell her I have her papers. Where's that cabron construction superintendent, and the policía? Hear that, policía? Now you must leave us alone! I found the papers for the house!"

"You found the papers?"

"In here," he indicated the grocery crate. "I took them from that dog, Carambita. Been trailing him since yesterday until I found him. I knew he had stolen them,and I knew also that I would get him."

"Christ, you had a fight all right. You're all banged up."

"He is banged up worse," grinned the old fellow.

Chan Li and Topo were hurrying towards them. Arsenio shouted to them, "Chan Li, Topo, look! The papers! Eh, where is Marquesa? Now we can kick those workers out of here! Marque-esa-a—" But his voice failed suddenly. He had looked up as he called her towards some place he evidently thought she was.

Probably the place where the razed tower had been, thought Jorge. Arsenio was standing motionless, his eyes fixed as though he were blind. Then he turned his gaze sharply, without moving his upturned head, not daring to face what he would see. He would have to look down now, for there remained no building silhouetted against the sky, nothing to see on high. His head slowly lowered, and you could see the shaggy old fellow taking it all in slowly, expressionless. The uprooted trees, the ruins, the bulldozer, the crowd. He tightened his hold on the crate, which seemed suddenly to stoop him with its weight. His head pivoted slowly toward the little group that stood silent, watching him. Chan Li, El Topo, Chori...his eyes searching out one that was missing.

"The Marquesa," he said. The tall Negro finally answered him by pointing mutely towards the figure under the columns. He looked at the indefinable thing and began to walk towards it heavily.

"Hey you, Grandpa! Get away from there!" shouted one of the policemen just arrived.

"Chico, let the poor devil alone. He's one of them that lived here, pitched out under one of those trees. They all lived here for years," Mateo told him. "He was away and didn't know they tore it all down."

"I'm telling you they're all cracked. Didn't you just hear him say he has important papers in that grocery box?" laughed the other policeman. "Hey, let's see the important documents you got there!" He approached the old man, who did not seem to notice when the policeman took the crate from him. A couple of others who could joke at anyone's expense ambled up for the fun. Jorge observed that the big Negro did also. But not to joke, judging from his expression. "That box belonged to her," the Negro Chori warned quietly.

The policeman looked up. "Oh, that so? You one of her friends too?"

"Just so," he replied.

"Aah," the officer enlightened the others, gently tapping his head. "Well, I know it has some very important things here. We'll just take an official look. Won't bother anything," he added, urged by something in Chori's expression.

They began to lift out its contents: a scrapbook of photographs. clippings, and children's drawings, an old rag-doll; a box of seashells; a jumble of half-torn written pages, evidently having suffered by the old man's scuffle to obtain them; an ebony walking stick. The onlookers exchanged amused glances.

"Yessir, Grandpa, this was surely worth fighting for," the policeman laughed. "Better hide it away good so nobody steals it. What sun! Let's clear out fast, Mateo, eh?" he called as they walked away.

The shaggy old man was alone. His companions, seeing there was no trouble about the box, had hurried off to arrange for the burial. Suddenly he noticed something lying on the ground near Jorge. He walked towards him and

with difficulty stooped to picked it up. The fellow was all done in. He stood staring at the object he held in his hand. It was one of the wooden gargoyles fallen from the tower.

The old man's eyes met Jorge's, whose expression held something that made him no stranger.

"They were hers. I do not know how to read," was all he said, and glanced at the box.

Jorge understood. "I read. Do you wish—?"

The old one nodded without smiling. "I think you will do this for me. Not now; tomorrow."

"Where? Here they will be working."

"There on the beach over the rocks."

"I will come."

The old man nodded wearily, and without more words picked up the box and the wooden figure and wandered off toward the sea.

Children were beginning to run over the mounds of ruins, and the sun shone on the uprooted pines still alive and exhaling their fragrant breath. The cement dust had settled pale and poisonous over the ceiba and laurel trees. Jorge turned and walked away.

25
THE NIGHT WIND

Mario had not yet returned but he had telephoned Lourdes long distance to say that he would arrive home the following day. Although he had walked right into the Labor riots in Santa Clara, his enthusiasm remained undiminished. In fact, referring to President Grau's obvious betrayal of the Revolution, he spoke of joining De Armas and the others in the organization of a new party with Eddy Chibás, the Cuban People's Party, popularly called the Ortodoxos.

It was a dizzying monologue! After they had hung up, Lourdes could not help wondering if Jorge might possibly be right: that with encouragement, this new Mario would endure

She tried to contemplate renunciation and to recall the old battle from which she had retired long ago, the battle to help Mario against himself. She summoned the courage to imagine life with him, to remember all they had had at the beginning. But it was futile. For he was not the Mario who had once existed in her own image of him; nor did she believe, as Jorge did, in his "rebirth." And she had never felt more shamefully naked than the other night that Mario had begun to make love to her. No, they were two strangers who, having once lived together on another planet, had now to bear proximity without communication, suffering the degradation of arbitrarily forcing together the past and the present. Oh, there was the sorrow for the lost years with him, for the hands outstretched and never touching. But that was all.

And was this to take the place of her life with Jorge? Never again to be able to hope, saying, as they so often did, "The day that we can truly be together...?"

That evening when they met, Lourdes read the strain of helpless waiting in Jorge's eyes. Farewell could be in every meeting. Is it now? his eyes questioned, or are you still hoping for the little miracle that will not happen? She was aware of something else, a change in him which she could not define, but she did not mention it. What for? If he wanted her to know, he would tell her. A tacit agreement spared them futile discussion. They wanted to make every moment together count. Each embrace, each surrender was defiance of an empty future.

Yet failure was implicit in the very intention. Before, ecstasy had risen from the deep earth-core of tenderness, and had taken them unaware. And when in the transport of creation, which is love, they had thought mortal ultimate had been reached, it had been borne even higher. Their union had been a constant metamorphosis of the familiar into the new. Without seeking, there had been always some unexpected delight! And no act, no deviation could defile this white flame.

But now like an impure element, what had been natural and spontaneous became willful pursuit. Insolently they would wrest their immortality from the gods. The enforced prison of the shabby little apartment had contained the world, but now it was not enough.

Although it was quite late, they decided to drive to the countryside. The wide clear night vibrated with life, and the warm breath of the earth rose and enveloped them. Finding a secluded country lane, they stopped and lay a blanket down on the grass.

Without knowing it, they were driven by the urge to be freed together, as though compelled to mingle their life fluid with the universe; to make certain that their union would be perpetuated, merged in all of nature. Yet the greater their sexual fulfillment, the deeper the consciousness of impending loss. Their passion had become an impotent cry of rebellion which left them no cleansing.

An abrupt chill seized Lourdes, as though their bodies had become two marble figures superimposed upon the living night. They no longer were an integral part of it...nor of each other. In sudden terrible revelation she understood. They had already left each other. Something had carried them beyond each other, and they could not help it. Jorge had recognized it, but she had refused to. They had seized and shaped and held fast to it, but now, whatever it was, that hidden force which was the center of their lives, was moving them in different directions and demanded recognition. And because she denied it, they were being torn from the universal harmony, isolated. Even now she could feel the palpable emptiness which surrounded them!

It must be ended now. It must, it must.

"Jorge!" He had been lying quietly at her side looking up at the night. Now, startled by the tone of her voice, he sat up abruptly.

"I want to tell you quickly," she said, "I know now that…" There was so much she wanted to say to him, but the implications rushed upon her in all their force, and she shook her head trying to dispel her emotion.

But Jorge had understood. His own hand was cold as he took hers, which she had stretched towards him for strength to say what she must.

Wordlessly he clasped her tightly to himself. What was there that could be spoken?

As they drove back to Havana, they did not know if they would see each other again, but the voice of the night wind rushing past their open car seemed to answer.

26
TELEGRAM

Within hours of Mario's return they descended upon him once again—his mother, his brother, his sister-in-law—to appeal to him to work something out with his father, who was still ailing. Certainly, they argued, he could find something more satisfactory than plunging into a new lake with a stone around his neck!

Miguel demanded to know if he was trying to prove something. Yes! Mario had retorted hotly, glad for the opportunity to unburden himself. His mother then asked Mario whether he did not think that it would be much more of an accomplishment if, instead of abandoning his father and brother who needed him, he would right whatever policies in the Company he so objected to?

Lourdes, a silent spectator, could not bear watching this any longer. When no one noticed, she slipped out. If Jorge were witnessing this, she wondered as she went upstairs to her room, would he recognize it as a portent of their own sacrifice wasted, or would he say, "Help him to win"?

And if he didn't win?

She stood there looking at her room which was so beautiful because it had reflected her own joy. Each object in it had shared her radiant thoughts. She wondered if she would know when it all became merely substance again: wood, crystal, mortar. But energy can never be destroyed, she mused, only transferred. Perhaps all the living vibrations which had filled the room would fly out the window, to go who knows where...

For some unknown reason she remembered an incident which had occurred during her residence in New York. She was leaning over the balcony of a very high office building that overlooked unending city blocks. The streets themselves were not visible. It was like an ancient long-abandoned empire of spires and jagged roofs, abrupt cliff-levels, and eruption of TV antennae, black tubes, pipes, and water tanks. Smoke rising from the chimneys was the last thin breath of a dying volcano. Unseen, the sun splashed silver and gold on the buildings. And there was not one green thing, no leaf nor broken stem to seek its light. There was blue sky and white cloud, and no lake in all this empire in which they could reflect. Only glittering dead windows and the sun going to waste.

And then she saw a bird circling the great abandoned valley. This sole bird! Rather than lose the power of its wings, it risked the shadowed broken planes of the concrete valley. How could it live? Perhaps between the cracks of the pavement there was a blade of grass, or in an old flowerpot. Perhaps there might be a few seeds on a rooftop aviary long deserted.

She could hear the voices in the drawing room below. Slowly she rose and turned to go downstairs.

§

Jorge went to meet Arsenio as he had promised. He parked as near as possible to the shoreline Arsenio had indicated, which lay beyond a flat wasteland utilized for the burning of rubbish. There was no one in sight, and although it was possible that the old man had forgotten, Jorge decided to wait rather than disappoint him. He sat in the car and watched the erratic curls of smoke rise from the mounds. It looked unreal, the bleak stretch, and the tenebrous curtain hung from this fiercely beautiful day.

As he waited, he thought about the telegram he had received that morning, which he had not answered. An urgent meeting was to be held in Oriente Province. He knew what it meant. Except for the stubbornly loyal Eddy Chibás, no one doubted any longer that the Revolution had been betrayed by its own Party. A new Party would have to be formed and led, hopefully, by Chibás, if he could be made to realize the truth. And if he did not, someone else then, someone like Eddy, who believed in the people.

And they were sure, as Jorge had been before, that if necessary there would be someone else because the time for Cuba had come. The time itself would create the person. They were sure the triumph of the Revolution of the '30s was just the beginning, and that present betrayal must not, could not stop it. Nor would the futility of hate and destruction have any part in it. It would continue as it had been conceived, and as Jose Martí had first conceived the nation.

Well, perhaps. But Jorge also recalled the passage which the lawyer Cipriano Salinas had quoted when they had said good-bye at the Carmelo.

How did it go? "...For the children of earth are wiser than the children of light." Who were they, "the children of earth"? The practical ones, like old Guzman? He had borne Jorge's insults, yet still offered him what he wanted in the future. With conditions, naturally. But perhaps the man was trying to lead him to what he sincerely considered "reality," the adjustment to limitations, finding the area between the ideal and the feasible. Maybe that was what Salinas meant: learning from the practical ones without getting lost.

He remembered with what scorn Guzman had spoken of men who wasted their usefulness rather than acknowledge the human condition. But then, wasn't the human condition also strength! Or was he confusing strength with stubbornness? Or with arrogance? Pride? Holding on to the impossible?

The acrid smoke from the dump reached his car, and he began to cough. He walked away from it towards the corner.

Had it not been for the unmistakable beard, he would not have recognized the strange-looking group that was crossing the street from the bus-stop and approaching him. But there it was: the beard, and the ones he had seen with the old man yesterday. He could only stare at the apparition. They were all dressed in what was evidently intended to be "street clothes," but the effect was so ludicrous that only the solemnity of their expressions prevented laughter. The old man, in a shirt and suit too big for him, was finding locomotion difficult in the unaccustomed shoes; and his pale gaunt companion walked stiffly, probably unable to bend his knees because of trousers that reached only a little below his calves. The Negro and the Oriental were not much better off.

They approached him and stopped, all four of them regarding him with somber recognition. "Thank you for waiting," the Negro said. "We have just come from the Funeral Home to meet you."

"Also to remove these garments for a while," added the old man as they walked towards the shore. Their awkward efforts to balance themselves in their shoes over the jagged rocks were futile. The old man almost fell.

"Confound it!" he roared, momentarily coming to life. "For twenty years I have been walking over these rocks! They are my own bones; I know them so well. But I am without feet in these cages! We will begin removing here." They all sat down with alacrity and took off their shoes, wriggling their toes to the sun.

"Even my bottom knows these rocks," he continued, referring to the sharp edge of ancient coral bed on which he sat.

The Negro Chori suddenly jumped to his feet. "Your bottom, Arsenio, but not Francisco-the-bodeguero's!" he cautioned. "Get up, all of you; we gonna spoil these fine clothes that don't belong to us."

The others hastily arose, and with concern felt the seats of their trousers for damage.

"Be doing them a favor," Arsenio mumbled, but he rose just the same.

Jorge followed them as they continued lightly over the rocks now that their shoes were off, except for Topo, who couldn't bend his knees much.

Arsenio was still thinking, but suddenly he stopped walking and waved his arms with the shoes and socks, shouting "Holy Mother of God! When I think that men got up early to work and kill each other just to have shrouds such as these."

They all turned toward him and Chori said, "Mighty strange you saying that, when you were the one got the idea to dress up for..." he couldn't bring himself to pronounce her name for that terrible nothing closed up in the coffin.

Arsenio's indignation vanished and he crept into himself again. The others, too, lost the joy of their freed feet and finished the walk to the shore slowly, as though they carried the box on their shoulders. They were careful not to look towards the left at all, where from the corner of their eyes they could see men working where their home had been.

Especially Chori. The first thing that bulldozer had run down yesterday, after the trees, was his shack. Right before his eyes he'd seen it turned into splinters, the little kitchen where Cachita was going to cook; the walls; the door that had the store-bought hinges; the garden fence that had taken a year and a half to collect and build. Worst of all was that zinc roof still shining under the bulldozer. And those little black kids in Santiago thinking the house was all ready for them. When they reached the cove where Arsenio had hidden away the papers, they sat down on the clean sand careful not to split anything and gravely now began to remove whatever clothes constricted then.

Jorge helped Topo out of his jacket which was so tight his arms couldn't get started. When he had taken off his shirt, and Jorge saw how hollow-chested and thin he was, it was startling to imagine what made him seem so big. The large bones? The expression of his eyes?

Arsenio seemed to have forgotten about the papers, and oblivious of the others sat staring toward the sea. They too remained silent, each one with himself alone, while the ocean tossed its mane and shook itself out. An exploding wave would have reached the borrowed pair of shoes and jacket Arsenio had negligently left on a rock, if Topo had not sprung up to save them. Chori walked quietly to Arsenio, and his powerful body leaned over the old man and addressed him softly, as though he were a child.

Arsenio, 'member what you said once? My junk-pickin' good for me, and your lazy tree good for you? 'Member?"

Arsenio wouldn't answer, but Chori know he was listening. "Well, Francisco's shoes and trappin's good for him."

"Cages," grumbled the old man, "cages."

"All right. But some people likes cages. You got to take care of those things until we give them back tomorrow." Seeing that Jorge was listening he explained to him, "Doc, that Galician Spaniard, Francisco—you know, one that has the bodega? He been real good to us. And you know who else? Policeman, name Mateo. Company gave us our money so we could, well, give our friend a proper funeral. And those fellows helped us with everything. But the funeral home didn't want very much to let us in, at our own funeral! We didn't look so good, I guess. But Mateo explained to them, and it was OK. But, uh," he lowered his voice so that Arsenio would not hear, "It wasn't OK with Arsenio anymore. He felt real bad, and said a great one like Marquesa or Antonia, I mean, must have a fine finishing up. And he was going to do the biggest thing for her he could ever do. He was going to put on proper clothes, with shoes and all. And us too, except that none of us had any! And you know what? Mateo and Francisco hurried home to find clothes for us, their own, their family's, we're all different sizes. And brought them to the Funeraria. That old goat there real proud when we squeezed into the shoes, for all his complaining. You saw us dressed, Doc. Think we look good for the Marquesa?" The others were listening intently.

"I'm sure she will be very proud of you. You look fine," Jorge answered.

Arsenio's left hand scratched the right side of his head the way he did when he was pleased

"Tell him about the flowers," Chan Li prompted. The eyes of the four companions glowed as they listened to Chori tell it.

"You should see it, Señor! We store-bought flowers and flowers with ribbons, and in circles like they do!"

"Whole damn place full of flowers," Arsenio added, proudly. "You see, she loves them... I mean..." he faltered, and turned from them. They were all silent again.

Jorge felt that it was an opportune moment to suggest, "Perhaps we had better look at those papers now."

Arsenio removed the box from its place of concealment as he explained, "The papers were torn in the fight. Maybe not much left to read." Jorge opened the box and shook his head at the hopeless confusion of torn letters, children's drawings, faded newspaper clippings, and photographs. But Arsenio said,

"Also that devil had this little box hidden under his shirt. But I got it from him," he nodded gravely, as he extracted it from under the jumbled contents of the crate.

Jorge, who had assumed that it was all worthless except in the imagination of the Marquesa, was surprised to note that the box was of fine marquetry. Arsenio gave it to him to open. Its contents were even more unexpected. He held up a gold medal with the inscription "To Don Rafael

Monte De Oca, First Award, Ministry of Agriculture, Santa Cruz de Tenerife, Canary Islands, 1889." Then he picked up a gold locket encrusted with garnets, suspended from a delicate pearl necklace. On the back of it he read, "To my beloved daughter, Antonia. Canary Islands, 1910."

"That is Marquesa. Not long ago, she told me her name," said Arsenio. "Antonia."

Jorge's doubt was short-lived as he opened the locket and regarded the oil portrait of a white-haired man with the same high forehead, strong nose and eyes of startling clarity that had so impressed him the first day he had seen the estate and met the old woman. But suddenly he noticed something that was more than an object of curiosity. In his hand, he held the Cuban "Carlos Manuel de Céspedes Citation for Distinguished Service to Leandro Camacho." He stared at it, affected and astonished. How had she come to have this in her possession? Had she found it in the house after it was abandoned, or had she known the man whose personality had so interested him?

Eagerly he picked up an envelope addressed to "Cipriano Salinas, attorney." There was a note attached to the outside:

"P.S. My dear cousin Antonia: this envelope is separate from the letter I have just written you, so that you put it in a safe place. My precipitate departure of course gives no time to draw up a will with our friend Cipriano. Take this to him at the first opportunity.

"As you already know, my wife and children are amply provided for, and it is my wish that, in seven years, at the pronouncement of my legal death, this house and all its land become yours. Cherish it. The dream which built it only you and I understand, and only you can save. My own presence is the obstacle. It seems that in order to realize dreams, men must sometimes bend with the wind. I would only break or cause the others to.

Again, God bless you,

Leandro"

Jorge had been so curious to know the contents of the note that he had forgotten to read it aloud. Now, dumbfounded he took the will from the envelope. He glanced over it and found it was just as Camacho had said.

Why had she never used it?

He looked at the others. They were waiting patiently. "You know, those papers the Marquesa was talking about," he began. His throat was dry with emotion.

"She sure did talk about 'em," Chori mused.

"Well, I'm going to tell you something about them," Jorge continued, but Arsenio interrupted to dispute mildly.

"Not so, Chori. She never made talk about them. Not once, until that company start coming around."

Jorge was suddenly interested. "You mean she never mentioned them to anyone before that?"

Arsenio shook his head.

"Once, though, that thief of a Carambita, wantin' to make fun, asked her 'If you got papers say this place is yours, how come you never go to the lawyer and claim it?' He was laughin' at her, but you know Marquesa! She never thinks anyone can be mean. She answered him real serious (like they was real people and not made up by her) that long as the family thought the house was theirs, there was hope they might come back to it some day and do what they supposed to do. And if they'd come back, then she was sure 'He' would too. Caramba!" Chori observed softly, "Marquesa always talking about that 'He.'"

So that was the reason! Jorge mused. Later he would have time to think about all this. Now he must tell them the news. "What I began to say before is that you thought those papers were lost!"

Arsenio again shook his head. "They were not lost," he said.

"There never were any papers," Chori affirmed. "We all know that."

Jorge looked at them incredulous. "You 'knew' there were no papers?"

They almost smiled as they nodded.

"I don't understand," he pursued. "I have been told that none of you would accept the money offered you by the company because you thought Marquesa would be able to prove the property was hers. Isn't that correct?'

No one answered. They shuffled uncomfortably and looked at each other.

"Well—?" Jorge waited, puzzled.

Chori finally took it on himself. "No señor, that's not it. We just pretended we thought so."

"'Pretended!' But if by doing that you knew that everything was going to be taken from you, why didn't you?"

"Because she believed it was true," Arsenio intercepted.

Jorge looked at them stunned. On their faces was written no conflict, no regret. It was just a logical fact to them. No more explanation seemed necessary, even now, when her death had made their sacrifice futile.

As though reading his mind, Arsenio reminded him, "She died believing it."

"Eh! Francisco is gonna wonder what happened to us!" Chori suddenly remembered. "He's staying with her there, so we could come to meet you."

Jorge was going to interrupt them to make them understand the truth. But suddenly he thought, why? What good would it do them or anybody, something that was now worthless, and had happened so long ago! They had their own truth, and were happy with it.

Deeply moved, he watched them as reluctantly they all began to get dressed again.

"What will you do, now that you have no place to go?" Jorge asked.

"Oh, we gonna sleep in the funeral home tonight, like we did last night."

"But after the funeral? What will you do?" They paused for a moment. They had not thought about that.

The wind was ruffling the scraggly bushes like dust mops, and shaking out the waves that scattered a crystal spray over them: day shaking out happiness over the blue and white figure of the afternoon.

Finally Chori said, "When I was working on the new road I saw a real nice stretch, right there by the ocean. Think maybe it would be a good place for my shack. Hasn't got a dump heap, though," he added regretfully. "But plenty of space for you to make charcoal," he informed Topo.

"Caray," Arsenio grumbled, "you going to start that all over again: calling me every two minutes to come and see some old junk, bothering me from my thinking."

"Who's inviting you?" Chori teased.

"Never mind," Arsenio retorted, as he struggled to fit into the shoes. "There are still plenty of trees left in Cuba. They are just waiting for me," he grinned.

Jorge suddenly looked at the old man intently, and then rose. "I'll be back shortly," he said. "There's something urgent I must take care of."

He couldn't do anything else. Maybe it would lead to destruction again; maybe he was stubborn, arrogant, or whatever; but then, so were Arsenio and the others. And they were getting along.

He hurried to his car. There was a telegram to answer.

THE END

Berkeley, California
April, 1969

211

ABOUT THE AUTHOR

Lorna De Sosa was born Lorna Done Newman August 19, 1913 in Cincinnati, Ohio. She studied at Tulane University in New Orleans, the University of Cincinnati, Columbia University, and the Cincinnati College of Music and Dramatic Arts. She acted in New York, Chicago, and New England theater companies, and became the founding director of the Cincinnati Civic Theatre.

In 1938 she married Dr. Salvador Bonilla-Sosa, a physician, and moved to Cuba; the couple had a son and a daughter and divorced in 1952. As Lorna De Sosa, she was a co-founder and director of the Academia de Artes Dramáticas in Havana. The celebrated Spanish playwright Antonio Buero Vallejo gave her exclusive rights to produce his plays in the Americas, and the Cuban government appointed her in charge of the national dramatic festival. In addition to working in the theater, Lorna was a pioneer directing and producing television and radio programs in Cuba and taught drama at the Catholic University of Santo Tomás de Villanueva. She was made a member of the Order of José Martí, one of the highest honors awarded in that country.

In the 1950s, Lorna went to Europe, serving as Latin American representative in the International Theatre Institute in Paris and working with the renowned dramatist/actor Louis Jouvet. After relocating to Manhattan in 1955, she completed the first draft of this novel. She moved to Berkeley in 1965 and taught drama at San Francisco State University. Later she also taught liturgical drama at the Graduate Theological Union in Berkeley and oversaw the Lector Training Program at St. Albert's Priory.

Her first book of poetry, Who Turned the Grass On? (Concord, CA:

Small Poetry Press) was published in 2003 when she was 90. Some of the poems in it had appeared earlier that year in pamphlet form as "The Something Little Christmas Tree." Long before that, though, Lorna had written lyrics for the works of composer Felix Guerrero, including his "April for Voice and Orchestra." While in Cuba she had also translated plays into Spanish, and in 1958 she translated (with Chesley Martin Hutchings) Poetical Diary of a Journey of a Galician Through the U.S.A., a collection of poems by her friend Father José Rubinos, SJ.

Lorna's last years were passed at the Salem-Luther Home for Rehabilitation in Oakland, California. She died on April 17, 2009.

A NOTE FROM THE EDITOR
Anita Susan Grossman

When I first met Lorna De Sosa, she was ninety years old and had just published her first book of poetry, *Who Turned the Grass On?* She was living at the Salem Lutheran Home for Rehabilitation in Oakland, California, largely bedridden and with failing vision, but her mind was sharp as ever. I helped distribute and publicize the book and organized a couple of events where local poets generously gave readings of her work. Many of them were old friends and colleagues from the California Writers' Club. I soon learned that Lorna had also written a long novel called *Infinite Corner*, set in pre-Castro Cuba. In 2004 she loaned me a copy of the typescript to read; at slightly under 500 pages, it fit exactly into a ream box of paper. It was an impressive work--one that reflected the language, the history, and the ethos of the Cuban people.

Lorna continued to tinker with the unpublished manuscript up until the time of her death in 2009. A few years later I was invited by her son, Victor Bonilla-Sosa, to edit *Infinite Corner* for publication, and gladly assented.

This enormously ambitious novel employs a multi-layered narrative to portray a cross-section of Cuban society. In it we are introduced to a world whose landmarks have a deep symbolic resonance. Most notably, the ruined Camacho estate suggests the fate of Cuba itself, seemingly doomed to alternating cycles of revolution and corruption. The mansion was built in a uniquely eclectic style employing Classical, Gothic, and Moorish motifs, and topped with carved wooden gargoyles. Designed by Leandro Camacho, hero of the 1898 Revolution, it still preserved even in decay traces of its former beauty. Much of the novel concerns the struggle over what is to become of the estate, which overlaps with the question of Cuba's future as a nation. In both cases we encounter idealists who struggle to maintain their integrity and escape the traps life sets for them.

This is not to reduce the novel to a political allegory, however. It is much richer than that. The characters are vividly realized with insight and compassion, and the author avoids cliché in her depiction of the curiously evolving relationship between its main protagonists, Lourdes, Jorge, and Mario. More generally, this is an authentic representation of Havana of the 1940s by someone who lived there at the time. De Sosa knew many of the real-life figures who appear in the background of the novel, and unerringly guides us through the physical geography of Havana. Last but not least, there is the language that conveys the flavor of idiomatic Cuban speech to the English-speaking reader.

When she was writing this book, Lorna De Sosa had been an actress, stage producer, and director for many years; much later in life she became a poet. Both gifts—the dramatic and the lyric—are evident in her writing. The prose is full of fresh imagery, natural, and yet surprising; within a story that is richly symbolic. As a stage director, she is careful to orchestrate her scenes, with each character, no matter how minor, distinctly imagined; and as in a play, we are aware of each character's entry and unique voice.

From what Lorna told me, *Infinite Corner* was begun in Cuba in the late 1940s, and the first draft was finished ten years later when she had moved to Manhattan. Poet John Ciardi at the Bread Loaf Writers' Conference in Middlebury, Vermont praised it highly as a work in progress; later Paul Engel, founder of the Iowa School of Writing, was so impressed by it that he sent letters to all his celebrated former students saying that the novel was deserving of their attention. In the late 1950s the editor of a major publishing house in New York was so interested in the unfinished novel that he sent a messenger from the office every few days to the author to pick up the latest few pages that she had written. However, in light of sensitive relations with Cuba at the time, the publisher also wanted to omit passages in the novel that were critical of the U.S. government's policy toward Cuba. This the author refused to do, and as a result the novel was not published.

Lorna's son Victor Bonilla-Sosa recounts how she was inspired to write the novel in part by the sight of a beautiful old mansion in the Vedado suburb of Havana that probably dated from the period of World War I. Other experiences of hers also entered into the making of the novel. She gave the character Antonia, who grew up in the Canary Island, the same background as that of her mother-in-law, who spoke of her youth there and of her father, a gentleman farmer. The character Jorge De Armas was inspired by a number of Cuban personalities, including Félix Guerrero, the Cuban composer and conductor. Lastly, the character Arsenio, who lives in Antonia's garden, may have been modeled in part by José María López Lledín, the elegant vagrant known in Havana as "El Caballero de Paris"; but for Lorna her chief inspiration for Arsenio was her friend Fidelio Ponce de Leon, the famous Cuban painter. Although Arsenio is a cheerful ne'er-do-well and not a painter, the two share a hand-to-mouth lifestyle and a philosophy of living for the moment. "He often dropped in to visit me in Miramar because he was intrigued by my face and wanted to paint me," she wrote. Ponce did two preliminary sketches of Lorna in different poses, one of them with an eagle perched on her, but died in 1949 before he got to turn either into a painting.

Welcome to the world of *Infinite Corner*.

ACKNOWLEDGMENTS

Books do not see the light of day without the collaboration of many hands. This novel is particularly indebted to a number of people who over time aided, encouraged, and made possible its publication. Thanks to her work with the author, Anita Susan Grossman as the final editor brings a great understanding to the development of the story, reflected in her judicious trimming and correcting of the manuscript while respecting the original text.

Grace Mott of the Bethesda Writer's Center in Maryland assisted with the book's print publication, insightfully choosing both the style and format. Additionally, she worked closely with me to create an appealing cover that reflects the spirit of the work. Her enthusiasm and undaunted can-do attitude have been a godsend.

The author's former New York agent, Rene Spodheim, kept the project alive in the midst of challenging personal circumstances. Mention must be made of Paul Engle of the Iowa Writers Conference, who encouraged the author and recommended her to the attention of several publishers and agents. Chief among them was Sherman Baker, VP and Editor at St. Martin's Press, who asked for the latest installments of the novel as it was being written, and Mel Berger of the William Morris Agency who also expressed great interest. Palomar College Dean of Humanities, Dwight Boehm, a dear friend and constant advisor, provided praise of the author's work and encouraged her writing. And finally, Lloyd Eric Reeve of Berkeley, California energized the author with his encouraging critiques, some which are reflected in this book.

Thanks to the invaluable effort of these dedicated individuals, *Infinite Corner* is at long last a triumphant reality, a fully-realized dream, a consummate achievement now in a print version that the author would undoubtedly be proud to hold in her own hands.

GLOSSARY

AGUILERA, FRANCISCO VICENTE AGUILERA (1821-1877): was a Cuban patriot born in Bayamo, Cuba on June 23, 1821. He was the richest landowner in the eastern region of Cuba, owning extensive properties, sugar refineries, livestock, and slaves. He never bought any of the slaves that were regularly brought from the African coast and offered for sale. Upon the outbreak of war in 1868, Aguilera freed all 500 of his slaves. Aguilera held many positions in the Cuban Army, including Major General, Minister of War, Vice President of the Republic, and Commander-in-Chief of the Eastern District. While in command of the army he was distinguished for courage and ability, taking part in person in many engagements and skirmishes. See Wikipedia.

AHORA, BIEN: Equivalent to "Well, now" when embarking on an explanation

AJIACO: in Colombia, a potato soup with chicken and corn; in Cuba, a stew with many ingredients.

ALMENDARES & HABANA: Two of the fabled Cuban national baseball teams, perennial archrivals.

ANDA! Expression meaning, "go on."

ANON-FRUIT: The sugar-apple, or sweetsop, is the fruit of Annona squamosa, the most widely grown species of Annona and a native of tropical climate in the Americas and West Indies. The flesh is fragrant and sweet, creamy white through light yellow, and resembles and tastes like custard. See Wikipedia.

ARROZ CON POLLO: a traditional Latin American dish of rice with chicken.

AUSENCIA: absence

AUTÉNTICO PARTY: The Partido Auténtico had its origins in the nationalist Revolution of 1933. It was made up in February 1934 by many of the same individuals who had brought about the downfall of Gerardo Machado in the previous year to defend the changes caused by the Revolution of 1933. Its candidate, Ramón Grau, went on to win the presidency at the 1944 general election, which also saw the Partido

Auténtico win the most seats in the Chamber. The party also won the 1946 mid-term election with 30 seats. It was the most nationalistic of the major parties that existed between the Revolution of 1933 and the 1959 Cuban Revolution. It had as its slogan Cuba para los cubanos ("Cuba for Cubans"). Its electoral program contained corporatist elements It supported numerous efforts to strengthen the power of the labor unions, some of the party's biggest supporters. Also, some of its members supported the management of the economy through tripartite commissions with businessmen, labor leaders and government bureaucrats. For the 1948 general election the party formed an alliance with the Republican Party, helping Carlos Prío Socarrás win the presidency, and also winning both the Chamber and Senate. and this alliance too won. However, the Partido Auténtico lost the 1954 general election to Fulgencio Batista's National Progressive Coalition. See Wikipedia.

AZABACHE: Or jet black, a hard crystalized black mineral made from petrified carbonized wood, famously used in Spain's northwest Celtic region, known as Galicia for centuries. Prized for its black sheen often employed in jewelry.

BARANDILLA: Rail.

BARGUEÑOS: a classic style of desk originating in Renaissance Spain.

BAYAMO: Founded in 1513 by the Spanish conquistadores, it has come down in Cuban lore as the epitome of sacrifice. During the Ten Year War 1868-1878, rebels conquered the city after a bloody siege. It was here that Carlos de Céspedes formed the government of the Republic in Arms commemorated in the Cuban national anthem.

BENAVENTE'S PLAY ROSES OF AUTUMN: Jacinto Benavente y Martínez (12 August 1866 – 14 July 1954), one of Spain's greatest playwrights and writers of the 20th century and winner of the Nobel Prize for Literature. His Rosas de otoño is among 170 plays he wrote, some semi sweet dramas critiquing the bourgeoisie and its mores. In this 1905 play Isabel whose husband's roaming eyes cause a series of marital mishaps ultimately salvages the relationship.

BERNABEU: Born in Havana one of the great Cuban designers along with Luis Estévez one of the most successful Hispanic designers in the United States.

BILTMORE: the Biltmore area was the poshest and newest luxurious suburban neighborhood in Havana's outskirts surrounded by golf courses, and huge estates. It is where the Cuban Castro elite and some diplomatic missions now reside.

BOHEMIA MAGAZINE: Also known as *Revista,* Bohemia was a weekly large format publication, one of the oldest of its genre in Latin America. It was started in 1908 by its founder, Miguel Ángel Quevedo Pérez. A cross between *Life* and *Time* magazines in the U.S., it provided news and commentary on Cuba's politics, society, sports, and business.

BOHIO: Cuban palm frond round building or hut inherited from the Taino aborigines. Traditionally the humble housing common to the campesino in the countryside.

BOLÍVAR: Simón José Antonio de la Santísima Trinidad Bolívar y Palacios Ponte y Blanco (24 July 1783 – 17 December 1830), the great South American Independence hero who liberated from the Spanish Empire what latter became Venezuela, Colombia, Ecuador, Peru, and Bolivia. His dream of a united confederation of South America remains a guiding star to this day for Latin America's statesmen.

CABALLEROS!: "Gentlemen!"

CABRÓN: Cuban expression literally male goat. Used as an epithet for a cad.

CALIXTO GARCIA HOSPITAL: named for the Independence War hero and among the foremost public medical facilities.

CALLE 23: Also known as La Rampa; described by Wikipedia as a street in the Vedado district of Havana. La Rampa runs from the Malecon to Calle L. Built in 1930, the end was the location of the Battery of Santa Clara that protected the city from attack. Along it is found such landmarks as the former Havana Hilton, renamed by the Revolution as Habana Libre. It is one of the most famous arteries of the capital, often the location of movies and novels. On the corner of 23rd and L is the Radio Centro CMQ Building, the pre-Castro radio and television headquarters of Cuba's principal broadcaster and where the author worked as a director and producer.

CALZADA: One of the old main thoroughfares of Havana. It runs parallel to the Caribbean shoreline from behind the US Embassy to the Chorrera Fort at the mouth of the Almendares River separating the old from the post-WWII Havana.

CAÑA BRAVA: bamboo.

CANEY: At El Caney, Cuba, 514 Spanish regular soldiers, together with approximately 100 armed Spanish and Cubans loyal to Spain under the command of Brigadier General Joaquín Vara de Rey y Rubio were instructed to hold the northwest flank of Santiago de Cuba against the American 2nd Division, Fifth Army Corps, commanded by Brigadier General Henry W. Lawton. Denied promised reinforcements from Santiago, Vara de Rey and his forces held over 6,000 Americans from their position for nearly twelve hours before retreating, preventing General Lawton's men from reinforcing the U.S. assault on San Juan Hill. Though eventually successful, the attack on the fortifications of El Caney had proved to be of little real value. The attack on two strongly defended points at both El Caney and San Juan diluted the strength of American forces, resulting in delays and additional casualties.

CARAJO: Literally- male genitals, commonly used as an expression of surprise, or scorn, not unlike the expletive used in English of crap or balls.

CARAMBA: A mild term of exclamation expressing surprise. A polite form instead of the vulgar coño.

CARAY!: Expression of surprise or acknowledgement.

CARIÑO: Common term of endearment meaning "Darling."
Carmelo: A high end restaurant the epitome of the bourgeoise hang out. Rare in its day, it was air conditioned – a luxury, and to this day, though a shadow of its former self, draws habaneros and tourist who have heard of it. It is across the street from the National Philharmonic Hall, thus a place of gathering before and after performances.

CARMELO CHURCH: Situated in the Carmelo neighborhood extending from Calle 23 to the Caribbean and from the Almendares River to the Avenida Paseo. As the city expanded in the 19th century the Count of Pozos Dulces gifted the land for a church which was begun in 1872 using the same quarry that was employed in the building of the famous Colón Cemetery. The family ran out of money and subsequently the unfinished church suffered various disasters, earning that name. In 1918 Father Reginaldo of the Dominican Order going from house to house obtained the funds to finish the church, some of the work which he did himself.

CARMELO RESTAURANT: "Without a doubt Cuba's most distinguished restaurant...long been the favorite gathering place of Havana society as well as the Anglo-America colony," according to its advertising. Located on Calzada and and D streets in the Vedado neighborhood. It advertised its fashionable air-conditioned interior, a rarity at the time, spacious dining and glass enclosed indoor as well as outdoor covered terrace.

CASA BLANCA: is a ward of the city of Havana in the borough of Regla. It is situated to the east of the entrance to Havana Harbor. After the British captured Havana, the later part of the 19th century navigators and carpenters who repaired merchant ships lived there. A ferry links Casablanca with the dock at the foot of Santa Clara street in Old Havana. This is also the western terminus of the Hershey Electric Railway. Wikipedia.

CEIBA TREES: a genus of trees in the family Malvaceae, native to tropical and subtropical areas of the Americas (from Mexico and the Caribbean to N Argentina) and tropical West Africa. Some species can grow to 230 ft. tall or more, with a straight, largely branchless trunk that culminates in a huge, spreading canopy, and buttress roots that can be taller than a grown person. The best-known, and most widely cultivated, species is Kapok, Ceiba pentandra, one of several trees called kapok. Wikipedia

CÉSPEDES: Carlos Manuel de Céspedes del Castillo (April 18, 1819 – February 27, 1874), leader in 1868 of the Ten-Year War of Independence from Spain and the slave holding plantation class. His rebellion laid the groundwork for the latter successful Independence struggle.

CHANGO, THE SEA-GOD: In the African Yoruba language: Ṣàngó, also known as Changó or Xangô in Latin America; is an Orisha, a type of spirit in Yoruba religion. Genealogically speaking, Shango is a royal ancestor of the Yoruba as he was the third Alaafin of the Oyo Kingdom prior to his posthumous deification. Shango has numerous manifestations. But his identification is with thunder, lightning, and fire. He is considered to be one of the most powerful rulers that Yorubaland has ever produced. In the New World, he is syncretized with either Saint Barbara or Saint Jerome.

CHARANGUITAS: Not to be confused with the South American instrument resembling an upside-down guitar, with the body of the instrument nearer to the head of the performer, like a violin. In Cuba it refers to a traditional ensemble that plays Cuban dance music. They made

Cuban dance music popular in the 1940s and their music consisted of heavily son-influenced material, performed on European instruments such as violin and flute by a Charanga orchestra. (Chomsky 2004, p. 199). The style of music that is most associated with a Charanga is termed 'Danzón' and is an amalgam of both European classical music and African rhythms. Wikipedia

CHICHARRÓN: Crisps made of burnt pig skin or crispy rind.

CHURROS: A pastry made of fried dough, usually elongated and normally to which powdered sugar is added.

COCHINO: A reference to a pig. Also, as the name implies, used to describe a filthy person or thing.

COFIO: Also spelled gofio. A roasted maize meal often stirred into coffee or used as a main ingredient in diet. Prevalently used in the Canary Islands.

COMPARSA: a celebratory street procession consisting of conga dancers followed by a band.

COMMANDING GENERAL BROOKE: John R. Brooke (1838-1926) served as military governor of Cuba from 1898 to 1902.

COÑO: One of the most common Cuban epithets and is vulgar Spanish slang for "female genitalia" à la the English pussy, often used in everyday speech with the versatile force damn or fuck.

CRUCERO DE LA PLAYA: A major intersection leading west of Havana where Quinta Avenida crosses several main roads leading to the Country Club Suburbs, home of some of the most sumptuous mansions, including the American Ambassador's residence, the road to Rancho Boyeros Airport (now Jose Marti International Airport), the Biltmore Country Club and Golf Links, and several public and private beach clubs.

CTC LABOR SYNDICATE ROW: The Confederación de Trabajadores de Cuba." I did a very brief internet check but didn't find anything particular for Havana for the early part of 1947, although later in the year there were factional battles in Cuba between the Communists and antis.

CUBILETE: A round or cylinder-shaped leather container from which the dice are cast.

CUIDADITO!: "Careful!" or Watch out!"

CURRO: A diminutive of name Francisco but used in the sense of reference to someone of Spanish origin.

DAIQUIRI: Derived from a Taino word. Not to be confused with the popular cocktail of the same name based on rum and lime juice allegedly invented by an American mining engineer at the turn of the 20th century. It is a village, 14 miles east of Santiago de Cuba which became a focal point of the United States invasion of Cuba in the Spanish–American War.

"DANCE OF THE MILLIONS": Known also as the Sugar Boom of 1918. During World War I a shortage of sugar on the international market produced an enormous economic boom in Cuba which had since colonial times been a major producer of sugar and its derivatives (bagasse, alcohol, rum). It all came to a crashing halt in the 1920s leaving many prosperous plantation owners and their factories destitute.

DANZÓN: Classic Cuban dance known as the habanera or contradanza. Its history is long and involved having Afro, English, and even French influences. In its purest form it is stately, elegant, and like the tango, miraculous. See: CHARANGUITA.

DOS RIOS: Depicted in the Cuban coat of arms between the Royal palms. Place in Santiago de Cuba province where supreme revolutionary leader, Jose Martí was killed in the first skirmish of the second and final war of independence on May 19, 1895.

EDUARDO CHIBÁS: Eduardo René Chibás Ribas (August 15, 1907 – August 16, 1951) was a Cuban politician who used radio to broadcast his political views to the public. He primarily denounced corruption and gangsterism rampant during the governments of Ramón Grau and Carlos Prío which preceded the Batista era. He believed corruption was the most important problem Cuba faced. In 1947 he formed the Orthodox party, a strongly anti-communist group, which had the goal of exposing government corruption and bringing about revolutionary change through constitutional means. Chibás lost the 1948 election for president, finishing in third place. He was an extremely strong critic of that election's winner, Carlos Prío Socarrás. He was considered a favorite in the 1952 presidential election but committed suicide a year before Fulgencio Batista seized control of the Cuban government during one of his regular radio broadcasts. See Wikipedia.

EL CERRO: is one of the municipalities or boroughs (municipios in Spanish) in the city of Havana. Considered a lower working-class neighborhood.

EL COCO: a ghostly monster, the Cuban Santeria version of the boogeyman.

EL ENCANTO: Literally, "the enchantment," the famous Havana store going back to 1888. It became the largest department store with a number of satellite branches in the 1950s. Situated in the heart of the fashionable downtown, it mysteriously burned in a fire after the Cuban Revolution expropriated it in 1961.

EMILIO BALLAGAS: Considered by some a neo-Romantic poet of the Afro-Cuban movements associated with the 1930s.

ENRIQUE JOSE VARONA: 1849-1933. Considered by many as the "outstanding Cuban polemicist now that Marti was dead," according to Hugh Thomas's magisterial history of the island. In 1885 he was elected representative for Puerto Principe in the Spanish Cortes. In 1885 he founded the Revista Cubana, a literary, scientific, and philosophical review.

ESTIRADO: A term used to denote a snob. Literally means "stretched."

FAROLES: Lanterns usually enclosed in a square set of glass shade mounted on a long pole traditionally used in the pre-Lenten season festival of Shrove Thursday. It also forms part of the equipment carried by penitents in Holy Week processions and other religious celebrations in Cuba and the Spanish heritage culture in Latin America.

FILETE: Side of beef, sometimes pounded thin and marinated in lime juice and garlic. A traditional Cuban dish usually accompanied with fried plantains and black beans and rice (known as moros y cristianos).

FINCAS: Extension of rural holding such as a farm or ranch.

FONDA CHINA: A Chinese dinner, usually of more common food. Havana had a large population of Chinese.

FOSA: Spanish means a mass grave.

FRAMBOYAN: Also known as flamboyan (Delonix regia), is a tree originally from Madagascar, but found elsewhere. As a tropical tree it can grows as high as 36 feet spreading its dense foliage. The large flowers have startling vivid color ranging from orange through lilac, red and yellow. The seed pods of the framboyan are often used in the maraca.

FRITA: literally means fried and can apply to a Cuban-style hamburger or fried plantain.

GENERAL CASTELLANOS: Adolfo Jimenéz Castellanos (1844-1829) was the last Governor-General of Cuba.

GENERAL GARCIA: Calixto García Íñiguez (August 4, 1839 – December 11, 1898) was a Cuban general in three Cuban uprisings, part of the Cuban War for Independence: the Ten Years' War, the Little War, and the War of 1895, itself sometimes called the Cuban War for Independence, which bled into the Spanish–American War, ultimately resulting in national independence for Cuba. See Wikipedia.

GENERAL LEE: Fitzhugh Lee (1835-1905), nephew of Robert E. Lee, was a Confederate general and later Governor of Virginia; he led the Occupational command in Havana 1898-1900."

GRAU: Ramón Grau San Martín (September 13, 1887 – July 28, 1969) was President of Cuba (1933–1934, 1944–1948). A medical doctor by training he participated in the disturbances leading to President Machado's demise in 1933. A leading voice in the rewriting of the document that became the much-vaunted Constitution of 1940, one of the most socially advanced in the 20th century and a supposed lodestar for the later rebellion against the dictatorship of President Fulgencio Batista. The two politicians' personal rivalries were intertwined in a series of Presidential contests. Notwithstanding, Grau's administrations were accused of widespread corruption. He ran twice more unsuccessfully against Batista engineered elections.

GUA-GUAS: a public minibus used in Cuba. In Peru's Aymara language it refers to children.

GUANABACOA: a colonial township in eastern Havana, and one of the municipalities (or boroughs) of the city. It is famous for its historical Santería and is home to the first African Cabildo in Havana. It was the site of the Battle of Guanabacoa, a skirmish between British and Spanish troops during the Battle of Havana during the Seven Years' War. Wikipedia.

GUANABANA: the term can refer to (1) a flowering tree also known as "soursop" or (2) its fruits or (3) a flowering ground plant of the genus Oxalis. A delicious fruit drink is made from it.

GUANCHES: the aboriginal Canary Islanders. Their origins are shrouded in speculation, but some anthropologists believe they are descended from Berber people.

GUARACHA: is a genre of music that originated in Cuba, of rapid tempo and comic or picaresque lyrics. Guarachas were played and sung in musical theatres and in low-class dance salons. They became an integral part of bufo comic theatre in the mid-19th century. The guaracha survives today in the repertoires of some trova musicians, conjuntos and Cuban-style big bands. See Wikipedia.

GUAYABERA: The classic Cuban shirt. It traditionally was made of linen and is all white and long sleeved which is worn outside the trousers. It has four patch pockets and vertical rows of fine pleats sewn closely together running along the front and back of the shirt ending in a straight hem with slits on either side. The pockets also come with identical lined pleats. There are any numbers of accounts of its origins. I prefer the one ascribing it to the shirt worn by agricultural workers in the Spanish countryside, transplanted to the New World. Today, they range from the Philippines to Mexico and come in any number of colors, pleats, and lengths of sleeves.

GUAYAQUIL: Capital of Ecuador and the scene of one of Liberator Simon Bolivar's greatest triumphs during the South American wars of Independence from Spain in 1812.

GUAYO: Also known as the guiro is a hollow gourd open at one end and with parallel cuts or ratchets across which a stick is scraped to make a scratching rasping sound. Of Taino Cuban Indian origin, it probably originated in the Amazon area in pre-Columbian times. It is one of the quintessential percussive instruments used in Cuban popular music ensembles.

HACENDADOS: The wealthy landowning class derived from the Spanish word hacienda or ranch.

HOMBRE! Expression literally meaning man. It is used as an exclamatory.

HOTEL INGLATERRA: Havana's classic hotel, build in 1875 that faces the Marti Park on the stylish Prado Boulevard that sweeps from the entrance to the harbor up to the Capitolio, or Congress building.

JACQUES FATH: Parisian fashion designer (1912-1954), a contemporary of Balmain and Dior.

JIPI: a brimmed hat made of woven palm fiber, more commonly called a Panama hat.

JOSÉ MARTÍ: José Julián Martí Pérez (January 28, 1853 – May 19, 1895) was a Cuban poet, philosopher, essayist, journalist, translator, professor, and publisher, who is considered a Cuban national hero because of his role in the liberation of his country, as well as an important figure of the "Modernist" school in Latin American literature. Through his writings and political activity, he became a symbol of Cuba's bid for independence from the Spanish Empire in the 19th century, and is referred to as the "Apostle of Cuban Independence."

JUDIAS: Kidney beans. Literally translates as "Jews" because of their association in Spain with a staple in Jewish cooking. In Spain they are referred to as "judias blancas" or white kidney beans, or "judias verdes," green lima beans.

LÓPEZ, NARCISO LOPEZ (1797-1851): Venezuelan-born former Spanish colonial officer and advocate of Cuban independence, executed by the Spanish administration after a failed insurrection.

MACEO: Lt. General José Antonio de la Caridad Maceo y Grajales (June 14, 1845 – December 7, 1896). Cuban born major figure of the Independence movement and second-in-command of the Army of Independence. Sometimes referred to as the "Titan de Bronce" or Bronze Titan in reference to his mulatto ancestry and military prowess.

MACHADO: Gerardo Machado y Morales (September 28, 1871 – March 29, 1939) though he played a role in the Cuban War of Independence, it was as President of Cuba (1925–1933) that he gained notoriety for corruption and ruthlessness, exemplified by installing Martial Law. Communists made inroads during his two terms and he was finally overthrown in a general strike. He died an exile in Miami where he is buried.

MAINE INCIDENT & SPAIN'S HUMILIATING OVERTURES:
In January 1898, a riot by Cuban Spanish loyalists against the new autonomous government broke out in Havana. They destroyed the printing presses of four local newspapers that had published articles critical of

Spanish Army atrocities. The U.S. Consul-General cabled Washington with fears for the lives of Americans living in Havana. In response, the battleship USS Maine was sent to Havana in the last week of January. On February 15, 1898, the Maine was rocked by an explosion, killing 260 of the crew and sinking the ship in the harbor. At the time, a military Board of Investigations decided that the Maine had exploded due to the detonation of a mine underneath the hull. However, later investigations decided that it was likely something inside the ship, though the cause of the explosion has not been clearly established to this day.

In an attempt to appease the United States, the colonial government took two steps that had been demanded by President William McKinley: it ended forced relocation of residents from their homes and offered negotiations with the independence fighters. But the truce was rejected by the rebels. Notwithstanding the war party in the US Congress fueled by the Yellow Press, mainly of William Hearst clamored for war which resulted in the so-called Spanish-American War. To this day Cubans consider that their triumph fighting Spain was stolen by the US intervention.

MALANGA: A tropical flowering plant in the Arum family.

MALECÓN: A road and crescent shaped seawall bordering Havana's Caribbean flank ending at the Vedado; Havana's equivalent of the Copa Cabana esplanade.

MAMBI UNIFORM: The uniform or clothing worn by the Mambises, who were rebel soldiers that fought against the Kingdom of Spain during the Cuban War of Independence (1895–1898). The mambí forces were made up of volunteers who mostly had no military training and banded together in loose groups who acted independently to attack the Spanish troops during the Ten Years' War. Known for their cunning, fierceness, and bravery. It is estimated that 8,000 poorly armed and underfed mambises inflicted close to 20,000 casualties on the well-trained Spanish soldiers during the Ten Years' War. See Wikipedia for a full account.

MANOLO FERNANDEZ: Not clear if it refers to the death of Havana's Mayor Manolo Fernandez Supervielle, (23 September 1894 – May 5, 1947, who according to some contemporary reports in 1947 claimed he was murdered. Or to the official version that he committed suicide. Also, another M.Fernandez, a professor of the University of Havana who was murdered in 1947 by a rival University student gang. The novel makes some allusions to student activists, particularly at the University of Havana located in the heart of the city. Its main entrance, a neo-classical esplanade and giant stairway referred to as the "Escalinata" the focal point of student demonstrations. Known as a breeding ground for revolutionary student groups, in which the then law student, Fidel Castro was a participant, which later played a key role to the 1959 overthrow of the Batista regime.

MANZANILLO, ORIENTE PROVINCE: A port city founded in 1784 and at one time taken by the French. It is in the eastern province of Oriente at this time and approximately over 400 miles east of Havana as the crow flies. It is also the site of three naval engagements in the War of 1898 between Spain and the American forces. The last a decisive defeat of the Spanish on July 18, 1898.

MENDIETA, CARLOS: President of Cuba 1934-1935, when the Platt Amendment was rescinded.

MENOCAL: Aurelio Mario Gabriel Francisco García Menocal y Deop (December 17, 1866 – September 7, 1941) was the 3rd President of Cuba, serving from 1913 to 1921. His terms as president saw Cuba's participation in World War I. He went to boarding schools in the United States, and then to Cornell University graduating in 1888 from the School of Engineering. As a young man he was involved in Cuba's fight for independence from Spain. When Cuba did receive independence following the Spanish–American War, García Menocal became a leading conservative politician.

MERENDERO: The Buffet.

MERENGUITOS: Hardened sugar and egg white based confections.

MERIENDA: a light late-afternoon meal, comparable to the English tea, but less formal.

MI PRIETO: a term of endearment, literally "my dark skinned one."

MIRAMAR: a prosperous Havana neighborhood, part of the post WWI urban extension of Havana beyond the Almendares River. Only to be outdone by the "Country Club" further out where palatial residences displayed the wealth of the elite. Now the cordoned residential area of the elite of the Revolution and of Ambassadorial residences, including the United States Ambassador.

MOJITO: is a traditional Cuban cocktail using five ingredients: white rum, sugar, lime juice, soda water, and mint. One of several Cuban origin drinks like the Daiquiri, also using rum. See Wikipedia.

MUERTOS DE HAMBRE: bums. Literally "dying of hunger."
MULATO/A: A person of mixed African and European descent.

NEGRITOS: Little black ones. A term of endearment, referring to children by their father.

NOVIOS: Lovers and commonly to denote betrothed.

OCHUN! CHANGO! YEMAYA!: Yoruba deities that form part of the Cuban Santeria pantheon. Ochun (Oshun) is an Orisha, a spirit, an important river deity, or a goddess that reflects one of the manifestations of the Yoruba Supreme Being in the Ifá oral tradition and Yoruba-based religions of West Africa. She is one of the most popular and venerated Orishas. She is the goddess of divinity, femininity, fertility, beauty, and love.

She is connected to destiny and divination. Yemaya (Yoruba: Yemọja) is a major water spirit from the Yoruba religion and associated with the moon. She is an orisha, in this case patron spirit of the oceans and/or rivers - particularly the Ogun River in Nigeria. She is often syncretized with either Our Lady of Regla in Afro-Cuban Santeria, or various other Virgin Mary figures of the Catholic Church, a practice that emerged during the era of the Trans-Atlantic slave trade. Yemọja is motherly and strongly protective, and cares deeply for all her children, comforting them and cleansing them of sorrow. She is said to be able to cure infertility in women, and cowrie shells represent her wealth. She does not easily lose her temper, but when angered she can be quite destructive and violent, as the flood waters of turbulent rivers. SEE Chango. Wikipedia has extensive background notes.

PACT OF ZANJÓN: Ended the Ten Years War (1868-1878) in which Cubans sought independence from Spain. By that time, the rest of Spanish America had gained theirs. Signed in the village for which it is named between Spanish General Arsenio Martínez Campos and the Cuban rebels. While it did not result in independence a number of concessions were granted by Spain including representation of Cuba in the Spanish parliament, a date certain for the abolition of slavery, political amnesty, and the release of prisoners on both sides, as well as the freedom of association and of the press. More important among the Cuban independence leaders freed were Jose Marti, Calixto Garcia, Juan Gualberto Gomez, and Antonio Maceo. However, it was short lived and guerilla warfare ensued leading to the second and final war of independence beginning in 1895.

PEDRO DOMECQ: A famous Spanish brandy.

PERSIANAS: Venetian blinds.

PICUALA: Quiscualis indica, a blooming creeper vine

PIRULI: A Cuban hard candy in various flavors shaped like a pointed cone on the end of a stick.

PLATT AMENDMENT: One of the most controversial legacies of the American occupation of Cuba after the defeat of the Spanish 1898. Passed as an amendment made in 1901 to a resolution of the United States Congress. It contained a number of provisions among which it required for all treaties with Cuba had to be approved by the U.S. Senate. It also gave the United States the right to interfere in Cuba's affairs if order broke down within Cuba. It also declared Guantánamo Bay to be U.S. territory.

POGOLOTTI: Marcelo Pogolotti (Havana 1902 – 1988). An influential painter and leading exponent of a nationalist style depicting social conditions, especially in the Cuban countryside. He studied in Italy, Paris, Amsterdam, and the United States in 1923 at the Art Students League in New York. He participated in a number of exhibitions in Havana in the 1920s. He was influenced by the Futurist movement in Italy, and later by Abstractionism.

PUERTO BONIATO: Is a port engineered by the American occupation forces under General Wood in 1901. It is a dependence of Santiago de Cuba in the eastern side of the island.

PUNTA DEL VEDADO: refers to a projection of land into the Caribbean in the Vedado neighborhood.

QUITRIN: a gig or light chaise in Cuban usage.

REFRESCOS: Refreshments or drinks.

REGLA: A municipality across the Havana Harbor, is a district inhabited largely by Afro-Cubans, many of whom practice Santeria.

RESURGENCE OF CUBAN IDEALS: refers to the general political movement Leandro and Antonia are involved with harkening to the pre-U.S. occupation struggling for Cuban independence and autonomy free from foreign interference.

RHUMBA PALACE: A popular Havana dance club in Marianao.

SACRED HEART: An allusion to Manhattanville College of the Sacred Heart, now simply called Manhattanville College New York that Lourdes is said to have attended for three years. The leading Catholic women's college in the area at the time (the alma mater of four Kennedy women, Ethel, Eunice, Jean, and Joan), it was located in the upper west corner of Manhattan until 1952, when it moved to its current site in Purchase, NY. There is also the Convent of the Sacred Heart on East 91st St. in Manhattan, a school for girls from nursery through the last year of high school, founded in 1881. It remains to this day one of the exclusive Catholic Schools run by the Madams of the Sacred Heart, a French order of nuns, located across the street from the Metropolitan Museum of Art on Fifth Avenue.

SAN MARTIN: José Francisco de San Martín (25 February 1778 – 17 August 1850), Argentine leader of the 19th century struggle for independence from Spanish colonial domination and with his contemporary, Bolivar, liberated Peru, Chile and eventually Argentina. He died in France after several attempts to return to Argentina failed.

SENSERRO: cow bells.

SERVANDO DIAZ TRIO: "There's Nothing Philosophic About Sofia's Hips" refers to lyrics in one of their popular songs. One of several groups that were in the traditional style of music making like boleros, son, guaracha, etc., and other "trova" style ensembles.

SOFRITO: a sauce used as a base for many Caribbean dishes. The Cuban variety features onions, garlic, and bell peppers.

SOLARES: Empty land lots in urban areas often supporting squatters.

SOMOZA: Anastasio ("Tacho") Somoza García (February 1, 1896 – September 29, 1956) was President of Nicaragua (January 1937 - May 1947 and May 1950 - September 1956). The quintessential banana republic despot after eliminating other opponents including the renowned Yanqui hating guerrilla leader Julio Cesar Augusto Sandino in 1934, he established a four-decade dynasty of rule, with the last Somoza, the young Tachito Jr., overthrown by the Sandinistas in 1979.

SPANISH SIDRA: generally defined as hard cider, although in this case it is referred to later as champagne.

SUGAR-BOOM OF 1918: SEE the Dance of the Millions.

TATA: a niñera nanny, nurse.

TENIENTE: Lieutenant.

THE PLAYA : Refers to Orquesta Casino de la Playa, founded in 1937 in Havana, was a band that bridged Cuban popular music and the sound of American Jazz Big Bands. It was led by tres player Arsenio Rodríguez and launched the career of many important musicians in Cuban music. The group took its name from the name of the casino where they worked. Wikipedia

THE TROPICAL: The estate was built in the late 1800s by the Herrera family, owners of La Tropical brewery, by 1912 it became a tropical gem on the outskirts of Havana and an immensely popular place for the citizens of Havana that featured the most popular orchestras of the time. In its prime, the grounds were scattered with waterfalls, gazeboes, and a small palace in the style of the Alhambra in Granada. There was also a huge ballroom.

TIMBALES: a percussion musical instrument consisting of a pair of drums and cowbells; figuratively used as a synonym for male genitals.

TINAJÓN: a large earthen jar of a type traditionally used in Camagüey.

TOMEGUÍN: Wikipedia describes it as: "The Cuban Grassquit (Tiaris canorus) is a small bird formerly placed with the Emberizidae. It is now recognized as a tanager closely related to Darwin's finches. It is found in Bahamas, Cuba, and Turks and Caicos Islands. Its natural habitats are subtropical or tropical moist lowland forests, subtropical or tropical moist mountain forests, subtropical or tropical dry scrubland, and heavily degraded former forest."

TRIGUEÑA: A term of affection; literally someone of tri-racial ancestry."

VARADERO: A world famous seaside resort approximately 87 miles from Havana.

VEDADO: Also, Vedado Point. One of the first bourgeois neighborhoods in the expansions beyond the colonial walls to the West of Havana.

VIBORA: La Víbora was founded in 1689, as a small town where the exchange of horses would occur for caravans traveling from Havana to

Güines. The town grew rapidly, and by 1698 it began to appear in local maps and chronicles. Today, it is Havana's most populated "barrio", with 23,118 inhabitants. Wikipedia

VICTORY OF LAS TUNAS: The reference is confusing, though, because "Victory of Las Tunas" was the name for a hundred years of the town which commemorated a victory of the Spanish forces over the Cuban rebels. To speak of Menocal's participation in "the Battle of Victoria de las Tunas" makes more sense. Lorna has abbreviated the phrase, which is understandable but puzzling to the neophyte in Cuban history.

VIEJO: "old" (adj.); as a substantive, an affectionate term of address, "old one" or "old man."

VIRGIN OF THE CARIDAD DEL COBRE: Cuba's legendary patron saint. Her shrine in Santiago de Cuba, the easternmost province is venerated much like the Virgin of Guadalupe is by Mexicans. The legend says she rescued three fishermen from drowning in a storm. She is often depicted as Black.

WELLES, SUMNER WELLES: an influential State Department representative in the Franklin Delano Roosevelt administration was Under-Secretary of State 1937-1943.

WEYLER THE-BUTCHER: Valeriano Weyler y Nicolau, Marquis of Tenerife, Duke of Rubí, Grandee of Spain, (September 17, 1838 – October 20, 1930). William Hearst's press gave him the derogatory title during his governorship in 1897 for his policy of placing up to 300,000 Cubans, including women and children whom he suspected of aiding the independence rebels, in "reconcentration" camps. Though reviled in Cuba he later played prominent roles in quelling a number of Spain's revolutions until his death.

YEMAYA: SEE OCHUN.

ZARZUELA: traditional Spanish type of musical drama comparable to light opera.

NOTE: Some of the entries relied initially on information in Wikipedia in English which are otherwise only found scattered in a number of sources in Spanish. Two useful publications for further study are Hugh Thomas, *Cuba: The Pursuit of Freedom* (1971) and *Historical Dictionary of Cuba, Second Edition* (2001) by Jaime Suchlicki.

Made in the USA
Las Vegas, NV
14 February 2022

43927129R00138